Skin IN THE GAME

A CAIN/HARPER THRILLER (#1)

D.P. LYLE

SUSPENSE PUBLISHING

SKIN IN THE GAME
A CAIN/HARPER THRILLER
by
D.P. Lyle

PAPERBACK EDITION
* * * * *
PUBLISHED BY:
Suspense Publishing

D.P. Lyle
COPYRIGHT
2019 D.P. Lyle

PUBLISHING HISTORY:
Suspense Publishing, Paperback and Digital Copy, October 2019

Cover Design: Shannon Raab
Cover Photographer: Shutterstock.com/ Arlo Magicman
Cover Photographer: iStockphoto.com/ dlewis33

ISBN: 978-0578516950

BOOKS BY D.P. LYLE

Jake Longly Thrillers
Deep Six (#1)
A-List (#2)
Sunshine State (#3)

Dub Walker Thrillers
Stress Fracture (#1)
Hot Lights, Cold Steel (#2)
Run to Ground (#3)

Samantha Cody Thrillers
Devil's Playground (#1)
Double Blind (#2)
Original Sin (#3)

Royal Pains: Media Tie-in Novels
Royal Pains: First, Do No Harm (#1)
Royal Pains: Sick Rich (#2)

Anthologies
For the Sake of the Game
It's All in the Story
Thriller3: Love is Murder
Thrillers: 100 Must Reads

Non-Fiction
Murder and Mayhem: A Doctor Answers Medical and Forensic
Questions From Mystery Writers
Forensics For Dummies
Forensics For Dummies, 2nd Edition
Forensics and Fiction: Clever, Intriguing, and Downright Odd
Questions From Crime Writers
Howdunit Forensics: A Guide For Writers
More Forensics and Fiction: Crime Writers Morbidly Curious
Questions Expertly Answered
ABA Fundamentals: Understanding Forensic Science

ACKNOWLEDGMENTS

To my wonderful agent and friend Kimberley Cameron of Kimberley Cameron & Associates. KC, you're the best.

To John and Shannon Raab and all the wonderfully dedicated people at Suspense Publishing. Thanks for your creative insights and hard word to make this book the best it can be.

To my writers group for helping make this story work. Thanks, Barbara, Terri, Craig, Donna, Sandy, and Laurie.

To my always first reader and editor Nancy Whitley.

To my long-time friend Jim Fabrick for his knowledge and experience with SERE Training.

To Nan for everything. And for offering some truly creepy ideas for this story.

PRAISE FOR D.P. LYLE

"Unputdownable. Bobby Cain wields both his knife and tongue with lethal expertise. Lyle's seamless prose, gritty voice, and whiplash pacing culminate in an unforgettable climax, showcasing a heartwrenching exposé into the world of human trafficking. And what a wild ride along the way. *Ray Donavan* meets *Deliverance!*"
—K.J. Howe, International Bestselling Author of *Skyjack*

"D.P. Lyle's novels are chillingly authentic. An expert technician just keeps getting better. Packed with edge of the seat tension, *Skin in the Game* takes hunting to an astonishing, and frightening, new level."
—Robert Dugoni, *New York Times* Bestselling Author of the *Tracy Crosswhite* Series

"*Skin in the Game* is a bracing and blisteringly original thriller that challenges old genre rules while making up plenty of its own. D.P. Lyle has fashioned a tale sharply edged enough to leave our fingers bleeding from turning the pages as fast as we can. His intrepid protagonists are among the best drawn and richly realized of any heroes seen in years, with echoes of both David Baldacci and C. J. Box, making *Skin in the Game* a winner from page one. A smooth and sultry tale that shoots for the moon and hits a literary bull's-eye."
—Jon Land, *USA Today* Bestselling Author of the *Caitlin Strong* Series

"From the first line of *Skin in the Game*, D.P. Lyle grabs your attention and your imagination, and never lets up. This is a masterpiece of suspense that is built upon strong characters, solid plotting, and excellent scene setting. Lyle uses misdirection as expertly as did Raymond Chandler, and builds tension that will cause the reader to turn on all the lights and lock the doors. Don't miss this one."
—Joseph Badal, Tony Hillerman Award Winning Author of *Natural Causes*

Skin IN THE GAME

A CAIN/HARPER THRILLER (#1)

D.P. LYLE

CHAPTER 1

APRIL

She had a plan.

Not much of one, and not likely to succeed. But she had little choice.

That he was going to kill her was a given. No question. She knew that shortly after their lives intersected. At first he had been a Good Samaritan, a knight in shining armor. Polite and kind and helpful. When her car gave up, sputtering to a stop on the grassy shoulder of the winding, rural road, middle of nowhere, dead of night, as she was returning from a birthday party, berating herself for staying so late when she still had papers to grade. There he was. His SUV sliding up behind her, washing her in its headlamps, him stepping out, approaching, saying, "Car trouble?" An easy smile on his face.

In the darkness, she couldn't peg his age, could be thirty, could be fifty, but she could see that he was handsome, well-dressed in slacks and an open-collar dress shirt. Harmless, soft-spoken. He popped the hood, rummaged around, told her it looked like her distributor had given up. Offered her a ride home.

Sure. Thanks. He seemed so safe.

Then things changed.

The Taser to her shoulder, the foggy and helpless way she lay

13

there, back of the SUV, knowing he was binding her, gagging her. Yet her muscles wouldn't respond to the silent screaming inside her brain. *Run, fight, resist.*

Then she was here. Wherever here was. A barn, large, drafty.

What she feared never happened. No rape, no touching, at least not that way. He had stripped her, tied her to a table, and shaved her. Completely. Even her long, dark hair was gone. She begged and pleaded, asking again and again what he was doing.

Making you perfect.

Those words shot a chill through her.

No doubt, he would kill her.

He had to. He'd made no attempt to hide his face. No concern that she might later identify him. The unmistakable truth was that there would be no 'later' for her.

Then, that same night, she curled on an air mattress, blanket pulled to her neck to ward off the damp chill. Her handcuffed left wrist tethered to a massive support pole by a thick chain. She had tried everything: squeeze her hand from the cuff, dislodge it from the chain, loosen the chain itself from the tree-like stanchion.

Nothing worked.

The next morning, it began. Back on the table, each extremity restrained, the hum of the tattoo machine, the sharp pricks of the needle.

Again, she asked him why.

"To make you the masterpiece you deserve to be," he said while gently cupping her chin.

Now, her fifth night in captivity, wrapped in the blanket, waiting. Right wrist tethered now. Too bad. She had hoped for the left.

She had a plan.

One she had hatched last night as she lay in the dark, trying everything to slip her hand free. Working until the bones ached, the flesh raw, sweat covering her, making no progress.

That's when she realized that to escape, to survive, she had to sacrifice her hand. Not in a coyote gnawing off a leg way—she could never do that—but still a sacrifice.

Too bad it had to be the right. She almost laughed at that. Worrying about which hand when death was the endgame.

The weather in Tennessee in April could be anything. Sweltering, or as cold as deep winter. Most of the day, fat rain drops had hammered the tin roof, echoing inside the cavernous space, dragging the temperature lower.

Hard shivers racked her. She wound the blanket tightly around her naked body, legs drawn up so that her feet were covered. Still her toes felt almost frozen.

So she managed to slip her bonds, then what? Were the doors—the large one ahead of her, or the smaller one to her right—locked, bolted, chained? And once she was outside, into the cold night, where was she? She had no idea. She pictured open land, trees, no civilization in sight. Was that the case? Did it matter?

Doing nothing was a death sentence.

Earlier, as he gathered his tools, she had asked when this would end. "Soon," he had replied. "Two days at most." Once her transformation was complete.

"What then?"

"Your presentation to the world."

His unhurried footsteps faded, leaving her in an eerie darkness, faintly blushed by the glowing coils of the electric heater he left on for some measure of comfort.

Timing was everything now.

She waited, listening, inhaling the damp, musty air laced with the faint electric aroma of the heater. Had he really gone? The last two nights she had thought so, but within minutes he had returned, muttering about forgetting something. Yet he hadn't searched for or picked up anything. One final check on her. He was nothing if not meticulous.

She envisioned him nearby, waiting, just in case. She did not turn or move and willed her breathing to slow. Let him believe she was asleep, that she had accepted her captivity, that this night would be like the others. She would sleep and wait for his return.

Exhaustion tugged at her. She fought it. She had slept only in fits and spurts over the past five days. Was it only five days? Seemed an eternity.

Her eyes burned and her entire body ached with fatigue. A few more minutes, she told herself.

She jerked awake.

Where was she? Her confusion only momentary. The support pole, only inches from her face, reflected the red glow of the heater coils; its humming, the only sound she could hear. She rolled to her back and then her other side, the chain that bound her rattling. How long had she slept? What time was it? She had no idea. Time was a lost commodity in the massive barn.

She sat up, directing her gaze toward the side door. The one he used to come and go. Was he out there waiting? Did it matter? She had to act now. Had to take that one-in-a-million shot. Otherwise, all would be lost. There was no Hollywood ending here. At least not the kind where the armored knight rides up, slays the beast, and lifts her onto his pure white stallion. If this script had a good ending she would have to write it herself.

She had a plan.

She stood, angry at herself for falling asleep while a growing panic filled her chest.

Time to act.

She grasped her right hand with her left and squeezed. Hard. Ignoring the pain, she called on all her strength but the bones proved more resilient. Tears collected in her eyes. She banged the hand against the pole but that did little, except abrade her skin, blood now oozing along her fingers. Again she squeezed and yanked, hoping the blood would serve as a lubricant. It didn't.

Plan B. Something more drastic. She had feared it would come to this. She steeled herself, closed her fist tightly, settled it against her buttock, took a deep breath, jumped straight up, retracting her legs, and landed hard on the floor. The lubrication of the blood now worked against her, her hand sliding from beneath her as she struck the floor hard. Pain shot up her spine, her breath escaping in a whoosh.

Goddammit.

She stood, set herself again, this time concentrating on pressing her fist even more tightly against her right buttock and repeated the jump/fall.

The pain was horrific, the cracking of the bones audible. She rolled to her back, tears welling in her eyes, her breathing deep and raspy. Nausea swept through her followed by a cold, hard sweat.

Two deep settling breaths.

Move.

She grasped the chain and tugged, the cuff further crushing her damaged hand. The pain was too much.

Do it.

Again, she tried. The angry ache worse.

Could she do this?

She stood, backpedaled, the chain and her arm now extended before her. A deep breath, a fall backwards. The chain snapped taut. The bones of her hand resisted before finally collapsing through the metal ring. She hit the floor hard. Fire shot up her arm. The world spun. She gulped air until the dizziness settled. The pain didn't.

Time to move.

She climbed to her feet, momentarily wobbling. She held her breath and listened, half-expecting to hear his footsteps. Nothing.

The side door. Locked. Toggle on the inside. She twisted it, eased the door open, and stepped outside.

Above, a nearly full moon peeked between fluffy clouds. No rain. Cold.

She examined her mangled hand. In the moonlight, it appeared blackened and swollen. A deep throbbing spread upwards into her shoulder.

She scanned her surroundings. A patch of open field to her left, dense woods ahead and to her right.

The pines offered cover so she headed that way. Naked except for the blanket she wrapped around her shoulders, feet bare. The ground cold and hard against her soles. She covered the two hundred feet to the trees before turning and looking back.

A house. A large house. Two lights on inside.

His house.

Was he inside, asleep? Was he aware she had slipped away? Was he standing at a window watching her every move?

No time to ponder that. She scurried deeper into the trees, pine needles and small rocks biting at her feet. The uneven terrain sloped downward. Toward a road? A stream? Would this path lead her to civilization? No way to know but now she was committed.

She moved more quickly. Through the trees, their branches clutching at the blanket, slapping against her exposed legs and arms. In and out of ravines, over masses of limestone, thick clusters of pine trees, small open areas, up and down.

Fifteen minutes later she stopped at the edge of a shallow ravine. The cold air burned her lungs. Her hand throbbed. The soles of her feet felt as if the flesh had been ripped off.

How far had she gone? A mile? Maybe more?

The rain returned. A soft sprinkle, tapping against the pines above her. The occasional splat of a drop against the protective blanket.

Then another sound. Behind her. Like a rock tumbling down a slope.

She spun that way.

A shuffle, a scrape.

Footsteps. No doubt.

No, no, no.

She turned and ran. Down into the ravine. Twigs and cold, hard rocks cut into her already damaged feet. She ignored the pain and picked up her pace. The channel she followed turned right and then left, the darkness thickening with each step. Then she reached the edge of the trees. Maybe a hundred yards of open land before her. A recently plowed field. Neat rows of tiny sprigs, a few leaves.

She looked back, holding her breath, listening. Silence.

What now? Cross the open area? Exposed. Back into the trees and continue downhill?

Think. Make a decision.

The field. Open the gap as much as possible and then figure it out.

Head down, blanket pulled around her shoulders, she burst out into the open. The moon slid from behind a cloud, silvering the sprouts. She locked her gaze on a single pine, bent and misshapen, distinguishing itself from the regiment of trees that hugged the far side of the field. She picked up her pace, reaching it in less than a minute.

Back into the trees. Rockier here, with even more piles of limestone boulders and ledges. She weaved through them, deeper into the trees.

Where was she? She stopped, considering whether to climb the rocks, get a better view of her surroundings, or stay low to the ground. Out of sight.

Behind her, a sharp snap. A twig breaking. Her heart did a dance and she spun toward the sound.

There he was.

Standing on a limestone outcropping fifty feet away, looking directly at her.

She discarded the now wet and heavy blanket and ran. Swerving through another shallow ravine, scattered with limestone rocks that excoriated her feet. The pain excruciating. She pressed onward.

Don't look back. Just run.

But she did glance back.

He followed, now in the ravine. Not really running. More a lazy lope. As if he knew she had no way to escape and running her down was simply a matter of time. He held something in one hand but at this distance she couldn't tell what? A gun?

She scurried out of the ravine, weaving, slipping past and beneath pine and cedar boughs, stretching out the distance between them. The forest rose and fell, the trees thick here, less so there, and always masses of limestone to deal with. Her feet screamed, her chest burned as if the cold air had frozen something inside. She kept moving. Pine branches slapped and clutched at her, raising welts on her arms and face. Her legs heavy, her feet on fire.

She rounded a twenty-foot high ledge of limestone, and descended to where a stream cut through the forest, tumbling downhill to her right. She stopped, bending at the waist, sucking air.

What now? Keep running? To where? Could her feet hold up much longer?

She straightened and looked around. Nothing but trees and more trees. Then she saw a crevice in the limestone that seemed to give birth to the stream. It appeared just wide enough for her to slip inside. Hiding seemed a better tactic than running in circles.

She stepped into the stream. The shock of the cold water initially soothed the fire in her ripped soles but that relief quickly became a deep ache, as if her feet were literally freezing. She eased into the crevice.

This better work, or she was trapped.

The scraping of his feet came from above. On the ledge.

She stood in the frigid water, plastering herself against the cold rocks of the crevice wall, her shivers now shaking her entire body. She clamped the web of her good hand between her teeth to soften their chattering.

The silence suddenly felt heavy. What was he doing?

Then footsteps, growing fainter, moving away.

It had worked. Tears welled in her eyes. Her mangled hand throbbed, her feet ached, she was lost and might even freeze to death, but she had beaten him.

She waited ten agonizing minutes before slipping from the crevice and climbing out of the stream. She moved to where a slant of moonlight slid through the trees and lifted one foot and then the other, examining the soles. Ripped flesh and fresh blood.

Following the stream downhill seemed the best bet. But after only a few steps, something slammed into her left side. Hard. Sharp. She staggered. A spasm of coughing produced sprays of blood. She collapsed to her knees, confused. Then she heard his footsteps. Close. Right behind her. She swiveled toward him and looked up into his eyes,

"You shouldn't have done that," he said.

"Please."

"You were to be my first masterpiece. But now? You're nothing. A wasted canvas."

CHAPTER 2

MAY

"Will not."

"Will, too."

Billy Clowers shook his head. "You don't know nothing."

"I know that if you leave those there it'll jump the tracks," Benjie Crane said.

"And we'll be in big trouble," Misty added.

"So you're on his side now?" Billy asked.

Misty jammed her fists against her hips. "When he's right, I am."

"You're so lame." Billy squatted beside the metal rail. "Both of you are."

Misty stepped up on the rail, balancing on her frayed tennis shoes, faded gray with new pink laces, and looked down at her brother. "Well, since we're twins, if I'm lame so are you."

"Not hardly."

"I'm smarter anyway."

"You wish."

"Want to compare report cards?"

Billy rolled his eyes. "Like that means anything."

"It means I'm smarter."

"Whatever." Billy settled two more quarters on the rail.

"You better take some of those off there," Benjie said.

"It will not jump the track."

"My cousin said if you used more than five pennies it would definitely cause a wreck," Benjie said. "And you got six pennies, two nickels, and three quarters."

Billy spun on his haunches. "Is this your cousin from up in Ohio?"

"Yeah," Benjie said.

"He's lame, too."

"Is not. He's five years older and in high school already. He knows stuff."

"That only means he's had five more years of lameness." Billy returned to adjusting coins. "You just have to make sure they're lined up down the middle. If they hang over the edge then they could derail it."

"See, I told you," Misty said.

Billy stood. "Do something useful. Take a listen."

Misty dropped to her knees on the gravel rail bed and pressed one ear against the metal. Her brow wrinkled.

"Well?"

"I don't hear nothing."

"Cause you don't know what to listen for." Billy dropped to his knees and pressed an ear against the other rail. "I hear it. It's coming."

"Is not. If it was I'd of heard it."

He stood. "Get Mom to clean your ears."

"It ain't coming."

Billy pointed down the tracks to where they curved right and disappeared into a stand of pines some two hundred yards away. "It'll come around that bend in about five minutes. If you want your coins flattened, you better get them lined up."

Misty and Benjie hesitated, looking at each other, and then began digging through their pockets. Soon a total of fifteen pennies, four nickels, and three quarters lined the rail.

"I feel it now," Benjie said, his hand resting on the track.

"Here it comes," Billy said, pointing.

The train chugged around the bend. Its horn sounded three short blasts.

"Let's go," Billy said.

They ran down the graveled slope and settled among thick wads of Johnson grass and shrubs.

Billy raised up and peered over a hydrangea, pushing one of its bright white flowers aside.

"Stay down," Misty said. "If the engineer sees you he'll stop."

"He ain't going to stop for nothing."

"He might," Benjie said. "My dad said that train engineers are kind of like cops. For trains, that is."

"Your dad's lame, too."

"Is not." Benjie slugged Billy's arm.

Billy hooked his arm around Benjie's neck and spun him to the ground, pinning him there.

"Stop it," Benjie said. "You're going to miss the train."

Billy rolled off and stood, brushing grass and dirt from his jeans. "Don't hit me again."

Benjie regained a squat. "Don't talk about my dad like that."

Billy started to say something but the train arrived, rumbling and roaring, vibrating the ground, creating a wind that rustled the grass and shrubs around them. The stench of the diesel fumes filled the air.

Once it passed, without jumping the rails, they scurried back up the incline. The coins that had been dull and lifeless were now flattened and shiny. Most still lined the track, only two having fallen off onto the gravel bed. They collected them.

"This is so rad," Benjie said, holding what had once been a nickel, now a wafer-thin shiny disk, in his palm.

"And the train didn't even know those coins were there. Just like I said." Billy looked at his sister. "Want to tell me I was right?"

She stuck out her tongue. "More like lucky."

"Not luck. Smarts."

"Really? You almost failed history."

"It was hard."

"I made an A. Didn't seem so hard to me."

"Whatever."

After they divvied up their booty, they walked the track, toward home.

"What do you want to do now?" Benjie asked.

"Don't know," Billy said. "Maybe go throw the football around?"

"Okay."

"Look." Benjie stopped, pointed.

Misty and Billy followed the angle of Benjie's arm and extended finger. At least a dozen buzzards circled in the distance.

"Something's dead," Misty said.

"Let's go see," Billy said.

"Looks like it's a long way," Benjie added.

"No, it ain't. It's just beyond those trees."

"That's across the county road. I ain't supposed to go that far."

Billy let out a short snort, shaking his head. "Then why don't you run on home to your mama and Misty and I'll check it out."

Benjie rolled one foot up on its side, head down.

"Come on," Billy said.

He and Misty crunched down the slope, waded through the Johnson grass, and angled toward the distant woods. Billy glanced back. Benjie skittered down the slope and followed them.

Ten minutes later, they had crossed the county road, marched between the rows of knee-high cotton plants, wound their way through the trees, and stepped back into the bright mid-day sunlight.

Billy raised a hand to block the glare from his eyes. "There they are." He pointed.

"There's a bunch of them," Misty said.

"What do you think it is?" Benjie asked.

"Something big. Maybe a dog." Billy lowered his hand and gazed across the furrowed, rich red dirt. TVA lines sagged between two massive metal towers and soared overhead, their electric hum barely audible.

"Or a cow," Misty said.

"A cow?" Benjie said. "That'd be so cool."

"Looks like whatever it is is over near those pine trees."

Billy started across the field. "We better step on it if we're going to see what it is and get back in time for lunch."

"We'll never make it," Benjie said. "It's a long way over there."

Billy stopped and turned. "We won't make it at all if you keep whining." He continued his march between the neat cotton rows.

Benjie caught up with him. "I'm not whining. But you said

they were around this bunch of trees, but they're way over there. And you know Old Man Wilson don't want us on his property."

Misty looked at him. "I swear, you're afraid of your shadow." She marched past them, head down. "Let's get going."

"Watch out for the plants," Benjie said. "We mess with those and Old Man Wilson'll be mad for sure."

The distance proved deceptive, the pines much farther than they appeared. It took them another ten minutes to cross the undulating field, the red clay soil glomming on their sneakers, making them heavy.

When they ascended the last wrinkle in the land, Billy suddenly stopped. A half dozen buzzards were clustered on the ground, maybe fifty yards away, the others still circling overhead. The birds now appeared larger, as big as a Thanksgiving turkey, and more menacing than when they were dark silhouettes against the bright, blue sky. A couple of them raised gnarly heads and inspected the trio.

"Boy those guys are ugly," Misty said.

"And big," Benjie added.

"What are we going to do?" Misty asked.

Billy hesitated, looking around. "Let's go this way. Around them. Through those trees. We can sneak up on them."

"Do they bite?" Misty asked.

"I don't think so."

"You don't think so? Don't you know?" Misty glared at her brother. "I thought you were the smart one."

"I am. But I don't know nothing about buzzards."

"They look dangerous," Benjie said.

"Let's go." Billy veered to his right, giving the feeding buzzards a wide berth. Once in the shade of the trees, the pungent odor of pine needles greeted them. They kicked their shoes against tree trunks and used the coarse bark to scrape away most of the red clay. They worked their way through the trees, the bed of brown pine needles cushioning each step.

Benjie pointed. "There they are. We're close now."

Billy bent low, ducked beneath a couple of branches and moved to the edge of the trees. The musty pine odor was now joined by another smell, richer and sweeter. Billy squatted, Misty and Benjie beside him.

Two of the buzzards raised their heads, turned their way.

"What is it?" Misty asked.

"I don't know," Billy said. "I can't see from here."

"What are we going to do?" Benjie asked.

Billy searched the ground until he found a cluster of pine cones. He snatched up the largest one. Stepping into the sunlight, he wound up and hurled it at the buzzards. They hopped away, but not very far, now all of them looking his way with dark eyes and wrinkled, prehistoric faces.

"Don't make them mad," Misty said.

"They're just stupid birds," Billy said.

"But big," Benjie said. "And ugly."

"Still stupid birds."

Billy rushed toward them, arms waving, shouting. The buzzards scattered, each taking long strides, leaping into the air, and with squeaky grunts and whooshing wings rapidly gained altitude toward their circling mates.

Billy watched them and then turned. "See. Just stupid birds."

They cautiously approached the area where the buzzards had been.

"Oh my God," Misty said, one hand flying up to her mouth. "What is that?"

CHAPTER 3

It was a beautiful May morning when Bobby Cain left the condo he shared with his sister Harper. The penthouse floor of the trendy St. Germain Place, a twenty-floor complex in downtown Nashville's SoBro area. Near the Omni Hotel and not far from Printer's Alley, the Country Music Hall of Fame and Museum, and the boisterous Lower Broadway. A street where food and alcohol were staples and where established and up-and-coming country music stars could be heard nightly.

Cain crossed Broadway, quiet now, and continued into the maze of towering office buildings that comprised Nashville's vibrant financial and business district.

He had an appointment with attorney Marcus Milner. Which meant that somebody had a problem. Something that needed fixing. He didn't yet know what, but he was sure of two things: it would be off the radar, way off, and it would pay well. The way it always was.

The law offices of Milner, Martin, and Rowe were plush and then some. The entire 30th floor of a glossy high-rise. Quiet, spacious, soft colors, expensive furniture, and pricy artwork. Soothing jazz hung in the air like a sweet fragrance.

Two sharply dressed people sat in the waiting room: a woman, working her laptop, and a man, shuffling through papers in his open briefcase. Both glanced up but quickly returned to their work.

Receptionist Margaret Porter smiled from behind her spacious, gray marble desk. "Mister Cain? What brings you by?"

Margaret, forty-ish, straight dark hair, gray suit over a white blouse, glasses hanging from a gold chain, had been with the firm for as long as Cain had worked with senior partner Marcus Milner. Almost four years now. Had it really been that long?

Cain leaned down, flattening his palms on the marble. "Let me guess. He didn't tell you I was coming."

She rolled her eyes. "He never tells me anything."

"He's a busy man."

"No, he's brain dead." She laughed. "Been that way forever. Good thing he's got me to handle the details." She picked up the phone. "I'll let him know you're here."

Cain walked down the hallway to Milner's office. Corner, of course. Window walls that looked down on the city. Expansive desk, and with today being no exception, littered with papers and folders and law books. Ensconced in his high-backed leather throne, phone to his ear, Milner waved Cain into the chair that faced him across the desk. Also leather, thick, supple, expensive.

Milner wore his usual three-piece suit, this one dark gray, with a crisp white shirt, yellow tie, and gold cufflinks. He swiped his thinning hair over the top of his head as he listened.

"Let me get back to you," Milner said. "I've got an important meeting just now." He waited a beat. "Sounds good. We'll chat then." He hung up the phone. "How're you doing?"

"Fine."

"How's Harper?"

"I left her on the stair climber."

"Too bad. I'd love to see her. It's been a couple of months."

Cain smiled. "I know better than to interfere with her workouts."

Milner laughed.

"What's up? You didn't say much when we talked."

Milner shuffled a stack of papers out of his way. "Sorry about the secrecy. But this is a delicate situation."

"Aren't they all?"

"This one especially so."

"Tell me."

"I believe you know General William Kessler?"

Who didn't? At least anyone who had ever served in the military or worked in the spook world. Cain had done both.

William "Wild Bill" Kessler was a legend in the military and spy worlds. His stellar resume included over three decades of military service, six tours in various war zones, four stars, a stint as Assistant Director of the NSA, and a long history of involvement in some of the most secret missions in US history. Things no one could ever talk about. Cain had been involved with half a dozen such special ops deployments. Not that Kessler was often present, rarely shoulder to shoulder or face to face with Cain, but Kessler's dense shadow had fell across each mission. The rumor was that he could have had the Chairmanship of the Joint Chiefs but turned it down, opting for civilian life instead.

The other rumor was that nearly fifteen years earlier Kessler had plucked Cain from the thousands of US Army recruits and launched him on the convoluted path his military career had taken. No one talked about that either. Mainly because most, actually all, of Cain's missions didn't exist. Anywhere. Never had. No trail left behind. Cain had never looked into the rumor and the few times he had been in the General's presence had never broached the subject. Some things were never discussed. Not even in private.

"I do know the General."

"He's the client."

Cain and Harper had worked with Milner on dozens of cases over the years. Mostly securing information, or planting information, or supplying incentives for someone to alter their behavior. Physical or psychological incentives. Sometimes this required wet work. Elimination of a threat, settling a score, taking out the garbage, whatever was needed. There was a time such work would have bothered him, given him pause. Those days were long gone. Any reservations he harbored evaporated years ago in Afghanistan. Tyler, Texas, too.

"What's the problem?" Cain asked.

"His granddaughter is missing."

"You know we don't do lost and found."

"Did I mention this was General Kessler?"

"And?"

"And he specifically requested you."

"Why?"

Milner shrugged. "I guess you'll find that out when you meet with him."

"If I meet with him."

"You will." Milner smiled. "I know you. You're already grinding over what he might have to say."

Cain had no argument for that. "What do you know so far?"

"She's a sophomore at Vandy. Apparently headed off for a hiking trip in Colorado. A week ago. No word since then."

"A college kid goes AWOL and that's news?"

"According to the General she's very reliable. Always checks in. Almost daily."

"We still don't do runaways."

"Just talk to him. Then decide." Milner picked up a silver Mont Blanc rollerball and tapped it on his desk. "But I should add, he said he would pay whatever it took."

Cain nodded. "That always helps."

"He's already put up a fifty grand retainer. And given us an open expense account. No restrictions."

"Sounds like he's pretty sure we'd take the case."

Milner shrugged, laid the pen on the desk. "He's very persuasive. Used to getting things done. His way."

"That's indeed his reputation."

Milner offered a quick smile, saying, "You don't get to his station in life by taking no for an answer."

"You said she's his granddaughter. What about her parents?"

"Deceased. Plane crash. Returning from an Aspen ski trip many years ago. The General and his wife then raised the girl."

Cain hesitated, mulling the situation. Distraught grandfather. Missing college kid. Who knew what family dramas were in play? Could be a total cluster fuck. But he had to admit that seeing General Kessler again was intriguing.

"Okay. When does he want to sit down?" Cain asked.

"Now."

"That urgent?"

Milner hesitated and then sighed. "I'm sure he'll tell you this, but he doesn't believe she's still alive."

"Based on?"

"A full week. No communication. No nothing. Means this might not be a lost and found situation. It might be something in your wheelhouse."

Cain stood. "Where's his place?"

"Down by Franklin. Leiper's Fork."

Leiper's Fork. Tiny town, big bucks. Open farmland that had morphed into the current hot spot for Hollywood's A-List and the Music City's megastars. Huge estates that, if you have to ask the price, you should move on down the road. Way down the road.

"I'll give him a call," Milner said. "When can he expect you?"

"Give me a couple of hours. I need to do a few things, then Harper and I'll drive down that way."

"I'll text you the directions."

Cain stood.

"Oh," Milner said. "I forgot to ask. How many blades do you have on you right now?" He smiled.

"That you could find?"

Milner laughed.

Cain left.

CHAPTER 4

Bobby Blade, Age 7

Everyone has a story. Where they hailed from, how they were raised, what goals they set, achieved, failed to reach. Most often, a simple, linear, mundane tale.

Not so for Bobby Cain, that being the name he ultimately inherited.

Truth was, his birth name was never known. Not to him, not to anyone. His real parents were likewise unknown. He didn't become a Cain until age twelve when he was adopted by Wilbert and Ruth Cain. After the FBI shattered his gypsy family, the culmination of a two-year investigation where they dogged the group, gathered evidence, and finally—on a misty and cool morning—materialized from the woods, guns drawn. After, Cain and Harper were packed off to a juvenile detention center, then to separate orphanages. After he was ripped away from Harper, not knowing at that time that their paths wouldn't cross again for fifteen years. On the other side of the planet.

At the tender age of two months, he had been abandoned in a Houston train station, where the woman who would become his aunt plucked him up. At least that's the story everyone told. Aunt Dixie and Uncle Al Broussard named him Bobby. A good name as names go, but probably not his. So he became Bobby Broussard.

Uncle Al and Aunt Dixie gave him a home, of sorts. They belonged to a transient group that at various times was called a family, a clan, or a gypsy band. Those of true Roma origin might have had issues with the latter, but Bobby never heard any complaints. Never even saw a real gypsy. But they lived like gypsies. Motor homes, trucks, trailers, always on the move. During Bobby's twelve years with the group, he visited a dozen states, from Texas to South Carolina.

The band, around sixty strong, consisted of three dozen adults, the remainder children, ranging from teens to Bobby, the youngest. The children were divided among the adults in no pattern Bobby ever saw. He and his "sister" Harper were under the wing of Al and Dixie. Harper was a year older. The family story was that she had been purchased from a young, unmarried girl for $200 and three bottles of Wild Turkey. Her mother a half breed, according to Uncle Al—white and Cherokee—gave Harper her almond complexion, dark eyes, and silky black hair. A distinct contrast to the blond Bobby.

The family never settled in one place more than a few months, more often only a week or two. Odd jobs, mostly in construction, brought in some money, but more came from the shows they performed. Never in big cities, where their itinerant nature and Bohemian appearance often drew hostility. Smaller communities were more tolerant of their camping on the town's periphery, and their performances, often at the local fairgrounds or the corner of some hospitable farmer's land.

Singing and dancing, some magic, fortune telling, and games of skill dominated. The games were of course rigged. Like tossing baseballs at balanced wooden pins. Seemed simple enough. Unless the pins were secured with wax, making a direct, solid hit necessary to tumble the pyramid. Or tossing coins toward the mouths of assorted glassware, arranged haphazardly on a wooden table. No problem. Except each was so shallow that the coins were rarely collected. Still, people lined up to take their chance. All for prizes such as cheap stuffed animals, necklaces, bracelets, and other trinkets lifted here and there, or wood products manufactured by the family—whittled whistles, slingshots, and the like. A dollar here, another there, it added up.

But the family's major source of income came from various cons, picking pockets, panhandling, and burglary. Thus, the need to keep moving.

Bobby's young life swerved on his fourth birthday. Not a turn anyone would have predicted. Uncle Al gave him his first knife. A folding six-inch blade with a deer antler handle. His fascination was immediate. Its weight and precision. The sharp blade that sliced through wood effortlessly. Whittling instruction followed. Bobby proved to be a natural. Small animals, whistles, necklace bobs, slingshots, he created each with ease. Not without a few nicks and cuts along the way. Thin, pale scars he carried into adulthood.

He collected more knives. Throwing lessons followed. From Aunt Dixie. Something she could do adeptly. This also came naturally to Bobby. Overhanded, underhanded, over his shoulder, between his legs, even blindfolded, he could hit every target.

Then, under Uncle Al's tutelage, he moved to axes, where he also displayed amazing skill. And, of course, bows. He was taught to hunt. A necessary skill as the family often lived off the land. Hunting, fishing, and nighttime raids of farmers' fields and chicken coops, fed the troupe.

They possessed guns, rifles and shotguns mostly, but bows were the predominate devices for hunting. Some small towns became nervous with guns blazing in the surrounding area. And local hunters didn't tolerate the intrusion. Bows allowed for what Uncle Al called "stealth hunting." No one ever knew they were there. Rabbits, possums, squirrels, and the occasional deer. Rarely turkeys.

By age seven, Bobby Broussard became Bobby Blade, the centerpiece of the shows. Balloons, shiny tin disks, scraps of colored paper, walnuts and pecans, became his targets. Much to the delight of those who came to the shows.

Harper entered the picture. She held the tiny targets as Bobby pierced each with a perfect throw of a knife or axe. He could easily crack a pecan held between her thumb and index finger.

That led to the board. Harper would stand against it, arms and legs spread, while Bobby peppered her outline with his blades. Uncle Mo built a circular platform that spun. Harper strapped into place, Bobby throwing in rapid succession while the audience oohed, laughed nervously, and occasionally shrieked, hands flying up to cover their eyes.

Word spread. The legend of Bobby Blade exploded. Folks scrambled to see the shows. The money rolled in.

CHAPTER 5

Early May in Tennessee is typically mild. A bridge between the cold dampness of winter and the oppressive heat of summer. But May can be tricky, wavering back and forth as if undecided which season would rule the day. And it can do so in no predictable pattern. Case in point—two days ago it was 60, raining, and windy; today, 88 and calm beneath a lid of clear blue sky. Humidity way up there. Enough to plaster your clothing to your skin, make you seek out the shade of a tree, or the churning of an air conditioner, definitely a sweating glass of lemonade or sweet tea.

Police Chief Laura Cutler's day had begun like most others, with a couple of phone calls and a stack of notices to sort through, but then rapidly veered toward boring. When she finally gave up pushing paper clips around her desk—making patterns, messing them up, creating new designs—and staring out her office window, she walked down to Flo's Diner for lunch.

Flo's, a weather-worn wooden structure with big windows and a massive deck, sat just above the marina and looked out over Tims Ford Lake. Best breakfast, lunch, and happy hour in town meant it was always crowded.

The aroma of sweet, smokey barbecue, the murmur of voices, and the jangle of forks and knives against plates, greeted Cutler as she entered. So did the cool air that seemed to push her damp shirt against her, causing a slight shiver. She nodded to the covey of old timers who daily occupied "Liar's Corner," the round table for eight snugged up against a windowless corner beneath an array of black and white photos of Moss Landing from "back in the day." Back when it was nothing more than a couple of houses, one being Jeremiah Moss's old place, and a rickety boat dock. Back before big money discovered the area. Built it into a thriving town of 8,000 with an active tourist trade and a large marina that hugged the western end of the lake.

She climbed on one of the bar stools. Flo Mason, the owner, swiped a bar towel across the counter, and clapped down an empty coffee cup. Flo, fifties, short and stocky, ran a tight ship that churned out great coffee and even better food. She wore jeans and a lime green tee shirt with "Flo's Dinner" in white script across the front.

"How's it going Chief?"

"Fine. Quiet."

Flo poured coffee. "The usual?"

The usual meaning tuna salad, lettuce, and tomato on wheat toast. "Sure." Cutler took a sip of coffee. "Where's Jimmy? I thought he'd be here."

Jimmy Rankin. Her best officer and the guy in charge when she was away.

"He was." Another swipe of the counter. "Got a call. Said he had to leave. Maybe an hour ago now."

"Any idea what it was?"

Flo shook her head. A strand of graying hair fell loose and she tucked it back behind her ear. "Said something about some kids. That's all I heard."

"Hope it's not the Tilton boys again."

Flo laughed. "Poor Eunice sure does have her hands full with those two."

Cutler ran a finger around the lip of her cup. "Ain't it so. Last time they dismantled a section of Jed Downings' picket fence. Said they needed the slats to make a raft."

"Them boys are going to do themselves in someday. Drown or whatever."

Cutler's sandwich appeared at the pass-through window from the kitchen.

"Here you go," Flo said as she placed the plate before Cutler. "Got some real good tomatoes."

They looked it. Deeply red and fresh.

Flo refilled Cutler's coffee. "Anything else?"

"This'll do. Thanks."

Another order came up. Three plates. Flo lined them up on one arm and headed toward a table near the back.

Cutler finished her meal, left cash on the counter, waved to Flo, and stepped outside. She slipped on sunglasses and looked up and down the street. As she walked toward her office, she called Jimmy.

"What's up?" she asked.

"Something weird."

"Want to expand on that?"

"Got a leg up here. On Clovis Wilson's spread."

"A what?"

"A leg. Human."

"And you didn't call me?"

"I was just fixing to. Wanted to sniff around first."

"Just a leg?"

"That's all so far. Bet there's more nearby somewhere."

"Who found it?"

"The Clowers twins. And Benjie Crane."

"Did you call Wally Spicer?"

"Sure did. Said he'd be here as soon as he loaded up Grace."

Wally Spicer ran a kennel. Raised mostly hunting dogs— Beagles, Setters, and Labs. He also had Grace, a black lab trained in cadaver location.

"Where are you?"

"Up off the county road on one of Clovis Wilson's plots. You'll see my car. Near the power lines."

"On my way."

Ten minutes later, Cutler turned off the two-lane black top onto the rutted dirt service road that lapped Clovis Wilson's property. Near a thick stand of pines, she saw Jimmy's silver Ford Taurus and Wally Spicer's red truck with stenciled white lettering that read "Spicer's Kennels, Lynchburg, TN, 931-555-9291."

Cutler climbed from her department-issue black Ford Bronco, abandoning its churning air conditioner for the sauna-like heat.

Not a breath of breeze. She should've grabbed a to-go lemonade at Flo's.

No sign of Wally, but she saw Jimmy near Ben Crane's green Chevy sedan and Dennis Clower's metallic blue Suburban, talking with Dennis and his wife Pat, and Ben. Behind them stood Benjie Crane and Billy and Misty Clowers. They looked scared. Their parents didn't look happy. She suspected the kids had been outside their boundaries.

She walked that way. The kids eyed her warily, the parents offered grim expressions. She nodded to them and said she needed to chat with Jimmy and get a handle on things and then they could talk. Ben Crane checked his watch. Impatient as usual but he'd just have to deal with it.

She and Jimmy walked the forty yards to where the leg lay. It appeared to have been ripped away from the hip and gnawed on by some creature.

"Jesus Christ," Cutler said.

"Ain't that the truth," Jimmy added.

"You ever seen anything like this before?"

"Nope. And I'm here to tell you I don't ever want to again."

"Looks like the predators got to it," Cutler said.

"Most likely wild pigs," Jimmy replied. "Those marks on the bones are probably tusk gouges. Then the buzzards got at what was left."

Feral pigs in many rural areas of the South posed a major problem. They escaped farms, formed packs, and generally wreaked havoc. Smart, fast, aggressive, predatory omnivores that would eat anything. Not just plants and grubs, though they could tear through a garden and leave behind few remnants. Destroy a hen house in minutes and even take down calves. Every now and then they became such a nuisance, and danger, that the local farmers formed their own pack and hunted them down. Last time was a couple of years earlier. If she remembered the details, eight of an estimated dozen pigs had been killed. Looked like the pack might've reformed, likely with some new members.

She squatted next to the leg. The odor of decay wasn't as strong as she thought it might be but it was plenty enough to cause the tuna sandwich in her stomach to do a couple of flips. Much of the flesh of the thigh had been removed and the toes and half the foot were missing. The calf was more or less intact and appeared to have been tattooed with thick black and white stripes that spiraled upward.

"What the hell is all that?" Cutler asked.

"Looks like one of those aboriginal tattoos the kids seem to like nowadays."

She stood and looked around. "Is this it?"

"So far. Wally's got Grace sniffing around in the trees. Maybe she'll find some parts that are more useful."

"Let's hope. It'll be a bitch getting an ID if this is all we have."

"Sure will."

"Looks like a female to me," Cutler said.

"That's what I thought."

"Been dead a while."

Jimmy nodded. "I bet on a week or two. Maybe more. Last few weeks have been cold and damp. Not like today." He looked up toward the sun. "Must be a hundred out here."

"Only ninety," Cutler said. "According to the radio."

"Those guys are never right." He swiped his shirt sleeve across his forehead. "I think they sit in some air-conditioned studio and make all that up, anyway."

She turned and scanned the open fields. "How much of this belongs to Clovis Wilson?"

Jimmy pointed. "His property line is just inside the tree line there, over that way to county road, and then up to the rail line easement. But that's just this parcel. He owns a patch work of land around here."

Cutler knew Clovis owned large parcels of farmland spread over two counties but she never could keep all the boundaries straight. Not that it was important to know. Until a leg popped up on one of them anyway.

"He aware yet?" Cutler asked.

"I called but he wasn't home. Probably out working one of his other fields. I called his cell. Didn't answer that either. Left a message."

"Jimmy." A shout from deep in the trees. Spicer. "Got something here."

He did. Spicer, Grace at his side, stood over the upper half of a body. Mostly anyway. Essentially skeletal, with only small bits of dried flesh here and there. No internal organs, left arm missing, a partially denuded right arm hanging by a couple of dried tendons. What flesh was left showed similar tattooing as she had seen on the leg. Half of the empty rib cage was missing, the remaining ribs splintered and crushed from the pigs' feasting. No head in sight.

Cutler knelt. "Definitely pigs," she said.

"How so?" Jimmy asked.

She reached down and picked up half a tusk. Obviously broken during the feeding frenzy. She handed it to Jimmy.

He examined it. "Looks like a young one."

She nodded, took the tooth and slid it into her shirt pocket, then returned her attention to the remains. "Got half a hand and three fingers. Maybe the ME can get some prints." She looked up at Spicer. "Good work. Anything else?"

"Nope." He nodded toward a shallow depression at the base of a pile of limestone. "Looks like the body was buried there."

Cutler walked that way. The grave site had been disturbed by excavation marks from where the pigs had retrieved their meal.

"Expand your search," she said. "Maybe we can find more remains."

"Will do." He scratched an ear. "I'd bet dollars to donuts the pigs ate the rest."

Cutler hoped that wasn't true. The more body parts they found, particularly if they could locate the head, the better chance they had of identifying the victim. "Keep looking anyway."

Spicer gave a quick nod. "Will do. If there's anything else to find, Grace'll find it. You can bet on that."

She watched Spicer and Grace melt into the trees, the dog leading the way. She turned to Jimmy. "Call Sara and Ray. Get them out here. Photograph the scenes and remains and then sift through the soil. You call the ME?"

"Sure did. They're sending a crew down."

She nodded, then walked to where the families stood. She knelt to get down on the kids' level.

"You guys doing okay?" she asked.

Silence. None of them lifted their gaze from the ground.

"Pretty scary finding that, wasn't it?"

No response, though she detected a slight nod from Misty.

"I hear you guys saw the buzzards and came to see what was dead."

A quick glance from Billy but nothing else.

"Talk to the chief," Dennis said.

Billy wiped his eyes with a pair of balled fists. "We didn't do nothing."

Cutler smiled. "Sure you did." Three pairs of eyes snapped up toward her. "You found this...person."

"We was just curious," Benjie said.

"And that's good. Maybe you'll grow up to be detectives some day." The eyes looking at her brightened. A little anyway. "Good cops are always curious."

That seemed to break the dam.

"We saw all those buzzards," Misty said. "A bunch of them. More than I've ever seen."

"Yeah," Billy said. "We knew it must be something big. Maybe a cow or something."

"Never thought it'd be somebody," Benjie said.

"Not to mention you weren't supposed to be over here," Ben Crane said. "This far from home."

Tears welled in Benjie's eyes, "It was farther than it looked. We thought it was just over by those trees. But when we got there we still had a piece to go."

"That's why you can't find the pot of gold at the end of the rainbow," Cutler said. "It keeps moving away from you."

"That's exactly what it was like," Billy said.

"That's no excuse for being here," Dennis said. He looked at Cutler. "They aren't supposed to cross the tracks. And definitely not the county road." He looked at his son. "Not for any reason."

"But, Dad..."

Dennis raised a finger. Billy fell silent.

Cutler smiled. "Well, you did break the rules. But I'm glad you did." She stood. "Otherwise we might've never known about this." She saw Wally Spicer and Grace come through the trees a couple of hundred feet away, then turn and disappear into them again. She looked back at the kids.

"Are we in trouble with the law?" Benjie asked.

"No." Cutler smiled. "This person—that you found—had a family and friends. I'm sure they're missing her. Wondering what happened. Once we identify her we'll be able to let them know."

Benjie smiled—almost.

Cutler looked at the parents. "You guys can head on home. If I have any more questions, I'll drop by."

She watched as they drove away. She didn't envy the kids. Grounding was definitely in their future. But she was indeed glad that they had stepped over the line.

CHAPTER 6

Cain returned home to collect Harper for the drive to Leiper's Fork. A trip that raised ambivalent feelings. Sure it would be good to see General Kessler again. It had been many years. On the other side of the world, each with sand and grit in their hair, eyes, everywhere; Cain with fresh blood on his hands.

But, under these circumstances? Kessler obviously adored his granddaughter. And with her parents succumbing to premature deaths, he and Miriam had essentially raised the girl. If she was truly missing, and not off on some college kid's adventure, they would be crushed. Even a tough, old bird like Kessler.

Cain heard the hiss of the shower coming from Harper's room, indicating she had finished her workout. He knew she'd be ready to roll within minutes of stepping from beneath the spray. Harper wasn't one to primp. Or waste time.

Three years ago, a year after they had started their consulting—that nowhere near covered what they actually did—not sure there was a word for that—they had purchased the entire top floor of St. Germain Place. Before it was built out. They designed the space as a single unit with four bedrooms, an office, and a well-equipped gym that included a throwing area for Cain to remain proficient with his knives. A shooting gallery for Harper and her weapons would have been nice, but that would have violated a dozen city codes. It was all wrapped in 360-degree views of the city's heart, the football stadium, and the Cumberland River.

"What's this about?" Harper asked as Cain pulled from the underground parking.

He had called her as he left Milner's office, telling her to get ready for a road trip. Probably just for the day but, as usual, to prep for a couple of more. You just never knew.

"Cindy Grant. General Kessler's granddaughter has gone missing."

"Gone missing in a bad way?"

"Maybe."

Cain avoided the interstate, as traffic there was unpredictable and most often snarled, instead following a more direct route. Highway 431, then 46, which melted into the one-street village of Leiper's Fork. Calling it a village was a stretch, the "downtown" area being a couple of blocks long and the stores and restaurants sparse. Beyond, the highway resumed, becoming Old Hillsboro Road, a two-lane blacktop that wound through rolling fields and thick stands of pines and gums and oaks. A half mile south of town, General William Kessler's estate came into view.

"Impressive," Harper said.

As Milner had described, its stone construction brought to mind a medieval castle. Backed up against a hillock of dark-green pines, it possessed a commanding view of the General's acreage, plenty of that, and the valley below. Civilian life had been good to the Kesslers. Cain knew their money had come from real estate and shrewd investing. Not to mention the various boards the General sat on.

They were buzzed through the gate that stretched between two thick river rock columns and continued up 200 yards of winding drive that ended at a paved parking circle. A stone archway led to a pair of massive wooden entry doors. As Cain reached for the buzzer, one door swung open.

Miriam Kessler. Thin, gray hair trimmed short, she wore black slacks and a lemon silk shirt. Cain knew she was sixty-eight but she appeared a dozen years younger. Less so today. Miriam had been at the General's side through everything. Countless state dinners and military processions. Now she devoted her time to charities and fundraising.

"Bobby Cain," she said. "It's been a long time."

"How are you, Miriam?" They hugged.

"We've definitely been better."

"I don't think you've met my sister, Harper."

"I've heard about you though," Miriam said, shaking Harper's hand. "Please, come in."

Cain and Harper entered and she closed the door.

"Thank you for coming," Miriam said. "On such short notice."

"Anything for the General."

"It's been a tough week," Miriam said. "Bill is beside himself."

Cain remembered Miriam as always appearing fit, healthy, alive. Now, she wore a haggard, exhausted mantle. Stress lines cut into her face, her hair gray and tired. Her eyes held an irritated redness and a hint of puffiness. She looked like someone enveloped in a personal hell. Yet through that mask a glow of strength and resiliency persisted. Like so many military wives, she was a warrior.

"Bill's in his study."

She led them through a voluminous foyer and into a great room, which was exactly that. Ceilings that soared 25 feet above them, maybe more, and a massive stone fireplace, large enough to park a car inside. Plush sofas, antiques everywhere, and twenty-foot windows filling one wall.

"Can I get you something?" she asked over her shoulder. "I'm sure Bill will want some lemonade."

"That would be fine," Cain said.

They entered the General's equally impressive study. Kessler stood and came around his desk, hand extended, now silhouetted against cathedral windows that looked out over rolling hills of green grass and wads of thick pines. He wore gray slacks and a dark blue shirt. His hair silver, eyes deeply blue.

"Bobby Cain," he said. "It's been a long time."

"Yes, it has."

They shook hands. Cain introduced Harper and they took seats facing Kessler who again settled into his oxblood leather chair.

"Wish it were under better circumstances," Kessler said. "Did you have any trouble finding us?"

"None at all."

"Good, good."

Miriam returned with three glasses of lemonade.

"Anything else?" she asked.

"No," Kessler said. "Thanks." He offered her a sad smile.

"Then I'll leave you to talk business."

Kessler watched her go, waiting until the door closed behind her. "She's taking this harder than me. And that's pretty hard."

"I imagine so," Cain said.

"You know about loss."

Cain stared at him.

"First being abandoned at—what was it? Two months?"

"That's what I was told."

"The murder of your adoptive parents. While you were overseas."

Cain nodded.

"And you, Harper. Abandoned, actually sold, by your mother."

"You've done your homework," Cain said.

"As I'm sure you have. And will." Kessler studied them for a beat, sighed. "The upshot is that I know each of you understand loss."

"From what I was told, your granddaughter is missing," Harper said. "That doesn't mean something has happened to her."

"I wish that was true." He folded his hands before him. "But I'm a pragmatic man. Always have been." He glanced at the door again. "I know the odds of her being alive are remote. Essentially nonexistent. It's been a week now and she hasn't responded. Her cell phone no longer receives calls. Something has happened. Something…unpleasant."

Cain wanted to reassure him but knew he really couldn't. Mainly because the odds dictated he was correct. Still, he tried. "She's a college kid. They do stupid things all the time. Like going away and forgetting to call."

"Not Cindy. Even when she was in Europe a couple of years ago, she called. Every day. Like clockwork. It's in her nature."

"Do you have any evidence that something's happened?" Harper asked.

"Specifically? No." Kessler shook his head. "I did call her roommate. A girl named Kelly Whitt. She said Cindy told her she was going to Colorado for a few days. She hasn't heard from her since she left."

"Did she?" I asked. "Go to Colorado?"

"She didn't fly. Or take a train. Or rent a car, or use any of her credit cards. And her cell phone went out after about forty-eight hours. It's last known position was in Nashville."

Cain was impressed, but not surprised. A retired General who had spent much of his life in intelligence, who ran dark ops in many of the most treacherous places on Earth, could get his hands on just about any information he needed.

"Milner was a bit cryptic when we spoke. Exactly why are we here?" Cain asked.

"Because I want you to find her. Or discover what happened to her." He hesitated. "And make things right."

"I'm sure Milner told you that we don't do missing persons."

Kessler leaned back in his chair, spun it slightly so he could gaze out the windows for a beat. He sighed; a deep, mournful sigh. "Let me ask you something," He swiveled back around. "How many knives do you have on you right now?"

"That you could find? Three or four."

Kessler nodded. "The tools of your trade."

Cain remained silent.

"Let me tell you a story," Kessler said as he leaned back. "There was boy. Raised by a wandering gypsy band. Became an expert with knives. At a very early age. He put on knife throwing exhibitions all over the South. Part of the traveling show. He also became an expert second-story thief. He had many talents." He steepled his fingers before him. "An arrest, an orphanage, and an adoption followed. Then on to the US Army. He was eighteen." He scratched the back of one hand and then re-steepled his fingers. "His military career was destined to be bland, normal. But then his SEREs training drew some attention. If memory serves, he stayed off the radar for a week. And then suddenly appeared in his CO's office. Something like that, anyway." Kessler offered a half smile. "Ruffled more than a few feathers."

Kessler had definitely done his due diligence.

"But our hero's shenanigans attracted the attention of the Pentagon, a few other agencies. And his military career took a sudden turn. Ranger School, Seal and Delta training, followed by various Special Ops missions. Intelligence gathering, communication and supply disruptions, and a few targeted eliminations. Most, but not all, sanctioned." He held Cain's gaze a beat. "Yet, each necessary." Kessler leaned back again, arms folded over his chest. "Then his parents were murdered. By three men. Each later met an unexpected and not so pleasant demise."

Again, Cain said nothing.

"Our protagonist in this little tale then left the military. But not, for lack of a better term, special ops. Only his employers changed. Private, rather than military. His methods? Well, let's just say the military—his gypsy family, too—trained him well."

Still, Cain remained silent.

"Then, there's another tale. Child sold to an itinerant family. By her alcoholic, half-Cherokee mother. Smart, precocious. Family disrupted when their past caught up to them. Orphanage, adoption, also military. Intelligence, PsyOps, CIA. Our heroine proved quite adept at running off-the-grid ops. The kind that could slam you in front of a Senate subcommittee." He gave a half shrug. "Then, a chance reunion. In a hell hole."

Cain wasn't really surprised that Kessler knew his background in intimate detail. They had a history. Kessler had run several of Cain's missions. But Harper? Kessler didn't know her. No military connection. Yet, Kessler had gone deep.

"So, let's get down to it," Kessler said. "I know—I can feel it in my bones, and my bones are always right—that I will never see Cindy alive again." Another glance toward the door. "I know that for a fact. She didn't run off somewhere. Forget to call. This isn't money driven. Not a ransom. This is something much worse. More final."

"Are you sure we're the right people for the job?" Cain asked.

Kessler leaned forward, his fists balled on his desk before him. "We're soldiers. Each of us. Trained to do the tough jobs. The ones no one else will do." He locked on Cain. "I know about Afghanistan. I know about the ones that killed your family in Tyler, Texas." Now, his attention turned to Harper. "I know about deeply secret CIA ops. Most well below the threshold of visibility. I know much of the work you've done together over the past few years." His fists relaxed. "So, yes, you're the ones for this mission."

Mission? Interesting word choice. But not unexpected coming from Kessler.

Cain nodded. "What do you want us to do?"

Kessler's blue eyes took on an extra intensity. "This is a military operation. A war, if you will. One where we, not the enemy, dictate the rules of engagement. You know me. Know I'm more of the General George S. Patton school. Stonewall Jackson, too. Never wait. Take the battle to the enemy. I want Cindy found. Dead, alive, whatever, I want her found. I want those who took her to feel the full weight of their actions. If she's been harmed, I want those responsible harmed. If she's been tortured, then pain and mortal fear should come their way. If she's been murdered, I want them to suffer a similar fate." His face darkened. "That's what I want."

CHAPTER 7

Bobby Cain, Age 18

That Bobby Cain made it into the military was a minor miracle. For one thing, he had a criminal record—juvenile, sealed, and later expunged—but still a record. Surely the military had access to that part of his life. He had limited formal education. Some homeschooling as his gypsy family scurried from town to town, thanks to Aunt Dixie, and his adoptive parents, the Cains, had pushed him to a high school diploma. But his education had always felt haphazard, incomplete.

Degree in hand, he enlisted in the US Army. Amazingly, they accepted him. Even though his final two years of school were at a military academy, he had no real "military connections" to smooth the path. Everything indicated that his Army career would be uneventful.

Things changed a few months in. Thanks to the not-so-formal education he had received from his gypsy family.

Several of the "parents" in the troupe had offered lessons that aren't available in a real school. Things like how to run a con, or lift a wallet, or a watch, or empty a purse in a heartbeat. Day, night, alone, in a crowd, each required a different approach and skill set.

For Cain, these lessons most often came from Uncle Al, Aunt Dixie, and Uncle Maurice, known as Uncle Mo.

Fighting lessons were particularly intense. "No fight is fair," was Uncle Mo's mantra. "The guy who fights fair, loses." He taught Cain to box, wrestle, and what he called "grappling." The art of taking someone of any size down with a single punch, or the literal snap of a finger, or out cold with a choke hold. Most of Cain's "brother" opponents back then had been years older, and much larger and stronger. But, he learned quickly. The key, according to Uncle Manny, was hand strength. *Strong hands win fights.*

Uncle Al taught him that in a fight, everything was a weapon. Fists, feet, elbows, knees, your head. A stick, a stone, a chair, a lamp, and, of course, a knife. He showed Bobby where to hide knives in his clothes and shoes, even how to construct those that could be secreted in belts, hats, pocket linings, seams.

Aunt Dixie gave him a master class in the art of throwing.

Uncle Al taught him how to climb. Trees, at first, then poles, trellises, whatever it took to get inside a house to "go shopping."

Then, it all ended. The FBI swooped in. The family had pending charges in several states. Mostly Texas, but also in Oklahoma, Arkansas, Louisiana, and a few other adjacent states. Essentially everywhere they traveled.

Home schooling was over. But it was his gypsy training—the skills he had learned from his various uncles and aunts—that pushed his military career in an unexpected direction.

SERE's training. SERE stands for Survival, Evasion, Resistance, and Escape. Basically, newbie soldiers were dropped in woods just outside of camp, given a basic backpack and a five to ten minute head start, and then hunted down. The recruit's task was to evade, survive, and if captured, refuse to talk. Evading was difficult, capture and the mock prisoner of war camp wasn't pleasant. Nor were the tiny boxes they folded "detainees" into. Or the bright light interrogations, or the water boarding, or the isolation, or all the inventive PsyOps techniques the "interrogators" imposed on those unfortunate souls who were captured.

Which was eventually everyone.

Except Bobby Cain.

Uncle Albert had taught him a bag full of evasive techniques. You just never knew when a B&E would go south and the cops would be on you. When a tree, basement, shed, drainage pipe, even partial self-burial could be a friend.

Cain's SERE's training took place at Camp Mackall, part of the massive Fort Bragg complex in North Carolina. In July. Hot and humid didn't cover it. Neither did oppressive.

Cain thought the entire set up was borderline ridiculous. Sure they would be released, given a few minutes head start, and then tracked down. Okay, that worked. But if by noon you hadn't been located and captured, you were supposed to come out of the woods and turn yourself in. The military didn't want anyone to miss the pain and humiliation of interrogation. A rigged game. Cain wasn't interested in playing ball. If they wanted evasion, he planned to supply it.

He and his fellow recruits were released in small groups, Cain's consisting of six guys. They ran, weaving through the trees, maybe two hundred yards. Then the squabbling over which way to go broke out. Cain left them to their debates and melted into the forest. Better to be alone if flying low is the goal.

Uncle Al often said that most pursuers assumed you would run on a track that would put the greatest distance between you and them. In many cases this was the best strategy. Quickly create a gap and then go to ground. Sit tight. Let the pursuers scratch around until they give up. Other times, getting close was best. Backtracking. His thoughts were that they wouldn't even start looking for you until they were beyond your last known location. "Who would run toward the hunters?" he always said.

That's the tactic Cain chose.

He guessed he had five minutes max. He worked through the trees toward the main installation, toward his pursuers. In a heavily wooded area, he found what he sought. A depression in the landscape, between two scraggly pine trees. He fisted some soil, added a bit of water from his canteen, and lathered the resulting mud on his arms, neck, and face. He wriggled into the depression and covered himself. Leaves, pine needles, dirt, rocks, anything he could find. He began with his feet and worked his way upward, making sure the surface looked undisturbed. He finally balanced a pine bough over his face, inhaling its sweet, pungent aroma.

He waited.

At first the cool, damp earth drove a chill into his back, but soon his body heat warmed his cocoon. He closed his eyes, slowed his breathing, and tuned in the sounds of the forest. Tree branches rustled in the breeze, a squirrel clawed up a tree above him, knocking loose bits of bark that tapped against his covering of leaves.

Wasn't long before the first troops shuffled by. A good thirty feet away. He couldn't tell how many but guessed four or five at least. Talking, laughing, making no effort to be secretive, not on the hunt yet. Thinking there was nothing to see until they got past the drop point.

Then they were gone.

Still, Cain waited. Insects crawled over his legs, arms, face, exploring, seeking food or a nesting spot. He ignored them, hearing Uncle Mo in his head: "When you go to ground, stay to ground. Movement can be seen and heard." Bees and wasps buzzed the air above. Even the sonorous hum of bumblebees. The breeze shook loose pollen and leaf bits, which fell through the pine branch over his face, triggering the need to cough and sneeze, watering his eyes. He remained still, silent. He turned inside, slowed his breathing, floated on a calm lake. Another trick from Uncle Mo.

Two more small groups came by, each farther away, maybe two hundred feet. Then nothing. The forest sounds fell into their natural rhythm.

The light that filtered through the trees and his coverings showed that noon came and went. He remained "buried" until nightfall, then crawled from his "grave," and worked his way toward the camp. He was now officially AWOL.

A nearby tangle of brush offered him cover and he slithered inside, waiting for the camp to settle into slumber. Midnight arrived. He knew his time was running out. At daybreak, his CO, a burly, whiskey-drinking, cigar-smoking, by-the-book guy named David North, would be furious, and getting nervous. Fearful something had happened to Cain, he would bolster the search efforts, probably bring in the dogs.

But Cain had a plan. One that suited his skills perfectly.

No place is completely secure. One of Uncle Al's truisms. Not a house, a high-rise apartment building, a bank. Nothing. There was always a way in—and out. This was also true for military bases. Cain found several exploitable defects in Camp Mackall's perimeter security. A barrier undergoing repairs, a shallow depression that left a small gap beneath a chain-link fence, an unmanned gate that was easily scalable. He opted for the low road, and crawled beneath the fence.

Once inside the compound, he had the run of the place. It was two a.m. Any guards on duty worked the perimeter, not the inner buildings. He knew a couple of the barracks were not in use. Probably waiting for the next wave of recruits. He showered, first in his smelly clothes, and then out of them. He squeezed water from them as best he could, then redressed. They would dry. He grabbed two blankets from the storage rack at one end of the sleeping quarters.

Back outside, he scurried between buildings until he found the one he wanted. Provisions were stored in a large metal quonset-like structure behind the mess hall. Entering was a snap. No alarms, no guards, and the door lock was simple, standard issue. Less sophisticated than many of the houses he had breached. He went shopping. Bread, cheese, salami, candy bars, and bottles of water, another of Jack Daniels. The building possessed an attic area. Access by way of a staircase along one wall. It was empty. Just dust and solitude. His new home. Until he decided to give up the game.

He dumped his provisions. One more thing to do. Back downstairs he lifted the wall phone and called his adoptive parents, Wilbert and Ruth Cain, both well-respected and successful attorneys. Told them all was okay, but if the military contacted them, to simply act concerned, but know that he was in no danger. Neither was happy. His mother questioned the wisdom of such a move. But after Cain explained the entire plan, his father, who Cain knew had a streak of outlaw in there somewhere actually laughed, seeing the humor in it. Which garnered a rebuke from Ruth.

"Don't encourage his bad behavior, Wilbert. What if they toss him out?"

"They won't," Cain said. "They need the bodies."

He returned to his new quarters, ate most of his provisions, drank from the Daniels bottle, rolled onto a blanket, and slept.

He remained there for a full week. His major discomfort was the heat during the day. The building was air-conditioned, and some did seep into the attic, but not enough to make things comfortable. Just tolerable. Regardless, he ate well, slept well, and during the day listened to the camp noise. And read. He had found a cache of books, a flashlight, and a pile of batteries.

Almost reluctantly he decided it was time to come in.

At five a.m., he returned the blankets, showered, and entered his CO's office. And waited.

The look on Sergeant North's face when he walked in early that morning was priceless. Cain sat behind his desk, the detritus of his breakfast, muffin wrappers and a banana peel, littering its surface, feet propped on the corner. Glass of bourbon in one hand, a smoldering cigar—one of his North's bootlegged Cubans he found in the desk drawer—in the other.

Anger didn't quite cover it. North's face purpled as if it might explode, his thick neck pulsed, the veins roping.

"Cain, what the hell are you doing?"

Cain smiled. "Surrendering."

"Where have you been?"

"Evading. Wasn't that the purpose of the exercise?"

North's entire body coiled, vibrated. "Do you have any idea how much time and manpower we've consumed looking for you?"

"Quite a bit, I imagine."

North stepped forward, teeth grinding almost audibly. "You're going to love the fucking brig."

"On what charges? Wasn't I supposed to try to win the game?"

"The game?" The words exploded. North spun toward the door, yanked it open, and bellowed down the hallway. "Get the fucking MPs in here."

The brig followed. For a few days anyway.

Then a guy showed up. Scrambled eggs on the shoulders of his uniform. A bird Colonel. Told Cain someone wanted to see him. In Langley, Virginia.

CHAPTER 8

Chief Laura Cutler stood atop a limestone outcropping and scanned the area. The scent of damp leaves and pine needles permeated the air. To the east, she could hear Wally Spicer working his dogs, their snorting and occasional yaps echoing toward her. She had called in a couple of officers—the department only had nine, including her and Jimmy Rankin—and they were searching to the west and south. So far, nothing.

Rankin pushed through the trees.

"Any luck?" she asked.

"Nada. If Wally's dogs can't find nothing, I doubt we will either."

"That's true." She skittered down from her perch, a few loose pebbles tumbling behind her. As she crunched onto the pine needles her cell sounded. She answered, listened for a beat, and disconnected the call. "ME's techs just showed. Clovis Wilson, too."

Cutler and Rankin exited the trees. Clovis stood near his blue pick up and the white ME's van, watching the two techs, one male, one female. They squatted, examining the pig-mauled leg. Clovis's face was ghostly pale and sweat peppered his forehead. The heat, or what he was seeing? Probably a little of each.

"Clovis," Cutler said with a nod. "You okay?"

He looked up. "Yeah. Just a bit shocked."

"Us, too."

"What is all this?"

"Looks like we got a body dumped on your property."

He shook his head. "I can't believe it. Who is it?"

She jerked her head toward the two techs. "That's what I'm hoping these folks can tell us."

Moss Landing, like most towns in this part of the state, contracted with the ME's office in Nashville for their forensic work, including body recovery and autopsies. Budget didn't allow for any other arrangement. Farming it out was much cheaper than supporting a local coroner or crime lab. Which was rarely needed. The truth was Cutler couldn't remember the last time the ME's office had been summoned to this neck of the woods.

She stepped toward the pair. "I'm Chief Laura Cutler." She flicked a thumb toward Rankin. "This is Jimmy Rankin."

The guy spun on his haunches and looked up at her. "I'm Sean Baker. This is Melinda Wurst."

"Thanks for coming," Cutler said.

"What is all this?" Baker said, pointing to the leg.

"Tattooing, it looks like."

"Never seen anything like this," Wurst said. "Definitely not something that'll be in our gang database."

"I doubt this is a gang-related thing," Cutler said. "They don't come down this way." She shrugged. "At least not yet."

"Looks more fashion statement to me," Rankin said.

"We'll get our tattoo guy on it," Baker said.

"You have a tattoo guy?" Cutler asked.

Wurst smiled. "We got a guy, or a gal, for just about everything it seems. But, yeah, we have someone who's more or less an expert in tattoos. Helps us identify gang members and occasionally ID remains. Like this."

Cutler nodded.

"These the only remains?" Baker asked.

"Got a partial rib cage and arm in there." Cutler pointed toward the trees.

"Let's take a look."

They did. Baker and Wurst went through their *in situ* examination, took several photos.

"If it's okay with you we're going to start packing things up?"

Wurst said.

"Fine with me."

"Looks to me like the body was buried here, and predators got to it," Baker said.

"Pigs most likely," Cutler said. She pulled the tusk remnant from her shirt pocket and handed it to him. "Found this near the ribs."

Baker raised an eyebrow.

"Yeah, I know. Shouldn't have touched it. But after I picked it up, to identify it, I figured I'd better hold on to it. So it wouldn't get lost."

Baker passed the tusk to Wurst who pulled a plastic evidence bag from her pocket and slipped it inside.

Took another twenty minutes for them to pack the remains into body bags and load them in their van. Cutler watched them drive away, then turned to Clovis.

"You see anything unusual around here lately? Past couple of weeks?"

"Nope. And I'm here pretty near every day." He waved a hand toward the neat rows of green-leafed plants. "Cotton's shooting up. Got to keep the bugs away."

"You haven't seen anyone stomping around out here?" Cutler asked. "Maybe in the woods? Or a strange vehicle parked nearby?"

"Ain't seen nobody."

She nodded.

"Strange is what it is," Clovis said. "I mean, who'd drop a body here on my place?"

"That's the question me and Jimmy'll have to figure out."

Clovis pulled a handkerchief from his back pocket and wiped his face. "Gonna be a hot one today."

"Already is."

Now he swiped his neck. "Well, I better get at it. We're working my soybean field over by the highway."

"Thanks for coming over," Cutler said. "We'll be clearing out of here soon. Let me know if you do see anyone, or anything out of the ordinary."

"You can bet on it." Clovis climbed in his truck and cranked it to life. He rolled the window down. "Let me know if you find out who it is."

"Will do."

Clovis drove away.

"What do you think?" Rankin asked.

"I think we got a killer on our hands."

"You don't think she was just walking in the woods. Maybe fell and hit her head. Something like that?"

Cutler looked at him. "We didn't find any clothing, so that'd mean she was out here buck ass naked."

"I suspect so," he said. "But folks do some strange things."

"You mean like getting themselves killed and eaten by pigs?"

He smiled. "Something like that." He turned back toward the trees. "We got any missing persons around?"

"Not here. They had that school teacher go missing a few weeks ago. Maybe a month back. Over near Lynchburg."

"That's right. I forgot."

"And as far as I know, she hasn't turned up anywhere," Cutler said.

"Doubt this'll be her. All those tattoos. Don't seem very teacherly to me."

"Teacherly?"

"It's a word."

Cutler gave him a skeptical look.

"What? It is."

She shook her head. "Wouldn't try to use that in a game of Scrabble."

"What about that teenager?" Jimmy asked. "The one that disappeared four, five weeks ago?"

"They found her. Hitched up to see grandma in Michigan. Traverse City, if I recall." She looked at Rankin. "Didn't you get that memo?"

"Probably on my desk somewhere."

"It's the somewhere that's the operative word here."

Jimmy Rankin wasn't one to fuss with keeping his office neat. Desk, book shelves, even a couple of chairs were stacked with papers and books and probably a few living things. Looked like Dresden, 1945. It was a department joke—one of the secretaries had even put a Hazmat sign on his office door—and Cutler never missed a chance to give him a ration about it.

"I could get the fire department to come over and hose it down, if you want," she said.

"I got my own system. I know where everything is."

The irony was that he did. Could always pull whatever she asked for from the rubble.

"What now?" Rankin asked.

Cutler looked down, kicked at a loose stone, sending it tumbling. She looked up at the sky. "I don't know for sure." She eyed Rankin. "Since we don't know who this was, I'm not sure we have anywhere to look. Not yet anyway."

That was the truth of it. Unidentified victims offered no clear path for investigation. You never knew which way to look, who to talk to, much less create anything resembling a suspect list. They were stuck on square one with no dice to roll.

"Maybe the ME can help us out there," Rankin said.

"Let's hope."

CHAPTER 9

To gather intel, best to start at ground zero. Cindy Grant's roommate Kelly Whitt. Harper called her as they drove back toward Nashville, catching Kelly between classes. She said she was headed to her last session of the day and would meet them after at the Starbucks on the Vanderbilt campus, off 21st Avenue near the famous Music Row.

That gave Cain and Harper time to review the materials Kessler had given them.

They parked a block away. Once inside, the heat of the day evaporated under the cranked-up air-conditioning. Cain assessed the room. Coffee bar at one end, several students in line to place their orders. A cluster of high tables and stools in the middle, many filled with small groups or individuals working their computers and iPads, thumbs dancing on phones. Along the far wall sat a series of deep, comfortable chairs and small, round coffee tables. These were mostly empty.

Cain grabbed a Venti dark roast and a blueberry muffin; Harper, a mocha and a yogurt parfait. They settled in the comfy chairs near one corner. That gave them a view of the room and the entrance and placed them far enough from other activity to allow some semblance of privacy. Not ideal, but Harper had said she wanted Kelly to feel relaxed, not threatened. And this apparently was a place Kelly considered home turf.

Two girls walked by, one complaining to the other about a professor. Apparently he expected her to study and come to class prepared. The nerve.

They tuned out the chatter as best they could and opened the file folder Kessler had given them. An 8X10 photo of Cindy Grant greeted them. Blonde, blue-eyed, a beauty. A welcoming, wholesome smile. Behind the photo were a half-dozen loose pages. The first had Cindy's vital info. Birthdate, current address, cell number, driver's license info, car registration, college transcripts.

Cindy was 20, lived in an apartment just off campus, and drove a three series BMW. Finishing her sophomore year. Majoring in graphic design with a minor in communication. Straight As according to her grade printouts. She ran on the cross-country team, waitressed part time at a popular restaurant called Southern Hospitality, and volunteered with a crisis hotline outfit called Talk To Me. Busy girl. And apparently on a straight and narrow path to success.

Another page contained info on Kelly. A 3X5 photo was stapled to the page. Cindy and another girl, standing side by side. Someone had handwritten "Cindy-Kelly" near the bottom. Kelly was also a beauty. Long dark hair, green eyes, a mischievous smile. Each wore jeans and halter tops and stood next to an ATV, which rested on a rutted dirt trail that slanted away into a grassy pasture, a thick stand of pines in the far field. Apparently taken late in the day as the sunlight slashed from their left, darkening half of their faces, casting long, lean shadows to their right. The typed page showed that Kelly, like Cindy, was 20 and a sophomore. She also worked part time at Southern Hospitality.

The next page was a handwritten list of the folks Kessler had contacted. His script was elegant, yet strong. No flourishes. No bull.

Kelly Whitt—roommate
Captain Lee Bradford—Nashville PD
Missy Mulligan—Manager, Southern Hospitality
Craig Williams—owner/director Talk To Me
Olivia Johnston—track coach

Cain finished the muffin and sipped the dregs of his coffee as he mulled what he had read. Cindy seemed to be a normal college girl. Pretty, smart, athletic. Worked when she didn't really have to, did community service. No wonder her grandparents were so proud of her. The classic overachiever. A lot on her plate.

Kelly, on paper, seemed to be cut from similar cloth. But he'd reserve judgement until they chatted with her.

Cain glanced at his watch. She was fifteen minutes late. Did she get cold feet? Decide that talking with a stranger about Cindy might not be the best tact? He hadn't gotten that impression over the phone. When he said that General Kessler suggested they talk, she seemed completely on board. Even eager to do so.

"She's late," he said.

"She's a college kid," Harper said. "Give her time."

Then he saw her. Standing just inside the front door, gaze flitting over the crowd. He gave her a small wave and she headed their way.

"Kelly?"

"That's me."

"I'm Bobby Cain. This is Harper McCoy."

She nodded, slipped her backpack from her shoulder, settling it on the coffee table to her left, and sat across from them. "Sorry I'm late. My prof got longwinded today."

"No problem," Harper said. "Thanks for coming."

"You said you wanted to chat about Cindy. Has something happened?"

That seemed an odd question. Cindy had been missing for a week.

"She's missing, if that qualifies as something."

Kelly hesitated a beat. "She's in Colorado. Hiking."

"So you've talked to her?" Cain asked. "Recently?"

"No. Not since she left." She looked around. "Who are you again?"

"Bobby Cain. Harper McCoy. We've been asked by Cindy's grandfather to see if we can find her. The General and his wife are worried. He said she's very good about keeping in touch. And they've heard nothing."

Kelly brushed a strand of hair from her eyes. "She's hiking.

Probably doesn't have cell coverage up there." She shrugged. "And he does worry about her a lot. Too much, I think."

"Does Cindy?" Harper asked. "Think he's too smothering? Anything like that?"

She shook her head. "No, I wouldn't say that."

"Who'd she go with on this trip?" Cain asked.

"Some dude."

"He have a name? This dude?"

"I'm not sure I like your tone," she said. She leaned back in her chair and folded her arms over her chest.

"He's mostly harmless," Harper said.

Cain smiled. "The General is very worried. He fears something might've happened to her." She didn't respond so Cain went on. "All we're asking is if you know the guy she supposedly took off with?"

"No. All she said was that she met this cute guy and they were going to Colorado."

"Is he a student?"

"She didn't say."

"And no name, I take it?"

She shook her head.

"To summarize," Cain said, "she left on some trip to Colorado with some guy and hasn't been heard from for the past week?"

"That's about it," Kelly said.

No, that wasn't about it. The forced innocence on her face, the way her eyes cut away for a brief moment, the hand that increased its grip on the chair arm. Kelly was lying. She knew more.

"And you're not worried?" Harper asked.

Her brow wrinkled, her gaze dropping toward the floor. "Not really."

Cain tapped a finger on the arm of his chair. "How did she get to Colorado? Drive?"

"No. Her car's still at the apartment. She probably flew."

"She didn't. Or take a bus or a train."

"How do you know that?"

"We know. Let's just leave it at that."

"Whatever." She looked away, as if buying time. Then she said, "Maybe the dude drove."

Her lying was now even more obvious. Face, body language, lame ass answers. She hadn't thought this through well enough to create a believable story. Or deliver it well.

Cain sighed and leaned forward, elbows on his knees. Time to crank up the heat. "You're lying."

"What? I am not."

He held her gaze. "You're lying. I want to know why."

"I don't have to do this." She grabbed the strap of her backpack and started to stand.

"No, you don't. But let me tell you what will happen if you walk out of here."

She halted, settling back in the chair. Her eyes wide now. He'd at least gotten her attention.

"We'll begin to dissect your life. Your friends, your family, your professors, your employers over at Southern Hospitality. Anyone and everyone you know."

"You can't do that."

"We can and we will," Harper said. She gathered in Kelly's gaze, held it. "Or we can quietly go about our business and do our job off the radar."

"Which is?"

"Finding Cindy," Cain said. "By whatever means are necessary."

Kelly's eyes moistened. She glanced around the room. "Why are you doing this to me?"

"Kelly, it's not about you. And it's not just you. We're simply starting here. Because you know Cindy as well as anyone. You live with her. You know her habits, her friends—and you know where she really went."

"I don't. I swear."

Cain stared at her. Unwavering. No blinking.

Kelly's gaze dropped to her hands, now folded in her lap. Her fingernails were painted a dark green and she worked one cuticle with her thumbnail.

"Kelly, listen to me," Harper said. "We aren't your enemies." Kelly looked up. "We're on the same side here. We, and the Kesslers, are afraid something's happened to Cindy. Or she's in trouble and needs help. I think you believe that, too."

Kelly took a deep ragged breath, forked her hair back from

her face. "This is so fucked."

"Tell us," Harper said.

Another raspy breath. "Something's not right. I feel it. But I promised her I'd never say a word."

"About what?" Cain asked.

She looked around the room again, then leaned forward. Her voice dropped a few decibels. "There's this guy. He hooks up college girls for dates."

"I see."

"Mostly with older guys. But really all kinds."

"Voice of experience here?" Harper said.

She sniffed. Nodded. "Only twice." She rubbed her nose with the back of her hand. "Made a ton of money but I just couldn't do it. I really hated it."

"I take it these dates involved sex?"

Tears collected in her eyes. "Yes." She rummaged in her backpack, came out with a tissue, and dabbed each eye. "And trips. All over from what I hear."

"And this is what Cindy did?" Cain asked.

She dabbed her left eye again. "She's been seeing guys for six months."

"I get the impression she doesn't need money."

"True. But this is her money. Not her grandparents."

"What are we talking about here? Money-wise?" Harper asked.

Kelly gave her a half smile. "Three or four grand a night. Ten or more for a trip."

"Is that where Cindy is?" Cain asked. "On one of these trips?"

She nodded.

"How long? With who?"

"It was supposed to be for the weekend. When she didn't return, I assumed the guy simply extended the date."

"But now you're not sure?"

Two girls came by. Talking, laughing. One gave us a quick glance but that was about it. Kelly waited for them to pass before responding.

"When I didn't hear from her for a few days, I called the guy who set it up. He said she was heading to Europe with the guy."

"She didn't," Cain said.

"How do you know?"

"Her passport. It hasn't been used."

"How do you know all this?"

"It's our job to know," Harper said.

"Who are you?"

"We told you. Interested parties. Hired by General Kessler."

Cain smiled, adding, "Let's say that we fix things. And right now we're trying to solve a puzzle."

Another ragged breath. Her lips trembled when she spoke. "What do you think?"

"What we think doesn't matter," Harper said. "It's what actually happened that counts."

Kelly nodded.

Harper leaned forward and laid a hand on Kelly's arm. "We need for you to be honest here. Cindy's life might depend on it."

Kelly sniffed, nodded again.

Harper pressed on. "Who is this guy? The one that set up the date?"

Kelly looked around. "He comes in here a lot. Don't see him now. His name's Adam Parker. He's a grad student."

"Did he arrange your dates?"

She nodded. "Not directly. I mean, he's the one I talked with. Cindy, too. But I think he has a partner or somebody who handles the money and arrangements. All I know is that I was told where to go and when to be there."

"Hotels?" Cain asked.

"Both of my dates were."

"Local?"

Another nod. "He asked me once about going away with some married guy. To Miami. I was scared. Told him I couldn't."

"Smart move," Harper said.

"Are you going to go see him?" Kelly seemed animated now. Her eyes wide, gaze surveying the room as if she feared she was being watched.

"Any reason we shouldn't?" Cain asked. He also scanned the room but saw no one locked on them or even giving them a second glance.

"Please don't tell him we talked," Kelly said. Almost pleading.

"We won't." Her shoulders and face seemed to relax, her relief evident. "Why? Is he a bad guy?"

"Not him. His partner. So I hear."

"Oh?" Harper said. "Care to expand on that?"

"Another girl I know. She went on several dates. One time she met a guy at the airport. Supposed to go to New York for the weekend. But the guy was a creep. She told him she wasn't feeling well and split. Adam's partner got all twisted out of shape. Made some threats."

"Anything happen?"

"Not that she could prove. But she began getting a lot of hang up calls. Someone broke into her condo. Stole some jewelry and stuff."

"Did she call the police?"

"She was too scared." She let out a quick laugh. "Besides, what was she going to say? Her pimp stole from her?"

"We'd like to talk with her," Cain said. "What's her name?"

Kelly shook her head emphatically. "No way. She's out of that world and wants nothing to do with it."

"Might be important."

"No. I can't do it."

"Tell you what, I'll give you my number," Cain said. "You pass it to her and tell her to call if she's willing to talk. Privately and completely confidential."

She nodded. Cain gave her his number and she put it in her phone.

"What about Adam's partner?" Harper asked. "Do you know his name?"

"No. I never saw him. All I ever heard was that his name is Carlos, I think."

"I don't want you to say a word about us," Cain said. "Or this conversation. To anyone."

"You can bet on that."

"Except your friend who had the trouble with Adam's partner," Harper added.

"Okay."

"Mainly, we don't want this Adam guy to know who we are or what we're doing. Got it?"

"What are you going to do?"

Cain smiled. "Best if you don't know. And best if you don't know us."

"You're not going to hurt him are you?"

"I'd rather not."

"But you don't know for sure?"

"Depends on whether he was involved in Cindy's disappearance." Cain glanced toward the front door where two young women came in, one laughing loudly. "But my gut tells me he was."

Now Kelly forked the fingers of both hands through her hair. "This is a freaking nightmare."

"Look, Cindy's apparently involved in some dirty business," Harper said. "You were smart enough to walk away. She wasn't. Things don't always go well for young ladies who move in those circles."

"I suppose."

"If we need any more info from you, we'll call, or arrange a meet," Cain said. "Somewhere private. If you hear anything or if Adam contacts you, play dumb. You know nothing. And call me." She gave a single nod. "In fact, if you see him here, call me. Immediately. Okay?"

"And then what?"

"We'll handle it from there."

CHAPTER 10

No more mistakes. No more impulsive behavior. Focus.

He felt a lingering anger. With himself. So stupid.

First off, grabbing someone off the street. Even if she had presented herself right to his doorstep—so to speak. Car broken down. Lonely road. Late at night. No one around. It was all so easy.

And so reckless.

She turned out to be a local teacher. Her disappearance created a stir. In the community, the newspapers. He had even heard Chief Cutler talking with that other cop, the guy, the one that she always hung out with. Jimmy Rankin. Over at Flo's Diner. Some local had found her car along the old Lynchburg road, right where he had left it.

And now her body had been found. That was the rumor floating around anyway. And he knew it was so. Who else could it be? On Clovis Wilson's property. Where he had buried her.

Should have done a better job.

He had planned for many months—and truth be told had mentally prepared for years—but then he had acted impulsively, grabbing her. He wasn't yet fully committed, fully prepped. Hadn't really thought it through. He had a place. He had all his equipment, ready to go. But chaining her to a pole was stupid. Of course she escaped. Predictable, actually. Anyone could get out of such an arrangement. Given enough time—and sufficient motivation.

With his purchase of the large animal cage, up near Lexington, anonymous and cash only, of course, that problem was now solved. Strong, titanium and steel, no way his new acquisition could escape.

And she was an acquisition. No more abductions—way too dangerous and unpredictable. He had purchased this one. Just like selecting a can of soup from the grocery aisle. Of course he hadn't known that was even possible a month ago. And had it not been for that article he found online, he still wouldn't know. Who could imagine that people actually sold women? Amazing. The article had been about a Ukrainian group that kidnapped American girls and sold them all over the world. Mostly the Mid East, but really everywhere.

But how do you go about buying someone? Who do you call? What would that even cost?

He hadn't known the answer to any of these questions—but he knew who just might. And he did.

Hispanic guy. Named Luis. In Vegas. A Caesar's valet who ran hookers on the side. High end girls. He had used his services many times on his trips to Sin City. Had always paid top dollar. Had a good relationship with Luis. "Favored customer" status was how Luis termed it.

But this was different. Buying wasn't like renting.

Luis hadn't blinked. Said sure, that could be arranged. Said he knew a guy. And luck of all luck the dude ran girls out of Nashville and Memphis. Local.

Luis smoothed the path and he contacted the dude. Told him what he needed. The dude agreed. Said they should meet. No. He had to remain anonymous. A little back and forth but finally the dude emails him some photos. Sort of a portfolio of his girls. Like a glitzy restaurant menu. Take your choice, pay the freight, and walk away. Simple and easy.

Amazing.

Of course, the guy initially balked at selling the one he selected. Saying she was like an annuity. Brought in top dollar. Worth a lot to him. The counter argument: she could walk away, quit the business at any time. Maybe better to take the cash and move on.

A price was negotiated. Fifteen grand. But, she was worth it.

She was perfect. Blonde, fit, stunning. An even better canvas than the school teacher.

CHAPTER 11

"Why are you doing this?"

She was strapped to a metal table as she had been every day since he brought her here. He had shaved her body. Completely. Even her head. And then he went to work. Maddening hours of the buzzing. Like a dental drill constantly assaulting her senses. The relentless pain of the needle. She had screamed, cried, begged, fought, even told him she would pay him whatever he wanted. All to no avail, his calm demeanor never wavering. Four days in, she felt her sanity wobble.

"You ask me that every day."

"I just don't understand."

"To make you beautiful."

"You said I was already beautiful."

"And you are. Near perfection." He smiled. "But I'll make you even more perfect."

The device buzzed to life again, the needle invading the tender skin of her abdomen. She took in a sharp breath and tightened the muscles of her stomach.

"I know it's uncomfortable but you must remain still."

"It's not that. It's…I don't understand. Why?"

"You're a beautiful young woman. Athletic and toned. A flawless canvas."

"Is that what I am? An art project?"

He laughed softly. "You might say that."

She whimpered.

"It's no accident that you're here." He patted her arm, as if he were a comforting father. "My dear, you were chosen."

"Please. Don't do this."

"You'll feel differently once your transformation is complete. When you become what you were meant to be." He gently squeezed her arm. "Once I have finished my work, you'll see."

Tears formed in her eyes, the barn's ceiling high above becoming swirls of brown and tan. He was insane. No doubt about that. But she had known that from the moment she arrived here.

What began as a simple "date" a week ago—god, it seemed much longer—had become…what? Nightmare? Purgatory? Hell itself? None of those captured the true depravity of her situation.

There had been no date, a reality she had discovered much too late. What infuriated her most was that the entire process should have stopped her. But it was a big payday. Three day trip to New York, four thousand a day. Too much to pass up. Besides, she loved New York.

It had been uncomfortable from the beginning. Adam had said someone would pick her up. A block from her apartment so she could walk to the pick-up point. The parking lot of a coffee shop. When she asked why, she was told the customer insisted on it. That he needed complete anonymity.

That had made sense. On some level. Many—hell, most—of the guys she had seen were married. Made sense they'd want to stay low to the ground, no real names, no personal info. But this one felt off. A parking lot for Christ's sake. She should have walked away.

The black SUV, tinted windows, the two Hispanic guys inside, set off alarm bells, but they assured her all was okay. That they would take her to her client, then on to the airport. They had been well-dressed, smiled, even opened the door for her.

She hesitated but climbed in the back, tossing her weekend bag and purse on the seat next to her. They told her to sit back, relax. That it'd only take a few minutes. Freeway out of town, three or four miles, then off into an industrial area. She didn't recognize it.

A metal door rolled up and then they were inside an empty warehouse. The SUV stopped. The two men climbed out and one opened her door. She stepped out and looked around. Cavernous, high windows along one side, dirty, muting the sunlight.

"Where are we?" she asked.

No one answered. She heard a car approach the open door. Just as it came into view she saw movement to her left. Then the Taser. Against her shoulder. The jolt, the pain, and she was down. She was aware of being bound and blindfolded, a ball gag strapped over her mouth, but her brain could only process bits and pieces of it. A confusing jumble of sensations. She tried to resist, knew she needed to, but her limbs, her entire body, refused to cooperate.

The men spoke briefly, their voices muffled. Her brain couldn't sort out the words. She was sure she heard something like, "the money's all there" and "tell him thanks."

Then she was in the trunk of the car and it was moving. Over bumpy roads, gravel pinging the undercarriage, and then accelerating on a smoother surface. Freeway? Which one? Which direction? A longer trip. Seemed like an hour, could have been more. Or less.

Still blindfolded, hands bound behind her, jaw aching from the ball gag, she was brought here. To a large metal cage. Her bindings and blindfold were removed.

And she saw him.

Not what she expected. He was fit, trim, handsome, calm. His age was difficult. Could be thirty or late forties. One of those guys who would look young well into his sixties.

Was this some kind of joke?

"Who are you?" she asked.

"Professor Higgins."

"Professor? Of what?"

He smiled. Relaxed. "Sorry. Bad joke. *My Fair Lady*?"

"What's that supposed to mean?"

"Just as Professor Higgins transformed Eliza, I will do so with you."

She stared at him through the bars. She wrapped her fingers around them. "Let me out of here."

"All in good time."

"You can't keep me here. Kidnap me like this."

"Really? I'd say I already have." He walked to the bars. One hand closed over hers. She jerked away. "But just to be clear, I didn't kidnap you. I purchased you."

"Please. Let me go. I won't say a word."

"Oh, I will. Let you go. When you're prepared. When the time is right."

A chill worked up her spine. Who was this guy? What did he want?

Now she knew. She had been here for—what? A week? The days ran together, never ending. He had not covered his face or attempted to hide in any way. Which meant she wouldn't leave alive. No matter how much he reassured her. What chilled her most was his maddening calmness, the efficient way he went about his work. Tattooing her with thick orange and black stripes. Calling her his "Tiger Lily."

Would she ever see her family and friends again?

The barn was large, a loft at the far end, a soaring beamed ceiling above her. She was lit by a trio of bright lights on metal stands that looked down on her like electronic sunflowers.

The buzzing stopped, as did the incessant pain. "Time for another color," he said. He walked to the nearby wooden bench where an array of ink bottles stood like multicolored soldiers. As he busied himself mixing another hue, she looked around.

She wasn't sure what she hoped to see. She had examined every board, nook, cranny, electrical conduit, and other than the two doors—one a large, double; the other a smaller, more standard door—she had seen nothing that offered an escape route. She decided the smaller door was likely the weaker of the two. But so what? She'd never get to it. The metal cage that was her new home was solid. No way to escape it. She had tried, and no joint, no door hinge so much as budged.

He returned, pulling the stool he sat on up close. "All ready."

"What is it I'm supposed to transform into?"

Again he patted her arm in that fake paternal manner. "Would Da Vinci have showed an incomplete painting? Would Shakespeare have passed around an unfinished manuscript? I think not."

"Please." A sob racked her.

"Patience, dear girl. We…you and I…have many hours of work ahead. Then you will see my true genius. The entire world will see."

Another sob. She twisted, but the restraints that bound her offered little give.

The tattoo machine buzzed to life. She flinched, anticipating the pain. "Stop," she screamed. "Don't do this." She arched her back and jerked against the restraints.

"I told you to hold still."

She broke. "Fuck you, you psycho."

"Now, Tiger Lily, don't be that way. We're going to make history."

"I'm Cindy. My name is Cindy Grant."

He smiled, calm, even pleasant. "That's who you were. You're changing. Reaching your full potential. Becoming Tiger Lily."

"You are massively disturbed."

"NO I'M NOT." He tapped a finger sharply against her forehead, emphasizing each word. "I am a genius. An artist. I'm making you beautiful. And famous."

"You're none of that. You're a fucking psycho."

His lips thinned, jaw tightened, his voice now a ragged whisper. "Don't make me hurt you."

A sharp laugh escaped. "Hurt me? You're going to kill me. I know that. You haven't disguised yourself. I can identify you. You won't let that happen. So why should I cooperate with your insanity any longer?"

"Have it your way."

He laid the tattoo machine aside and walked to the table again, this time returning with a small, black object and a plastic bag. He held up the object and pressed a button. It sparked to life, electrical flashes dancing between two metal nubs on its end.

"Remember this?"

She glared at him.

"Which will it be?" He held the device in one hand, the plastic bag in another. He then leveled the stun gun just a few inches from her face and again it flashed to life. She could almost feel the sparks.

"Please. Don't."

"You're right. Too violent. Let's go with the bag."

He quickly slipped it over head. She twisted her head away, but he crushed one edge of the bag's mouth in his fist, tightening it around her neck. She struggled to breathe, each gulp sucking the plastic against her face.

He was going to kill her. Suffocate her. Panic took over. She yanked against the thick leather restraints around each ankle and wrist, across her chest. She tried to bite the plastic, create an opening for air, but couldn't capture it between her teeth. She looked into his eyes. Calm, cold. Her lungs burned, her heart like a tight fist hammering against her chest so hard that she feared it might explode. Through the breath-fogged plastic his face blurred, but not so much that she couldn't see his smile. As if they were having a polite conversation over dinner.

Oh God, I'm going to die.

Dizziness swept over her and she felt as if she were fading into a black abyss. Her arms and legs felt rubbery, her body weightless as if she were floating in calm, warm water. Struggling was useless. Maybe death wasn't the worst that could happen. She felt her body relax.

"That's better." He pulled the bag away and she gulped air. "Can we proceed?"

A sob racked her as she sucked in deep, strident breaths.

"There, there." He patted her arm again. "Don't you see? I'm really your salvation."

She sniffed. "Pardon me if I don't see it that way."

"Once we're done, once your true beauty is revealed, you'll see it differently."

Arguing with him was impossible. He was crazy. Dangerously crazy. She saw no way to avoid whatever he had planned for her. To think that her life had been almost perfect. With a clear future. Now? She had nothing. She would die here in this barn in the middle of nowhere and no one would ever know what happened to her.

"Do I really have a choice?"

"No, my precious Tiger Lily, you don't."

CHAPTER 12

Cain didn't hold out much hope that they would hear from Kelly's friend. Why would she call? She had apparently extricated herself from the prostitution ring and had weathered the retribution that visited her. The calls, the B&E. Did she feel she remained under some threat? Worried, scared? If so, would she reach out to them, total strangers? Cain suspected it all depended on the picture that Kelly painted when they talked.

Miracle of miracles, she did. Her name was Ella Hamilton. She sounded stressed, and hesitant. Like she wasn't sure she had made the right choice in calling. Cain couldn't say he blamed her. Made sense on many levels. Cain explained what he and Harper were doing and why they needed to talk with her, ending with, "Can we meet? Have a chat?"

"Isn't that what this is?"

Phone conversations aren't like face to face encounters. No facial expressions, micro tells, pupillary reactions, body language, all the indicators that someone was being honest, or lying, aren't available. And they needed to test the veracity of whatever Ella said.

"I'd rather do it face to face," Cain said.

"I'm not sure I'm comfortable with that."

"It's important. Or could be. You can pick the time and the place."

Ella relented and the meeting was arranged for a couple of hours later.

After he disconnected the call, Cain said to Harper, "I think you should handle this. She seemed spooked."

"And you think I'll be less threatening?"

Cain smiled. "She doesn't know you like I do."

Harper opened her laptop. "I'll see what I can find on her."

"I have a sit down set with Olivia Johnston. Cindy's track coach."

"Sounds good. Then we can hook up and go see Captain Bradford."

Took Cain only fifteen minutes to reach the Vanderbilt Athletic Department and the office of Olivia Johnston, the women's cross-country coach. When he had called earlier, she had said her afternoon was fairly open so any time would work. She had asked what he wanted to chat about, but Cain said it was a private matter and would be better handled face to face. She had hesitated but when Cain added it was about one of her athletes—Cindy Grant—and his inquiries were on behalf of her grandfather General Kessler, she agreed.

She looked up from behind her desk when Cain rapped a knuckle on the open door's frame.

"Coach Johnston?" I asked.

She stood. "You must be Mister Cain."

"Bobby, please."

"Olivia." She extended a hand, her grip firm. She waved him to the folding chair that faced her, and sat. "What can I do for you?"

"Like I said, I want to talk about Cindy Grant."

"I should've told you on the phone that I can't discuss any of our athletes. But I must admit you made me curious. You said you were working for her grandfather. General Kessler?"

"I am. And believe me, I have his full blessing in this."

"I understand. The General is a generous donor to the school. But that doesn't really change things. I still can't say anything about Cindy."

"I appreciate that. But you should know that Cindy is missing."

Confusion settled over her face. "What do you mean?"

"No one knows where she is. No one has heard from her for a

week. And her grandparents say that would never happen."

"I see."

"Have you seen or heard from her?"

She looked up, her brow furrowed, as if thinking. "Now that you mention it, I haven't seen her at any of our workouts lately. This is our off season, but our girls work out almost every day. When one of them doesn't show for a week, it's usually an illness, flu, things like that, or academics. Tests, projects. The bane of all college students."

"So her absence didn't really alarm you?"

"No. I thought she was simply ill or busy."

"I wish it were that simple."

She picked up a blue ballpoint and clicked it a couple of times. "Want to explain that?"

The whole truth and nothing but the truth wouldn't work here. Just some version of it. "She told friends she was going away. To Colorado. Hiking. With some dude that no one seems to know. That was a week ago. No evidence she actually did that and her cell phone is essentially dead." Cain opened his palms toward her. "So I think you can see why her grandparents are worried."

"And they hired you?"

Cain nodded.

"Who are you?"

"I investigate things. I fix problems. The General and I go back to our military days."

She nodded. Clicked the pen a few more times.

"I understand privacy rules," Cain said. "Appreciate them. Respect them. But I'm not here to invade Cindy's life—any more than is necessary. But I fear she's either in serious trouble or something untoward has happened."

"Untoward? I hate that word. So euphemistic."

Cain shrugged. "Seems appropriate here."

"Code for she could be dead? Is that it? You think she's been abducted? Maybe murdered?"

"That's one fear. Or that she's somewhere against her will and needs help."

"Lord." Two more clicks of the pen. "I never suspected anything like that."

"What I need to know is what she was like. From your perspective."

She stared at her desktop for a full half minute, obviously wrestling with what she could, or should, say. Hold to the rules and regs, or do the right thing? Finally, she looked up. "Smart, tough competitor, hard worker, dedicated. Reliable."

"So her disappearance goes against character?"

"That would be my take. She's just finishing her sophomore year so she's been on the team for two seasons now. I've seen nothing but focus and hard work."

"Which I assume means you don't believe she'd run off somewhere and not tell anyone."

"I can't imagine that."

"Neither can her grandparents. Which fits with what I've learned of her so far." Cain sighed. "So it leaves us with a decidedly uglier picture."

She dropped the pen. It clacked against the desktop. "I can't believe this."

"I've talked to her roommate already. Not much help." Not exactly the truth but Cain saw no need to get into that here and now. "Can you think of anything that might help? Her habits? Where she might have gone? Or with who?"

She shook her head. "Nothing."

Cain gave her his number and she promised to call if she thought of or heard anything that might help.

Cain had time before he was to meet Harper so he made two more stops: Southern Hospitality, where Cindy had waitressed, and Talk To Me, the crisis center where she volunteered. At the former, he talked with manager Missy Mulligan, and at the latter owner Craig Williams. Each told a story similar to that of Coach Olivia Johnston. Cindy was hard working, dedicated, dependable, and would never simply disappear.

Dead ends. But not completely. Each had reinforced his belief that something had happened to Cindy. She hadn't run away, or fallen in love and eloped, or gone away with some high roller for a week of sex and fun. And money. Of those choices, the latter would be the most likely but Cain didn't buy it. Not the Cindy Grant he pictured. Even if she were off on some sex junket, she would have called—someone. The Kesslers, Kelly, someone.

And then there were Cindy's fingerprints. Kessler had told him that he believed Cindy had been printed as part of her job at the crises center. Cain had asked Craig Williams about it.

"Yeah, we require all our employees to be printed. Background checks, the whole thing."

"Makes sense."

"Don't want anyone with a criminal or psychiatric record working here. So we have everyone visit the Nashville PD and get printed. They run the prints through their databases. To make sure we don't have any surprises down the road."

Good news. If a body were found, any prints could determine if it was Cindy or not. Cain hated that ugly truth. That a body recovery, not a rescue of a kidnapped girl, was the likely outcome. After a week of silence, the odds of Cindy being alive were progressively diminishing.

CHAPTER 13

The place Ella Hamilton chose to meet was The Blue Plate Café, a diner just off campus. Sort of a cross between 50s retro and a country kitchen. Crowded and noisy, it was obviously popular with the college crowd.

When Harper arrived, she saw Ella sitting in a booth along a row of windows that looked out on the gravel parking area. Alone. Cup of coffee before her. Her thick, brown hair was slightly longer than on her Facebook page but her over-sized brown eyes were just as captivating. Like Kelly and Cindy, young and beautiful, Ella was even more so. Nashville had more than its share of attractive young ladies, but Ella had that thing—that electric beauty that made young men do stupid stuff. And attracted the attention of predators. Like Adam and his crew.

"Ella?" Harper asked as she approached.

She nodded.

Harper sat across from her. "Thanks for seeing me."

"I thought I was meeting with Mister Cain," she said. "That's what Kelly said."

"We're partners." Harper smiled. Ella didn't. "We're also siblings."

"Really?"

"So we go way back. Talking to one of us is talking to both." Ella didn't respond so Harper continued. "I'm glad you came."

"I almost didn't," Ella said. "And I'm still not sure it's a good idea." She took a sip of coffee. "I hope I don't regret it."

"It'll be okay. Your secrets are safe with us."

"How do I know that? I don't even know you."

"I understand. Just trust me. I'll keep you off the radar. Completely."

She didn't respond.

"Ella? You okay?"

"No. I'm scared."

"Of Adam and his partner?"

"Yes. And now with Cindy missing…." She sniffed. "Why the hell did I ever get involved with these guys?"

"We all do things that in hindsight look stupid, or crazy, even dangerous."

"I think this would meet all those criteria."

A waitress appeared. Young, probably a college kid, brown hair pulled into a bun, round glasses that made her look smart. If she went to Vandy, she probably was.

"What can I get you?" she asked.

"Just coffee. Black," Harper said.

She walked away but returned in a few seconds, glass pot in one hand, a cup dangling from a finger. She filled it, topped off Ella's cup, and left.

"Tell me how you got into this?" Harper asked.

Ella hesitated, as if considering what to say, if anything. She took a sip of coffee, glanced around. "Adam I knew. Casually, anyway. Saw him around a lot. We had lunch one day. He asked if I wanted to make some serious money. Sure, why not." She ran a finger around the lip of her cup. Shook her head. "So stupid."

Harper waited her out. Letting her gather her thoughts. Tell it her way.

"At first, I told him no way. That I wasn't for sale."

"But?"

"He told me I could make a couple of grand a night." Another sip. "Doesn't seem like enough now. Anyway, Adam hooked me up with a guy. The one that actually set up the dates."

"And he is?" Harper asked.

"Carlos Campos."

"He a student, too?"

"Not that I know."

"But he ran the show?"

"Seemed that way. I don't know if he had other partners."

"Did you meet him?"

"Only once. Very briefly." Ella twisted a strand of hair with one finger. "He was with these two other guys. Tough looking. Also Hispanic. He, Carlos, did all the talking."

"Did you get the names of the other guys?"

Ella shook her head. "No. They sort of stood to the side. Didn't say a word."

"Like bodyguards or something?"

"Exactly. Carlos seemed normal. Not a bad looking guy. But those two made me uncomfortable."

"So let me get this straight—is it Adam or Carlos or both that set everything up?"

"Carlos. Adam was more or less out of the picture once I started seeing clients. At least I never really talked to him again."

So, Adam was the procurer and Carlos the pimp. She wondered if Adam's parents had any clue what their son's side job was. Not likely.

"How did this work?" Harper asked. "Carlos would call and tell you where to be and what time?"

"Exactly. Usually it'd be the same day. The place was either a local hotel or maybe a motel just out of town." She shrugged. "Most of the guys were married so I guess they felt a remote motel made it safer. For them, anyway." She stared at her coffee for a few seconds. "But I never liked leaving the city. Motels seemed less safe."

"I understand you never went on a weekend trip. Is that correct?"

"Yes. Again, everything seemed safer if it was local. Short term, so to speak."

"I understand you finally agreed to take a trip but in the end bailed?"

"This guy was a true creep. Old, mostly bald, fat, thick lips, puffy cheeks, bad teeth. Dandruff everywhere." She looked around again. "He looked dirty." She continued to wind the strand of hair near her right ear. "Made me feel dirty."

There it was. End of the road. Where most young ladies who made such choices ended up. What seemed like easy money became something else again. Ella's eyes glistened with moisture.

"And Carlos took issue with you refusing the trip?" Harper asked.

"That would be an understatement. He called. All agro, angry. Threatened me. Said I was damaging his reputation." She gave a head shake. "His reputation? Can you imagine?"

"Some folks have a warped self-image."

She actually smiled at that. Briefly. "So the calls and the break in—I'm sure it was him—or one of those guys he was with."

"Do you know how to reach Carlos? A number or anything?"

She shook her head. "No. He would call when he had a job for me. Give me the info. That's it. I never had a way to contact him."

"No caller ID number I take it."

"His number was always blocked."

A burner phone most likely. Standard MO for pimps and drug dealers and other gutter crawlers.

"What if something came up?" Harper asked. "You had to cancel the date? You had no way to reach him?"

"That never came up, but if it had I would've called Adam. Let him pass the word to Carlos."

"When did you last hear from Carlos?"

"When all this went down. The last call I got was the one where he threatened me. That was a couple of months ago." She scooted the nearly empty cup to her left and folded her hands before her. Her fingers were long and thin, nails painted a light pink, a gold ring with a small opal on her right middle finger. "I think he finally got bored with fucking with me. After the break in."

"Probably felt he had delivered his message."

"Maybe. I hope so, anyway." Another glance around. "But I can tell you, I still look over my shoulder. And stay away from dark alleys."

"Wise move."

"Do you think he did something to Cindy?" Ella asked.

"I don't know. Possible."

"Dear God, I hope not."

"Me, too."

She sighed. "What now?"

"For you, nothing. We'll need to keep digging." Her eyes widened and she started to say something but Harper raised a hand. "Don't worry. This conversation never happened. That goes both ways. Don't tell anyone about this. Okay? Not anyone."

"No problem there. I never want to see that guy again. Never ever." She twisted the opal ring back and forth. "What are you going to do?"

"Whatever's necessary."

"Meaning?"

Harper shrugged. "Nothing that'll come back on you. That I promise."

CHAPTER 14

Cain waited for Harper's call. When it came, she was in her car on the way back home. Cain called Captain Bradford, who said General Kessler had called, saying Cain might drop by and that now was as good a time as any. He hadn't sounded enthusiastic, or thrilled. Maybe he was having a bad day. Maybe he didn't appreciate civilians sticking their noses in his business. But at least he hadn't said no.

Cain swung by the condo and picked up Harper. Cain's S550 Mercedes navigated the downtown traffic and then they sped out US 70 toward the Nashville PD's Headquarters. He felt the need to hurry in case Bradford changed his mind. He didn't expect the meeting would yield anything useful. After all, Bradford hadn't offered any news when they spoke. And Kessler would have called had Bradford given him any useful updates. This visit was more to get an inroad to someone in the system they could call on down the road if necessary. Judging from Bradford's attitude, that might be a pipe dream.

As Cain snaked through the thick freeway traffic, he asked Harper, "How was your chat with Ella?"

"Interesting. Similar story as Kelly. Adam Parker recruited her into the business but after that seemed to fade into the background. Guy named Carlos Campos actually ran things. Set up the dates, that sort of thing."

"She have any insight into their relationship? Parker and this Carlos?"

"Not really."

"So, Parker's the talent scout and Carlos the pimp."

"That's how I read it," Harper said. "Maybe Captain Bradford has some info on them."

"Might be best to leave him out of this."

"Why?"

"We don't know him. Don't know where he stands on crimes like this. He might not give a shit. Or worse, might be a zealot." He glanced at Harper. "I don't want Adam Parker or Carlos to know we're snooping into their lives. If Bradford makes a move, it might put them on alert."

"Good thought. I agree."

"Digging into Parker and Carlos is the key."

"I don't get it," Harper said. "These girls—Cindy and Ella and Kelly—they're pretty, bright, come from good families it seems. Not hurting for money. Why would they do this?"

Cain shrugged. "Excitement? Pushing the envelope? Why do kids that age do half of what they do?" He smiled. "Our childhood wasn't exactly legal."

She laughed. "Our adulthood either."

They found an empty slot near the front door. The officer behind the entry desk found their names on his clipboard and then led them down a short hallway to Captain Lee Bradford's office. After introductions, they sat facing him over his desk.

"Thanks for seeing us, Captain," Cain said.

"Like I said, General Kessler called. Asked if I'd talk with you."

"I assume you have no new information on Cindy Grant's disappearance?"

"Nope. No new and no old information. Nothing at all. Don't expect to either. You ask me, she probably ran off somewhere."

"Everyone we've talked to said that would be out of character for her," Cain said.

Bradford smoothed his tie; red, over a crisp white shirt. "With college kids, you never know. Besides, she's an adult. No way I could open a file on an adult that just wants to disappear."

"If that's what happened," Harper said.

"True. But without some evidence of a crime or some kind of foul play, I'm afraid my hands are tied."

"I understand," Cain said. "Let me ask you—do you get many abductions around here? Young women?"

"That depends. Most often, when it looks like someone might've been taken, they show up. Pissed at Mom and Dad." He waved a hand. "That kind of thing."

Cain nodded. "Those aside, do you get many that are actually abducted?"

"Sure. Nashville's like any other big city. Bad stuff happens."

"Any unknown females pop up in the past week or so?" Harper asked.

"Two. One was younger than Cindy Grant. Twelve. Still hasn't been located. The other was sixteen. Black girl. She was found three days ago. In a dumpster. Finally got an ID yesterday. Local prostitute. Had a sheet so we were able to match her prints. Looks like her pimp is the culprit." He scratched his chin. "Then I know a corpse—actually part of one—was found down near Moss Landing. Earlier today."

"Female?" Harper asked.

"That's what I hear."

"You said partial?" Cain asked.

"Yeah, the scuttlebutt is that she'd been dead a while. Apparently the corpse had been feasted on by wild pigs."

"Moss Landing? Down by Tims Ford Lake?"

"Yep. But I know the remains have been transported here. I think the ME will do the autopsy in the morning."

"Any ID on the remains?" Harper asked.

"Not yet. I guess it'll mostly depend on what body parts were found. Hopefully the ME can tell us something."

"Mind if we drop by the autopsy?" Cain asked.

Bradford hesitated. Considering. Cain knew that would break a bunch of rules, but hoped that the General's name in all this would help. It did.

"Since it's General Kessler that hired you, and since we have no ID on the remains, I suspect we can work that out. If it's on the QT."

"Of course."

"I'll see if the ME is in concurrence and give you a call in the

morning."
"Appreciate it."

CHAPTER 15

He had finished his work early. Mid afternoon. He returned her to the cage and put away his instruments. Said he had some business to attend to, but might be back later. Or maybe not till morning. Part of the game. Never letting her know when he would return. Then he left, securing the door behind him.

At least she now had clothes. Draw-string cotton pants, tee shirt, no shoes. The first two days, after he had completed his work, he had abandoned her naked, wrapped in a blanket. The flimsy garments were one of the few comforts he had allowed. Those and the air mattress and blankets, the toilet chair. Jesus. And the space heater. That had been a life-saver. Okay, bravo for him. Still, she remained a caged animal.

A cage for Christ's sake.

She examined her arms, lifted her shirt exposing her chest and abdomen. Now almost completely covered with thick orange and black stripes. She was a freak. His private stuffed animal.

She sat on the mattress, legs folded to her chest, cheek resting on her knees, and cried. So long and hard it hurt.

Stop it, Cindy. Don't give in to that self-pity crap. Think.

There had to be a way. She couldn't die here. She simply couldn't. But it seemed her mind only ran in circles, always returning to the same place. There was no way to escape this steel prison.

While her mind traipsed over familiar territory, discovering no new pathways that might lead to escape, she watched the shards of sunlight that stabbed through the cracks in the barn's walls creep across the floor toward her. When they winked out, darkness fell quickly. The temperature dropped. She wrapped herself in the two blankets and stretched out on the air mattress. But sleep didn't come. Her mind wouldn't relent as she relived the last few days.

She had fought him. Argued, pleaded, cried, anything that might melt his heart. She now realized that he didn't have one. At least not one she could reach.

Who would do this? Why?

Twice her protestations had led to the plastic bag being secured over her head. Pulled tightly against her face as she struggled for precious oxygen. Each time, just as she felt consciousness slipping away, he had removed it, smiling calmly as she gulped air.

Smiled.

As if this was some schoolyard game.

Fighting him, defying him, wasn't an option. But if not that, what? How could she possibly escape? Everything she thought of only led her back to the plastic bag. Or worse. The Taser was always nearby.

She jerked awake. Confused for a moment. She had apparently fallen asleep. For how long? She sat up, one blanket wrapped around her like a shawl. She could see light through the gaps in the wood. Faint, almost invisible. Early morning.

During the night, her brain had apparently sorted through her meager options and had stumbled on a different tact. Might not work. But maybe, just maybe, he was human after all. Wasn't he? He seemed intelligent, and at times almost normal. Soft spoken, kind—if in a fake sort of way. But would he respond like a truly normal person? Could she appeal to whatever sliver of humanity he possessed?

Her plan? Praise him. Admire his talent. Make him think she had bought into his madness. Make him complacent. Make him trust her. If so, would that offer her a crack, an open door, a way to escape?

Weapons were available. Not just her hands and feet and teeth. Not just her anger and fear, which given the chance she would unleash on him. If she could. She had never been violent. Never had to be. Always preferring a smile and a pleasant attitude to navigate life's problems. Wasn't sure she could reach that deep into her own darkness. Did she even have such darkness? Could she really release the anger she felt inside?

Other weapons? The tool box that sat in the far corner held a thick-bladed knife, a ball-peen hammer and a screwdriver, she knew for sure. She had seen those. But unless he let his guard down, made a mistake, she would never reach any of them.

She wasn't optimistic that flattery would gain her any advantage. But she saw no other options. She had nothing to lose by trying.

The door scraped open. He was back. Even earlier than usual. He walked toward her and handed her a bag. Her breakfast. This one from McDonald's.

"Thanks." She tugged the bag through the bars. Inside she found two bacon and egg biscuits. She was starving. She unwrapped one and took a bite. Then another. Seemed like only a minute and she had devoured both biscuits.

By the time she finished, he had arranged his tools, flicked on the bright lights that surrounded the table.

"Ready?" he said.

Like she had a choice.

She knew the routine. She stripped, he opened the cage. He strapped her to the cold metal platform. Then went to work on her left leg. The needle seemed extra sharp this morning, the buzzing an assault on her senses. She tried to block it out, going over her plan again. Still trying to see the pitfalls. Where it could all go wrong.

How to begin? What should she say? She had gone over this a dozen times but right now everything that in her dreams had seemed so clever, now felt weak and transparent. She knew she had only one shot at this. If he saw through her ruse, all would be truly lost.

Miraculously, he gave her an opening.

"You're very quiet today," he said in that maddeningly soft voice of his.

"I'm tired I guess. And embarrassed."

He lifted the needle from her skin and looked at her.

"Embarrassed? For what?"

"The way I've acted. I mean, all of this. You did all of this for me."

"That's true." He returned to his work.

"I should be thanking you, not fighting everything. You took me away from those other men. The two guys who tazed me, tied me up. I know they would have used me until there was nothing left. Then I'd simply disappear. No one would ever know what had happened to me."

"That's what men like that do. They don't create. They consume."

"But you saw something in me. You saw a potential beauty that even I didn't know existed."

He lifted the needle again and smiled. "You're a beautiful young lady. You know that. Beautiful women always do."

That was true. Her beauty had opened doors, offered her certain privileges. Garnered special attention, moved her to the front of the line. Cheerleader, homecoming queen, all that crap that now seemed so meaningless. But beauty was also the proverbial double-edged sword. Was it not her beauty that led her into the hands of Adam and Carlos? To Carlos' two thugs? To this place at this time?

No, that wasn't the complete truth. She had delivered herself here. On the proverbial silver platter. Why had she ever agreed to sleep with all those strange men? For money. Something she had never needed. But that wasn't it. Not really. More to color outside the lines. Do something exciting, foreign to her, dirty.

Stop it. Focus.

"But you saw more," she said. "Yesterday, after you left, I looked at what you've done. Really examined it for the first time. How you've transformed me. It's remarkable." She offered a smile that she hoped looked genuine. "You're truly talented."

"I know."

"I'm grateful that you chose me for your canvas." Canvas. She chose that word carefully. Mimicking his own choice.

His smile broadened. "And a lovely canvas you are. Your skin is flawless. A pleasure to work with."

"And all this. This barn. The preciseness of that cage. The electrical set up. That took vision and planning."

"It did."

"I can't imagine it was easy."

"It took a while."

"I'm sure. I mean, this must be in the middle of nowhere. Where do you find electricity out here?"

"We aren't that far removed from such things."

"Really? I assumed we were in the boonies somewhere."

Another smile. "Let's just say it's very private."

Could that be true? Was she actually closer to civilization, to help, than she had assumed? If she could find a way out, could she reach help?

Keep him talking.

"I'm sorry I've been so difficult," she said.

"That you have. At times, anyway."

"I just didn't understand. Didn't see your vision for me. Now I do. I'm flattered that you chose me."

"You were chosen. From many options. But your beauty and perfection made the ultimate choice easy."

"You're going to make me cry. I don't think I've ever felt so loved."

"Soon the entire world will love you."

The tattoo machine buzzed to life as he returned to his work. She lay there for several minutes before asking, "Am I the only one?"

"More or less."

What does that mean?

"I'm truly honored," she said.

"Soon you'll be ready for the world. You'll be breathtaking."

"When?"

"A few more hours. I'll finish this leg, touch up the other one, then your face, and you'll be complete."

"Then what?"

"The grand finale."

"What do you mean?"

"All in good time." He patted her thigh. "But your public will love you."

A tightness rose in her chest, her lungs suddenly stiff, unable to take even the shallowest breath. Her heart swelled as if it were an overinflated balloon nearing its rupture point. She struggled to tamp it down. Not let him feel her panic.

But it was too late. She saw it in his eyes. He knew. Saw the fear evident on her face.

Think.

"You said we were near an electrical source?" she asked.

"We are."

"And maybe a shower?"

"That, too. Why?"

"Before I meet my public I'd like to be clean. To show off your work better."

He smiled. "That won't be necessary."

"But, I'd feel better."

"We'll see."

#

She's a clever girl. Finally realizing that resisting him was impossible, she was trying to win him over. Flattering, praising, hoping he'd let his guard down. So transparent. Desperate.

Wasn't going to happen. He'd made that mistake before. Never again.

That teacher. He had wasted days working on her, making her special. And all for nothing. A partially completely canvas would never do. Not for his debut. All had to be perfect.

But he had learned. Replacing a tether with a cage. Buying a girl, a canvas, rather than taking what opportunity gave him. Cleaner, simpler, safer.

So let her think she could manipulate him. That her plan was working and that she could lull him into errors. Much better this way. Made her more compliant. More manageable.

He returned to his work. Another two hours and she would be complete. A true masterpiece. Better than he had hoped. Much better than the school teacher.

Then he could turn his attention to the evening's festivities. The final act.

CHAPTER 16

The call from Captain Lee Bradford came early. Just before seven-thirty a.m. The ME had agreed to let them see the remains. Cain hadn't been optimistic. With most medical examiner/coroner-types, jealously protected their domains. The weight of General Kessler's name no doubt.

Bradford introduced Cain and Harper to Dr. Walter Curry. A short, stocky guy, with thinning white hair and ruddy cheeks. Rimless glasses, tethered to his ears by almost invisible nylon loops, seemed to hover above the tip of his nose as if by magic. His handshake firm, smile inviting.

"So you're employed by General Kessler?" Curry asked.

"His granddaughter Cindy is missing," Cain said. "He asked us to look into it."

"You guys P.I.s or something?"

"We'd be under the 'or something' category," Harper said.

Curry nodded, a question, maybe several questions, in his eyes.

"The General and I go back to our military days," Cain said. "Harper and I do special investigations. That's what he hired us for."

"Special, huh?"

Cain nodded, letting it lay there.

Curry hesitated, obviously waiting for an explanation, but

when none came, he said, "Let's head down to the lab."

Autopsy rooms are not the most pleasant places to hang out. The *yech* factor alone makes most people squirm at the thought. It's not just the smell, that combination of astringent cleaning agents and the sick, sweet odor of death and decay, it's also the fact that the corpse had once been a person. A spouse, parent, child, friend, whatever. The loss was often palpable. Particularly if it were a child. Or, like now, a young woman.

A life ended.

Not from age or illness. Those deaths rarely found their way to the ME's table. Rather, it's the unexpected, unexplained, suspicious, and violent deaths that required the ME's skills.

And in this case, a young woman had most likely lost her life in a flurry of violence.

Cain had seen autopsies before. Not many, but he remembered each. Vividly. Watching a body sliced open is an unforgettable event.

This one was different. Only a leg, an arm, and part of a rib cage. The parts arranged on the examination table before him looked odd, unreal. Not human. But, they were.

Cain and Harper stood next to Bradford, across the table from Curry and the pitiful remains of Jane Doe.

"Not much to work with here," Curry said. "Female, for sure. I estimate mid-twenties, maybe up to early thirties, but not beyond that. About five-seven, medium build. Based on bone size, length, and the epiphyses." He pointed to the leg. "And then there are these tattoos."

Under the harsh lights, the tattooing was clear and stark. Thick, black stripes that spiraled from the ankle up the leg, ending near the knee where the pigs had gnawed and fed. A similar design wound up what tissues remained on the arm.

"Did Cindy have tattoos? Like these?" Curry asked.

"Not that we know. We'll check it out but I suspect the answer will be no."

"Based on?"

"Doesn't seem to be the kind of thing she'd do."

Curry gave a one-shouldered shrug. "These days you never know."

"Any prints?" Bradford asked.

Curry reached out a gloved hand and rolled the arm so that the partially destroyed appendage was now palm up. "Got three fingers remaining. Not in good shape." He bent forward, examined the hand more closely. "I might be able to get prints from them. Then I'll load them in the system and see if anything pops up."

"When will that happen?" Cain asked.

"I'll get to work on them as soon as we finish here. If she's in the system, I'll have something fairly quickly."

"DNA?" Harper asked.

Curry nodded. "I took some samples and they'll go over to the lab. Once they get a profile they'll load it into CODIS. Probably won't help. Young lady like this is not likely in the database, but you never know. Could have a history. Might get lucky."

"Still, the tattooing could help," Cain said. "Even if the prints and the DNA don't get us anywhere these might point you in the right direction."

Curry's brow furrowed. "Maybe. Not optimistic though." He waved a hand. "These aren't gang tattoos. We've got a pretty big database on those. These look like those aboriginal designs kids seem to like." He shrugged. "Fashion statement, I assume."

Cain glanced at Bradford. "Any local tattoo folks do this kind of work?"

"We only have two in town. That I know of. I suspect both have done this kind of thing."

Cain leaned forward and looked at the leg more closely. "These look fairly fresh. Still have sharp edges. Maybe you'll get lucky."

"Luck would help," Bradford said.

"Any clue as to the cause of death?" Harper asked.

"None. And with no cause, the manner will be impossible." Curry tossed her a look. "Probably have to sign it out as undetermined but my gut tells me we're looking at a homicide."

Bradford nodded. "Apparently no clothing was found, so an accidental fall, or something like that doesn't seem likely. Unless she was in the habit of stomping around naked in the woods."

"Drugs?" Cain asked. "Maybe she got sideways on LSD, or E, or something like that? Those people seem to fly out of windows from time to time, so a romp in the woods would be possible."

"I've seen crazier things," Bradford added.

"I took some tissues samples," Curry said. "We'll do a tox screen on it but muscle and skin aren't all that good for such testing. Without hair, urine, liver tissue, or vitreous fluid I'm not hopeful."

Time and decay were major obstacles in toxicological examinations. Dried and decayed flesh and a handful of bones weren't the ideal samples for such testing. Drugs don't tend to concentrate in either.

"No boney injuries?" Cain asked. "Other than that done by predators?"

"Not that I can identify." Curry turned to the table behind him that held several instruments and metal pans. He picked up a fractured tusk. Maybe an inch long. "Meet the predators." He extended it toward us. "Feral pigs."

"You think they might have killed her?" Bradford asked.

Curry laid the tusk on the table. "I guess it's possible. But pigs don't eat clothing. What are the odds that some girl running naked in the woods would encounter a pack of hungry pigs?"

"Not very likely," Bradford said.

"For sure, I wouldn't want to run into a pack of them," Curry said. "But to answer your question, I don't think they had anything do with this young lady's demise. They came along later."

"What makes you think that?" Harper asked.

"First off, the investigator's report stated that the remains had been buried. Pigs don't do that. Like squirrels and hickory nuts." He smiled. "Then there's the nature of the wounds. Or should I say chew marks? Not much blood. That means the blood was clotted before they went to work." He lifted the leg, exposing the bottom of the foot. "Also, there's this."

The sole was gouged and gashed, several chunks of tissue missing.

"From the pigs?" Cain asked.

"That's what I thought at first, but I believe these happened pre-mortem." He pointed. "See the blood settled in the lacerations?" He turned and retrieved something from one of the pans and held it up toward the overhead light. "I dug this bit of limestone out of one of the gashes."

"What does that mean?" Bradford asked.

"That the damage to her feet happened while she was alive. All this other," he waved a hand over the remains, "occurred post-mortem. When the pigs got wind of her."

"You're thinking she was running bare foot?" Cain asked.

"Sure looks that way. My best guess anyway."

"Someone chased her down and killed her?" Bradford asked.

No one said anything for a minute.

"Maybe she was with a boyfriend," Harper said. "Doing the sex thing in the back of the car. A fight broke out. She jumped out of a vehicle and took off. Buck ass naked. He ran her down, and…."

"That's a wild theory," Bradford said.

She smiled. "Just thinking out loud."

"That would be a hell of a story," Curry said. "Regardless, the key will be the ID. If we can do that we'll know who she is and what all her relationships were."

"Let's hope," Bradford said.

Curry looked at Cain, then Harper. "And you want to know if this is General Kessler's granddaughter?"

Cain nodded. "Right age, and size."

"But not the tattoos?"

"No. But she's been missing over a week. A lot can happen in that time."

"True." Curry raised an eyebrow. "I'd say these remains are at least that old. But, probably a bit longer."

"Hopefully the fingerprints will tell us," Bradford said.

"Does Miss Grant have prints anywhere?" Curry asked.

Cain nodded. "According to Kessler, and her boss over at the Talk To Me crises center, she was printed as a requirement to work there."

"Really?" Bradford said.

"Apparently it's company policy," Cain said. "And the printing was done by the Nashville PD, so her prints should be on file."

After thanking Doctor Curry, Cain and Harper followed Bradford into the parking lot. It was just after nine. The sun had started its climb, the heat already building. Clouds gathered to the west; it looked like rain might be coming.

"Thanks for letting us stick our noses in," Cain said.

Bradford shrugged. "That was Curry's doing."

"But you opened the door."

"Truth is, I'm a little surprised he allowed it. But I guess you can see what General Kessler's name means around here. Curry trained at Vanderbilt and Kessler is one of their biggest donors."

"Money does talk."

"Loudly." Bradford stopped next to his department-issued Chevy. "What's your next move?"

"I think we'll head down to Moss Landing. Get a feel for things."

"The remains might not be Cindy Grant."

"Maybe not. But it's a nice day for a drive."

"Except that it looks like rain."

Cain smiled. "I've got wipers."

Now, Bradford smiled. "The chief down there is Laura Cutler. She's a good cop. A real pistol, as they say. She can fill you in."

"I take it you know her?" Harper asked.

"I was one of her instructors at the academy. Tried to get her to hang around here but she wanted to go back home. Too bad, she's a good one." He gave a quick nod. "Be sure and tell her hello for me."

"Will do."

"And if you discover anything, I'd appreciate a heads up."

"You got it," Cain said.

CHAPTER 17

Back at their condo, Harper grabbed her laptop and settled on the living room sofa while Cain walked down the hall to the office and made two calls.

The first to Kelly Whitt, Cindy's roommate. Kelly's initial optimism, asking if he had located Cindy, crashed once he said they hadn't. He asked her if Cindy had any tattoos. No way. Cindy hated tattoos. Felt that anyone who did that was short-sighted. And stupid. According to Kelly, Cindy's mantra on the subject was that every style goes out of fashion sooner or later so why make it permanent? Smart girl.

Next he called Kessler and asked the same question.

"No. Not that I know of," Kessler said.

"These you wouldn't miss."

"These, what?"

"They found some partial remains. Young girl." Kessler's intake of breath was audible. "Down near Moss Landing."

"Is it Cindy?"

"I don't think so. Age and size are right but these remains seem to be older. According to the ME anyway."

"And they have tattoos?"

"Big, black stripes. Arm and leg."

"That's not Cindy," Kessler said.

"Her roommate said the same thing."

"She would know, I'm sure."

"I agree. The timeline doesn't seem to fit anyway. The ME thinks he can grab prints so we should know something later today."

"I see," Kessler said. "What now?"

"Harper and I are taking a drive down there and see what the story is. I'll get back to you once I know more."

"Good. Anything else?"

Cain considered the question. Yes, there was something else. Cindy had been involved in prostitution. A connection that had likely led her into trouble. Maybe worse. But did Kessler need to know that right now? What if Cindy turned up safe and sound? Why damage her relationship with her loving grandparents if all was okay? What she did with her life was her business. Who she told about it was her decision. Unless something had happened to her. That would change everything. But right now? Cain simply said, "That's all we know so far."

Cain returned to the living room, telling Harper of the conversations. He asked, "What are you doing?"

"Looking into missing girls in this area." She closed the laptop. "Hard to get a handle on the exact number but from what I could see it's not small."

"I suspect that's true of most big cities."

She nodded. "I have an idea."

"A con of some type?"

Harper had been blessed with a bagful of gifts. When they were kids, she had been an excellent pick pocket. No one ever saw her coming and definitely never suspected this pretty little girl would lift their wallet, or empty their purse. She was also the perfect distraction for Uncle Al and Uncle Mo. She could cry on demand. And really sell it. Usually with a fall and a scuffed knee and rolling around and sobbing. While the two men emptied a cash register or stuffed clothing under their jackets. She was a natural.

But her forte was running cons. She could sell anyone on anything. Make them fork over cash for some nonexistent service or product. Those big, innocent eyes melted everyone. They couldn't get their money out fast enough.

Harper smiled. "You might say."

Cain sat in a chair facing her. "Let's have it."

"I need to enlist some help," Harper said.

Cain smiled. "Mama B?"

"Mama B."

Mama B. In real life, Beatrice Baker. An icon in the spook world. Mama B, originally from Hattiesburg, Mississippi, had spent thirty years in Naval Intelligence until she retired. Mid-seventies, very smart, and access to corners of the intelligence world most didn't even know existed. Not to mention her complete understanding of the deep web, the dark web, probably a few other webs no one knew about. How could things like that even exist? Web networks so broad based and active, yet so far off the radar? How they worked and how someone climbed on board was a mystery to most. Cain, for sure.

But not to Mama B.

Harper knew her best. She had worked with her on too many missions to count. Cain had met her much later, after he and Harper reunited, learning that Mama B had been in the background of several of his own covert ops. After the trio left the military, they had spent a few evenings drinking bourbon in bars near Langley as well as Mama B's current home in Annapolis. Mama B could never be far from the Navy.

She had also helped Cain and Harper with several "civilian" investigations over the past few years.

Harper placed her iPhone on speaker and dialed Mama B's number.

"Harper McCoy," she said when she answered. "How the hell are you?"

"Fine. And you?"

"Hanging in there. Me and old Arthur-itis."

Harper laughed. "Old Arthur can be a bitch, for sure. I'm here with Bobby."

"How's it hanging, Cain?" Mama B asked.

"All good."

"I sense this isn't a social call."

Mama B could read people better than anyone. Voice changes, body language, micro expressions, you name it and she could decipher the signs like a Cherokee tracker. Truth was her bloodline did have a taste of Cherokee mixed in. She loved the fact that Harper was a quarter Cherokee. Gave them a special bond. Especially over a bottle of small-batch "firewater," as Mama B called it.

"We could use your help," Harper said.

"Name it."

"It's about General Kessler's granddaughter."

She let out a soft groan. "I'm not going to like this, am I?"

"She's been missing for over a week," Cain said.

"Lordy. Bill and Miriam must be beside themselves."

"They are. Kessler asked us to look into it."

"Cindy? Right?"

"That's correct," Harper said.

"I met her once. Maybe twice. I remember Bill and Miriam brought her to a political dinner. She was twelve or so. Wasn't long after her parents died. Very pretty girl."

"Yes, she is."

"Doesn't look good, I suspect."

"It doesn't," Cain said. "They found some partial remains down south of Nashville. Only an arm and a leg. Part of a rib cage. Fed on by pigs."

"You've got to be kidding."

"Wish I was. We're headed that way as soon as we finish here. But I'm not optimistic it's her."

"Why?"

"These remains are female, right age and size, but I think they're more than two weeks old. Also the arm and leg were tattooed. One of those aboriginal black stripe things."

"And that wasn't her style?" Mama B asked.

"Doesn't seem that way. Her roommate says she hated tattoos."

Cain told her of Cindy's side job. Prostitution.

"Do Bill and Miriam know that?"

"Not yet. Can't bring myself to tell them just yet."

"Hoping for good news that would negate sharing that little tidbit? Or at least soften it?"

"Something like that."

"So what's the story?" Mama B asked. "The party line on her disappearance?"

"Her roommate tried to kite the idea that she went off with some dude for a hike in Colorado," Harper said.

"But that never happened," Mama B said. "Right?"

"You never miss a beat. I'd say the odds of that are virtually zero."

Harper explained that no flights, train trips, passport or credit card use had occurred. That her cell phone was dead.

"College girl without a cell is never good news," Mama B said. "So, what're you thinking?"

"We know of a guy who set up dates for her," Cain said. "Did for a couple of other girls we talked to. They both split from the program. Cindy remained."

"Money?"

"Oh, yeah. She was pulling down several grand a night. But more than that, I suspect she enjoyed the excitement. The doing her own thing."

Mama B sighed. "You thinking something went awry and this guy is the key?"

"I think he can get us there," Cain said. "He apparently has a partner, though from what I gather, more likely a boss."

"I'm onboard. What do you need?"

"Look into these two guys. First is Adam Parker. A grad student at Vandy. He's the procurer. Finds the girls and drags them into the business."

"What?" Mama B said. "He's working on his MBA and this is his master's thesis?"

"Let's just say he has an entrepreneurial spirit."

"I'm sure that's it. And the other guy?"

"Carlos Campos. Don't know much about him but I gather he's not a stand up citizen."

"Okay. I'm on it. Anything else?"

Cain waved a hand at Harper. "Harper has a gag she wants to run."

"I'm sure she does. Okay, let's have it. What do you need?"

"A bunch of naked girls."

"Didn't expect that," Mama B said.

"I've been considering the best way to make a run at these guys," Harper said. "Parker's the entry point into this world.

Campos is the one that runs the girls. I figure a frontal assault might get us nothing but push back."

"And alert the enemy," Mama B said. "Never a good thing." She chuckled. "Unless it is."

Mama B understood PsyOps better than most. Such shenanigans were also another of Harper's skills. Thanks to her CIA training. Sometimes sneaking in the back door and disrupting things, causing confusion, turning bad guy against bad guy, dividing and conquering, was best. Other times, taking it straight up was the better choice.

"My first thought was to go in on Adam and this Carlos guy hard," Harper said. "Drop a healthy dose of fear on their heads. Show them the wisdom of giving up what they know about Cindy's disappearance. As much fun as that could be, I think a softer approach is better."

"Make them allies?"

"Exactly. Start with Adam. Feed his greed. Then climb the food chain. Shake the trees."

"Sounds like a decent plan," Mama B said.

"That's where you come in," Harper said. "I want to make Bobby a pimp daddy."

Mama B laughed so hard she began to cough. Once she collected herself, she said, "He'd make a good one."

"Thanks, I think," Cain said.

"You up for this, Cain?" Mama B asked.

"First I've heard of it. Harper doesn't tell me much."

"Blame it on her training."

"We need a website," Harper said. "One that caters to those looking for very high end girls. Bobby can then pose as representing a large network of suppliers from all over. Offer to expand their business. Fill their pockets with cash."

"I like it," Mama B said. "What cities you thinking?"

"Maybe LA, Chicago, New York, Miami, Houston. Big ones. The ploy will be that Bobby is enlarging his footprint. Moving into mid-sized markets."

"No problem. It'll look like a real bicoastal operation. I'll pull some photos off the deep web. Not ones that are out there much. Make up some profiles."

"Sounds perfect," Harper said. "Very high end. Very off the radar. Only known to those in the know. And very profitable, of course."

"A big carrot always works," Mama B said.

"Especially to greedy pond scum."

"Once I create the URL and e-mail address, I'll send you the link. With a little something extra."

"Let me guess?" Cain said. "A Trojan horse?"

"You got it. Just get this guy to sign on to the website and I'll be in his computer. We'll know everything he does."

"Perfect," Harper said.

"Same with the phone number. I'll set up a toll free number. For dates. If he calls, or even if he puts the number in his contacts, I'll be in his phone. I'll record all his conversations."

"Thanks," Harper said. "Anything we can do for you?"

"A bottle of Pappy Van Winkle would be nice."

"Consider it done."

CHAPTER 18

Neither Cain nor Harper had ever been to Moss Landing. Lynchburg, sure. Many times. The home of Jack Daniels and Miss Mary Bobo's Boarding House. No longer for boarders, Miss Bobo's was a popular family-style restaurant where reservations were needed months in advance. The lakeside town of Moss Landing was only fifteen miles farther down the road. According to MapQuest, a mere 87 miles from the condo.

As always, they packed overnight bags, because you just never knew, and, of course, an assortment of weapons. Neither went anywhere unarmed. It wasn't in their upbringing, their training, even their DNA to do anything else.

For Cain, a pair of throwing knives, their sheaths sewn into the side seams of his jeans, near the front pockets. Easily accessible. His large belt buckle secreted two T-handled, jabbing blades and a pair of four-inch ceramic knives were incorporated into the sole of each shoe. Another was strapped to his left ankle. In his left front pocket, the switchblade he had been given at age ten by Uncle Al. All this was a fairly standard arrangement for Cain.

Harper's ordinance needs were simpler. A Heckler & Koch VP9 slammed with a 15 round magazine. In the purse she slung over one shoulder, in a zippered interior compartment, were two extra clips and another pair of Cain's throwing knives.

Harper loaded Moss Landing in the GPS of Cain's Mercedes

S550, and they headed out. The guidance system mostly agreed with MapQuest, indicating it was actually 91 miles and would take just under two hours. Those Mercedes folks apparently didn't understand the insane Nashville mid-day traffic, so two hours was optimistic. After spending way too much time bumper to bumper with fellow Nashvillians, Cain finally climbed on I-24 toward Murfreesboro where he veered off onto Highway 231 toward Shelbyville, then south on 82 to Lynchburg.

The drive gave Cain and Harper time to run through everything they knew about Cindy Grant's disappearance. One thing for sure was that, sadly, the General was correct. With her missing and no contact for now a week and a half, the chance of her being alive was remote at best. Possible, just not likely. The remains found in Moss Landing would not be her. The timing, the tattoos, and their mutual gut feelings said this was a wasted trip. But they had time, so why not? Mama B wouldn't have the website up until tonight, maybe tomorrow, and they needed that before visiting the entrepreneurial Adam Parker.

They skirted Lynchburg and turned east toward Tims Ford Lake. The weather-worn, two-lane county road rose and fell through farm land and thick stands of pines and maples and gums. There was little traffic out here and soon the road hopped over a final rise and Moss Landing came into view. The compact downtown area was maybe six blocks by four, everything in neat rectangles, and nudged against the lake. A three-pronged marina held a couple of dozen boats. Out on the flat lake, a water skier cut a serpentine wake behind a blue and white power boat.

They did a lap of the town, getting a feel for its character. Quiet, little traffic, only a few people strolling about. The tree-lined streets were edged by the usual small town shops—restaurants, bars, a drug store, movie theater, hardware store, bait and tackle shop, and a central downtown square. The police department sat along its south side.

They parked in a slot labeled "Visitor Parking," and walked through the metal-framed, glass front door. Inside, the Moss Landing PD looked like any other small town department. Two rows of worn, wooden bench seats in a small waiting area, a railing with a swinging gate separating it from the business end of the department. A picture of the governor on the wall. An American flag stood in one corner. A young woman looked up from behind the reception desk. She had short-cropped, dark hair, wore a blue blouse and large, gold hoop earrings. She had been reading a book, which she closed on a finger marking her place, and offered a warm smile.

"Hello," she said.

"Hello. I'm Bobby Cain. This is Harper McCoy."

"Welcome. I'm Megan Butler. What can I do for you?"

"We're looking for Chief Cutler," Cain said.

"Is she expecting you?"

"No. We were hoping she'd have a couple of minutes."

"Can I tell her what it's about?"

"We're investigating the disappearance of a young lady and I hear she found a corpse nearby."

"I'll say. Everyone's buzzing about it." She slid a bookmark into the book and laid it aside.

"Is she available?" Harper asked.

Megan hesitated, then stood. "Let me check." She disappeared down a hallway, returning in less than a minute, saying, "She's in her office." She waved a hand. "This way."

They followed her to an open office door on the left. Chief Laura Cutler stood behind her desk. She appeared fit with dirty blonde hair pulled into a short ponytail, and wore jeans and a black department tee shirt, the city logo in gold over the breast pocket. Introductions and handshakes followed. Cain and Harper sat; Cutler settled into her chair.

Cutler got right to it. "I understand you're interested in the body we found?" she asked.

"Body parts."

Her chin elevated a notch, eyes narrowing. "How do you know that?"

"The ME," Cain said. "Up in Nashville. We saw the remains this morning."

"And you're looking for a missing girl that might fit?"

"Not likely. The missing girl didn't have tattoos as far as we know. Certainly not any like those on the remains. At least not when she went missing."

Cutler nodded. "The tattooing did look fresh."

"It did. But I still have my doubts that it's her."

"So what brings you here?"

"I guess you might say we're looking under all the rocks," Harper said.

"Are you guys P.I.s?"

"Not officially," Cain said. "We're working for General William Kessler."

That grabbed Cutler's attention. Her shoulders straightened. "Oh?"

"It's his granddaughter that's missing. She's a Vanderbilt student."

"How long has she been gone?"

"Just over a week," Harper said.

Cutler gave a half nod. "You think she came down this way?"

"No evidence of that but the truth is no one knows where she might've gone."

"A runaway?"

Cain shook his head. "Not the type, according to everyone."

"Isn't it often that way?" Cutler raised an eyebrow. "Everyone says, no way, they'd never do that. But, then they do."

Cain shrugged.

"What can I do to help?" Cutler asked.

"Maybe nothing. Like I said, we don't see the remains you found being her but you just never know."

She glanced at her watch. "I'm expecting to hear from the ME sometime today. If he can make an ID, that is."

"He was optimistic he could get usable prints from the three fingers that remained."

"Let's hope." She pushed a stack of papers to one side. "We don't get this kind of stuff around here. It's a pretty boring town. The occasional alcohol-fueled fight, a B and E from time to time. But murder is pretty rare."

"From your end you're sure this was a homicide?" Harper asked.

"Unless she was tear-assing around the woods buck ass naked, I'd say it was a good bet."

Cain smiled. He liked Cutler. Straight shooter it seemed. "I agree. Based on what we saw."

"I'm still not sure who you are. How do you know General Kessler?"

"We go back to our military days." Cain glanced at Harper. "We both do on some level. I take it you know him?"

"Yeah. Just about everyone in the great state of Tennessee does. He's big player in the real estate world. I met him a year or so ago. He came here to look at a project. A new mall over off the highway. In the end, he backed away. But he was here a couple of times. Seemed like a nice man. Smart for sure."

"He is that."

"This is what you do? Find missing college students?"

"Not usually," Harper said.

"What's usual?"

"I guess you could say we fix things."

She cocked her head. "That's intriguing. Want to expand on that?"

"Not really."

"Now I am curious," Cutler said. She glanced at her watch again. "You guys hungry?"

"Always," Harper said with a smile.

"Then you're in luck. One thing we have around here is good food." She stood. "Come on. The city'll buy you lunch."

"We'll buy," Cain said. "We have an expense account."

"Lucky you."

Cain had seen Flo's Diner during their cruise of the town. Looked inviting then and even more so as he and Harper followed Cutler through the door. The aroma of barbecue filled the air.

A woman carrying a tray of dirty dishes walked by, stopped. "Chief, you sitting at the bar or do you want a table?"

"Table," Cutler said. "This is Flo," she said to Cain and Harper. "She owns the place."

"Thus the name," Cain said.

Flo laughed. "I'd shake your hand but I'm what you might say indisposed at the moment." She nodded toward the tray. "Grab a spot and I'll be right there."

About half the tables were filled and virtually everyone there nodded to Cutler, a few saying hello, as they walked by. Each studied Cain and Harper as Cutler led them to a table in the far corner.

"Smells good," Harper said. "Bobby wouldn't stop on the way down." She smiled. "One of his character flaws."

Cutler laughed.

"Let's say his focus can be one-tracked," Harper continued.

"Pot-kettle," Cain said.

A smile from Cutler.

"What's good here?" Harper asked.

"Flo's pulled pork and meatloaf are legendary."

"That they are," Flo said as she walked up, wiping her hands on a towel.

"Flo, this is Bobby Cain and Harper McCoy."

Flo nodded. "What brings you to our fair city?"

"They're investigators," Cutler said. "Or something like that."

"Investigating what?"

"A missing young lady," Harper said.

"Maybe the one the Chief found yesterday?"

"Maybe."

"That poor girl," Flo said. "Everyone's talking about it." She pulled a pad from her apron pocket, a pencil from behind her ear. "What can I get you?"

Cutler, the pulled pork sandwich; Cain and Harper, the meatloaf.

After Flo left, Cain said, "Tell me more about the remains you found."

Cutler eyed him. "You first. I want to know about General Kessler's granddaughter."

Cain laid it out. Cindy Grant. Sole grandchild of William and Miriam Kessler. Sophomore at Vandy. Supposedly off on some hiking thing in Colorado. No evidence that happened and no one knows the guy she was supposed to have gone with.

"You're thinking she was abducted?"

Cain looked around, making sure no one was eavesdropping. He leaned forward and dropped his voice. "This isn't for public consumption. Okay?"

"Sounds intriguing."

"Lee Bradford said you could be trusted," Cain said.

"You know Lee?"

"Just met him. Seems like the real deal."

"He is. Known him for years. Hell, he tried to recruit me after I finished up my training." She shrugged. "But me and Nashville aren't a good fit."

"He asked us to tell you hello," Harper said.

Cutler nodded. "So, what's the big secret?"

"It looks like she might've been involved in a prostitution set up. Went off on a date and hasn't been seen or heard from since. Cell phone dead. No credit card activity."

"Jeez. These kids. Do they even think anymore?"

"Not always clearly," Harper said. "Anyway, we've got a line on the dude who set up the date."

"And he says what?"

"Haven't talked with him yet." Harper told her of their plan.

Cutler stared at her for a few seconds, her head giving a slow nod. "Setting up a fake website to make this guy think you're in the same business. I like that."

"Hopefully it'll get us in the door."

"You guys are pretty clever."

"It was all Harper," Cain said.

Cutler winked. "Never send a man to do a woman's job."

"Amen," Harper said.

The food arrived. Along with quart-sized Mason jars of sweet iced tea.

"My, this is good," Harper said, around a mouthful of meatloaf.

"Flo has it down for sure." Cutler took a bite of her sandwich, dabbed sauce from the corner of her mouth with her napkin. "So you get inside, then what?"

"From what we know so far," Cain said, "this guy—his name is Adam Parker—is in bed with some other dude. A tough guy. Named Carlos Campos. Ever hear of either of them?"

Cutler shook her head. "No."

"Didn't suspect you would. Nashville seems to be their stomping ground."

"The hope is to appeal to their greed," Harper said. "Offer them access to more girls. From out of the area. See who they have on hand. How they run things. Hopefully, learn about Cindy that way."

"Like I said, clever."

Cain smiled. "And your young lady? Any guesses as to her identity?"

"Not until the ME gets back to me." She glanced at her watch. "We have folks come and go around here all the time. Nothing like this, but every now and again we have to track down a runaway or two." She took a slug of tea. "Best bet right now is a school teacher. Went missing up near Lynchburg. That's where she lives and teaches. Her car was found abandoned on the side of the road just a few miles from here. Maybe four weeks ago, or thereabouts."

"That fits the timeline."

"Exactly." Another bite of sandwich. "Her car was actually broken down. I heard it was some electrical thing. Not sure what exactly. Regardless, it had to be towed. My thinking is that if someone grabbed her, it was likely a crime of opportunity."

"Good bet," Cain said.

"Did she have tattoos?" Harper asked.

"No. At least her parents and friends said so. But, like I said, the tattoos on the remains looked fresh. And four weeks is a long time."

Cain pushed his half-eaten meal aside. "I suspect that you're asking yourself, if the remains are your missing teacher, why would she have gotten tattoos and then run off into the woods?"

Cutler gave a slight shrug. "And here I bet you thought a small town cop never got any difficult cases."

"No. Not in the least."

Cutler raised an eyebrow. "Voice of experience?"

"You might say," Cain said. "We've worked quite a few cases in small towns. They're just like big cities, only smaller."

Cutler laughed. "Wish you'd have a chat with our mayor. See if I can get a raise."

"Gladly. Not sure I'd carry much weight, though."

"Never hurts."

They finished their meals, the table was cleared, and Flo brought each of them a cup of coffee. Everyone declined her offer of pie.

"Being a teacher, her prints are in the system," Cutler said.

"That should help."

"Cindy Grant's are, too," Cain said.

"Really? She have a record or something?"

"No. She volunteered at a crises center. They require all their people to be printed."

"I see."

"Where were the remains found?" Harper asked.

"Not far from here. Just west of town."

"Mind showing us?"

"Not at all."

CHAPTER 19

Cindy found herself, yet again, strapped to the table. Earlier, after a couple of hours of work, her captor had returned her to the cage and left, saying he had, "A few things to prepare." Whatever that meant. Based on the angle the sunlight slashed through the gaps in the barn's warped wooden walls, it was now mid-day. It was warm but the cold, hard table and her own fear conspired to send a chill up her spine, pebbling her flesh.

Would this never end? And when it did, what was next? She could see no way that this would end well.

Her captor busied himself at the adjacent table, mixing a new color. He moved calmly and slowly, maddeningly so. Her urge to lash out, scream, fight him, returned. But to what end? He was in complete control. No doubt there. She took a deep, calming breath. Better to stick to her plan. Her new one. Be calm. Flatter him. Let him think she had bought into his madness. Win his trust. Hope for a letdown, a break in his meticulous routine. An opening through which she could escape. To where, she had no idea. What was beyond these walls? Anything was better than where she was.

He returned to her side, scraping his stool up next to her. The machine buzzed to life. Cindy flinched.

"I know," he said. "But we're almost done."

"I don't know how much more I can take today."

"The face is always tender. That's why I waited until last."

"Then what?"

"Then you'll be the star of the show."

She felt tears press against her eyes, panic rose in her chest. She fought for control. Don't give him that. "What does that mean?"

"You'll see."

See what? She wanted to ask, but knew he would offer no explanation. What would being the star of the show consist of? Would he take her from this place? If so, where? Would that offer her a chance to escape?

"When?" she asked.

He smiled. "Tonight."

That soon? Was she ready for that?

The buzzing, the pain, continued for another forty-five hellacious minutes. Her face tightened, her jaw ached from gritting her teeth. Her breaths raspy gasps as sweat slicked her body, adding an even deeper chill.

Finally, he pushed back the stool and stood. "All done."

She couldn't cover her sigh of relief. Tinged with a dose of fear for the unknown she now faced. At least here, day after day, everything was predictable. But, what now?

"What do you think?" he asked.

She raised her head and looked down her body. Thick black and orange stripes twisted and enveloped her legs, arms, torso, her entire being. Again she fought back tears.

Her brain screamed 'hideous' and 'insanity' and 'monster,' but she calmly said, "Beautiful. You're a true artist."

He smiled.

"I'm so happy you chose me," she said.

"Are you?"

"Of course. Who wouldn't be honored? I mean, before I was just Cindy Grant. No one. Now?"

"Now, you are my Tiger Lily." He ran a finger along her jaw. "And you're perfect."

He began packing up his equipment. "I have things to take care of, but tonight I'll return and we will prepare for the grand finale."

"When will that be?"

"Soon." He patted her arm. "Soon."

He returned her to the cage. "You get some rest. We have a big night ahead of us."

Then he was gone.

She examined herself. Tattooing covered every inch of her. Even if she survived, what would she be like? A freak. How could she face her family and friends? Return to her life? Maybe death was a better option.

God, she had been so stupid. The easy money, the excitement, had lured her down this road. There was no one else to blame. Everything was on her. And now, she saw no way to unwind her mistakes.

She curled in a ball and let it out. Sobs racked her. So intense, her chest cramped, her stomach wound into a massive knot as if it might explode.

CHAPTER 20

Chief Laura Cutler hadn't yet decided how she felt about Bobby Cain and Harper McCoy. Her initial impression was that they were confident, smart, and she suspected good at what they did. Whatever that was. She couldn't shake the feeling that they weren't simply investigators. Not sure what, but there was an undercurrent of detachment. Maybe not the right word. They did seem to care about Cindy Grant. And General Kessler. But there was a decidedly clinical nature to everything they said. And something else. Darker. Again, not the right word. More a sense of a take-no-prisoners attitude.

Cain had suggested that he drive, and she let him. She climbed in the passenger seat of his Mercedes, Harper in back.

"Nice car," she said.

"I like it."

"This investigative stuff must pay well. Or are you a trust fund baby?"

Cain laughed. "A little of each. My parents left me some. Harper's, too. But we do have a few wealthy clients."

"Like General Kessler?"

Cain shrugged.

She watched him as he fastened his seat belt and cranked the engine. Handsome, in a rugged yet schoolboy way. Tall, six-three, she guessed, lean, even lanky, with sandy hair that flopped over his forehead, deeply blue eyes, with faint crow's feet at their corners. Like he laughed a lot. His long fingers slid the gear into drive.

"Where to?" he asked.

She pointed ahead. "That way to Elm, then left. It's a couple of miles."

Three blocks down Elm, civilization faded.

"Beautiful country," Harper said.

"It is," Cutler said. "It's why I live here."

Which was true. One of the many things she liked about Moss Landing. Sure, the lake was cool and fun, but for her the tree-covered hillocks and broad fertile valleys of crops and grassland were what she felt an affinity for. Probably came from growing up on a farm. Only a few miles away from the road they were on. She frequently found herself out here, out of the city, meandering through the countryside. She told herself it was part of her patrols but, in reality, she loved the terrain, and the solitude.

She twisted slightly in her seat. "What exactly do you do?"

"I told you," Cain said. "Private investigations."

"Actually, you said you fixed things. That could have a lot of meanings."

"True. Basically, we do whatever the client needs."

"Which includes?"

"This and that."

She waited but he said nothing for a minute. "Very cryptic. You hiding something?"

"You sound like a cop." He offered a smile. His crow's feet deepened.

She twisted a few more degrees, facing him more directly. He looked her way.

"What?" he asked.

"Give me something. I'm letting you sniff around my case and you haven't told me anything about yourself." She glanced back at Harper. "Makes me wonder who you really are."

Cain said nothing for a minute as he maneuvered past a pick up truck that had parked along the road's shoulder.

"Fair enough," he said. "Some clients need information. We get it. Some need information manipulated. We make that happen. Sometimes someone needs convincing to change their methods of doing business, or whatever."

Cutler absorbed that. "It's the 'whatever' I'm most interested in."

"Let's just say we don't like bullies," Harper said. "Or criminals. Or those who seek to harm innocent folks."

"At least we agree on that."

"Bradford said you're a good cop," Cain said. "A tough, good cop."

"Good to hear that."

Cain nodded. "He's a fan it seems."

"It's mutual. He's a good guy. And knows what he's doing."

"That was my impression," Cain said.

"He was one of my instructors back at the academy."

"Looks like he did a good job."

"You trying to flatter me?" Cutler asked.

"Just making an observation." Cain glanced at her and smiled.

"Let's get back to the whatever," Cutler said. "You ever bring harm to these bad guys?"

"Some folks aren't easy to impress. Sometimes words aren't enough."

"You sound like a hit man."

He shrugged.

"Come on? Really?"

"We fix things," Harper said.

"And the circle is complete."

Silence fell.

Then Cutler said, "Left, here."

Cain turned onto another blacktop road.

"Have you ever killed anyone?" Cutler asked.

"I spent a few years in the Middle East. We both did. Mostly Afghanistan. Lots of death and destruction over there."

"And your role in that?"

"Can't say. Most of what we were deployed to accomplish was off the radar. Buried in all that classified stuff."

"Sounds like CIA black ops shit to me."

Cain smiled. "Harper was Navy. I was regular Army."

That explained it. What she had sensed. They considered this a mission. The big question being—what was that mission?

"Jesus," Cutler said. "Did the General hire you to even a score or something?"

"He hired us to find his granddaughter," Cain said.

"And if she's dead? What then?"

"I guess we'll jump that chasm if and when it arrives."

She said nothing for the next mile. Tried to process what he had said. Were they bad guys? Or good guys with boundary issues? From where she sat it could go either way.

She pointed ahead. "When you cross the railroad tracks up here, take a right."

He did.

"That dirt road up there. About a half a mile. By the feed store sign. Turn up that."

CHAPTER 21

The uneven, deeply-rutted road gyrated the car. Gravel pinged beneath. Ahead, a trio of crows argued over what appeared to be an empty potato chip bag. One took to the air, the other two hopped to the side of the road, eyeing them with cocked heads as the Mercedes rolled by.

"We should've taken my Bronco," Cutler said. "I don't think this car was designed for off-roading."

Cain smiled. "It's German. They design them for everything."

As they approached a stand of pines, Cutler pointed to a grassy area. "Park there."

They climbed from the car. The sun had just crept past its zenith and the heat of the day was in full force. After the car's AC, it felt sweltering.

Cutler walked toward the trees, stopping twenty feet away. "The leg was found right here." She waved a loose circle with one hand. "Buzzards were feeding on it at the time."

"Who found it?" Harper asked.

"Some kids. They saw the buzzards and came to investigate."

"Bet that shook them up," Harper said.

"Oh yeah. And their parents weren't any too happy."

"Let me guess," Cain said. "They were beyond their boundaries?"

"Voice of experience?"

"You might say."

"I get the impression that's true."

Harper smiled. "Bobby never liked to color inside the lines."

"Me? Look at you. Acting all innocent."

Harper shrugged. "We had a rather unusual upbringing."

"We?" Cutler looked from Harper to Cain, back again. "You were raised together?"

"We're siblings."

Cutler seemed to consider that. "I'd never have guessed."

A common reaction. Cain was blonde with blue eyes; Harper, true to her Cherokee heritage, darker, black hair, expresso-colored eyes.

"Long story," Cain said.

"We were raised by gypsies," Harper said. "At least that's how the family presented itself."

Cain laughed. "Right up until the FBI came and hauled everyone away."

"The FBI?" Cutler asked.

"Let's say our family didn't follow the rules all that often."

Cutler shook her head. "Why do I get the impression that that rubbed off on both of you?"

"Nature and nurture," Harper said. "Bobby was born mischievous. I had to learn it."

"She was a good student," Cain said.

That got a laugh from Cutler.

Cain refocused on the task at hand. "The remains were found here? In this open area?"

"Just the leg." Cutler shielded the sun from her eyes. "The other remains were found in there."

She pointed toward the trees, then headed that way. Cain and Harper followed. Beneath the canopy, the temperature dropped twenty degrees. Thirty yards in, Cutler stopped near an excavation in the soil.

"The body had been buried here. Pigs dug it up. Ate most of it. Dragged the leg out into the field, I suspect."

"I'm sure you gave the entire area a thorough search," Harper said.

"We did. And sifted the soil. But what you saw at the ME's office is all we found."

Cain knelt and examined the shallow grave. "Actually not a bad place to dispose of a body."

"Yeah, unless a pack of feral pigs shows up."

"Best laid plans have a way of going sideways," Harper said.

Cain stood. "Who owns this property?"

"Clovis Wilson. A local farmer. Owns a lot of parcels around here."

"He offer any helpful information?" Cain asked.

"None." Cutler nodded back toward where they had come from. "That's one of his cotton fields. Past couple of months he was plowing and planting. Said he had been out here nearly every day. Saw nothing suspicious."

"The corpse was probably dumped at night," Harper said.

"That's a good bet. Not much nighttime traffic out here, so it wouldn't be difficult to sneak in."

Cain circled the grave site, examined the terrain around it. Dirt, pine needles, scattered with gravel and patches of limestone. Perfect for gouging the feet of the victim. He told Cutler of the ME's findings—the pre-mortem and post-mortem wounds.

"Whoa," she said. "You're saying someone chased that poor girl down and killed her?"

"Looks that way."

"That's pure evil." She looked around. "And changes everything." She shook her head. "I mean…." She stopped as if she had lost her train of thought. Or maybe hadn't completely processed everything yet. She looked at Cain. "Are you sure?"

"That's the ME's opinion. Sure looked that way to me."

"This kind of crazy crap doesn't happen around here."

"See?" Cain said. "Small town crimes can be as bad as they come."

"But, this?" She massaged one temple. "I knew it had been too quiet around here lately."

Cain didn't envy her. Small department, probably only a few officers, and now a crime that would stress their resources to the max. And scare the living hell out of the locals. Probably attract the media types like sugar does ants.

Once they returned to the car, Cutler's phone buzzed. She answered. Cain and Harper climbed in and waited. Cranking up the car, and the AC. Cutler walked back and forth, phone to her ear, brow furrowed. She ended the call and settled in the passenger seat.

"That was the ME," Cutler said. "The remains are Rose Sanders."

"Your school teacher?"

"Yep." She looked at him. "Sorry it didn't help your search."

"I didn't expect it would."

Cutler took a breath, pulsing out her cheeks as she exhaled. "Now I have the pleasure of trying to track down one malignant SOB."

"Anything we can do to help?" Cain asked.

She eyed him. "Don't see how. Unless you have the nose of a bloodhound."

Cain laughed.

"What now? For you?" she asked.

"Guess we'll head back to Nashville."

"We have a big barbecue down at the marina later this afternoon. It's an annual thing. You guys should stay. If you can."

Cain had seen signs that hawked the event but hadn't paid attention to the date. Didn't know it was today.

"We wouldn't want to intrude," Harper said.

"You wouldn't be. You'd be my guests. And you'd enjoy it. The food will be outstanding." She cocked her head. "Give you a chance to see that folks here in Moss Landing aren't all sociopaths."

"What do you think?" Cain asked Harper.

"Sounds like fun. This is a cool town and an evening out of Nashville would be welcome. And I never turn down good barbecue."

"That's the truth."

"Besides, we're out of moves until your pimp-daddy website is set up."

"Somehow I don't see you as a pimp," Cutler said to him.

"I'll take that as a compliment." Cain swung the car around and regained the gravel road. "Any place to stay around here?"

"We have a great B&B right downtown."

"That'll work."

"I'll call them. Make them give you a good deal."

"Remember? We have an expense account," Harper said.

"Wish someone would give me one of those."

CHAPTER 22

It looked as if half the town had turned out for the BBQ. Several hundred of them, anyway. Their collective murmurings were interrupted by bursts of laughter and screams from an adjacent open field, beyond an array of picnic tables, where wads of children played on brightly-colored playground equipment and chased each other in no discernible pattern. The frenetic energy of youth.

Three canopied pavilions squatted near the water's edge. One shaded a long table piled with platters of ribs, pulled pork, and chicken quarters, as well as massive bowls of potato salad, coleslaw, and cornbread muffins. Another contained tables scattered with pies, cakes, cookies, and what looked to be bread pudding. The third housed a bar, where folks collected cups of wine and beer to wash down the feast.

A pair of barrel-like barbecue pits, mounted on low trailers, pumped rich smoke skyward. The late-afternoon sun hung above a forested hill, its shadow creeping toward the gathering, while a gentle breeze off the lake chased away some of the heat. Still warm, but now with a tinge of coolness.

Since they had eaten lunch, they stood under a tree just outside the drink pavilion. Many of the people who walked by said 'good afternoon' to Cutler, while eyeing Cain and Harper with apparent curiosity. Asking themselves who these folks with the Chief were, no doubt. Cain was sure she would field more than a few questions over the next couple of days. Small towns always noticed strangers.

One couple stopped to chat. The man, heavy-set with thinning hair, full cheeks, and a mouth that turned down slightly at the corners, wore a Hawaiian shirt over tan Chinos. The fit-appearing woman wore fitted jeans and a rose silk shirt.

"This is our mayor," Cutler said. "Tom Mills. And his wife Emily." Cutler nodded toward us. "This is Bobby Cain and Harper McCoy."

They shook hands. The mayor's soft, his wife's firm.

"Welcome to our fair city," Tom said. He smiled as he surveyed the crowd. "As you can see, we like to have a good time around here."

"Looks that way."

"You visiting? Maybe looking to relocate?"

"They're investigating a missing person," Cutler said.

Concern creased Mills' face. "Someone from here?"

Cain shook his head. "College student from Nashville."

"You think they might've come this way? Something like that?"

"No. But she's been missing over a week. When we learned of the remains Chief Cutler found, we figured we'd better drive down and check it out."

Mills looked at Cutler. "That turned out to be that school teacher from Lynchburg. Right? Rose, something?"

"Sanders," Cutler said.

"That's so awful," Emily said. "We don't have things like that happen around here."

"I suspect that's true," Cain said. "But unfortunately no community is immune."

Mills nodded his agreement. "Is there anything the Mayor's office can do to help you two?"

"I don't think so," Harper said. "It's unlikely our young lady is down this way. It was a long shot to drive down." She glanced at Cutler. "But your Chief has been very helpful."

Mills smiled. "She is the best." He laid a fatherly hand on Cutler's shoulder. "We're lucky to have her."

"That's for sure," Emily said.

"You should give her a raise," Cain said.

He laughed and looked at Cutler. "You put him up to that?"

"No," Cain said. "I just know she works hard."

"That she does. But our budget only goes so far." Mills looked around, obviously ready to move on, ready to end this conversation. "We'll let you folks get some food." Then to Cain and Harper, "Nice meeting you."

Cain watched them walk away. They stopped to chat with another couple. "Seem like nice people."

"Emily's a real peach," Cutler said. "Tom can be a pain in the ass. Especially around budget time."

"In my experience that's pretty much universal. The battle between the police and the mayor."

"Doesn't make it any more fun, though." She looked at Cain. "But thanks for the plug anyway."

Cain and Harper grabbed a couple of beers, handed to them directly from an ice-filled wash tub. Cutler declined. They headed toward the collection of picnic tables. A woman at the far table waved, motioning them toward her.

Cutler halted her strides. "How tough are you guys?" she asked.

"Meaning?" Harper asked.

"My mother."

"Your mother? We need to be tough for your mother?"

Cutler shook her head. "You have no idea."

The woman looked like an older version of Cutler. She was working her way through a plate of ribs. They sat on the bench seat across from her.

"This is Bobby Cain and Harper McCoy," Cutler said. "Jean. My mother."

"Nice to meet you," Cain said.

Jean held up her hands. Decorated with barbecue sauce. "I'd shake your hands but then you'd need a shower." She laughed. "Where'd my daughter find you two?"

"Mother," Cutler said. "Be nice."

"Nice, schmice."

Cain smiled. "Actually, we found her."

"Well now, there's a story."

"They're looking for a missing girl," Cutler said.

"You cops, too?"

"No," Cain said. "More private."

"And this missing girl is here in Moss Landing?"

Cain shook his head. "I don't think so."

Jean licked her fingers. "Then it doesn't make much sense to look for her around here, does it?"

"Mother doesn't have much of a filter," Cutler said. "Whatever pops in her head comes out of her mouth."

"Well, it don't." Jean picked up another rib.

"They heard about the body we found," Cutler said.

"Parts," Jean said. "Body parts."

Cutler scowled. "See? Mother has a way with words."

"The remains weren't the girl we were looking for," Harper said.

Jean looked at her daughter. "I hear it was that missing school teacher. From over near Lynchburg."

Cutler nodded.

Jean took a sip from her beer. "That's terrible. I swear. The world's coming apart. Car breaks down and she ends up pig food."

"Mother."

Jean shrugged. "Well, it's true." She looked at Cain. "What's your story?"

"Be careful what you say," Cutler said. "Mother's a crime writer. You might end up in one of her books."

"A writer? That's great. Anything I might know of?"

"Probably not. I'm more of a local phenomenon."

"You're a phenomenon all right," Cutler said.

Cain smiled. "I suspect I can get your books at a local bookstore?"

"Better than that." Jean again licked sauce from her fingers, scrubbed them with a frayed napkin. She pulled a book from the bag on the ground beside her. "I've got one for you right here." A pen appeared. "I'll even sign it."

"He can afford to buy one," Cutler said. "He has an expense account."

"Shish," Jean said, and then to me, "How do you spell your name?"

"Cain with a C. Bobby Cain. And Harper McCoy."

She scribbled the personalization and handed Cain the book. He looked at it and passed it to Harper.

"Thanks," Harper said. "We look forward to reading it."

"It's about a serial killer."

"My favorite type," Harper said.

"Good. Mine, too. Enjoy it."

"I'm sure we will." Harper slipped the book into her purse.

A twinkle appeared in Jean's eyes. "I expect you to go to Amazon and give it five stars."

"You can bet on it," Harper said.

"Got to run," Jean said as she stood and gathered her plate and plastic flatware. "I need to chat with the mayor."

"Mother, leave Tom alone."

"I pay my taxes."

Cutler sighed. "That's not the point."

"Sure ain't. The point is he won't give me the green light on using the park for my fundraiser."

"Yes, he will. He told you he would. But you have to submit the proper paperwork."

Jean parked a strand of hair behind her ear. "I don't have a secretary do all that crap. He does. He should do it."

"It doesn't work that way."

"Guess we'll see, won't we?" She nodded to her daughter, then to Cain and Harper. "I'm sure I'll see you later." And she was off.

"Welcome to my life," Cutler said.

"She's feisty," Harper said.

"Not the word I'd choose."

They walked to the adjacent field. A group of girls were doing cheerleading routines, twirling and falling and laughing, while a dozen boys tossed a football around. Beyond, near the tree line, a group of older kids were firing arrows from long bows at a series of hay bales, maybe a hundred feet away, each fixed with targets and a dozen or so balloons. Cutler led them that way. A man, dressed in khakis, a black tee shirt, and a safari hat was directing the shooting efforts.

He turned as they approached. "Chief," he said.

"Martin. This is Bobby Cain and Harper McCoy. This is Martin Stenson. Our local archery expert."

Stenson was fit, trim, well-tanned, pleasant smile. One of those guys whose age was impossible to guess. Blue eyes, blond hair peeking from beneath his hat. Could be thirty or fifty. Probably would look the same until he was seventy.

A balloon popped. Martin turned. "Good shot, Danny." The thin, mullet-haired boy beamed. "You're getting better."

"Martin's a big bow hunter," Cutler said.

"There are several of us around," Stenson said.

"Bow hunting isn't easy," Cain said. "Takes a lot of patience."

Stenson smiled. "That it does."

"What do you hunt?"

"Deer and wild boar mostly. Sometimes we go up to Montana or Wyoming for Big Horn Sheep."

"That's serious stuff," Cain said.

"You hunt?" Stenson asked.

"Not since I was a kid."

"Let me guess," Stenson said. "Rifles and shotguns."

Cain nodded.

"You ever bow hunt?"

"Some. As a kid. Wasn't very good though."

"Bobby was better with knives," Harper said.

"What?" Confusion spread over Stenson's face. "How do you hunt with knives?"

Cain smiled. "Patience."

Stenson laughed. "I'd like to see that."

"Another time."

"Go ahead," Harper said. "You need the practice." She smiled.

Harper extracted the two knives she had from her purse, handing them to Cain.

"You always keep knives in there?" Cutler asked.

"Usually," Harper said. "Bobby's not very good at keeping up with things." She gave him a smile, an eyebrow bounce. "So, I'm his pack animal."

Part of their routine. They never exposed their real weapons. Unless they planned to use them. These were for show. Like now.

Cain nodded toward the hay bales. "What color balloons do you want?"

Stenson hesitated as if trying to decide if he was kidding.

"Pick two of them," Harper said.

Stenson pointed toward a bale that had a half dozen balloons of varying colors attached. "Red and yellow."

Cain turned that way. A flick of his right hand followed by his left. Pop, pop. Red, then yellow.

"That's amazing," Cutler said. "How'd you learn to do that?"

"Misspent youth."

Stenson shook his head. "I've never seen anything like that. Why don't you come out to the house some time. My guys would love to see that."

"Martin has a ranch near here," Cutler said. "He's got quite the archery set up out there."

"I do," Stenson said. "Come on out. We'll do a barbecue, shoot some arrows. And watch you throw knives. Maybe you can teach my guys a thing or two."

"I'd love to," Cain said. "Next time we're this way."

"Where do you live?"

"Nashville."

"Not that far." He watched as one of the girls burst a balloon with a well-placed arrow. "Good shot, Ellen." He looked back at Cain. "What brings you down this way?"

Cutler answered before Cain could. "They're private investigators. Looking for a missing girl."

"Someone from here?" Stenson asked.

"She went missing in Nashville," Harper said, shaking her head. "We heard about the body Chief Cutler found, but it wasn't the person we're seeking."

Stenson looked at Cutler. "I understand it was Rose Sanders."

Cutler nodded.

"Tragic. I didn't know her but I do know the principal over there in Lynchburg. David Walton. Good man."

"Yes, he is," Cutler said.

A brief moment of silence.

"I'd better get back to it," Stenson said. "Hope you guys enjoy your time here." He turned away, stopped and looked back. "The invite to my place is open any time."

"We'll do it," Harper said.

They walked back toward the pavilions. Cain noticed that Jean had the mayor and his wife cornered near the water's edge. The mayor seemed to be on the defensive.

Cutler followed his gaze. "That woman is going to be the death of me. Seems like half the time I spend with the mayor, or with the City Council, I'm cleaning up some mess she's created."

"She does seem to be a pistol," Harper said.

"She's a Gatling gun."

CHAPTER 23

After planning to hook up with Cutler later at a bar called Maxie's to listen to some local music, Cain and Harper headed to the B&B Cutler had arranged for them. They debated begging off and returning to Nashville but ultimately decided that until the website was up they couldn't approach Adam Parker, and maybe an evening of relaxation and small-town life was in order.

Lily's Creekside Inn, a perfectly restored Victorian, white with lavender trim, occupied a tree-shaded corner lot only a block from the PD. The owner, Lily Butler, a short, stocky black woman with a round face, bright eyes, and an infectious smile, greeted them when they entered. "It ain't often the Chief calls for reservations." She laughed, swelling her cheeks, reducing her eyes to slits. "You must be important."

"Only in our minds," Harper said.

Another laugh. "Well, I got the best rooms in the house for you."

"Any room will be fine," Cain said.

"You'll like these. Both corner, across from each other." She spun the ledger on her counter. "Just sign in and I'll show you the way."

The rooms were spacious, each with high ceilings, two large windows, a four-poster bed, and antiques everywhere. Everything smelled clean, fresh, and flowery.

"Breakfast is served every day in the dining room," Lily said. "Seven 'til ten. Don't miss it. It's the best in town. Make the biscuits my own self." Another belly laugh.

"Sounds perfect," Cain said.

"Got a great wifi system. We're all high-speed around here. The password's on that card there." She nodded toward an ancient roll top desk along one wall.

After she left, Cain tugged his MAC Air and iPad from his canvas briefcase, settled it on the desk, and fired it up. A dozen emails, mostly SPAM, but two of interest. The first from Milner, asking if he had anything to report. Cain fired off a reply that said this was a dead end and that they'd be back in Nashville in the morning. The next, the one he'd been waiting for, was from Mama B.

She wrote: "Here's your pimp daddy site" followed by a link, and then, "Call when you can. Got the skinny on the guys you inquired about."

Harper came in the room. "I like this place."

"It's very nice."

She nodded toward the computer. "Any news?"

"Mama B came through. Let's take a look."

Harper stood behind him as Cain clicked on the link. The world of high-end prostitution opened. Amazing. Mama B had hit a home run. The main page connected to several others revealing sub sites for various cities—New York, Chicago, Miami, LA, Houston, and Atlanta. Each had scores of pictures of scantily clad young women. Each beautiful, each a total fake. An 800 number was supplied for anyone looking for companionship.

"She's unbelievable," Harper said. "This looks legit."

Cain pulled out his iPhone, put it on speaker, and called Mama B.

"This is fantastic," Cain said.

"You expected less?" Mama B asked.

"Not even close," Harper said. "It's exactly what we need."

"The number will connect to me," Mama B said. "Anyone calls and I'll give them the old two-step and let you know."

"Perfect."

"When you dig into it you'll see it's packaged as a very private and exclusive club. Not for public consumption. Requires a membership. That way the carrot will be bigger."

"Great idea," Harper said. "Wish I'd thought of that."

"That's why you have me." A soft chuckle. "I figured that would end any questions they might have about it not being out there in their world. With the riff-raff."

"I like it," Cain said. "We'll be inviting them into a secret society."

"My thoughts exactly. If I read what I've learned about Adam Parker and Carlos Campos correctly, they'll love it. Make them feel important. Special. Eager to invite you into their set up."

"Exactly what we need," Harper said.

"What have you found on them?" Cain asked.

"Adam Parker is indeed a grad student. Smart kid. Straight As. He's in the MBA program now. Has a condo just off campus. I'll send you all his contact info."

"Good," Cain said. "I plan to track him down tomorrow."

"The other guy, Carlos Campos, is a different story. He's got a sheet with the local PD. Drug possession, a pair of assaults, a B&E, and was tagged for selling stolen items. TV's, phones, laptops, that sort of stuff. Did a couple of months in lock up. That was for one of the assaults. Three years ago. Also got popped for pimping but that was dropped due to lack of cooperation from the girl involved."

"Sounds like dependence or intimidation," Harper said.

"Probably both," Mama B said. "She initially agreed to come clean, be the good citizen. Changed her mind when it came right down to it."

"Not surprising," Cain said. "Seems these girls never roll on their pimps."

"Looks like Carlos has a crew of sorts."

"We know he has at least two," Cain said. "No names, but one of the girls had at least met them."

"I'm on it. I suspect they'll turn out to be small-time street miscreants."

"My favorite type," Cain said.

"Try not to hurt them too badly," Mama B said.

"That depends on them, I suspect."

"Doesn't it always. That's all I have right now."

"You're a genius."

"Of course I am. Later." She ended the call.

They had an hour before they were scheduled to meet Cutler so they walked around town. Pleasant and friendly, folks nodding and saying "howdy" more than once. Finally, they strolled into Maxie's.

To the left was a long bar, each stool occupied, and to the right a couple of dozen tables, also occupied. In the near corner a young man, hunched over, face hidden behind stringy hair, strummed country blues from a worn, acoustic Gibson amplified through a Seymour Duncan amp. He was in the middle of some catchy tune Cain didn't recognize. Maybe something he wrote himself.

Cain saw Cutler in the back, at a table beneath a picture of a narrow lake. Probably one of the many fingers of Tims Ford. She held a long-necked PBR, working the label loose with a thumbnail. A waitress followed them to the table. They ordered a pair of PBRs, too.

"Got it." She looked at Cutler. "You're food will be right up." She turned and left.

"Food?" Cain asked.

"Hot wings."

Cain rubbed his stomach. "Not sure I can help you there. After all the barbecue I ate today." Cain had had seconds.

After the knife throwing exposition, and meandering around the marina, Cutler telling them bits and pieces of Moss Landing's history, the trio grabbed some food and sat at one of the picnic tables.

"You some kind of wimp?" Cutler asked.

"Just need to watch my figure."

"I'm sure that's it," Cutler said.

"I'll help," Harper said.

"That a girl," Cutler said. She took a slug of beer. "Anything new with your investigation?"

"Our site's up and running," Cain said.

"That fast?"

"We have resources," Harper said.

Cutler eyed her, and then said, "I still don't get what you do." She shrugged. "Maybe I don't want to know."

The waitress placed two beers on the table. "Here you go. We got plenty more where that came from so drink up." She wiped her hands on the small towel tucked beneath her apron tie. "Anything else?"

"Wings," Cutler said.

"Got it."

Cain asked, "What's your wifi password?"

"MAX2013. That's the year we set it up." Then she was gone.

Cain opened his laptop, logged in, and headed to the page Mama B had created. He spun the computer toward Cutler. She studied the page and then looked over the screen. "I take what I said back. You'd make a great pimp."

"He would," Harper added.

"Funny," Cain said.

"This's amazing." Cutler clicked a few pages, going through the various cities. "It definitely looks official."

"Hopefully it's good enough to fool Adam Parker and get us up the food chain."

"It will. No doubt."

The wings arrived. Cain closed the laptop and put it away. Cutler grabbed a wing; Harper, too.

Cutler gnawed one to the bone, tossing it in the bowl provided, then licked sauce from her fingers. "You going to visit this Adam dude tomorrow?"

"That's the plan."

"I'd love to see that."

"We'll give you a call afterwards if you want. Let you know how it went."

"I'd like that."

CHAPTER 24

Cindy Grant sat against the bars of her cage, cotton pants and a tee shirt, a blanket wrapped around her shoulders. She had cried off and on all afternoon, to the point that her ribs burned. As the sun set, she regained some semblance of control over her emotions. Her sobs now low whimpers, eyes raw, nose dripping trapped tears.

What time was it? It had been dark for a couple of hours. Maybe longer. Time wasn't easily judged once the sun faded. The temperature had drifted downward and he hadn't turned on the space heater when he left. She tugged the blanket more tightly around her shoulders.

When would he return? And when he did, what next?

He had said she would be presented to the world. Be a star. What the hell did that mean? The dread that had held her for the past week deepened. Her mouth dry, sticky, acidic, her stomach a hard knot. The only thing she knew for sure was that she wouldn't survive whatever it was. No way he could or would allow that.

She stared at the door. Wishing he would come, fearing he might. This was purgatory. Not quite hell, not yet anyway, maybe close. Wasn't purgatory hell's waiting room? She thought she learned that once. Somewhere.

She drew her bare feet against her buttocks, tucked the blanket around them, and rocked gently. *Come on*, she wanted to scream.

Get this over with. Whatever is going to happen, let it begin. It couldn't be worse than the anticipation.

Or could it?

Then she heard footsteps and the metallic sounds of him working the lock. The door scraped open and he was inside. The two standing lights snapped to life. He smiled at her. Calm and casual. As if returning from a day at work. As if he might say, "Honey, I'm home."

A canvas duffle over one shoulder. With a heavy thunk, he placed it on the table. The one she had spent days strapped to.

"How are you?" he asked.

"Confused. Scared."

"No need for either. This is your night. You're the star."

She sniffed, swiped the blanket's corner across her nose. "The star of what?"

He walked to the cage. Looked down at her. "Art must be seen to be appreciated."

"I don't understand."

"You will."

He returned to the table and unzipped the duffle. She now noticed his combat-style pants, black, like the tight, long-sleeved shirt he wore. He removed a pair of handcuffs and then unlocked her cage.

"Take off your clothes."

She hesitated. It wasn't like he hadn't given that command before. Every day she had been there, in fact. Meant he was ready to work on her. But that was done. Every inch of her body displayed his grotesque tattooing.

His jaw tightened. "Now."

She slid from her clothing, her flesh pebbling from the cold and the fear that welled inside her.

"Turn around."

"Why?"

He grabbed one arm and spun her. "Do exactly what I say when I say it."

He twisted her arms behind her back and snapped the cuffs in place.

"Why are you doing this?" she asked.

"We have to take a little trip."

"Where?"

"Someplace special."

"No. Please." Her voice sounded foreign to her. Coarse, raspy. Stretched with the fear that tightened her chest. "Just let me go. I'll never tell."

"Far too late for that, don't you think?"

"Why? I don't understand. Why are you doing this?"

He studied her. "Are you sure you really want to know?"

What did that mean?

"But I guess you deserve that," he said. "Knowing what you are. Who you are. That you'll be admired and treasured forever."

"What are you talking about?"

He grabbed a ball gag from the table. "First this."

"What? Why?"

He stepped behind her and pressed the ball against her mouth. She clamped her teeth together, shook her head. The gag slipped beneath her chin. He tugged the strap, pulling her against him, the ball now compressing her neck like a fist.

He whispered in her ear, "Do I need to get the plastic bag?"

"Please." Her voice a mere whisper.

"Open up."

Did she have a choice? She parted her teeth. He secured the gag in place.

"That's better. I hate screaming."

She whimpered.

"You see, hunters, *real* hunters, always take trophies."

She stiffened. What was he talking about?

"You wanted to know how special you are." He clutched her arm and directed her to a table along the far wall. A canvas sheet lay over it. Tented up in the middle, something beneath it. "And so you shall." He lifted the canvas, folding it to one side.

At first she wasn't sure what she saw. A large glass container. Filled with liquid. Something inside. Then the pieces came together. A face. A head. Shaved. Black-striped tattoos over its surface.

Oh, my god.

She recoiled, staggering. His grip on her arm tightened. A wave of nausea, her heart rising into her throat. She tried to scream, to breathe. A savage trembling overtook her. Her legs wilted. She slumped, but he held her upright, his mouth now against her ear. His breath hot.

"She was to be my first masterpiece. But she was incomplete. Not worthy. But, you? You're so very worthy."

He helped her back to the table. The table where he had tortured her with those incessant needles. He lifted her so she was seated on its edge. He cuffed her ankles and tied a blindfold in place.

Then, his voice a gentle whisper, he said, "Relax. Don't fight it."

She tried. She really did. But her panic only grew. Her heart thumped audibly.

He wrapped a blanket around her, lifted her on to one shoulder, and carried her outside. The door clicked closed behind them. She heard gravel beneath his boots and sensed he was carrying her up an incline. Then a mechanical pop and she was rolled onto a hard surface. He adjusted the blanket, tucking it here and there. A door slammed shut. A vehicle door. She rolled to one side, then the other, extended her legs. Her heels rubbed against coarse fabric. The lining of a cargo area. Probably a SUV.

Another door slammed and the engine cranked to life.

The next few minutes the SUV rose and fell and swayed. The road beneath pinged with gravel and then the rough hiss of asphalt.

Where was he taking her?

More gravel, gyrations, and finally the vehicle jerked to a stop.

He climbed out, the vehicle rocking slightly. The door banged closed. Then two more car doors slammed. Footsteps on gravel. Then voices. Two, no three, all male. Muffled. She was unable to hear what they were saying.

The rear snapped open. Hands grasped her and lifted her to a standing position. The gravel cold and hard beneath her bare feet.

"Let's see what we have here?" Not her captor. Another man.

"Wow." Another voice. "She's magnificent."

"Got to admit, I wasn't sure you could pull this off. Especially after the fiasco with the other one."

"You have little faith." Her captor.

She sensed the men walking around her, inspecting her. The blanket was gone. She was completely naked, exposed.

Once again she was lifted over a shoulder. This one more muscular. Down a slope. She smelled water. Fish. Heard the unmistakable lapping of water against a shoreline.

An unceremonious drop onto another firm surface followed. The impact hollow, a rocking sensation. A boat. She attempted to roll to one side. A boot pressed against her chest, flattening her shoulders against the cold surface.

"Hold still," her captor said.

She tried to speak, to scream, but the ball gag prevented any intelligible sound. Her tears soaked the blindfold. Someone spread the blanket over her. It seemed even more coarse than it had earlier.

The boat's engine ground to life, then movement. First reverse, then a jerk forward. Water slapped the bottom, she bounced one way and then the other. Her back, shoulders, hips took the brunt of the impacts. It seemed forever but she knew it was likely only fifteen minutes before the engine slowed and then stopped. The boat crunched against something. The shore?

Someone snatched away the blanket, then removed the cuffs from her wrists and ankles. Again, hands lifted her, over the side, and placed her upright. In water. Only a foot or so deep. Cold. Silt and smooth rocks against her soles. The smell of fuel exhaust strong. A firm hand clamped on one arm and led her up the slope to dry land. Pine needles. The blindfold came off, then the gag.

Three men stood before her. Her captor and two others, one tall and thin, the other shorter, muscular. Each dressed in all black. Moonlight silvered their faces, the trees. She looked back across the water but saw no other lights. No signs of civilization. The only sounds were the waves against the shore, the gentle breeze that rustled the trees, and her own breathing.

"Where are we?" she asked.

"Where you were meant to be," her captor said. He smiled. "Turn in a circle. Let us see your beauty."

"Please," she begged.

"Do it. Now." His voice sharp, threatening.

She did.

"Amazing," the tall man said.

"What did I tell you?" her captor said.

The muscular man stepped toward her and ran his fingers over her face. She flinched. He smiled. His hand trailed downward, over one breast, down along her hip. "Perfect. You're absolutely perfect."

Tears streaked her face.

Her captor knelt, unzipped the duffle he had tossed from the boat, and lifted out an object. Then two more. He handed one to each of the other two men. At first Cindy couldn't tell what they were, but as they each reconfigured the devices, unfolding the parts, snapping them into place with sharp clicks, they took form.

Crossbows.

What the hell would they need…? No, no. Surely not.

"What is that?" she asked.

"Just what it looks like," her captor said, briefly holding her gaze. "It's time."

"For what?"

"This way." Again, a rough hand on her arm directed her into the trees, to a small clearing. She could see the terrain ahead was a mixture of thick trees, ravines, and patches of shrubs, some lit by the moon, others cast in deep shadows.

"And now it begins," he said.

She looked at him. "What?"

"The hunt."

She took a step back. He was insane. All of them were. Completely and totally. Her world blurred through the tears that collected in her eyes.

"Imagine you're a tigress. On the Transvaal." He waved a hand. "The entire world is your domain." Now he raised the bow above his head. "And we are the hunters. Seeking a trophy."

"You're sick. All of you are."

"I thought I was an artist." He smiled. "Or were you trying to play me?"

She groaned.

He shook his head. "So transparent."

"Please don't do this," she said. "I won't tell anyone about you."

Her captor shook his head, let out an exasperated sigh. "We've been through that. Over and over. Besides, the bets have been placed."

"What?"

The tall man spoke. "We each ponied up ten grand. Winner take all." He nudged the muscular guy with an elbow. "Means you're worth thirty K."

"Please." Her voice a weak, desperate, foreign rasp.

"You have ten minutes," her captor said. "Run."

She looked at the three men. "What are you talking about?"

"It's simple. You flee, we hunt."

"No, no, no." She shook her head. "I won't do this."

He clutched her arm, squeezed. "You will or I'll shoot you right here, right now. Your only chance, the chance of any prey, is to escape." He shoved her. "Now run."

She staggered and nearly fell. She spun back toward him. He raised the bow and aimed at her chest.

"Nine minutes."

She ran.

CHAPTER 25

Beautiful. Hideous. Spectacular. Disturbing.

A work of art.

A psychopath's dream.

All this raced through Cain's mind as he and Harper stood next to Chief Laura Cutler and Jimmy Rankin.

Cain's and Harper's plan to hit the road early, get back to Nashville and track down Adam Parker, hit a snag before it really began. They had loaded their bags into the trunk of Cain's Mercedes just after seven a.m., and then headed into the breakfast room where Lily Butler busied herself putting the finishing touches on a spread that included scrambled eggs, thick bacon and sausage links, a bowl of grits, and a platter of fluffy, golden-brown biscuits. As Lily had promised, it was spectacular. After thanking Lily for her hospitality, and the great breakfast, they headed north. Only made it three miles out of the city when Cain's cell buzzed. Cutler, telling them to meet her at the post office.

"Why?" Cain asked.

"Something you need to see."

"What?"

"I can't even describe it."

Cain disconnected the call with an amped up sense of dread. After whipping a u-turn where a gravel road spurred off the highway, they booked it back toward town.

The building was white clapboard with black trim. Keeping with that theme, a large, white sign with "US Post Office 37352" in black, block letters crowned the front door. Cutler's black Bronco, a silver Ford Taurus, and three patrol units squatted in the gravel lot just left of the building. Cain parked and he and Harper stepped out.

A semicircle of canvas screens on movable metal poles shielded the side of the structure from the public's prying eyes. Cain and Harper ducked inside.

The girl hung by her ankles from a large metal hook screwed into the wooden eave. Arms extended downward, reaching within a foot of the ground. Her lithe body imprinted with thick, black and orange stripes.

Her head missing.

"Jesus," Harper said.

Cutler turned toward her. "Jesus ain't nowhere to be seen in this mess."

"Who found her?" Cain asked.

"Norm Sweeney, the post master, when he came in to open up. Fortunately, he's an early riser, so we were able to do all this before the town cranked to life." She waved a hand toward the canvas barrier. "He entered through the back door so didn't immediately see her. Not until he hauled yesterday's trash out to the dumpster. He freaked. Called. So here we are."

Cain stepped closer to the body. Young, fit, very dead. He touched her cold leg. The tattooing amazingly detailed with crisp lines. He moved around her, examining the work. Whoever did this possessed an experienced hand.

"Any idea who it is?" Cain asked.

"Nope." Cutler let out a long breath. "I took her prints and sent them up to Nashville."

"How'd you do that?" Harper asked.

"We aren't all that backwoods. We have one of those scanners. The City Council sprung for it a year or so ago. So they're now in the hands of the Nashville PD."

"Give them a call," Cain said. "Tell them to check them against Cindy Grant. I suspect, they'll match."

"Why do you think that?' Cutler asked.

"A hunch."

Cutler pulled out her cell and did exactly that. "They'll get back to me shortly."

"I take it the ME will send someone down," Cain said.

"In the works," Rankin said. "Said it'd be an hour or two."

The rope that bound her ankles ended with a short loop that allowed the suspension. The knots simple, nothing distinguishing. Cain moved to where he could see the soles of her feet. Ripped and excoriated. Embedded limestone slivers. Just like the school teacher. He turned to Cutler. "We have a problem here."

"You think?" Cutler said.

"Worse than simply this."

"How so?"

"Whoever did this, did your school teacher, too."

Cutler hooked one thumb in her belt. "Why do you think that?"

"The tattooing is similar." Cain reached out and touched the girl's leg again, running his fingers over the smooth skin. "Black and orange stripes here. Only black on the teacher." He turned to Cutler. "But the similarities aren't accidental."

Cutler's face paled.

"Her feet are damaged the same way. Reinforces what I thought." He looked at Cutler. "She was hunted down. Both of them were."

"Come on," Rankin said. "You're kidding? Right?"

"Wish I was. We have two young women. Naked. Tattooed to look like animals. Both with injuries to the soles of their feet. The kind of damage that comes from running over rocky terrain. I don't think either would do that unless they had to."

"Okay," Rankin said. "This young lady is a tiger. What about Rose Sanders?"

Cain shrugged. "An unfinished tiger? Maybe he hadn't gotten to the orange part yet."

"Maybe the teacher was a zebra," Harper said.

Cain nodded. "Could be."

Rankin shook his head. "If that don't beat all, I don't know what does."

"Wait a minute," Cutler said. "You're saying we have some

psycho running around here hunting young women?"

"After he tattoos them," Cain said.

"What kind of sick freak does that?"

"The worst kind," Harper said.

Cain circled the corpse again, closely examining her chest and abdomen, found what he expected. "Here." He pointed.

Cutler, Harper, and Rankin stepped up beside him.

The first entry wound was easy to see. Near the left scapula, middle of an orange stripe. Small, round, clean. The second was more difficult, buried in a black stripe. Lower right chest. Also small and clean. No blood. He stepped down.

"Two entry wounds. No exits. The bullets will be retained so the ME should be able to grab them. That'll at least give us some ballistic information."

"When and if we find a weapon," Cutler said.

Cain pulled out his iPhone. "I'm going to grab a couple of photos. Send them up to one of the FBI profilers I know. Get his take on this."

"What are you thinking?" Cutler asked. "What are we dealing with here?"

"A serial killer," Harper said. "A narcissistic one."

Cutler twisted her neck one way, then the other. "Which means?"

"He's not finished. He's proud of his work. That's why he displayed her this way. Likely considers himself an artist. Wants the world to know how special he is."

"If that's the case, it begs the question," Cutler said, "why was Rose buried and this one displayed here?"

Cain shook his head. "I don't know." His gaze ran over the corpse. Even as grotesque as this was, she was beautiful. A work of art. Of sorts. "If I had to guess, I'd say he wasn't satisfied with Rose."

"Satisfied?" Rankin asked.

"Maybe she wasn't perfect," Harper said. "Not up to his standards."

"Some fucking standards," Cutler said. "This guy doesn't possess standards."

"Sure he does," Cain said. "This," he waved a hand toward the body, "was painstakingly done. It took time. He put his soul into it."

"He doesn't have a soul either," Cutler said.

"You know what I mean. He created this. He wants credit."

"Then he should come on down to my office and say so. I'll give him lots of credit."

Cain smiled. "I didn't say he wanted to be caught. He just wants to be known."

"This young lady's a tiger," Rankin said. "Rose Sanders a zebra or something. What's next?"

"Whatever he wants," Harper said. "But there's a theme here."

Cain wanted to believe something else. Not what he knew to be true. Not what the evidence clearly stated. Some guy was transforming women into exotic animals and hunting them. He could find no narrative that said otherwise.

"You have any big game hunters around here?" Cain asked. "Ones that travel to Africa for trophies?"

Rankin's brow furrowed as he considered that. "Not that I know. I mean, we got hunters of all kinds. I'd say half the folks in town. But other than deer and boar heads I haven't seen anyone with trophies like lions and tigers or anything like that."

Cutler stepped closer to the corpse. She lightly touched one leg, examining the tattooing. She turned back to Cain. "You ever heard of anything like this before? Some psycho creating his own prey and then hunting them?"

Cain nodded. "There was a case a few years ago. Kentucky, wasn't it?" he asked Harper.

"Yeah. His name was Peter something. I forget." She snapped her fingers. "Peter McCormick. He picked up hitchhikers and then hunted them."

"Did he do any of this kind of tattooing?" Rankin asked.

"No," Harper said. "If I remember correctly he went down in a shootout with the police."

"Good riddance," Rankin said.

"I guess it means we're looking for someone who has tattooing and hunting skills," Cutler said.

"Good bet," Cain said. "Could be a team but I doubt it. Team killers aren't that common, and this is personal. This guy sees himself as some kind of god."

"Creates and destroys?" Cutler asked.

"Exactly," Harper said. "It's all about power and control. And his omnipotent narcissism."

Cutler massaged her neck, twisted her head right and left, as if working out a kink. "I've read about those kinds of miscreants but I've never seen anything like this."

"Few people have," Harper said.

"You think he's a local?" Cutler asked. "Someone from around here? Or some drifter?"

"Local," Cain said. "Both victims were found in your backyard. Means it's his backyard, too."

"Yeah, but if this is Cindy Grant, she's from Nashville," Cutler said.

"Not that far away," Cain said.

"We don't have any tattoo parlors around here," Rankin said. "There're a couple over in Lynchburg. I'll see if they recognize the work. If not, we'll have to expand the footprint." He tugged at one ear. "Maybe all the way up to Nashville."

"I'll go over and chat with Lucas at the gun shop," Cutler said. "See if he knows anyone around who likes big game trophy hunting."

"Hard for me to believe this is the work of anyone around here," Rankin said. "We know everybody in town, hell, the whole county, and for the life of me I don't see this being any of them."

"Serial killers don't have scarlet letters," Harper said. "Many seem as normal as you and me. Bundy, Gacy, even Dahmer. Not all look like Manson."

Rankin shrugged.

"This guy knows the lay of the land," Cain said. "You can't just turn someone loose and hunt them anywhere. You have to know where the roads and the farmhouses are. The killer would need to know the victim couldn't escape. Or reach help."

"We got so much open land around here the hunting ground could be anywhere," Cutler said. "I wouldn't even know which direction to look."

"That's what they pay you the big bucks for." Cain smiled.

Cutler huffed out a breath. "I knew there was a reason I was rolling in the dough."

The next hour dragged by. They tossed around ideas, potential suspects—of which Cutler had exactly zero, and said so.

"There isn't a single person around here that would be capable of this," she said.

"There's one," Cain said.

Cutler sighed and shook her head.

Harper said that due to the organized nature of these crimes— the planning, the execution, the patience—the killer wasn't likely a teenager. At least mid-twenties, could be into his fifties. Those were her thoughts.

Finally the ME's van with two techs arrived. While they photo'd and examined the body, then with the help of Rankin began to loosen the rope that suspended the girl, Cain called Marv McBride, his FBI contact. Cain had sent him the pics earlier along with a note that he'd call soon. McBride's initial impression lined up with Cain's and Harper's. They had a very bad, very narcissistic, power and control driven dude. And he was nowhere near stopping.

After Cain disconnected the call, he told Cutler of McBride's initial thoughts. Cutler wasn't thrilled.

"Why the hell'd he have to choose my domain?" she asked.

"He had to choose somewhere," Cain said. Cutler frowned. "And, like I said, the odds are this is his domain, too."

"Great. Just fucking great."

"The tarps were a good idea," Cain said. "I suspect you want to keep this under wraps. No details."

"You got that right. Last thing we need is a media circus to break out."

"Not to mention all the cranks that'll come out from under the rocks," Harper said.

Cutler sighed. "I don't even want to think about that."

"Unfortunately, it's coming," Harper said. "Something like this can't be kept under wraps for very long."

Cutler seemed to consider that. "We'll do our best to keep the details out of the official reports." She shook her head. "For a while, anyway."

"What the hell's going on in there?"

Cutler spun. "Mother, don't come in here."

"What you got in there?"

Cutler pushed through the gap in the tarps. Cain and Harper

followed. Jean craned her neck, trying to see past them.

"Mother, go away."

"That's no way to talk to your mother." Jean looked at Cain. "I raised her with better manners but she don't seem to follow them all the time."

Cain smiled. Cutler didn't.

"This is a crime scene," Cutler said. "You can't be here."

"Sure I can. It's free country." Jean tried to move past her, but Cutler grabbed her arm.

"If you don't leave, I'll arrest you."

"Arrest your mother?"

"No, someone who's trying to contaminate a crime scene."

Jean's jaw tightened. "If that don't beat all."

Cutler directed Jean several steps into the lot. "Go home."

"When you tell me what's going on. Not before."

"I swear to God I'll lock you up if you don't leave."

Jean glared at her but spun on her heels and marched to her car, muttering, shaking her head. They watched as she drove away, launching another withering glare at her daughter.

"She'll be the death of me," Cutler said. "Unless I kill her first."

"She is a trip," Harper said.

"No. She's a circus of one."

Cutler's cell rang. She answered, walked away with the phone to her ear.

Cain helped the techs and Rankin cover the body and load her into the rear of the van. They secured the door, climbed in, and drove away.

"This's going to get uglier, isn't it?" Rankin asked.

"You can bet on it," Cain said.

Cutler walked up. "That was the Nashville PD. The prints match Cindy Grant."

CHAPTER 26

"What the hell were you thinking?"

Cindy's captor shrugged. He sat at the table on his patio, across from his fellow hunters. The pair stone-faced. He took a sip of lemonade.

"You hung her up at the Post Office, for Christ's sake."

"Isn't that the purpose of trophy hunting? Display your conquests?"

"You cut her fucking head off."

"A personal trophy."

They stared at him, speechless.

The captor continued, "If memory serves, both of you have a few trophy heads on your walls."

"Not this."

"Game is game."

"Are you trying to get us caught?"

The captor shook his head. "Never happen."

"Do you even know who she was?"

"Sure. Some working girl. Cindy something."

"Cindy Grant."

"Okay," the captor said. "Cindy Grant. Big deal."

"It is a big deal. A very big deal."

"Don't see how."

One of the men leaned forward, elbows on his knees. "You

162

know who General William Kessler is?"

"Sure. Why?"

"She was his granddaughter."

"How do you know that?"

"I know people. Down at the PD."

The captor hesitated, digesting that. "Okay, so what? No way she can be traced back to us."

"That's pretty arrogant thinking."

"Did you enjoy last night? Wasn't it the ultimate thrill?"

The two men stared at him.

"The perfect prey. Not some dumb animal. A human. Isn't that what you wanted?"

"Sure. It was great. But, I don't know that this kind of boasting will turn out well."

"It'll be fine." Another sip of lemonade.

"I don't like it. Why didn't you bury her like you did the other one?"

"The first one," the captor said, "the school teacher, wasn't complete. Not worthy of being displayed. Or even to hunt." He smiled. "Not like this one."

The two men exchanged a glance.

"Besides, she escaped. Changed everything. Won't happen again. Those mistakes have been corrected."

One of the men took a long, slow breath. "It's the mistakes that worry me. The unpredictable." Another breath. "I can't believe you're so calm about this."

"There's no need for concern here."

"I hope you're right."

"I am." More lemonade. "In fact, the next one has already been selected. Same source. Completely anonymous. No connection to any of us."

The taller man rubbed his neck. "I don't know about this."

"If you want out, that's fine." The captor smiled. "But I don't think you do. Either of you. I saw it in your eyes last night. The thrill of the hunt." He waved a hand. "Not to mention the thirty grand."

Silence ruled.

"If either of you want to walk away, it'll be okay. You have a good week or so to decide. It'll take that long to get the next one in hand and prepared."

CHAPTER 27

The Kesslers were broken. In a profound way that few could imagine and even fewer had ever experienced. Deep fractures that would never completely mend. Parents were not meant to outlive their children, much less their grandchildren. For the Kesslers, their only grandchild.

A thick layer of guilt clung to Cain. Guilt from being the one to deliver the blow. Messengers might not be responsible for the news, but they do bring the pain.

It had started with a phone call. Cain's first thought had been to simply show up at the Kesslers' home. Deliver the anguish cold. Like ripping off a bandage. But a two hour drive lay before he and Harper and he needed to be sure it wasn't a wasted trip.

He and Harper had business in Nashville. Cain had Adam Parker in his crosshairs and was anxious to get the hook in him. That he was involved in this was a given. Cain could see no scenario that didn't include Parker. Carlos Campos, too. They had roped Cindy into the business and had set up the date. Cindy's last. Whoever they handed her off to was the one Cain wanted. And the path to that person ran straight through Parker and Campos.

So as they pulled away, leaving Cutler to handle her end of the investigation, Cain called. It went like this:

General Kessler: "I take it you have news."

Cain: "I do."

Kessler: "From your tone I assume it's not good."

Cain: "It isn't."

Kessler: "Tell me."

Cain: "When I get there."

Kessler: "That bad?"

Cain, after hesitating to consider how to say it, deciding that clear and succinct would be best: "As bad as it can get."

Kessler: His jaw tightened. "I'll prepare Miriam."

And who will prepare you? Cain thought.

Now, he and Harper sat in General Kessler's study facing him over his desk. The room with the soaring windows and breathtaking views. No one was admiring that. Not now. Maybe never again.

Miriam stood behind her husband as Kessler stared at his large iMac, eyes drowning, cheeks slick with tears. Neither had moved, or said a word, for several minutes. After Cain laid out the scene, and after Kessler demanded to "see for myself," Cain emailed him the photos of Cindy. Kessler had opened them on the screen. Twice he raised a shaky hand and gently touched the image. Sobs racked Miriam as she clutched his shoulders with white fingers.

"Give me the details," he finally said.

Miriam took a ragged breath and then retreated to the sofa to Cain's right. She sat down heavily, her torso doubled in pain, gaze directed at her feet.

Cain rattled off what he knew. Or at least suspected. Two gunshots to the back. One just left of the spine, probably to the left lung, maybe the heart, the other along the right lower rib margin. No exit wounds so ballistics was in play. Feet torn and gouged—like the school teacher. The beheading seemed to have been post-mortem. Cain didn't know that for sure but felt the need to cast some sort of lifeline.

"Was the other girl treated similarly?" Kessler asked.

"We don't know," Harper said. "They only found partial remains."

"But the two are connected," Kessler said. A statement, not a question. "The tattooing, the damage to the feet. Both over near Moss Landing."

"That's likely," Harper said.

Kessler glanced at Miriam, then toward Cain. "They were hunted." Again. Not a question.

"I believe so," Cain said.

"Who would do that?" Miriam asked. "What type of sick person would do that?"

"A sociopath," Cain said. "One who split from humanity along the way." He looked at Miriam. "That's my take, anyway." He now turned to Kessler. "I reached out to a friend. An FBI behavioral analyst. Sent along the photos. He agrees."

Miriam squared her shoulders and stood. She walked to her husband and gave him a kiss on the top of his head. "I'll leave you to talk." As she walked by Cain, she squeezed his shoulder. "Do what you do." Her grip tightened. "With extreme prejudice." Then she was gone.

Extreme prejudice. Talk about a loaded term. Means different things to different people. Miriam was a soldier's wife. To her, only the military definition mattered.

Harper stood. She gave Cain a knowing look. "I'll go check on her." She left.

Cain knew what was coming. Knew Miriam and Harper left the room so there would be no witnesses to the words. Only he and General Kessler would ever know what was said. At least first-hand.

Kessler's fingers touched the screen one last time before he closed the image. He wiped his eyes with the heels of his hands, adopted an erect posture, his face stone. Then he spoke. "You know what I'm going to say."

Cain nodded.

"You remember Afghanistan? Juarez?"

Another nod.

"Whatever it takes. As long as it takes." Kessler stood, leaned forward, elbows locked, hands flattened against the desk top. His ice-blue eyes hardened. "Cindy was tormented, tortured, and murdered. Apparently in the most heinous manner." He took a deep, ragged breath, releasing it slowly. "I want the same visited on whoever was responsible." His chin came up. "With the most extreme prejudice."

Sir, yes sir.

The mission parameters were now set.

#

Harper studied Bobby. They were winding their way along the back roads toward Nashville. She twisted slightly in her seat to face him. His hands gripped the steering wheel, not exactly white-knuckled, but firm. His gaze, focused yet unfocused, on the roadway. Silence settled in for a good twenty minutes.

Growing up together, sharing the same bed or tent or sleeping bag under the stars, Bobby had been a happy, carefree child. Whether throwing knives or breaking into homes or helping her run a scam, he had always done so with a sense of fun, play. Nothing mean spirited. A game to him.

The military changed him. From what she had learned about his career, he had completed his missions efficiently. Coldly. Doing the jobs few were willing or able to do. Afghanistan, Iraq, Beirut, wherever he was needed. But those paled when compared to Juarez. His military ops had been sanctioned, for God and country. Juarez had been personal. Deeply so. And it changed him profoundly.

How many nights had she heard him roaming their condo, unable to sleep? How many times had she found him standing at one of the massive windows, staring out toward the dark river? They rarely talked about such things. There was no need to do so. Each understood.

"Where are you?" Harper finally asked.

"You know."

"Afghanistan?"

Cain shrugged, glanced her way. "Don't forget about Juarez."

CHAPTER 28

Bobby Cain, Age 27

After his SERE's training stunt, after his AWOL charges were imposed and then miraculously rescinded, Cain found himself in the DC area. The Pentagon, CIA headquarters, various NSA facilities. He was poked and prodded and put through an endless series of medical tests, including evaluations by three different military psychiatrists. Apparently he passed, since after a few months, he landed at Fort Benning, Georgia. Ranger School. For the next year he trained. It was hard, grueling, even dangerous, but he thrived.

He assumed he'd then be deployed with his unit. The military had other ideas.

For the next year, he trained with the Navy Seals and Delta Force and learned hand-to-hand combat from a series of instructors, the most important being an Israeli IDF Krav Maga instructor. Krav Maga. A combination of boxing, wrestling, Karate, Judo, and old fashioned street fighting. It fit well with what he had learned from Uncle Albert, whose philosophy was that there was no such thing as a fair fight. The Marquess of Queensberry didn't exist in his world. Anything and everything was in play. Knives, chairs, rocks, whatever. The only principle was to hit first, hit hard, and don't stop until your opponent was down and out.

Cain had no idea why the military put him through two years of this type of training and, true to the military, no one would tell him.

Then he found out. In a military transport somewhere over Eastern Europe. Inbound to Afghanistan. It seemed they had a problem with a well-ensconced Taliban general. The mission lasted less than 48 hours and ended with Cain on a low-flying stealth copter weaving through rocky mountains toward a secure CIA base and the Taliban general sprawled in a pool of his own blood.

For the next five years, Cain went on nearly two dozen other missions. If you can call sanctioned assassinations missions. Most in the dark of night, all requiring his unique abilities to get in, kill quietly, and get out without raising any alarms. Iraq, Afghanistan, even a couple in the heart of Beirut.

Each was carried out by small squads. Cain was mostly hooked up with Seals or Delta Force, sometimes with Marine specialists. The CIA never far away. No records were generated; ever. No written orders. Just pack up and go.

But just two weeks after his twenty-seventh birthday, Cain's life changed. Dramatically. On several levels. A reunion. The end of a career.

The hot desert wind buffeted the helicopter. The newest generation stealth version. They hugged the faceless terrain, invisible now in the moonless night. The pilot, a young Marine, relaxed, as if out for a routine training run. Cain sat in the back with two other Marines. Guy named Bart O'Keefe from Kentucky, and Mike Bolton, from the deep woods on Michigan's Upper Peninsula.

Their destination for this operation was some shit-hole village a few kilometers from Kandahar. Supposed to be mostly "friendlies," but with those guys you never knew. The Afghanis you trained could turn on you when least expected. When they could do the most damage. Happened all the time.

Cain had been added to the mission late in the game. Apparently things on the ground had morphed. The target a mullah, which always made things sticky, and could easily blow up into an international incident. But their target wasn't really a mullah. No sign of God or Allah, or whoever, around this guy.

Taliban all the way. A commander, a bomb maker, an intel guru, but not close to a man of the cloth.

The problem? He had proved difficult to track, had changed locations weekly, if not daily. Each time he blipped up on the radar, he quickly vanished, making each window of opportunity a narrow sliver. Now he had ensconced himself in a fortified house. Two days now. The fear, of course, was that he'd pull up stakes and bolt. If he hadn't already. But the latest intel said no.

Only two ways into his hideaway. A firefight, or Cain doing what he did so well. The brass opted for the latter, so here he sat.

The helicopter dropped Cain and his Marine escort in the desert two kilometers outside the village. It was nearly ten p.m. They worked their way through ravines and around towering sand dunes and ultimately into the bowels of the city. The so-called "safe house" was in a more residential area. They met four Navy Seals in the back room of a damaged and dusty structure.

"Any problems?" one of the Seals asked.

"No," O'Keefe said. "All five by five."

The Seal in charge introduced himself to Cain. "Louis McNamara."

They shook hands.

"Who's the CIA dude running the op?" Cain asked.

"McCoy."

"Where's he at?"

"She's right here." A woman's voice.

Cain turned. The world tilted. He couldn't believe it.

"Bobby Cain," she said.

"Harper?"

She smiled. They embraced, holding each other tightly for what seemed like several minutes.

Cain's mind raced. He had not seen her since they were removed from juvie and packed off to their respective adoptive parents. Cain had been twelve; Harper thirteen. He honestly thought he'd never see her again.

The Marines and Seals made nervous movements. Obviously, unsure what all this meant.

He and Harper released their holds on each other.

Harper said, "My brother."

"What?" McNamara asked.

"Bobby Cain. My brother. We were raised together but haven't seen each other since the family broke up. Fifteen years ago now."

Cain smiled. "Or was broken up."

She nodded. "True."

"So, how did you end up here?" Cain asked Harper.

"Long story. And one for later. Right now we have a mission." She shrugged. "Sorry you got dragged into it so late, but things here changed. The target moved to a more secure location. So, a change of plans." She looked at Cain. "They said they were sending in someone with special skills. I didn't know it was you until after you were airborne." She shook her head. "The truth is I didn't know you were in this line of work. Even that you were in the military."

"Speaking of long stories," Cain said.

"We'll catch up later." She nodded toward McNamara.

He unfolded a map and a schematic of the compound, spreading each on a wobbly wooden table. He went over the plan. Cain listened, absorbed. Then they were off.

The mission went well. Just after midnight. The guards, either asleep or drinking or smoking some of their own shit, left the target alone and vulnerable. Third floor of a ramshackle house on the western edge of town. Took all of fifteen minutes for Cain to slip inside the walls, scale the outside of the building, and take care of business.

Then they returned to the safe house, where Harper waited. Nearly three hours to kill before their extraction copter was due. Two kilometers away, four a.m.

The house where they were holed up was near the southern perimeter of the village. Rumor was the sector was populated by three hundred Marines, but Cain only saw a handful of them. Keeping a low profile until asked to do something high profile. Something bloody and deadly. Things they were good at.

One of life's basic truths is that everybody has a breaking point. An intersection of place and people and circumstances that tests their skills, judgement, and moral fiber. A series of events that forces a moment of decision. One that alters the trajectory of life.

Cain's came around two a.m. while he and Harper sat outside on a small enclosed porch, catching up. Harper's naval career, entry into the secret world of the CIA. Cain's training and black ops.

They had listened to the rape for half an hour. The cries, the whimpers, the begging that are the same in any language. Just across the street, three doors up, a group of "friendlies" were having their way with a young girl. Cain wondered what part of Islamic dogma covered that. Of course, dogma was for the sheep, not the wolves. Been that way for millennia.

Cain sat in a dark corner, knees drawn up. Every time silence fell he thought it was over. Either they had had their fun and moved on or the girl had died. But the begging and screaming always flared again. His nerves were like live wires. As if charged with pulses of electricity.

McNamara stepped outside. He twisted his neck as if working out a kink. "Somebody should do something about that," he said.

Cain stood. "Someone is."

"You?" McNamara asked.

Cain nodded. "I can't let this go."

"I hear you."

Harper stood, brushing dust and sand from the rear of her pants. "This isn't sanctioned."

"I know," Cain said.

"You could end up before a court martial. Worse."

Cain shrugged. "I'll worry about that later."

Harper smiled. "Good."

"So. You're okay with this?"

"This what? I don't see anything." She grabbed his arm. "I just wanted to make sure you were committed."

"I am."

"Me, too. I'm in."

Cain stared at her. "No. This is my deal."

She tightened her jaw. "No, it's mine. I'm in charge."

"But like you said, this is off the books."

Harper shrugged. "Everything we do is off the books."

And it was settled.

The house was dark, only an upstairs light on. The window open, the anguished cries spilling out. A guard stood just left of the front door, smoking a cigarette, his weapon propped against the wall.

Cain and Harper made their way up a trash-strewn alley, cut between two houses, crossed the street, and crept back toward the house, approaching from the rear. Most of the houses they passed were dark, but how the occupants could sleep through the girl's cries was a mystery. Maybe they were used it. And the occasional gunfire Cain could hear in the distance. Some Taliban dude firing into the air. Seemed they did that day and night.

They crept along the side of the house to the front corner. The guard, his back to them, took a final pull from his cigarette and crushed the butt beneath one boot.

Harper stepped into the open. Looked at the man. She said something to him in his native language. How did she know that? The man moved toward her. Eyes bright, a smile on his face. Harper had obviously propositioned him.

Cain moved quickly. Clamping a hand on the man's throat, squeezing him into silence, Cain dragged him around the corner. He struggled and kicked, but Cain's grip only tightened. Cain took him down, on his left side, pinning the now terrified man against his chest, never relinquishing the pressure on his larynx. He smelled of sweat and fear. Cain easily sliced through his pants at the groin, severing his femoral artery, and held him tightly as his life ebbed away. Took less than five minutes.

They entered through a rear door, finding the first floor unoccupied. At the top of the stairs, light and the girl's whimpers tumbled through an open door. Cain slowly ascended, Harper behind and to his left. He grasped a throwing knife in each hand. He peeked round the door jamb. Two AKs leaned in the far corner. One bad guy stood, tucking in his shirt; a second, pants down, climbed on top of the girl.

When Cain stepped through the doorway, the standing man looked up, eyes wide with surprise. A flick of Cain's wrist and the blade entered the guy's throat, just left of his trachea, puncturing the carotid on that side. He gasped, clutched at the knife, blood spouting between his fingers. His gaze locked on Cain for a second, then he collapsed. The guy on the girl twisted toward them, tried to rise. Harper's silenced handgun spit a hole in his forehead. He collapsed on the girl. She screamed.

Cain dragged the dead soldier off her and onto the floor. Harper said something in Arabic. The girl, now covered with blood, rolled from the bed, stood. Harper collected her clothing from the floor and handed them to her. She clutched them to her chest and bolted out the door.

Cain, Harper, O'Keefe, Bolton, and three of the Seals reached the extraction point fifteen minutes early, the stealth copter five minutes later. They were quickly airborne. Them, their mission, no longer existed. They had never been there. The mission that bore no name never took place.

When they reached the mountainous base, the CO was waiting for Cain. He took him in his office and delivered the worst news Cain had ever received.

His parents in Tyler, Texas had been murdered.

The funeral had been four days later, delayed so Cain and Harper could make their way from Afghanistan to Texas. Cain's pass was a given; Harper had to plead and threaten to get hers.

They each took a leave while Cain settled his parents' estate, with Harper's help. Along the way, decisions were reached and plans were made. Cain left the military; Harper, the CIA. His separation proved easier than hers, but in the end, they were again civilians.

The police had three suspects in the slaying of his parents. Guys tied to the Sinaloa cartel. Drugs dealers, killers, very connected. And now in Mexico.

They reached out to Mama B, their first of many collaborations. Mama B was also on the way out the door, winding down her four-decade career. She found the trio. Holed up in Juarez. A neighborhood of cheap stucco shit-boxes west of town. At one a.m., the street dark and quiet. But the trio had company. A pair of local prostitutes. Cain and Harper scaled the fence that encased the small backyard and settled along one side. A clear view through a dirty window. The party wound down around two. The girls, and they looked like just that—mid-teens as far as Cain could tell—finally slipped on their clothes, stuffed wads of pesos in their purses, and headed out. They watched as the pair giggled and staggered up the street, passing a bottle of tequila back and forth. Most likely their tip for services rendered.

Juarez is one of the most dangerous cities in the world. A cartel war zone. As bad as any place Cain had encountered in the Middle East. So, when the bodies were found, throats sliced to the point of near decapitation, the Sinaloas had no doubt it was the work of the rival Zetas. Retribution was promised.

CHAPTER 29

As soon as they got back into the molasses that is Nashville traffic, Cain's cell pinged an incoming text. Kelly Whitt. Cindy's roommate:

HAVE INFO ON ADAM. HEADING INTO CLASS. CALL ME AT 1 PM.

They reached the condo before noon. While Harper unpacked her bag, flipped on the Keurig and made them coffee, Cain called Mama B and brought her up to date.

"Let me guess," she said. "Kessler wants this rectified."

Rectified. The perfect word. "Exactly."

"So we're in full attack mode now?" Mama B asked.

"You got it."

"One thing—does Kessler know I'm involved?"

"No. I figure it's best if he doesn't," Cain said.

"I agree. I don't think he'd have a problem but I appreciate being off the radar on this one."

"Of course, he probably suspects you're lurking somewhere," Cain said.

"Lurking's what I do best."

"I might have a line on Adam Parker." Cain told her of Kelly's text. "Hopefully later today."

"I'm going to send you a couple of things. A link with your pimp daddy contact info. What name do you want to use?"

"William Faulkner."

"Always the jokester."

"And we'll see how well educated he is."

"I love it. Simply send the link to his phone, it'll add you to his contacts, and I'll be inside."

"Meaning?"

"I can tap his phone. Listen and record all his conversations and texts. Even if his phone's off."

"That'll help."

"The other thing is a link to the new site. Have him log on with his computer to see what you're all about, check out your girls, that sort of thing, and I'll be inside his motherboard. Same access."

"You're amazing."

"That I am. There're a dozen other ways I could access his electronics, but these will be easy and clean."

"I'll get on it when I meet with him."

"Later."

Cain dropped on the sofa. He told Harper the plan.

"So now we wait," she said. "Any idea what Kelly has for us?"

Cain shook his head. He checked his watch. 12:30. "Guess we'll know soon."

Mama B's email arrived. Cain checked it. He added William Faulkner to his own contacts so he could feed it to Adam Parker. He then bookmarked the URL for the site.

At exactly one p.m., he called Kelly.

"You got my text," she said. "Good."

"Where are you?"

"Just got back to my apartment."

"Are you alone?"

"Yes, why?"

"You better sit down."

"No. Please don't tell me something's happened to Cindy."

Cain sighed. "Unfortunately, something did happen. She was murdered."

"What? Are you sure?"

"Yes."

"Who? How?"

"Better you don't know."

"But…"

"Kelly, listen to me. We're going to try to keep all this out of the public eye, for as long as we can. You might hear about the murder on the news but the victim will hopefully be unidentified. It's Cindy, but we don't want to create any hysteria. It'll make the cop's job harder. Mine, too."

Kelly broke down. Cain let her get it out, though hearing her anguish wasn't easy.

"I don't understand any of this," Kelly said.

"You will. Later. But right now, this information can go no further. Understand?"

Silence.

"No one. Not another person. Okay?"

"Jesus, this is so hard."

"I know. But you'll be fine. It just takes time."

That was a lie. Kelly would never be fine again.

"So, what news do you have?" Cain asked.

Kelly sniffed, sighed, then said, "I started to call you this morning. Around nine. I saw Adam. At Starbucks. He was talking to a girl I sort of know. Not well, just to say hello. I managed to maneuver nearby so I could catch what they were talking about."

"Did he see you?"

"No. The place was packed."

"Okay. What did you hear?"

"Just a sec."

She covered the phone but Cain could hear her talking to someone. Muffled and not intelligible.

"Sorry. A friend just invited me to a party later. I'm not sure I'm in the mood though." Another sigh. "Adam was recruiting the girl. At least it seemed that way. It was a short conversation and I didn't have time to call. The good news is that he's meeting her again at four. At a place called Murphy's. A local hang out."

"I know it. On Broadway."

"That's it. I grabbed a pic of him and the girl. Her name's Tonya, I think. Could be Tina. Something like that. Don't know her last name. I'll text the photo to you."

"Good job."

"Thanks. I feel like a spy."

"You are. But now I want you to back away. I'll take it from here."

"Was it Adam? Did he kill Cindy?"

"I don't know. But I do think the trail to her killer goes through him. Nothing else makes sense."

"Then I want to help. I'll do whatever you need."

"I know. And maybe I'll need to call on you down the road. But right now, the best thing you can do is protect yourself. No way you want Adam and his friends knowing that you're involved here. Okay?"

"I guess so."

"No guessing. It's a fact. Stay low to the ground. I don't think it'll happen, but if Adam reaches out to you, play dumb. You know nothing."

"I will. I promise."

His cell chimed an incoming text. The attached pic showed Adam Parker, coffee cup in one hand, the other waving as if making a point, chatting with a beautiful black girl.

"Got the pic. Thanks."

"No problem."

"I'll call you if I have any more news."

CHAPTER 30

They had nearly three hours to kill so Cain called Captain Lee Bradford.

"Mister Cain," Bradford said. "Looks like your missing young lady is now my murder investigation."

"Yours?"

"She might have been found down in Moss Landing, but she went missing from my domain. So, yeah, mine."

"Have you talked with Chief Cutler?"

"Sure did. And she welcomes our help."

"She's a good cop," Cain said. "Seems to me, anyway."

"She is."

"Anything new on your end?" Cain asked.

"Maybe. Just got a call from the ME. Said he found something interesting."

"Like what?"

"Don't know yet. Getting ready to head over there right now."

"Mind if Harper and I join you?"

"Sure. I don't think Dr. Curry will mind."

"See you there."

"Oh, how's General Kessler taking the news?" Bradford asked.

"Not well. But he's a tough guy. He and Miriam are both resilient."

"But this? I imagine it's a bitter pill to swallow."

"True. See you in twenty."

Bradford was standing next to his car, phone to his ear, when Cain pulled into the lot and he and Harper stepped out. Bradford ended the call and they shook hands.

"Thanks for letting us tag along," Harper said.

"You haven't gotten by Curry yet." He smiled.

Dr. Walter Curry was in the autopsy lab, finishing another autopsy. The table behind him held a draped body. Cindy Grant, no doubt.

"Mr. Cain, Ms. McCoy," Curry said. "Good to see you again."

"Thanks for letting us be here."

Curry nodded. He waved toward the trapped corpse. "I'm afraid we found your missing girl."

"We saw," Cain said. "At the scene."

"Then you know how odd this all is."

"Never seen anything like it."

Curry tugged off his gloves and gown. "Me either." He slipped on fresh gloves and peeled the drape off Cindy's corpse. "Yes, very odd. The tattooing. The displaying of the body. The decapitation." He shook his head. "But there's more."

"So I hear."

"We have two entry wounds. Here and here."

"And the bullets?" Bradford asked.

"That's the strange part. No bullets."

"I didn't see any exit wounds," Cain said.

"Because there aren't any."

"You saying he dug the bullets out?" Bradford said.

"No evidence of that. The wounds are smooth and round. No evidence of any trauma like I'd expect if someone went rummaging around in there."

"Then, what?" Harper asked.

"She wasn't killed with a gun. No other explanation." He frowned. "Bullets don't typically evaporate."

"What are you saying?" Bradford asked.

"These wounds are from some type of stabbing weapon. Maybe a spear or an arrow."

Interesting. Cain glanced at Harper. She was thinking the same thing. Hunters. Arrows. Martin Stenson. Or someone in his world.

Cain examined the wounds. Now clean and easily visible under the harsh lights. "Not hunting arrows," he said. "Too clean."

"True. Maybe target arrows. Maybe a metal spike. Something like that."

"I'd bet on arrows," Cain said. "Her feet. Same injuries we saw on the other woman. The school teacher."

"Yes. Rose Sanders." Curry looked at Cain. "Before, when I suggested she might have been running over rocky terrain, I wasn't so sure." He waved a hand. "But here there were no pigs involved. Hard to indict tusk injuries here. And again, I found small bits of limestone in the plantar wounds."

"Pre-mortem damage?" Harper asked.

"Yes." He waved a hand. "The head removal was post-mortem. No doubt."

As he had hoped. As he had told Kessler. Some small favors are huge.

"They were both hunted," Cain said.

Curry nodded. "That'd be my guess."

"So you're thinking Rose Sanders was a zebra and here we have a tiger?" Bradford said.

"That's what it looks like," Cain said.

"Jesus," Bradford said. "This definitely connects the two cases. Women altered to look like exotic animals and hunted. What kind of person would do that?"

"A narcissistic sociopath," Harper said. "Power and control. A common combination in these types of killers. This guy creates his prey, hunts them, and then displays them. Like trophies."

"I'd bet he has the head somewhere," Curry said. "A personal trophy."

"Maybe Sander's head, too," Bradford said.

"Wouldn't surprise me," Curry added. "Don't know that for sure since we didn't find her head. Or neck."

"Rose Sanders wasn't displayed," Bradford said. "She was buried."

Cain walked to the other side of the table and looked down at Cindy. "Harper and I discussed this. Our thinking is that either she wasn't a satisfactory result—not up to his standards—or maybe she somehow escaped before she was completed."

Curry's brow furrowed. "That might explain it."

"If Sanders escaped, the killer lives in or around Moss Landing," Cain said. "Probably not far from where she was buried."

"Unless he transported both from somewhere else," Bradford said. "To confuse us."

Cain nodded. "Possible. But I don't think so. He's local. If Rose Sanders did escape, there would be no transporting involved. She was likely buried near where she died."

"Why do you think that?" Bradford asked.

"Let's say she got away and he had to hunt her down. Chased her into the woods. Killed her. Now he's got a corpse to deal with. Maybe some distance from his lair. Not easy to carry a body very far."

"But he could have. In a vehicle," Bradford said.

Cain nodded. "Maybe. But the grave site seemed hurried. Not very deep. As if he had to make do with what he had. No shovels or anything like that. Which is why the grave was shallow and why the pigs found her."

"That makes sense."

"Which means he's working in that area," Cain said.

"Also," Harper said, "he wants credit for his work. He would want to be near the chaos he created. Feel the tension that followed."

Bradford sighed. "I surely don't envy Laura Cutler."

Cain and Harper were barely out of the parking lot when she said, "Do you think Martin Stenson could be the guy we're looking for?"

"Could be."

"Not how I read him. But then we only saw him for a few minutes."

"And bad guys don't have 'GUILTY' tattooed on their faces."

"Tattooed? Interesting choice of words."

Cain shrugged.

"Sounds like we'll be back down there soon," Harper said.

"Sure does. As soon as we snare Adam and Carlos."

"Another interesting word choice."

CHAPTER 31

Laura Cutler knew what was coming. No way to avoid it, so she steeled herself to face it head on. They were scared, they were concerned and confused, but mostly they were scared. Maybe she could tamp that down somewhat. She wasn't optimistic. Only thing to do was to ride it out. It's not like they were going to fire her. Were they?

She met with the City Council in the Freeman Civic Center Building. Built and donated by Sam and Claire Freeman. Wealthy residents who no longer lived in Moss Landing. Or anywhere. They now resided in the nearby Pine Grove Cemetery, in the shadow of the same large oak tree where her father was buried. Heart attack, during her senior year of high school.

Mayor Tom Mills had called a special session of the council so Cutler could "bring them up to date," and waylay their fears. The former she could do; the latter, probably not. All eight council members were present. Something that rarely happened. Showed the depth of their concerns.

She sat in a chair, a not very comfortable one, facing the members who were gathered in a semi-circle behind the curved table. The goose-necked microphones before each were flexed downward, like wilting sunflowers. Not needed today. No public presence. This was a private meeting.

"Laura, thanks for coming in," Mayor Tom Mills said.

"Wish it were under better circumstances."

Tom nodded. "We all do. So tell us. What do you know so far?"

She examined the expectant faces. "What's said here doesn't leave this room. Okay?"

"Why?" Mills asked.

"I think you'll see when we're finished."

He shrugged, as if to say, "We'll see."

Cutler straightened her back. Took a breath. "We have two murders. Rose Sanders and now Cindy Grant. The granddaughter of General Kessler. It appears that each of them had been tattooed. With an animal design."

"What does that mean?" It was Noleen Jenkins asking. She owned a card shop in town and had been on the council for more than ten years. She had also been Cutler's nemesis. The one that continually raised complaints, and always voted against a pay raise or new equipment for Cutler and her crew. And right now she had that look. The one that said she was on the warpath. Tight jaw, creased brow, and the barest hint of a smirk.

Cutler wanted to shoot her.

Probably not a good idea.

"It's a guess," Cutler said. "At least in the Sanders case. But from the pictures Tom showed you, you can see that Cindy Grant was definitely tattooed as a tiger. I suspect Rose Sanders was a zebra. But since we didn't find many remains that might not be the case."

"How were they killed?" Noleen asked.

"It looks like Cindy was shot. Twice. In the back. With Rose, we don't know. Both bodies are with the ME. Up in Nashville. Hopefully, he'll be able to tell us more."

"Do you have any suspects?" Tom asked.

Cutler shook her head. "Not yet. But it's likely the killer is local."

Noleen jerked to attention. "Why do you think that?"

"Both bodies were found here. One, a more or less local. The display at the Post Office. He'd have to know the town. Know when it was safe to do that."

Noleen nodded as if she actually agreed with Cutler. There was a first for everything.

"Anything else?" Tom asked.

Cutler shrugged. "Truth is we don't know any more than that. But it's early in our investigation. Hopefully we'll have more in a day or so."

Tom nodded. "How do you think we should handle this? As far as the public is concerned?"

"Let out as little as possible. We don't want whoever did this to know what we have. And what we don't have."

"Shouldn't the public know?" Noleen said. "I mean, if someone is running around killing people they need to know."

Cutler knew this was coming. Knew she didn't have a great answer either. "I agree. Mostly. If anyone asks I'd say that two people have been killed. That we don't know why or even if they're connected." Noleen started to say something but Cutler went on. "Which is true. We don't know that. We suspect it, but we don't know."

"Aren't you parsing words?" Wilbur Starling joined the conversation. He owned the hardware store in town. This was his first year on the council.

"Maybe. But I think playing this close to vest—at least for now—is best." Cutler searched the faces before her. She saw no real disagreement staring back. "Cindy Grant was the granddaughter of General William Kessler. You all know the name. Everyone knows the name. I'd like her identity to remain in this room."

"Why?" Wilbur again.

"To prevent a media circus. It's going to come out. Probably sooner rather than later, but every day it doesn't gives us more time to look into this without having cameras following us around."

Mills nodded. "Any disagreement?" He scanned to his right and left. No one said anything. He tapped a pen against the tabletop. "Anything else?"

"I wish I had more but that's about it right now," Cutler said.

"What about this couple?" Noleen asked. "The ones with you at the barbecue? I heard they're involved in the investigation. Is that true?"

"No. Not really. They were hired by General Kessler to find his granddaughter. Now that they have, I suspect they're work is done."

"You trust them to keep a lid on this?" Wilbur asked.

"They seem to be seasoned investigators. I think they

understand how these things work. Besides, if I understand them correctly, General Kessler wants this to remain quiet for as long as possible."

"So, they're like P.I.s?" Noleen again.

"Something like that. Maybe not licensed P.I.s. They do more personal investigations."

And a whole lot more apparently. She still wasn't sure who or what Bobby Cain and Harper McCoy were. But the point was moot since she wouldn't likely be seeing either of them again. No reason for them to venture back this way since they had found General Kessler's granddaughter.

She wasn't sure how she felt about that. Bobby Cain was an interesting man.

CHAPTER 32

Murphy's was a just dive-y enough bar/restaurant on the north side of Lower Broadway, sandwiched between a Mexican restaurant and a popular music venue. Good drinks, good food, even had its own live music. Cain and Harper had been there many times. They walked the two blocks from their condo. It was just after four.

The bar was only half-filled, mostly college kids, getting an early start on happy hour. More industrial than Irish, as the name might suggest, the walls were plain concrete and the ducts and electrical conduits lay exposed along the ceiling and walls. A long bar down one side, manned by three fast-moving bartenders, the main dining area a collection of twenty or so four-tops. In one corner, a guy sat on a stool and strummed a black lacquered Gibson acoustic and sang Country standards.

Cain immediately saw Adam. At a corner table with the attractive black girl he had seen in Kelly's photo. He had a laptop open, showing her something. No doubt his business plan. She was laughing and leaning in toward him. Adam was quite the charmer it seemed.

Cain and Harper grabbed stools at the bar, ordered Stellas, and tried to melt in with the crowd while keeping inconspicuous tabs on Adam. Cain nursed the beer through the next twenty-five minutes until the girl checked her watch, stood, and walked away.

"Show time," Cain said.

As they had previously planned, Harper followed the girl out onto the street. To inform her that what she was getting into might not be a smart choice. Maybe alter her trajectory. Worth a shot.

Cain waved the bartender over, paid the bill. He weaved through the tables to where Adam sat, busy with stuffing his laptop into a canvas messenger bag. Adam looked up.

"Adam Parker?" Cain asked.

"Yeah."

"William Faulkner."

"Like the author?"

One point for Adam. "I get that a lot."

"What can I do for you, Mister Faulkner?"

"Bill." Cain sat. "I have a business proposition for you."

"What? Selling insurance?" He laughed.

"Something more profitable."

"I like profit."

"Don't we all?"

"So what is it?" Adam asked.

"Girls."

Obviously not what he expected. He visibly stiffened. "What does that mean?"

"Open your laptop." Cain nodded toward the bag.

"Why?"

"I want to show you something."

Adam hesitated, but curiosity won out. He pulled out the laptop and booted it.

"What's your email?" Cain asked. He slid his phone from his pocket. "I'll send you a link. So you can see what I'm offering."

Again Adam hesitated but recited his address. Cain fired off the link. Adam opened it. One eyebrow went up. Hooked. Now to reel him in.

"My group runs girls," Cain said. "All over the country. Even a few overseas. I think we could do some work together."

Adam glanced around the room and then back to Cain. "I don't see what this has to do with me."

"Good." Cain smiled. "We like discretion. What I'm offering is to expand your inventory."

"Why would I need that?"

"Money. For you and your partner."

Adam's back stiffened. One corner of his left eye twitched. "I don't have any partners."

"Look, I know about you and Carlos."

"How do you know—" He caught himself.

"Relax. It's my business to dig up these things. Particularly if my group is considering a working arrangement. I know you recruit college girls and Carlos sets up dates for them. I suspect you get a piece of the action along the way."

Another look round the room. "How do I know I can trust you?"

"You don't. But that goes both ways. I'm taking a risk, too. But nothing ventured, nothing gained. Right?"

Adam seemed to relax a notch.

"I know Carlos has other recruiters out there but college girls are hot commodities." Cain indicated the laptop. "Look around the site. Tell me what you think."

He did. Cain sat quietly and waited.

"This is your set up?" Adam asked.

"Me and a couple of others," Cain said. "You can see we're coast to coast. And extend into Europe and the Middle East. I run the domestic stuff."

"LA, Miami, Atlanta, New York, Chicago. That's a big operation."

"It is. And we're always looking for fresh girls. From different areas. Customers like choices."

Adam leaned back. "What are you proposing?"

"There are a few options, but for you I think it would be more to your liking if we folded you and Carlos into our group."

"We're doing okay. Why would we do that?"

"You said you liked profit. This will definitely boost your bottom line."

"How?"

Cain smiled. Greed comes in many forms but it all leads back to dollars. "We command higher prices. More choices. More profits. You'll get access to our girls. And we to yours. We do all the bookings. You'll simply find the talent and manage things locally." Cain gave a one-shouldered shrug. "Less hassle, more money."

"I don't see how."

Cain tapped his computer. "Check out LA." He did. "Scroll through the girls." He did. "You think these girls would be an easy sell?"

"Absolutely. But these girls are in California."

"We fly our girls around. Bring in a new crew for several weeks, they move on and more arrive. From all over. Definitely expand your inventory. And sales."

Adam gave a slow nod. His wheels were definitely turning. "I like that."

"Good. Why don't you take this to Carlos? Then we'll sit down with him and get into the details. I think you'll both see the profit potential."

"Okay. No promises though."

"I understand. What's your cell number? I'll text you my contact info. Cell and email. Once you sit down with Carlos, give me call or shoot me a text and we'll go from there."

Cain sent him the link.

And just like that Mama B was inside Adam's laptop and cell phone.

CHAPTER 33

"Choosing the right bait's what it's all about."

That was Uncle Mo's take. And he was the family's best fisherman. Since the group traveled constantly, always seeking better jobs, better scams, better communities to put on the shows, they often lived off the land. Everything from night-time raids on farms to pilfer corn, pumpkins, melons, and the like to snatching chickens and rabbits. Whatever was available. It wasn't like the itinerant group could grow their own crops. Spending a growing season in one location wasn't an option. Not only would most communities, once the novelty of the shows thinned, grow tired of having "smelly and thieving gypsies" in their midst, it wasn't in the group's DNA to drop anchor.

"For catfish and crappie use worms, for bass a good spoon or wiggler's best," Uncle Mo said one day, as he and Bobby sat on the bank of a muddy pond just outside of Corinth, Mississippi. The morning was hot and humid, the kind of day that melted your clothes to you skin. Cain was seven and held a cane pole, bobber and worm in position, waiting for a fat catfish to take the bait. "Fish are like people. Use the right bait and they'll come running. And once you hook and clean them, move on. Never over fish the water—or a town. Mother Nature and human nature won't allow for either."

One of the many lessons Cain had learned at Uncle Mo's side.

He had a true understanding of fish. And people. Whenever he waxed philosophical, as he did that day, he would tug at his mustache—a thick bristle that hid his upper lip and drooped past the corners of his mouth—and fix his gaze on something in the distance. As if playing back some memory in his head. They caught a dozen that day. Uncle Mo nine, Cain three. Cain could never come close.

For Adam and Carlos the bait was money. And they bit.

While Harper hit the stair climber, Cain sat on the sofa in the condo, the TV tuned to an A&E documentary on the devastation visited on the Everglades by Burmese Pythons. The face of a game warden filled the screen, the interviewer extending a microphone near his chin. "These big old nasty snakes have reduced the raccoon and possum population by ninety-five percent. And they ain't got a single natural predator. We've tried trapping them but that don't work. They like live bait running free. Never seen one crawl into a trap. So we drive the roads at night, looking for them stretched out on the asphalt soaking in the residual heat." He shook his head. "But we estimate there're more than thirty thousand of them and more being bred every day. It's a losing battle."

Cain wondered if the pythons might over fish the area and turn on each other to avoid starvation. He guessed it was possible but he didn't know much—as in anything—about such snakes. Rattlers and cotton mouths sure, but not exotic pythons. While he pondered that, his cell buzzed. It was Mama B.

"Adam called Carlos about a minute after you left," she said. "I tracked his cell to Carlos' place. Took about twenty minutes. Carlos logged on to your site so I got his computer in the network now."

She was amazing.

"They moved around your site for most of the next hour. Carlos definitely wants to meet you."

"How do you know that?"

"Because I used Adam's phone as a mic and listened to everything they said."

Of course she did.

"Carlos was skeptical but he did call. Gave me some lame story about visiting Miami next week and wanted to arrange a girl. Wanted to know the going rate."

"Gathering intel."

"Absolutely. Shows the boy at least has a brain. I told him it depended on the girl but the range was a thousand to six thousand a night. Weekends could go up to ten and a week could reach twenty."

"I bet that got his attention."

"Big time. He said that was too rich for his blood."

"Unless the money is flowing his way," Cain said.

"You got it. I could almost hear him panting. And it wasn't over the girls. As nice as they look on the site. Bottom line—expect a call. Soon."

The call from Adam came twenty minutes later.

"Bill Faulkner?"

"Yeah. Adam?"

"I talked with Carlos. Showed him your site. He wants to meet."

"I'm pretty free. Tell me when and where and I'll be there."

"What about now?" Adam said.

"That works.

He gave Cain the address. Cain already knew it but he played the game. Had Adam repeat it as if he wanted to make sure he had it right.

"Okay, give me thirty minutes and I'll be there."

CHAPTER 34

Carlos ran his business from a small house in a neat and clean neighborhood, fifteen minutes from the Vandy campus. An interesting choice. Actually, clever. Hidden in suburbia. Cain wondered what his neighbors would think if they knew the nature of his endeavors.

The tree-lined street was quiet, except for six boys playing touch football in a vacant lot a half block from Cain's destination. The house was craftsman style, light gray with white trim, the yard well-maintained. The kind of place where a family would reside. Not a predatory scumbag.

Cain was fifteen minutes late. On purpose. He wanted Carlos antsy.

A black BMW 535 sat in the driveway. No doubt Adam's ride. Cain parked at the curb.

Adam answered the door. He led Cain past a living room where two young women in shorts and halter tops watched TV. They glanced Cain's way but said nothing. Adam made no introductions. Cain wanted to grab them, shake them, tell them to get the hell out. Not the time, not the place.

They entered a den that had been converted into an office. Four desks, two on each side, held iMACs—three dark, one displaying Cain's newly-minted website. A stocky Hispanic male spun his chair toward them. Carlos for sure. Looked like a poster boy for a diet of beer and burritos. Neck thick, belly thicker. His jeans rode low and a yellow sweatshirt, sleeves ripped off at the shoulder, revealed a colorful tattoo of a toucan on one bicep.

He stood and extended his hand. They shook.

"Mister Faulkner. A pleasure to meet you."

His English was southern, Texan even, but no hint of his south-of-the-border heritage. Of course, according to Mama B, he had been born in San Antonio.

"Call me Bill," Cain said. "Thanks for seeing me."

He waved a hand toward the computer. "An impressive business you have."

"Thanks. We've worked hard at it."

"We?"

"I have two partners. One in LA and one in Chicago."

"Something to drink?"

"Whatever you're having is fine," Cain said.

He nodded to Adam who headed out of the room. Carlos sat down, hooked another chair with one foot and spun it toward Cain. "Have a seat."

Cain did.

Adam returned with a frosted bottle of Patron and three shot glasses. He poured two shots.

"You're not joining us?" Carlos asked Adam.

Adam glanced at his watch. "Got a meeting with a new recruit. I'm already late."

Carlos smiled. "Don't want to hold that up." He glanced at Cain. "New talent's the name of the game."

Cain gave a quick nod. "It is indeed."

Adam left.

Carlos raised his glass. "Hopefully to a new beginning."

"Hopefully," Cain said.

Cain drained the shot. As did Carlos. Carlos refilled the glasses.

"Your site," Carlos said. "Very classy. How many girls do you have on board?"

"Total, we have over four hundred. Mostly in the US. Some in Europe. A few in Asia, the Mid East. It's an international operation."

Carlos smiled. "I like the sound of that."

"We only take the best. The ones that can bring top dollar. No low end stuff."

"So I saw."

Another wave at the computer screen. It displayed Cain's fake LA page. A dozen women smiling back. Each beautiful, mostly blonde. Hard to believe Mama B had built the entire set up in a few hours.

"And you?" Cain asked. "How many girls do you have?"

"It varies. Right now twenty-five or so. They come, they go. I'm sure you have the same problem."

"Some. But we take care of our people so the attrition rate is actually minimal."

"What's your secret? For keeping them in line?"

"We set up savings accounts for them. Help them keep a bit of what they work for. Makes them feel like they have a stake in things."

Carlos nodded as if considering that. "Smart. I can learn something here, I think."

"I take it you're mostly in the Nashville area?" Cain asked.

"Yeah. I have a few girls over in Memphis. Nothing big. So yeah, definitely a local operation."

"Maybe we can fix that. Expand your base."

"That's what I want to know about," Carlos said. "How would we work together? If we decide to move that way."

"In each city we have local handlers," Cain said. "We set up the dates and collect the money. The local guys handle transportation, security, and, of course, recruit new girls. That's not only more efficient but it takes the handlers out of dealing with the cash. Allows a layer of insulation if the police snoop around."

"What do you mean?"

"If the customer doesn't hand over cash to the girls, and if you don't take it directly from them, it's harder to get dinged for pandering. The authorities follow the money. Our way puts a couple of layers of protection in place. The girls and the money are never in the same room, so to speak."

"Clever."

Cain shrugged. "We try to think of everything."

"Looks that way."

"One thing you should know. We're set up as a private club. Membership is required."

"Seems restrictive. I mean, how do you get new clients?"

Cain smiled. "Recommendations. We don't advertise. You won't find us in the public domain. Search engines rarely stumble over us. It adds another level of security and it protects our clients. Clients who pay top dollar and demand privacy."

Carlos nodded.

"We screen the clients. Make sure we have no bad actors. With the money we charge, our members are mostly corporate types. Politicians, lawyers, professionals of all types."

"Still seems you're missing out on some business."

"My father always told me that in any venture you need to carve out your territory. Either be the best, the most expensive, the most exclusive, or the cheapest and deal in volume. Those in the middle die off." Cain nodded toward the computer. "We opted for the top of the mountain."

"I know. I called to check it out. Up to six grand a night? That's big money."

"Exclusivity isn't cheap."

A grin split Carlos' face. "What do you see for me and my crew? If I decide we can do business."

"You'd run the Nashville area. And take a piece of the action. All the action."

"You mean of the entire operation?"

"I do. That's how we do things." Cain held his gaze. "Again, it's a loyalty issue. We want everyone on the same team."

An even bigger grin. His eyes almost flashed dollar signs.

Use the right bait and the fish will come.

"What are we talking about here?" Carlos asked. "Money-wise?"

Time to set the hook.

"I don't know what your take is but, as you saw, we get top dollar. I suspect we could triple your take. Maybe more. And you'd have less work to do. Not to mention a rolling stock of girls."

"What's that mean?"

"We move the girls around to all our locations. Offer the

customers more choice. Not the same faces all the time. A few weeks at a time. We would bring girls from other cities into Nashville and move yours into other cities for temp work." Cain smiled. "So to speak."

"Love that."

"We rent a couple of condos in each city. For the girls. Like a sorority house. They like it. Let's them see more of the world. Of course, they all want to go to Paris or London. We have a set up in each. As well as Budapest, Rome, and Brussels, to name a few."

"You weren't lying about being international."

"We are definitely that," Cain said. "Show me what your operation looks like."

Carlos worked the keyboard and opened up his home page. It was fairly vanilla. Cain's was much better. Thank you, Mama B. He clicked on a link titled DATES and a page of thumbnails appeared. Cain scanned them. He immediately saw Ella Hamilton's image. Cindy's friend who had said she no longer worked for Carlos. Cain pointed to her image.

"Very pretty girl."

"One of my favorites." He laughed. "She's on leave right now."

"Leave or left?" Cain asked.

"Oh, she said she was done with the life but I've heard that before. Once they spend all the money, they come back."

Cain laughed. "Seems to be the case, doesn't it?"

Carlos scrolled down the page. Cain resisted the impulse to take in a breath when Cindy Grant's image rolled up. He pointed out a couple of other girls, diversionary, and Carlos gave the thumbnail of each. Then Cain indicted Cindy.

"She's exceptional," Cain said.

"Yes, she was." Carlos shrugged. "She's no longer with us."

Was this a confession of some kind? "What do you mean?"

He hesitated. "Let me ask you—do you ever get your girls more long-term gigs?"

"Such as?"

"Something more permanent. Like for months. Even years."

It struck Cain. He hadn't considered this before. Should have. Carlos wasn't talking about matchmaking. Nothing as mundane as that. He was saying they trafficked some of the girls. Sold them on the open market. Cindy might have thought she was going off on some date to Europe with a high-rolling married dude, but that was the cover. The one she told Kelly. The one that got her isolated. Where she could be abducted. Sold. By Carlos. To her killer.

Cain held his expression flat, then smiled. "You mean like selling the girls?"

Carlos gave a half nod. "That's right."

Cain nodded. "Yes, we do have a system for that."

"A system? What does that mean?"

"It's really quite lucrative. We sell mostly to the Middle East. For big money."

Carlos smiled, rubbed his hands together. "I like that." He cracked the knuckles of one hand. "We haven't done that but a few times. All more local."

"You're not worried about them popping up somewhere?" Cain asked.

"A little. But in each case the buyer was taking the girl out of the country. Usually to Mexico."

"Seems risky," Cain said.

"But the money's good." He indicated Cindy's picture. "Got ten grand for her. The buyer was taking her to Mexico. Acapulco, I think. He said he had another buyer down there."

"Did he?"

"It's what he said." Carlos shrugged. "No reason not to believe him."

"Your buyer?" Cain asked. "A local guy? Someone you know?"

He shook his head. "Not really. In fact, I never met him."

"How did that work?"

"The girls think they're heading off on a weekend date. Sometimes longer. So they won't be missed too quickly. I got a couple of guys who pick them up. Tell them they're headed to the airport." He smiled. "But that's not the case. They Taser them, wrap them, and make the delivery."

"Where does the exchange take place?"

Now a broad grin appeared. "There're a bunch of old deserted warehouses not far from here. They meet the buyer there. All done under cover."

"How do you know you can trust the buyers?"

That caused a hesitation. He glanced at the floor, then back to Cain. "I don't I guess."

"My point," Cain said. "We would have some reservations about selling locally. Too many ways it could come back on you."

Carlos smiled. "Got that covered. My cousin. Down near Juarez. He's with the Zetas. He handles everything. Even the transportation."

Juarez. A place Cain never wanted to see again.

"Including the girl you just told me about?" Cain nodded toward Cindy's pic. Still up on the screen.

Another quick glance at the floor, buying time, deciding what to say, how to say it, no doubt. "No." He strung the word out. "That was different."

"In what way?" Cain asked.

"Dude contacted me. Out of the blue. Said he'd heard about me from some guy in Vegas." He shrugged. "I do know a few folks out there. Anyway, he told me this guy I know—guy named Luis Orosco—he's a valet at Caesars—had suggested he contact me about his needs."

One of the hidden secrets about Vegas is that valets are well connected. You need a night club or restaurant recommendation, they have it. Need drugs? Covered. Need a girl? They can hook you up with that, no problem.

"He vouch for the guy? Your man in Vegas?"

Carlos hesitated a full half minute. "Not really. I didn't call him and ask or anything like that. The dude simply said he had talked with Luis and Luis'd told him to call me."

"But you didn't know the buyer? Beforehand?"

Carlos shook his head.

Cain nodded. "You do see where that could have gone sideways? Right?"

"I suppose. But the money was good. Ten grand a pop. Not bad."

"No offense, but that's what my father called chump change." Cain sipped the tequila. "If we work together, we'll have to insist that no further local sales take place. Is that a problem?"

"Not if you have a better way."

"We do."

"I'm listening," he said.

"First off, we only sell to foreigners. Those who will take the girl, or girls, to places where they'll never return. The Middle East and Asia mostly."

"Oh?"

"Saudi Arabia, Kuwait, Indonesia, Hong Kong, even Iran."

"How do you work that?"

"We have a guy." Cain smiled.

"What's your going rate?"

"It varies. Never less than a hundred grand. Most are well north of that."

"Wow. That's amazing."

"So, we're good here?" Cain asked. "No more local sales?"

Carlos hesitated, glanced at the floor. "For now. Assuming we can work out a deal."

"We can. Then you'll do a lot better on any sales."

Carlos slapped his knee. "Count me in on that."

You just have to choose the right bait.

CHAPTER 35

Cain left Carlos, saying he had a good feeling about them working together. Carlos, giddy, animated, agreed.

Cain climbed in his car with the feeling that he needed to go home and shower. The thought that Carlos and Adam weren't much above the Taliban fucks Cain and Harper had dispatched crossed his mind. They seemed to have the same regard, and use, for young women. Merely commodities. Cattle to be moved around at will, used, abused, sold, killed. Disposable items. It was all he could do not to flick a blade into Carlos' fat neck. Maybe the time would come. Maybe not.

As he drove, he called Bradford. He answered on the second ring. Cain could faintly hear traffic noise in the background.

"We need to talk," Cain said.

"Okay." Then to someone there, "I need to take this."

Cain heard his footsteps. Hard surface. Then Bradford was back.

"About what?" he asked.

"Our guy. He bought Cindy Grant from Carlos Campos."

"You know this how?"

"I just left his place. He told me."

"What? How?"

"Let's meet," Cain said.

"Okay. I'm in the field. Finishing an interview. Say, twenty minutes? Sally's Country Kitchen? Haven't eaten all day and a meat and three sounds good about now."

"See you there."

Next Cain called Mama B and brought her up to date, telling her that the website blew away Carlos and Adam. And that he was inside their operation.

"You sure?" she asked.

"Oh yeah, they bit hard." He then told her about the valet in Vegas. "Stay on them. Adam and Carlos. See what you can dig up on this Luis Orosco."

"How does God create such creatures?" Mama B asked.

"Not God. This is the work of the fallen angel."

"I'm on it," she said.

It was just after five-thirty and a fine drizzle had kicked up as Cain pulled into the lot at Sally's Country Kitchen. The lot was already filling. He had ten minutes before Bradford would show so he sat in his car and called Laura Cutler.

"Your life is about to get more complicated I fear," he said.

"Well, you're just making my day."

"Our guy. He bought Cindy from Carlos Campos. Local dirt ball and pimp."

"And he brought her down here?"

"Sure did."

"Any leads on who that might be?" she asked. "Someone I should go shoot?"

Cain laughed. "Nothing solid."

"But you're still convinced he's down this way?"

"I do."

"Can't say I disagree," Cutler said.

"I'm having a sit down with Lee Bradford. Then I'll be heading your way."

"When?"

"Tomorrow."

"Okay. Jimmy and I'll continue sniffing around."

"Cautiously," Cain said. "We don't know where to look and stirring the water might not be a good choice right now."

"Lord, you're just making my day." She sighed. "Anything you need me to do?"

"Keep your eyes and ears open, but don't start digging in too aggressively."

"I don't even know where to begin."

"And that's the problem," Cain said. "If he even suspects you're on to him, he'll clean up his work place."

"Where he kept Rose Sanders and Cindy Grant? And worked on them?"

"Exactly."

"Okay. That makes sense to me. Anything else?"

"I want to visit Martin Stenson."

"Why?"

The wounds Cindy Grant had suffered. To Cain's eye they had been inflicted by arrows. Nothing else made sense. Not bullets, for sure. If these girls were hunted, why not with a bow? Stenson was an expert. And a hunter. Maybe he was involved. At least he might have an inside track on who to look at.

"I'll explain when I see you. Keep it low key. Something like, Harper and I are back in town and want to take him up on his invitation to see his place."

"Okay. When?"

"I need to swing by and see General Kessler on the way down. I should be in Moss Landing by noon. So tomorrow afternoon, or whenever he can."

"You know this makes me crazy. You not telling me anything."

"Let's say it has to do with Cindy's autopsy," Cain said.

"That's it?" Cutler said. "That's all you're going to say?"

"It's complicated. Tomorrow you'll know everything."

"And I was just starting to like you."

"That would put you on a short list."

"I'm beginning to see that. Want me to have Lily Butler hold you and Harper rooms?"

"That'd be nice. And tell her to whip up some biscuits."

Cutler laughed. "Will do."

CHAPTER 36

As he disconnected the call to Laura Cutler, Bradford pulled into the lot. Cain met him as he stepped out. They hurried through the drizzle and pushed through the front door. Sally's Country Kitchen was half filled. The aroma of home cooking and the clatter of forks and knives filled the air. They found a table in a corner, near the back.

They ordered beers, Cain a Stella, Bradford a Bud Lite. Then food. Cain settled on pot roast, turnip greens, squash, and pintos; Bradford meat loaf, mashed potatoes, corn, and green beans. Their waitress scribbled it down and walked away.

"What do you have?" Bradford asked.

"First, what do you know about Carlos Campos?"

"Before your call I'd've said he's a small player in the prostitution world. Pimping out college girls for the most part. But it sounds like he's more than that."

Cain nodded. "No evidence he was selling girls?"

"If I had anything like that he wouldn't be out breathing free air." He rubbed his wrist. "Setting up dates is one thing, but trafficking—and that's what we're talking here—is another thing altogether."

"He said he had sold a few girls. Has a cousin in with the Zetas. Sells the occasional girl through him. All down in Mexico."

"Except for our guy. Right?"

"Right," Cain said. "Carlos sold Cindy Grant to him."

"You sure?"

"I just had a sit down with him. He wasn't bashful about saying so."

The food arrived. They began to eat, though Cain's appetite had evaporated. Not so for Bradford. He dug in with relish.

"My favorite place," he said.

"I can see why."

He dabbed gravy from the corner of his mouth. "What you're telling me is Campos sold Cindy to a serial killer?"

"I'm not sure he knows that, but, yes."

"And you still have no clue who that might be?"

"Not yet. But I'm inside his organization now so hopefully that'll come out."

"Want to explain 'inside'?"

Cain told him of his site and their approach to Adam and Carlos. How he had offered them a business proposal they simply couldn't resist.

"That's pretty smart."

Cain cut off a piece of roast and forked it into his mouth. "I thought so."

"My instinct is to bring him in, put him in a hot box, twist his tit until he squeals."

"That might work."

Bradford tapped his fork against the edge of his plate. "But you have other ideas?"

"Let me work him. From the inside. Our best chance of finding the buyer is to play Carlos."

"And if he sells him other girls in the meantime?"

"I don't think he will. I've shown him that I have a better program. One that will funnel a lot more money his way. He jumped on that."

"Greed is a great motivator."

"Particularly to a miscreant like him."

"I don't know." Bradford sipped from his beer. "Still seems that squeezing him might get quicker results."

"Except I don't think he knows the guy he sold her to. Not really. I'd be surprised if our guy used a real name or even looked the same when he made his purchase."

Bradford sighed. Laid his fork and knife across his plate. Apparently his appetite had diminished, too. "That makes sense. I doubt our killer would be that stupid."

"All I'm saying is give Harper and me a little time. I'm deep inside his business. He can't make a move I won't know about."

"How's that?"

"Not sure you want to know. Plausible deniability and all that."

He leaned forward. "But if I'm going to hang my weenie in the wind on this, I need to know what you're up to."

Cain thought about that. Bradford would indeed be at risk if he didn't act on what he knew. If Cain had read Carlos wrong and he did, indeed, sell other girls to the killer, it could be a career ender. Of course he had a right to know, but was that safe? Would word leak out? Would Campos get wind and be put on alert? Or lose confidence in their new venture? It came down to whether or not Cain could trust Bradford to keep this off the radar. He decided he could. Mostly.

"Let's say I have an inside track to his cell phone and his computers. Adam Parker's, too. They can't make a move without me knowing. In real time."

"Want to explain?"

"Can't. It goes deep into the spook world. Sources would be compromised."

Bradford nodded, let out a long breath, and leaned back in his chair. "I looked into you."

"I'd be surprised if you hadn't."

"Odd thing is, I couldn't find much. A non-distinguished military career. No offense."

"None taken."

Cain didn't say that it had been planned that way. What he did for the military, and the CIA, and all the other dark world initials, wasn't for public consumption. He had been invisible for a reason.

"Reading between the lines, your missions to the Mid East, the blanks in your resume, so to speak, seem pretty shadowy."

"It was. And it's why I can't elaborate on any of it."

"Thus your connection with General Kessler?"

Cain shrugged.

"You're asking a lot."

"I am. And I know the risks. But if we spook Campos or Parker, we can lose everything."

Bradford seemed to consider that, gave a quick nod, then said, "I suppose so."

"If they get the slightest whiff that you're on to them, that you even know they exist, they might shut down the entire operation. Dump everything that might incriminate them."

"And pass that news on to the guy we're really looking for."

"Exactly. But if they're comfortable, fat and happy, they just might lead us to our guy. He might not know him, but he's connected to him. Done business with him. He might yet lead me to him. And if so, you'll be there."

Bradford said nothing for a good minute, digesting what Cain laid out, weighing the good, the bad, and the ugly.

"Okay," he said. "I see the wisdom in that. We'll do it your way."

"Thanks."

"For now. But if another girl gets taken, sold, whatever, I'll have to move in another direction."

"I understand." Cain took a slug of beer. "Maybe this will help. In the end, I can hand you Carlos' operation. Even his entire hard drive."

"You can do that?"

Cain smiled. "I already have."

"I probably don't want to know how."

Cain smiled. "You don't. Couldn't tell you anyway."

Bradford nodded. "What's your plan?"

"Harper and I are heading back down to Moss Landing tomorrow. Hook up with Laura Cutler. Check out a big bow hunter down there."

"Bow hunter?"

"I think that's what happened to Cindy. Probably the school teacher. To me, the evidence suggests they were hunted. Likely with a bow."

"Based on Cindy's autopsy?"

"Right. Those wounds didn't come from a spear or a spike or anything like that. They were made by arrows."

"Maybe."

"No maybe about it. Hunters like projectile weapons. Particularly if the prey is on the run. Only a bow fits that scenario."

"Want to give me a name? The bow hunter?"

"Not yet."

Bradford eyed him. "You think he might be our guy?"

"Don't know. Only met him briefly. I don't yet have a feel for him." Cain wadded a fist, then relaxed it, wiggled his fingers. "At least he'll know the hunters in the area."

"Makes sense."

"Then maybe a trip to Vegas. See the guy who referred the likely killer to Carlos."

"Need the LVPD's help with that?" Bradford asked. "I know a couple of guys there."

"Definitely not. We can't afford any stumbles here. I'll handle him."

"He might give Carlos a heads up. If they're friends."

"He won't."

He stared at Cain.

"I can be very persuasive," Cain said.

Bradford shook his head. "I don't even want to know what that means."

CHAPTER 37

Last night the drizzle had turned into a full-on electrical storm. Cain and Harper had watched it roll through, standing at the floor-to-ceiling windows in the condo. Lightning strobed their faces and thunder rattled the walls.

"I love this," Harper said.

"I know you do."

They both did. As kids, whenever such storms kicked up, they would huddle in a tent, front flap open, wrapped together in a blanket, rain slapping against the canvas, and watch the dark sky, the dancing lightning. That and the cool wind on their faces always pebbled their skin. And freshened the air with ozone. Great memories.

This morning, all was calm and clear. No clouds, a warm breeze, and the promise of another scorcher.

Took just over an hour to fight the Nashville traffic and to reach the Kessler's estate. They met with the General in his study. He handed Cain a newspaper, folded to page two. Lower right corner. The headline stated: **General Kessler's Granddaughter Dead**.

Cain scanned the article. No real details. Nothing about the manner of death or the tattooing. No mention of murder. A not so small blessing. Didn't want any of that out. Just said that her body had been found in Moss Landing and that the local police were investigating and weren't sure what the cause of death was.

Cutler had done her job.

"It's worse when I see it in black and white," Kessler said.

"I imagine that's true," Harper said. "How's Miriam?"

"As you might expect. She crawled back in bed. Doesn't want to face the day." He shook his head. "Me either."

"You'll both get over it," Cain said. "Eventually."

He offered a grim smile. "That's what they say, isn't it?" He sighed. "Not like we have a choice."

"At least the news hounds don't know the truth," Harper said.

"Not yet," Kessler said. "But they will. We've been getting calls. I shunted them all to our attorney. She's doing a good job running point. Prepping a statement right now."

"Good," Cain said. "But, I'm afraid I'm not going to make your day any brighter."

"I didn't expect you came out here with good news. Tell me."

Cain brought him up to date.

"You're telling me Cindy was sold like a piece of meat?"

"I'm sorry."

Kessler stood and walked to the large window that looked over his domain. Cain sensed he'd trade it all for Cindy to be alive and well. The General now seemed older, smaller, more frail. An image no one had ever seen. He turned back toward Cain and Harper. Pain etched his face.

"What kind of people do this?" he asked. "Sell women? Torture and kill them?"

"The worst kind," Harper said.

He walked back to his desk. His chair creaked as he fell into it. "Each of us has seen some shit. Very bad shit. People with no morals. Sick souls. Jihadis who'll do anything to anyone if it fits their agenda. But this? I'm having trouble getting my mind around it."

"Consider this guy—Adam and Carlos, too, for that matter—a domestic terrorist," Cain said.

"Oh, they're all that and more."

Cain shrugged.

"What's the plan?"

"We're headed over to Moss Landing. Have a chat with Chief Cutler."

"You think he's there? Moss Landing is his stomping ground?"

"I'm sure of it. Both women found there. Cindy, displayed like she was. He wants to see, feel the reaction. That means he's close by."

"I'm sure you're right."

"He is," Harper said. "These narcissistic types like to see their work, like to feel the electricity that surrounds it. They feed on the fear and terror they create."

"He might have procured Cindy in Nashville but he took her back to his domain. Moss Landing."

Kessler sighed. "I take it back. This guy's worse than the jihadis."

Cain's mind raced back to the night he and Harper had dispatched the rapists. Off the books. Not sanctioned. Solely because they had to. "Not sure that's possible. But this guy, whoever he is, is just as dangerous."

Kessler nodded. He tented his finger before him. "That's why he has to be exterminated. This is not a situation for the courts."

Cain glanced at Harper, back to Kessler. "We're on the same page."

Kessler held their collective gaze.

"We have a few things to look into over in Moss Landing, then I think a trip to Vegas would be in order," Cain said. "Lean on the guy who referred him to Carlos. Maybe he knows who we're looking for."

"I can have my plane ready in an hour. Just say the word."

"That would help." Cain stood. "We better get moving. I'll call later."

CHAPTER 38

Chief Laura Cutler wasn't in her office. Where she said she'd meet us.

"She's down at the marina," Jimmy Rankin said from behind his desk. "Some shenanigans going on down there."

"What?" Harper asked.

"Not sure. Some kids doing something."

"We'll walk down there," Cain said.

"I'd go with you, but she's got me catching up on paperwork." Rankin waved a hand over the files before him. "And she's not in a good mood so I know better than to get my butt out of this chair before I'm done."

Cain and Harper found Cutler standing on the dock, talking to two teenagers. Boy and girl. She didn't look happy.

They waited. Cutler finally wagged a finger at the pair. They walked away, heads down. Cutler came their way.

"Kids," she said.

"What's the problem?" Harper asked.

She sighed, looking toward the teenagers now climbing in their car. "They broke into a boat here. One of the newer cruisers. Belongs to Mac Stanley. Looking for a place to make out."

Cain laughed.

Cutler smiled. "Bet you never did anything like that."

"He did worse," Harper said. "Much worse."

"Doesn't surprise me." Cutler smiled. "Anyway, they got lucky. I called Mac. He said as long as they didn't damage anything to let it go."

"Whatever I did, or didn't do," Cain said, "I never got that kind of break."

"Not that you ever deserved any rhythm," Harper said.

Cain shook his head. "We're going to tell tales now."

Harper raised an eyebrow. "Probably not."

"So, what do you have for me?" Cutler asked.

"Quite a bit," Cain said. He eyed the people hanging out on the pier and the small park near the marina. "Maybe we should sit somewhere."

She led them to the collection of picnic tables where they had sat during the barbecue. Deserted now. They sat.

"Okay," Cain said. "Here's what we know. Or at least what we think. Your teacher and Cindy Grant were probably killed by the same guy."

"We don't know that," Cutler said.

"No, but hear me out. I think both were hunted. The damage to their feet surely suggests that. That means we have a guy tattooing young women, turning them loose, and hunting them."

Cutler examined her hands, twined before her, knuckles white. She said nothing.

"The wounds weren't from a gun," Cain said.

"What?"

"No exit wounds. No retained bullets."

Cutler looked from Cain, to Harper, and back to Cain.

"These were done by some sort of round, cylindrical object." Cain hesitated a beat. "An arrow."

Cutler's wheels were turning.

"Not the typical hunting arrow," Cain said. He described the nature of the wounds he had seen. "No serious hunter would use target arrows. My guess, it was likely a crossbow."

"So we have a bow hunter who likes to decorate and hunt humans," Harper said.

Cutler looked toward the water. "Jesus Christ." Then her head whipped back toward Cain. "Surely you don't think Martin Stenson has anything to do with this?"

"Do you?"

Cutler's shoulders jerked. "No. No way."

Cain shrugged.

"Martin's a good man. He does a lot for this town. He's a friend. I've known him forever." She pressed a knuckle against one temple.

"Sociopaths don't wear labels," Harper said.

Cutler seemed to mull that. "Is this why you wanted to see him again?"

Cain nodded. "I want to get a feel for him."

"You're on the wrong track."

"You sure?"

There it was. Cutler knew the man. Or thought and hoped she did. And now he had dropped napalm into her lap. Cain saw tension gather in her face. The lines at the corners of her eyes deepening even as she considered the possibility.

"He's an expert with bows," Harper said. "He's a hunter."

Cutler shook her head. "I can't buy that."

"We're not saying it is him," Cain said. "In fact, we have absolutely no evidence that he's involved. But, he just might know who is."

"I don't buy that either. If Martin knew anything about this, he'd say so. He's that kind of guy."

"Is he?" Harper said.

"Yes. I have no doubts."

Cain leaned forward. He captured Cutler's gaze. "You might be right. On all counts. But, I want to see him. And the guys he hangs with. The other hunters. Maybe something will fall out."

"Well, you got lucky there," Cutler said. "He's having a cocktail party later today. At his place. Most of his buddies will be there. They'll be drinking and shooting."

"Sounds dangerous," Harper said. Then she smiled.

"You're both invited," Cutler said.

"Good."

Cutler looked at Cain. "Can I trust you?" Her gaze slid to Harper. "Both of you?"

"What does that mean?" Harper asked.

"Me taking you there puts me in a bad situation if you go in there and rattle cages."

"Not our intention," Cain said.

"I'm sure that's true." Cutler shook her head. "But if you betray some agenda, or prejudice." She opened her hands, palms up.

"Trust us," Harper said. "This isn't our first rodeo. We know what we're doing. All we want to do is get a feel for things. Gather a little intel."

Cutler sighed. "Do you really think our guy is part of Martin's circle?"

Cain shook his head. "No evidence of that. But Stenson, from what I gather, is more or less the big dog in this little group. Seems to me he would be a good place to start."

"Martin Stenson's a bright guy. If you go fishing, he'll figure it out."

"That's always a concern," Cain said. "But our goal here is to simply meet the players. See who's who in his world." He shrugged. "It might be a lost lead, but it's worth a shot."

"Okay," Cutler said. "I hope this isn't a mistake."

"It's not," Cain said.

"I'll give you directions."

"We'll pick you up," Harper said.

Cutler considered that. "Okay. Swing by the station about three."

CHAPTER 39

The past twenty-four hours had been a living hell for Chelsie Young. She knew when she started prostituting herself that there were risks involved. Sex and alcohol made some guys mean. Even abusive. She had been lucky, though. Most of the guys she had hooked up with were nice, mostly shy, in fact. Usually married. Couldn't afford to make waves was her thought.

And the money was good. No doubt about that. Not to mention the trips. New Orleans, New York, even Cancun and the Bahamas. Places she might never have seen otherwise.

But this?

This was never part of even her worst nightmares.

The trip, this one with some older guy. A week on Maui. Six grand plus all that sun and beach time, and great dinners. And all she had to do was make him happy. She could do that.

Meeting in the parking deck at the mall was odd, but not all that unusual. A couple of the guys had met her in such places. One even in a church lot on a Friday night. He had actually been a nice guy.

When the SUV pulled into the slot opposite her car and those two Hispanic guys stepped out, her pulse quickened. Something was off. She should have fled then. When she had a chance.

But the big one smiled. Easy, relaxed. Said they would take her to the airport and she would meet the guy on the plane. All she had to do was act casual. Like they were simply seat mates. The guy had a high-profile job and feared seeing someone who knew him. Would be awkward if they boarded together, appeared to be traveling together.

That made sense so she let her guard down.

Big mistake.

They loaded her bags in the back, laughing, saying they were jealous she was getting to go to Hawaii. She climbed in the back seat. The smaller one making sure she was comfortable. Leaning in, smiling, making sure her seat belt was secure, saying they were all about safety. A soft laugh.

She saw the Taser in his hand too late to react. The jolt hit her hard. The next thing she remembered clearly, she was bound, gagged, and blindfolded, curled up in the rear cargo area, like she was another piece of luggage.

Twenty minutes later the rear popped open and she was lifted out. Her balance off, she stumbled, nearly fell, but then felt herself lifted and rolled into a small space. Rough carpeting tugged at her clothing. A door slammed and what light she could sense through the blindfold vanished.

As soon as she heard the engine crank to life, she knew. She was in a car trunk.

What the fuck was happening?

Then she was here. Restraints, gag, and blindfold removed, she was shoved into a cage. When she turned, she saw him. Not what she expected. He looked normal. Even handsome. He smiled. For a brief moment she had thought maybe it was some sex game. But she quickly realized that wasn't the case.

He had indicated the sweat pants and tee shirt neatly folded in one corner and, for the first time, had spoken.

"Change into those. I'll be back later."

Then, he was gone.

She shook the cage's door. Tried to pry the bars apart. Nothing gave an inch. She paced, taking in her surroundings.

She was in a barn. A large empty space with two large support poles, wooden walls that let long shafts of orange sunlight knife though the gaps. She sat, cried, tried to make sense of everything. The sun faded, darkness enveloped her.

Then, he was back. Lights snapped on. She asked him what was going on. He said nothing but began laying out tools of some sort on a small stand next to a heavy, metal table. Thick leather straps attached to each corner. Then she was on the table, wrists and ankles secured. She cried and begged and pleaded.

Next, he shaved her. Completely. She tried to resist. Twist away. But the straight razor he scraped across her skin made her freeze, tighten every muscle until her entire body ached.

When she saw the tattoo gun she screamed at him. Called him crazy. He only smiled and patted her arm.

"You'll feel differently once your transformation is complete."

Her nightmare was now complete. He was crazy. Beyond that.

The buzzing, the pain, electrified her nerves. He spent the next four hours working on her right leg; the higher he worked, the greater the pain.

He said little. Only responding to her questions with "All would become clear" when his work was completed.

Now, it was light outside. Had been for several hours. Where was she? Where was he? What if he never returned? She would die in this cage. No one would ever know.

She had slept little, maybe not at all. She could only remember roaming her cage, looking for some weakness, finding none, before curling up on the air mattress, wrapped in the blankets he had provided. Maybe she dozed.

She rolled up one leg of her pants. Examined her calf. The tattooing was perfect. Tan with random black spots. Like a freaking leopard or something. *What the hell?*

Then, she heard him. Footsteps, the door cracking open, his form silhouetted against the sunlight.

He handed her a bag. Inside, a cheese sandwich and two bottles of water. She hadn't eaten in twenty-four hours. She unwrapped the sandwich and took large bites, washing it down with the water.

He busied himself with setting up his tools again.

"Ready to begin?" he asked.

"No. Please. I can't take anymore."

He walked to the cage. "You'll do just fine. Relax."

"Why are you doing this?"

"To make you beautiful."

"You said I was beautiful. Last night."

"You are. In fact, you're perfect. Even better than I hoped." He smiled. "But even perfection can be made more perfect."

"I'm begging you. Don't do this."

"Take off your clothes and we will begin."

"Please."

"I won't ask you again." He pulled a Taser from his pocket. "You can either strip and climb on the table, or I'll carry you there."

She whimpered.

He tapped the bars with the device. "We have much to do today and not much time. I have somewhere to be later and we're a little behind schedule."

"That makes no sense."

"It will."

She had no choice. She stripped off her clothing. He opened the door, grabbed her by the arm, and led her to the table.

Now was the time.

She slammed her palm into his chest. His breath exploded and he stumbled backwards. She ran toward the door. Didn't make it. He hooked her with one arm, lifted her. He was strong. Stronger than he appeared.

He strapped her to the table and slipped a plastic bag over her head. She gasped, struggled, jerked her head back and forth, tried to bite through the bag. Nothing worked. Dizzy, the bag fogged, the world beyond fading away. Then the bag was gone. She wheezed in deep breaths.

He smiled and spoke slowly, with a maddening calmness. "You resist me again and the bag will remain. I'll dump your body in the lake."

Sobs racked her.

He patted her arm. "Take deep breaths and relax. It'll be easier that way."

She sniffed. "Why me?"

"Look at you," he said. "Long arms, longer legs, a tight body. The perfect canvas. The perfect Chelsie Cheetah."

"What are you talking about?"

"You'll see."

But she knew. He was tattooing her to look like a cheetah. The spots on her leg.

He now began work on her other leg. She tried to go away, imagine herself lying on a sugar-white beach, the sun warming her skin.

CHAPTER 40

Cain and Harper checked in at the Creekside Inn. Lily Butler had reserved the two best rooms in the house. Same as before. They dropped their luggage and headed back downstairs.

"Hope your rooms are okay," Lily said, from behind the reception desk.

"Only perfect," Harper said.

Lily beamed. "I put some fresh flowers in there for you. And a box of taffy."

"I saw," Harper said. "You're going to spoil us."

"It's what I do." She smiled. "Where you off to?"

"Maybe grab some coffee," Cain said. "Take a drive."

"Where's the best coffee?" Harper asked.

"What are you talking about, young lady?" She tossed them a mock frown. "I make the best coffee in the state."

"And biscuits," Cain said.

"That I do. That I do."

Lily filled a pair of large paper cups with coffee and handed Harper a small paper bag.

"What's this?"

"A little something for the road."

The 'little something for the road' turned out to be two waxed paper-wrapped biscuits, each enveloping a thick slab of ham. As Cain turned the car from the lot, Harper unwrapped one and took a bite.

"Wow. These are great." She picked a crumb from her shirt and placed it in her mouth. "I forgot we hadn't eaten all day."

She unwrapped the other for Cain and handed it to him. He took a bite as he turned out of the parking area. "This hits the spot."

They left town behind and took the same route they had before. Toward Clovis Wilson's land where the body of Rose Sanders had been found. Cain saw Wilson and another man standing in the field; Wilson with one hand shading his eyes as he inspected the rows of green cotton plants. Cain turned down the same road as before, stopping just behind Wilson's truck. He and Harper climbed out. Wilson turned and looked toward them, said something to the other guy, and walked the fifty feet to where Cain and Harper stood.

"Your crops look good," Cain said.

Wilson nodded. "Looks like it'll be a good year. What brings you folks by?"

"Just driving around," Harper said. "Enjoying the day."

"Saw you out here and thought we'd say hello," Cain said.

Wilson kicked at the dirt. "I hear they identified the girl they found here. That school teacher that went missing."

"That's right."

"It don't make no sense." Wilson shook his head. "I hear she might've been murdered and dumped here."

"Something like that," Cain said. "No way to know for sure."

"Then that other girl. General Kessler's granddaughter?"

Cain nodded.

"We don't have stuff like that happen around here," Wilson said. "Not ever." He again shaded his eyes and glanced toward the stand of trees where Rose's corpse had been found. "You think one's got something to do with the other?"

"It's possible," Harper said.

Wilson pursed his lips. "You think that means there might be others coming?"

"I hope not," Cain said.

"That makes two of us." Wilson gave a quick nod. "Sometimes I wonder about my fellow humans."

"How much of this land is yours?" Cain asked.

"I got several plots around here. This one runs from the county road." He extended a finger that way. "And runs to those trees over there. Across that field." His arm swept to his right as he spoke. "Then on over to the railroad easement. It's a shade over five hundred acres."

"Who owns the land around yours?" Cain asked.

"Beyond the rail line is city property and private homes. And a park. That a way, down across the county road, would be Luke Nash's place. Or one of them. Luke owns several plots round the area, too." He scratched an ear. "That way there," he pointed, "beyond that stand of trees, is Martin Stenson's property."

"He own much land?"

"Sure does. Nearly two thousand acres."

"That much?" Harper asked.

"Yep."

"Does he farm it?" Cain asked.

"No. The story was he was going to build a couple of communities on part of it but he never did. Still might, I reckon."

"I imagine it's fairly valuable land," Harper said.

Wilson nodded. "As acreage around here goes, it is. But Martin don't need the money and, if you ask me, the aggravation of overseeing the construction of a bunch of houses." He gave a half smile. "I can't even imagine."

"Probably easier than farming," Cain said.

"Maybe. But I don't have to deal with plumbers and electricians and the like." He smiled. "And all those county regulations."

"Just the weather and bugs?"

"Ain't it so."

CHAPTER 41

"Turn left up there," Harper said. "Looks like that'll take us past the group of pines and toward Stenson's property." She pointed to the Mercedes' navigation screen.

Two hundred yards ahead, Cain hung a left onto a patched, two-lane road that rose and fell, twisting between a thick stand of pines on the left and open rolling fields on the right.

Cain's burner cell chimed. He pulled it from his pocket and answered, activating the speaker function. He raised a finger to Harper, indicating she should remain silent.

"This is Faulkner," he said.

"Mister Faulkner. This is Adam Parker."

"Hey, Adam. I told you, call me Bill."

"You alone? Can you talk?"

"Yeah. I'm in my car."

"I got some good news. Carlos says he's in. Wants to do some business together."

"That's excellent. We'll make a lot of money."

"I like the sound of that. Anyway, he wants to sit down and work out the details. When's good for you?"

Cain considered that. "I'm tied up today, but tomorrow should work."

"Okay."

"I'll call in the morning," Cain said. "We can pick a time. I'll go over how it all works. Who does what, how the money's handled, all that."

"Which brings up something I wanted to ask," Adam said.

"What's that?"

"Just between me and you," Adam said.

"Okay."

"How do you see my role in this? I mean, Carlos runs the show. He makes all the decisions and sets up the dates, the transportation, the money, all that."

"And you find the girls," Cain said.

"Exactly. I recruit them."

"Don't you think that's an important job? Without the talent, the business doesn't fly."

"I definitely agree. I'm not sure Carlos sees it that way. He says he can find girls on his own."

"He can. But can he find the college girls you bring in? The ones that snare top dollar?"

Harper had been working her iPhone but now looked his way, raised an eyebrow.

"I'm glad you see it that way," Adam said.

"I do. My partners do. You're a valuable asset. And you'll be paid accordingly."

Use the right bait.

After he hung up, Harper twisted in her seat and looked at him. "You're actually an accomplished pimp. Snare? Top dollar?"

"Simply playing the role."

"Oh, I'm not criticizing. I'm impressed."

Cain smiled. "Why wouldn't you be?"

She shook her head. "Turn right up here." She looked back at her phone. "I found Stenson's address. It's just under five miles down this road."

Another two-lane black top. More undulations through forests and open land. On the left, a paved drive appeared. It disappeared over a rise in the land. No buildings or signs of civilization were visible. Cain slowed.

"Is this it?"

Harper shook her head. "No. Still got a couple of miles."

Cain continued. Sure enough, another mile and a wooden

rail fence appeared on the left. It hugged the contours of the road. The land beyond, more manicured. They reached an impressive driveway. Similar to General Kessler's. Cain slowed. Stone columns flanked the entrance, the drive rising up to a massive ranch-style home. Several cars and trucks sat to one side and beyond them a large, red barn.

"Nice place," Harper said.

"Sure is. Looks like the crew is already gathering."

"We got a couple of hours. Let's go get ready."

"What's to do?" Cain asked.

"You need to shave. I need to re-do my make-up."

"You don't use make-up."

"Oh yeah, I forgot." She laughed. "I do want to change into my party dress."

"You don't wear dresses either."

"You know what I mean. We need to look professional."

Cain sped up, pulling away from the Stenson estate. "Call Mama B. See what she has for us."

Harper did, putting the phone on speaker.

"Harper?" Mama B said. "How're you guys doing?"

"We're down in Moss Landing. Going to a party over at Martin Stenson's place."

"You got anything on him?" Cain asked.

"Of course I do. He's fifty-two. From the photos I've seen, a good looking guy. Looks much younger."

"He does," Cain said.

That's one of the things Cain had noted about Stenson when he met him. His age was hard to peg. Could've been fifty, or thirty. Good genes no doubt.

"Has one son. Tyler. Looks like his dad. The wife, and mother, died five years ago. Cancer. Martin Stenson owns two businesses. One is real estate. High end properties. Both residential and commercial. It's based out of Nashville. Has thirty employees and a manager. So he doesn't have to do much except cash the checks. The other's an internet based software wholesaler. Basically they bundle products from a bunch of companies and offer discount packages. His son seems to run that one."

"So, Stenson has a lot of leisure time?" Cain asked.

"Sure does. And a very healthy bank account. Net worth just over thirty million."

"We're in the wrong business," Harper said.

"Isn't that the truth," Mama B said. "More to your needs, he heads up a group they call the Southern Bow Hunter's Society. Got around sixty members. Scattered all over but most are in the western Tennessee area."

"How many in the Nashville area?" Cain asked.

"I knew you'd ask that. I searched a fifty mile radius. Looks like twenty four at this time."

"Lots of suspects."

"You thinking that group is the key?" Mama B asked.

Cain sighed. "Not sure. But it's a good place to start. I'm convinced the girls, at least Cindy Grant, was hunted and killed with a bow."

"From what you told me, probably the other girl, too."

"That's why we want to meet Stenson and his crew."

"Sounds good. I'll keep digging."

"Anything on Luis Orosco?" Cain asked.

"He is indeed a valet at Caesar's. And seems to do some pimping. Been arrested twice but neither case went anywhere. The girls refused to cooperate and, of course, neither would the johns. So, he's more or less clean. As clean as you can be in that business."

"Or in that city," Harper said.

"True. I'll send his contact info your way."

"You're the best," Cain said.

"Yes, I am. One more thing. You're in with Carlos."

"That's what Adam Parker said when I talked with him earlier."

"He wasn't lying," Mama B said.

"Tell me."

"I've been listening in to his cell. He and his two guys were talking. A lot. About you, the deal, everything. They're already planning how they'll spend the money."

Earlier, while at Carlos' place, Cain had texted him his contact info, as he had with Adam, thus giving Mama B access to Carlos' phone, too. Meant she could turn on the microphone whenever she wanted. And Carlos would have no clue she was listening to everything said.

"Got to love greed," Harper said.

"The universal motivator," Mama B said.

CHAPTER 42

If Martin Stenson's estate looked impressive from the road, it was more so on closer inspection. After turning between the stone columns Cain and Harper had seen earlier, a broad paved drive flanked by shrubs and wildflowers led them to a sprawling wood and stone ranch-style structure that clung to the apex of a low hill. Gave Stenson three-hundred-and-sixty degree views of his domain—acres and acres of undulating fields and clusters of pine forests. Cain saw no farmed land. As Clovis Wilson had said.

Cain parked near a collection of other cars and trucks and he, Harper, and Cutler climbed out.

"Impressive," Harper said.

"Martin doesn't do anything second rate," Cutler said. "They'll be out back. This way."

A stone pathway led them around the left side of the house. The barn he had seen earlier sat on lower ground at the end of a dirt and gravel drive two hundred yards away. Its pair of massive doors, as well as the smaller ones to the loft, were closed. A gray Chevy pickup sat to one side.

A flagstone patio ran the length of the house. Looked as big as a carrier deck. At the far end, a large barrel smoker pumped gray puffs into the blue sky. An Olympic-sized pool and a large Jacuzzi hugged the patio. Beyond, Cain saw several men with bows facing a series of six targets, maybe fifty yards away.

Stenson and two other men sat around a low table on deeply cushioned sofas and chairs in the shade of a wooden overhang. Stenson looked up and then stood as they approached.

"Chief, glad you could make it," Stenson said. He gave Cutler a brief hug. "Mister Cain, Ms. McCoy, good to see you both."

"Harper," Harper said. She shook his hand. "Thanks for inviting us.

"My pleasure." He shook Cain's hand. "Bobby, right?"

"That's right."

"Let me introduce you to a couple of friends." Stenson motioned toward the other two men, who now stood. "Ted Norris. Hank Dixon."

They shook hands.

Norris was taller, lanky like Cain, with a soft handshake. He had shaggy blond hair and strongly resembled Stenson. Were they related? Dixon, shorter, thicker, had a heavy grip. A tough-guy statement of sorts. His hair was short-cropped and dark, as were his eyes.

Cain, Harper, and Cutler settled on one of the sofas.

"Something to drink?" Stenson said. "Maybe some lemonade?"

"Sounds good," Harper said.

As if conjured, a middle-aged Hispanic woman appeared through a door.

"This is Juanita," Stenson said. "She runs things around here."

"And it isn't easy," she said with a laugh.

"She pours a mean drink if you'd prefer something harder," Norris said.

"Lemonade will do," Cain said. "For now."

Juanita nodded. "Back in a sec."

"I'm sorry to hear about General Kessler's granddaughter," Stenson said. He nodded toward Norris and Dixon. "Bobby and Harper are private investigators. They were hired to find the girl when she went missing."

"Didn't turn out as we had hoped," Harper said.

"I bet he and Miriam are beside themselves," Stenson said.

"They are," Cain said.

"I take it you know them?" Harper asked.

Stenson nodded. "Sure do. Not very well. Just through business.

We tried to do a project around here a few years back. Kessler and a couple of other guys wanted to put together a high-end community. They looked at a parcel I own. Didn't work out." He shrugged. "At least not yet. I understand there's still some interest."

"I heard she was murdered," Dixon said.

Cain nodded. "She was."

"What happened?" Stenson asked.

Did he know? Was he the one? Was his question intended to deflect and cover?

"We don't know everything yet," Cain said.

Dixon tapped Norris's shoulder. "We heard she was painted or something. Dumped over by the post office."

"Where'd you hear that?" Cutler asked.

"Over at the service station," Norris said. "A couple of the guys were talking about it."

Cain glanced at Cutler. She closed her eyes, opened them, sighed.

"We were hoping to keep this off the radar," Cutler said. "But it sounds like it's already out of the bag." Another sigh. "So, yeah. She was tattooed. Like a tiger. And hung by ropes from the post office eaves."

"Jesus," Norris said. "Who would do something like that?"

Cutler shrugged. "We don't know."

"Any suspects?" Stenson asked.

"None."

Juanita appeared with a tray loaded with glasses of lemonade. She distributed them. "I'll have some chips and guacamole in a couple of minutes." She headed back inside.

"I don't envy you your job," Stenson said to Cutler. Then to Cain and Harper, "I can assure you things like this don't happen around here."

"Unfortunately bad things happen everywhere," Cain said.

"I understand she was a student at Vandy," Norris said. "Any idea how she ended up down this way?"

"College kids are hard to keep tabs on," Cain said.

"Ain't that the truth," Dixon said. "My son was a hell raiser. Had to bail him out of trouble too many times to remember. He went to UT, over in Knoxville. Over there they consider hell raising a sport. Even an academic major. They damn near expelled him, but somehow he made it through. Even did well enough to make it to law school. Now he's married, got a couple of kids, and practices over in Atlanta." He shrugged. "Go figure."

"Martin never had to worry with anything like that," Norris said.

Stenson shrugged. "I got lucky. My son Tyler was a good student. Never got into trouble. He went off to Princeton. Got an MBA. Now he runs my software business." He gave a quick nod. "Actually, it's more his now. I gave him most of the company."

"Speak of the devil," Norris said.

A young man walked up. He was a younger version of Stenson. Norris, too, for that matter. Same thick, blonde hair, same blue eyes, same smile.

"You guys talking about me again?"

"All good, but yeah."

Stenson introduced his son. He took a seat.

"You guys joining Dad's little hunting club?" Tyler asked.

"No," Cain said. "We're just visiting."

"They were hired by General Kessler to find his granddaughter," Stenson said.

"I heard about her," Tyler said. "I'm sorry."

"It's a tough situation," Cain said.

"You're not a hunter?" Harper asked.

Tyler shook his head. "Not a chance."

"Tyler was a good archer as a kid," Stenson said. "But he's what you might call anti-hunting."

Tyler waved a hand across the pool toward where several men were firing arrows at targets. "Target shooting's okay. That I enjoyed when I was younger. No time for it now. But hunting defenseless animals doesn't seem a fair sport to me."

"That's because you've never tried turkey hunting," Dixon said.

Cain knew that to be true. During his hunting days, when he and Harper were still part of the gypsy family, turkeys were by far the most difficult game to bag. Smart, tough, stealthy. Getting even a single shot at one took great skill and patience. Cain had only ever taken down three in all the hours he and Uncle Al had spent scouring the woods for game.

Tyler smiled. "Maybe if you guys hunted each other it'd be fair. A more even playing field."

"Like *The Most Dangerous Game*?" Harper asked.

Tyler nodded. "Richard Connell's story. One of my favorites." He shrugged. "Of course, General Zaroff didn't exactly play fair. He had home field advantage."

"But, Rainsford did turn the tables on him," Harper said.

"You know the story," Tyler said. "I'm impressed."

Harper smiled. "One of my favorite stories, too."

"Didn't you tell me you'd done some bow hunting as a kid?" Stenson asked Cain.

"I did. But that was long ago."

"Sort of like riding a bicycle though," Norris said. "You never forget."

Cain smiled. "Just get rusty."

Dixon stood. "Let's go thump a few targets."

"I'm in," Norris said. "Bobby, want to join us?"

"Sure."

The group followed the two men and Stenson around the pool.

Cain and Harper met the three men who were shooting. They said they had to hit the road.

"Before we eat?" Stenson asked.

"My wife's doing lasagna," one of them said. "She'll kill me if I don't bring home an appetite."

The other two had similar excuses. The trio began packing up their gear—four bows, two crossbows.

Harper pulled out her iPhone. "Can I grab a group picture before you go?"

"Harper likes vacation pictures," Cain said.

"That would be good," Stenson said. He smiled at Harper. "If you send me a copy."

"Of course."

Everyone except Cain and Cutler lined up and Harper snapped a couple of pictures. Cain noticed Harper work the phone as she scanned the group back and forth.

"All done," Harper said.

After the three men lifted their gear bags and left, Stenson picked up a crossbow. "Ever use one of these?" he asked Cain.

"Can't say I have."

A lie. In fact, one of the Marines he had deployed with was an expert. Taught Cain the ins and outs of the weapon. More than simply an expert bowman, the Marine, a kid from South Carolina, was an assassin. Like Cain. Cain employed knives, he a crossbow. In a tiny shit-hole village near Kabul, Cain saw him take down a Taliban sniper from two hundred yards. At night. Wind blowing hard across. One shot. Done. The kid was good.

"It's pretty easy. Let me show you."

Stenson hit the red circle just right of center.

"Nice shot."

Stenson held up the bow. "This one's my favorite." He handed it to Cain. "Give it a try."

Cain did. Missed the center by six inches. As planned.

"Not bad," Norris said. "First time I tried one of these I missed a barn." He laughed.

CHAPTER 43

Tyler, Harper, and Cutler left the men to play with their bows and walked back around the pool to the patio. Harper and Tyler sat. Cutler said she needed to make a couple of calls and wandered toward the grill at the far end. Phone to her ear. Juanita brought more lemonade along with a bowl of guacamole and a basket of chips.

Once they were alone, Harper said, "Can I ask a personal question?"

"Sure."

"Are you and Ted... What's his name?"

"Norris."

"Are you two related?"

Tyler laughed. "No. But we get that all the time. People think we're brothers or something. Or sometimes they think he and Dad are brothers."

"Your dad does look young."

Tyler looked that way. "He does. I hope I inherited his genes."

Harper smiled. "I'd say you did."

Tyler almost blushed. He nodded toward her. "Hope you're right."

"I understand you went to Princeton," Harper said.

"I did. Got an MBA. Now I run our software company."

"You create software?"

Tyler laughed. "Neither Dad nor I are that smart. We bundle software packages from several companies and offer discounts. That sort of thing."

"Bet that keeps you busy."

"Some. But I've got good people so I can do most of my work from home. Online."

"Where do you live?" Harper asked.

"Couple miles south of here. Dad gave me about twenty acres so I built a house on it."

The road she and Cain had passed.

"Sounds wonderful," Harper said.

"Not this kind of wonderful." He waved a hand. "Dad likes grandiose. I like simple."

"Nothing wrong with simple."

Tyler looked across the pool to where his father stood, crossbow resting on one shoulder, talking with Cain. "Tell that to my father." He shrugged and looked back toward Harper. "He thinks I should have bigger appetites. For more stuff. More adventures."

"Such as?"

He looked down at his feet, his head shaking slightly. "His hunting trio would be one thing. He and his buddies, mostly Ted and Hank, go on hunting trips all the time. Deer in Michigan, Bighorn sheep in Wyoming and up that way. Even wild boar hunting."

"And you don't go along?" Harper asked.

"No. I did once. I was fourteen. Hated it." He smiled. "I mean, sleeping in tents when it's cold and wet, and trying to prep food on an open fire? Not my idea of fun."

"You like things more comfortable?"

"I do."

She raised her lemonade glass. "I'm with you there."

She flashed on a few nights spent in Iraq and Afghanistan, curled in the basement of a bombed out building, bad guys scouring the streets for her and the operatives she oversaw. Waiting for their pursuers to rush down the stairs, or an IED to tumble to their feet. A tent and a campfire would've been nice. Even a cold and wet one.

"Not to mention the actual hunting," Tyler said. "That was

the worst part."

"In what way?"

"That first hunt—actually the only one I went on—Ted bagged a Bighorn. It wasn't pretty." He again glanced back to where his father stood, Ted Norris nearby. "He used a crossbow. The first shot struck its hindquarters. Needless to say, it bolted. Took well over an hour to track it. Following the blood trail, we found it. Cornered, hobbled, weak from blood loss. It was pathetic. Ted shot it in the heart."

"No wonder you don't like hunting."

"I don't. Like I said, it's not exactly fair."

"Like it would be if they hunted each other?" Harper smiled.

"Exactly."

Again she tilted her lemonade glass his way. "To your more pastoral life."

"I like that," Tyler said. "Pastoral. The perfect word. You should come by my place and see it some time. I'll cook dinner."

"On a campfire?"

"No." He laughed. "I even have indoor plumbing. And a commercial stove."

"Love a man who cooks," Harper said.

"I do know my way around the kitchen." He smiled. "In fact, this guacamole is one of my creations."

"Then I better try it." She scooped some on a chip and ate it. Dabbed her lips with a napkin. "That's excellent."

He gave a mock bow. "You should try my chicken cacciatore."

"Is that an invitation?"

"It is."

"Maybe," she said. "Not sure how much longer we'll be around."

"Since the girl you were looking for was found? So to speak?" She nodded.

"Do you think Chief Cutler will ever find out who did it?"

"Eventually."

Tyler raised an eyebrow. "Really?"

"Killers always screw up. Get caught."

"Don't some go unsolved? Become cold cases?"

Harper shrugged. "Sometimes the bad guys do get lucky."

"Isn't luck part of just about everything?"

Harper laughed. "That's true."

"Dad said you and Bobby are siblings," Tyler said.

"Yes."

"You don't look it." He smiled.

"We get that a lot."

"Where'd you grow up?"

"All over," Harper said.

"Military?"

"That came later. Navy for me, Army for Bobby."

"Makes for an interesting Army-Navy game, I imagine."

"Sure does," Harper said.

He took a sip of lemonade. "So why all the moving? When you were growing up?"

"Our family was a little unusual. We moved around a lot."

"Doing what?"

"Putting on shows. Living off the land."

"Which explains the hunting," Tyler said.

"Had to if we wanted to eat."

Tyler studied her. "That I get. Hunting for food has been part of human history since the cave days. It's the trophy hunting Dad and his buddies do that I have a problem with."

"So you said."

He looked back across the pool. "Seems cruel."

"You the sensitive type?" Harper asked.

He turned back to her. "You sound like Dad."

"If it helps any, neither Bobby nor I would hunt anymore. And definitely not for sport."

"You hunted too?" Tyler asked.

"Sure did. Not as much as Bobby and the men in the family, but some."

"The men? How big was your family?"

"About sixty."

"What?"

Harper shrugged.

"Sounds like a gypsy troupe or something," Tyler said.

"Exactly."

"Wait a minute. You're saying you guys are gypsies?"

Harper laughed, shook her head. "Not really. But we sure lived that way. Town to town. Putting on shows. Scratching out a living."

"What kind of shows?"

"A bit of everything. Bobby was known as Bobby Blade. He was a knife thrower."

"Dad mentioned that. Said he was very good."

"Lucky for me that's true."

"What does that mean?"

"I was the target." She told him about the show, the board, the spinning wheel.

"You're very brave," Tyler said.

She smiled. "I was young and stupid."

"I'd love to see it."

"You have a spinning wheel?" Harper asked, smiled.

Tyler grinned. Easy, relaxed. "No. But, Dad does have targets."

Harper opened her purse. She pulled out a pair of throwing knives. "Let's go."

"You carry knives in your purse?"

"And lipstick."

That drew a broad grin from Tyler.

"They're Bobby's," Harper said. "He doesn't carry a purse. So, lucky me."

As Harper and Tyler circled the pool, Cutler, sliding her phone in her pocket, joined them.

"Get your calls made?" Harper asked.

"Yeah. Jimmy broke up some fight down by the marina. Couple of high school boys."

"The life of a cop," Tyler said.

"Better than paperwork, I guess."

They joined the men just as Cain fired a crossbow bolt into the target. Several inches from the red center circle.

"Good shot," Dixon said. "You're getting good at this."

Harper buried her smile. Bobby screwing with them. He could handle anything with a point. Or a cutting edge.

"Even a blind dog gets the bone every now and then," Cain said.

"Here," Harper said, handing him the two knives. "Tyler wants to see you do your thing."

"I told Ted and Hank about your throwing skills," Stenson said.

"Yeah," Dixon said. "I want to see that."

Cain took the knives. "You got a balloon to hold?" he asked Harper.

"Yeah, right." Harper looked at Tyler. "He's not as good as he used to be." She slugged Cain's shoulder. "And I'm not as stupid."

Cain faced the target, ninety feet away. He flicked his right hand, then his left. Thump, thump, the two knives struck the center circle, only an inch between them.

"Wow," Norris said.

"Didn't I tell you?" Stenson said.

"How'd you do that?" Norris asked.

"Misspent youth," Cain said.

That garnered a round of laughter.

"I think it's time for some barbecue and whiskey," Stenson said.

Cain retrieved his knives, handing them to Harper. The group settled around the patio table Juanita had set up. Two platters of ribs and brisket, large bowls of potato salad and marinated green beans, and a basket of corn muffins appeared. Looked and smelled wonderful.

Harper sat next to Tyler. She snugged her chair a couple of inches closer to his. She could play the game. Keep him interested. He was an inroad to Stenson's world and maybe, just maybe, the killer. Any pathway angled that way was worth exploring. Besides, he was handsome and charming. Spoiled, for sure. And, of course, living off daddy's money. But, if he could offer anything that pointed them to Cindy Grant's killer, it was worth a shot.

The barbecue was spicy, the whiskey smooth, and the meal was relaxing, even fun. Of course, it crossed Harper's mind she might be dining with a killer. But who? There were several candidates at the table.

While she chatted with Tyler—okay, flirted—she kept an ear in the other conversations. She heard nothing that suggested guilt or even a passing interest in Cindy's murder from anyone. Maybe this was a dead end. Maybe the killer wasn't part of Stenson's group. Maybe he was one of the guys who packed up right after they arrived. Maybe she and Cain were running in circles. The wrong circles.

Afterwards, Tyler walked them to the car. Cutler jumped in the back seat. Cain climbed in and cranked the engine. Tyler grabbed the passenger door handle but, before opening it, said to Harper, "I meant what I said about dinner."

"That sounds wonderful," Harper said. "I think we're headed back to Nashville in the morning, but I'm sure we'll be back." She smiled and touched his arm. "I will, for sure."

"When?"

"Not sure. But I love this town. I can think of worse places to spend a weekend."

Tyler smiled. "I'd love that."

PsyOps came in many forms.

CHAPTER 44

"Look at this," Harper said.

"I'm driving."

Cain was. Back to Nashville. After another great breakfast thanks to Lily Butler.

"Here." She extended her iPad his way.

He gave it a quick glance. The main website page of *The Tennessean*, Nashville's major newspaper. The headline: **VANDY STUDENT DEFACED, MURDERED.**

"We knew this would happen," Cain said. "Sooner or later."

"I was hoping for later."

"What does it say? How much do they know?"

Harper scanned the article, relating the high points to Cain.

Cindy Grant was named, and her relationship to General Kessler was spelled out but that the General could not be reached for comment. That her body had been found in the "small, bucolic town of Moss Landing." That a homicide investigation was "underway" but no suspects had been identified. Thankfully, there was no mention of how she was murdered, how she was "defaced" or displayed or, most importantly, that she had been hunted.

"That's better than I thought," Cain said. "It's going to be big news but less so than if they knew she had been stalked and killed with a crossbow."

"How do you know it was a crossbow?" Harper asked.

"Don't. But yesterday, while shooting with Stenson and his crew, it all made sense. The wounds could only have come from target arrows or from crossbow bolts." He glanced at Harper. "I don't think any hunter worth his salt would go after game of any sort with target arrows."

"Game?" Harper said.

"You know what I mean."

"Makes sense. Not the game. The crossbow."

"Of course it does."

"Don't let it go to your head. What now?"

"Better give General Kessler a call. See how he's handling this."

Harper lifted Cain's iPhone from the console tray near the Navi screen. She scrolled though his favorites until she found Kessler, and tapped it.

"Bobby Cain." Kessler's voice came through the Mercedes' speaker system.

"It's Harper. We're in the car."

"Headed up to Nashville," Cain said. "I take it you saw the paper this morning?"

"I did."

"Any fallout yet?" Harper asked.

"Alice Shaw, my attorney, has been grabbing the calls. Apparently she's already received over a dozen. From all over. And it's not even ten yet."

Alice Shaw was a name everyone in Nashville knew. Founder and senior partner of Shaw, Merkel, and Marks, one of the largest firms in the city. And the most expensive.

"At least they don't know the details," Harper said.

"Not yet," Kessler said. "Any idea who might've leaked this much?"

"No," Cain said. "But I suspect it came from either the Nashville PD or over in Moss Landing. Apparently some guys at a service station down there were talking about it."

"Really?"

"Not in any great detail," Harper said. "They simply know she was tattooed and dropped at the post office."

"That's too much," Kessler said.

"You knew it would happen," Harper said. "This story can't be controlled. Only delayed."

They could hear Kessler's sigh through the speaker. "How'd it go over there? In Moss Landing?"

"We spent much of yesterday with Martin Stenson and his crew," Cain said. "At his home. I'd say we have a suspect pool of sorts."

Kessler hesitated as if absorbing that. "You think Stenson's involved somehow?"

"Don't know. But if not, it could be one of his group."

"At least they might be able to lead us in the right direction," Harper added.

Ten miles out of Nashville, the traffic thickened. As usual. Cain maneuvered around an eighteen-wheeler only to fall in behind a tiny electric death trap, cruising well below the speed limit. One of those with only an expanse of glass between the driver and another car, a power pole, or a bridge abutment. Harper called them "Donor Cars." The passengers wouldn't survive the impact, but some of their organs might.

"I don't see Martin being this kind of animal," Kessler said. "But I don't know him all that well. Just a couple of brief business meetings. But, to me, he seemed... What's the word? ...Ordinary."

"It's the ordinary ones that are dangerous," Harper said. "Sociopaths don't wear labels."

"Speaking of sociopaths," Cain said. "When we get up to Nashville, I'm going to arrange a meeting with Adam Parker and Carlos Campos. We know they're involved."

"But neither is likely the killer," Kessler said.

"No, but they know who Cindy was sold to. And the buyer is the guy we need."

"You sure?"

"I am," Cain said. "It's why he bought her."

Kessler puffed out a breath. "And I thought Afghanistan was a shit-hole. How are you going to handle them?"

"Gently," Cain said. "Unless that doesn't work."

Kessler sighed. "You know my feelings on that."

The next two calls were to Chief Cutler and Captain Bradford. Chief Laura Cutler wasn't a happy woman.

"Yeah, I saw the article. So did everyone else. Right now I've got folks from a half a dozen newspapers wandering around here, harassing everyone. Not to mention news crews from CNN and ABC. The sharks are circling."

"You have any idea who might've leaked the story?" Harper asked.

"No one in this department," she said. "At least, they better hope not. If I found out one of my guys did it, I'll crack their skull."

"Anyone come to mind?" Cain asked.

"No. And truly I don't think it happened on this end."

"What about your mother?" Cain asked.

"Trust me, I asked. Told her if she opened her mouth, I'd shoot her. Right after a couple of these annoying reporters."

Cain laughed. "Sorry. But I had to ask."

"So did I," Cutler said. "Mother wasn't amused."

"I can picture that."

"My main concern is that this guy might already have another victim. Every time my phone rings I expect it to be another tattooed girl hung up somewhere." She sighed. "This is a royal mess."

Could he? Have another victim on his tattooing table? Cain didn't relish that possibility. Harper jumped in, breaking that thought chain.

"Probably not yet," Harper said. "But you can bet he will."

"What does that mean?" Cutler said.

"Most of these guys have a cooling off period. The killing satisfies something inside. The driving need. So they tend to sit back and enjoy the euphoria. But eventually the demons stir and they go on the prowl again."

"Pleasant thought," Cutler said. "How long are we talking here?"

"No way to know," Harper said. "It varies greatly. Our guy waited a couple of months between visits. So, it could be months again."

"Unless he accelerates," Cain said.

"Possible," Harper said. "Bottom line is that there's no way to know. His timeline is his timeline."

"Thanks," Cutler said. "You made my day."

Harper ended the call, saying they'd keep her updated on

anything they learned.

Captain Lee Bradford wasn't happy either.

"Of course the leak could've come from here," Bradford said. "We're a big department. Too many folks know the details. Not to mention over at the ME's office."

"Anyone in mind?" Cain asked.

"No. But I got my sniffer working."

"What about the media?" Harper asked.

"Oh, yeah. They're around. Not as bad as what I hear is going on down in Moss Landing. Laura Cutler must be beside herself."

"She is," Cain said. "We just talked with her."

"You down there?"

"We were. Just getting back into Nashville."

"And then what?"

"Sit down with Carlos and Adam Parker. One or both of them know who bought Cindy."

"I'd still like to lean on them," Bradford said.

"Not yet. Let me meet with them first."

Bradford hesitated. "You do know the clock's ticking?"

"We do. I'll call you after I meet with them."

Cain's next call was to Adam. On his William Faulkner phone.

CHAPTER 45

He hadn't signed up for this shit. No way. Sure the money was good. And being the man, the one that seduced these air-headed college chicks into turning tricks, was perfect. He'd proven his worth, over and over. And now with a new venture coming his way, one that would increase his cash flow substantially, or so it seemed, things couldn't be better.

Except.

Adam Parker sat in his car. He had pulled to the curb several blocks from Carlos' to re-read the front page story. Cindy Harper murdered? Carlos said she had gone off to Europe. Probably wouldn't be back. So how the hell did this happen?

He remembered when he recruited Cindy. He knew she was General Kessler's granddaughter, and that did give him pause. But, the choice was hers, wasn't it? He simply made the offer. She could've said no. If she was ever arrested, or word leaked that she was a prostitute, that wasn't really his problem. And dragging her roommate, Kelly Whitt, and her friend, Ella Hamilton, into the mix had been a good thing. A profitable thing. Even if Kelly and Ella had jumped ship. They'd be back though. No doubt. The money was too easy.

But now, with Cindy murdered, would the General stir things up? He was powerful, extremely wealthy, and connected. He could make things happen. Could any of this lead back to him? Would the police show up, wanting to know if he knew anything about what had happened? Would he be a suspect? How deeply into his life would they go?

This was totally fucked.

He had a more immediate problem. How would he handle Carlos? What should he say? Nothing? Maybe that was smart but he had to know how this all went down. For his own protection, if nothing else.

He tossed the newspaper on the passenger seat and pulled from the curb.

"Here," Carlos said. He handed Adam a wad of hundreds.

"What's this for?" Adam asked.

"It's your share of Cindy's last gig."

"She's dead."

Carlos shrugged. "That's too bad. She was a money maker."

"I thought she went to Europe," Adam said.

Carlos laughed. Glanced at Alejandro Reyes and Hector Munoz. "Change of plans."

Adam didn't like the two—what were they? Muscle? Enforcers? Whatever. They were bad news and he had never felt comfortable around them. A darkness, a sense of violence dripped off them. They rarely smiled. Had he actually ever seen either one of them show any humor? He couldn't remember if they had. Now they sat on a sofa in Carlos' living room, their dark gazes leveled on Adam.

"How did this happen?" Adam asked.

He sat in a chair at one end of the coffee table, the duo to his right, Carlos in an identical chair across from him.

Carlos shrugged. "It happened."

Adam leaned forward. He pinched his nose. Thinking maybe a simple nod, acceptance, might be the best tact. But, he had to know.

"Look, this is going to make waves. Maybe big waves. I need to know the truth."

"Might be best if you don't."

"Come on, Carlos. We're in this together. If I don't know what happened, I won't know how to answer any questions coming my way."

"Don't say nothing," Hector said.

Adam looked at him, then to Carlos. "Not knowing could lead to saying something that doesn't fit. With whatever you say. Don't you think it's best if we're on the same page?"

"You're assuming anyone will ever connect us."

"They might. If they dig deep enough. We are connected. I've brought you, what? Over a dozen girls? They'll talk. It only takes one to open that door."

Carlos considered that. "Okay. The truth? I sold her."

"What?"

Carlos shrugged.

"To who? Why?"

"The 'why' was for ten grand. That's where your cut came from. The 'who' is unimportant."

"Is it? What if the police track down that person?"

"They won't."

"How can you be sure?"

Carlos smiled, nodded toward Alejandro and Hector. "We know what we're doing."

"You know who her grandfather is? General Kessler has powerful friends. Don't you think he can mount a fucking army of folks to find out?"

"We'll simply say that as far as we know she went on a trip to Europe."

"With who?"

Carlos stared at him. Apparently he didn't have an answer for that. Not a good one, anyway. He simply said, "With some dude."

"So, what? They say: 'Oh, okay, some dude. Why didn't you say so in the first place? We'll go look for some dude.' Don't you see the breakdown in logic there?"

"You want out?" Carlos asked.

Did he? Shouldn't he just walk away? While he could. The truth? It was too late for that. He was in this way too deep. And there was this new venture. One that could bring in a boatload of money. Adam sighed. "No. I don't want out."

"Then let us handle this end. You take care of recruiting."

Adam nodded. His cell buzzed. He pulled it from his pocket and examined the screen.

"It's Bill Faulkner. He said he'd call when he got back into town.

Probably wants to set up a meeting to finalize everything."

"Good. Tell him to come on by."

CHAPTER 46

After hanging up, telling Adam he'd be by within the hour, Cain drove home. Two minutes after he and Harper walked into their condo, Mama B called.

"Adam's getting wonky," she said.

"How so?"

"He sat down with Carlos and his two guys—Hector Munoz and Alejandro Reyes—and confronted them about Cindy. Carlos admitted he had sold her to some guy."

"How did Adam take that?"

"Not well. But in the end, he remained onboard. Carlos said he'd take care of things and that Adam should stick to recruiting."

"Okay. I'm on my way over there," Cain said.

"How you going to play it?"

"We'll see. But my bias is straight up."

"I'd expect nothing less."

After he hung up, he said to Harper, "Airdrop me the photo on Stenson's group."

She did. He checked it. "Looks good."

"How are you going to use it?" Harper asked.

"According to what Carlos said, his two guys were the only ones who saw the buyer."

"And the guy in Vegas."

"And him. But, I might see if they'll cop to knowing any of

the guys in the picture."

"That could get prickly."

"More than prickly. I'll play it by ear."

Thirty minutes later Cain was seated in Carlos' living room with Carlos, Adam, Munoz, and Reyes. Adam had greeted him at the door. He looked stressed, spooked. No small talk, no smile.

"Thanks for seeing me," Cain said, shaking Carlos' hand. He sat.

Carlos smiled and rubbed his palms together. "Let's get this done."

"Let's do it."

Cain explained again how everything would work. His group would handle the girls, the appointments, the money. Carlos and crew would do the recruiting and take a cut. A big cut.

"I like it," Carlos said. He looked at Adam. "Sound good to you?"

Adam nodded.

"Okay, what's next?"

"Needless to say," Cain began, "there can't be any formal contract. Nothing in writing. No paper trail. It'll all be on a handshake."

"No problem," Carlos said.

"There's just one thing."

Carlos' eyes narrowed. "Like what?"

"The girl you sold. Cindy Grant."

Cain felt more than saw Adam stiffen.

"What about her?" Carlos asked.

Cain sighed, fixing a look of concern on his face. "That's something that could come back on us."

"I don't see how?"

"You do know she was the granddaughter of General Kessler?"

"So?"

"He's a powerful man. Lot's of connections. Could cause trouble. Expose the entire thing."

"Never happen," Carlos said.

"But it could. My partners have some hesitation because of that." He looked at Carlos. "Unless we can fix it."

Carlos nodded toward Munoz and Reyes. "We can handle

that."

"I thought you didn't know him? The buyer?"

"I don't. But we'll find him. Eventually."

"Eventually is a long time."

"He'll be back. When he does, we'll fix it."

Cain decided to take the leap.

"This isn't for public consumption," Cain said. "Cindy was tattooed. Like a tiger. She was hunted and killed."

Carlos sat up straight. His gaze cut to his two guys, then back to Cain. "I didn't see anything like that in the paper. How do you know this?"

Cain smiled. Hoping to decompress Carlos. "We're in an illegal business. My organization is large. International. We know people. Own people. Cops, judges, even a couple of FBI guys. We have resources."

"I see."

"So, we know what happened. The details. We need to find this guy. The buyer. Now. Before the temperature rises."

"I'm not sure how to do that?"

Cain pulled out his phone. "We know Cindy was hunted by some guy with a crossbow."

"What?" Carlos asked. "They still make those?"

"They do. And folks hunt with them. Like the guy who hunted Cindy Grant."

Carlos took a deep breath and exhaled loudly, puffing out his cheeks.

Cain opened the photo he had downloaded from Harper. He extended it toward Munoz. "You guys recognize any of these guys?"

"What is this?" Munoz asked.

"There's a bow hunting group down near Moss Landing. Where Cindy was found. These are several members of that group."

Carlos stood and walked around behind Munoz, examined the photo. "How'd you get this?"

"Like I said, we have resources. The guy might or might not be one of these guys. Take a look. Anyone look familiar?"

Munoz and Reyes stared at the screen. A quick glance to each other.

That's all Cain needed. The glance. The way their shoulders squared. The hesitation. The show of carefully studying the photo. The killer was there.

Munoz shook his head. "I don't recognize any of them."

"Me either," Reyes added.

"You met the guy twice, so I suspect you'd know."

"It was dark," Munoz said. "We met in a warehouse. I think maybe he was disguised."

"Disguised? How?"

"Nothin' big," Reyes said. "Not like he wore a mask." He glanced at Munoz. "He did have a cap on. Like a baseball one. Plain blue. Had it down low." He shrugged. "Like we said, it was dark."

Cain nodded. "It was a long shot." He looked up at Carlos. "He called you though. Right?"

Carlos nodded. "A couple of times."

"No number in your phone?"

"It was blocked. I figured it was one of those throw away phones."

Cain already knew that. Mama B had searched Carlos' phone. The calls did come from a burner. One purchased a month earlier, in Vegas. Cash. No ID. No security camera at the store. She had checked everything.

"That would be smart," Cain said. He looked at Munoz. "You sure no one in the photo looks even remotely familiar?"

He shook his head. "None of them looks like anyone I ever met."

CHAPTER 47

Chelsie was exhausted. It had already been a long day and now he was back at work. He had started early, near sunrise, worked for a few hours. How many, she couldn't work out. Time meant little in here. Long enough to complete her entire lower back. The pain, the incessant needle, had ramped her nerves to the breaking point. She had cried and pleaded and he finally relented, saying they'd take a break. He left briefly, returned with a PB&J sandwich and two bottles of water. Then, he left.

Two hours later he returned. Strapping her to the table. Face up. Now working on the sensitive areas around her breasts.

"How much longer?" she asked.

"Two, maybe three days. Then you'll be perfect."

"I meant today. I'm not sure how much more I can take."

That was true. She felt a vibration throughout her entire being. If her nerves had been frayed before, they were now nearing the break point. Didn't he ever tire? Weren't his hands, his back, aching and knotted? He'd spent hours perched on a stool, hunched over her. His concentration seemed almost superhuman.

He smiled. "You're doing just fine."

"No, I'm not. Please."

He placed the tattoo gun on the table, near her hip. He sat up straight, twisted his torso one way and then the other. "Another hour."

"I can't."

"Sure you can." Another smile. "You're a real trouper."

"Do I have a choice?"

His eyes narrowed. "I'm working hard to make you perfect. How about some gratitude?"

Was he fucking kidding? She wanted to rip his eyes out. Bite his face. Kick his balls into his throat.

Pipe dreams. She saw no way any of that could ever happen.

"When you're finished, what then?" she asked.

He patted her arm, causing an involuntary jerk. "All in good time."

"Why? Why me? Why this?"

"We've been over this."

They had. Several times. He was the artist, she the canvas. She becoming truly beautiful. In his eyes. In his madness.

He had said she would be his Chelsie Cheetah. And she looked like one. Much of her skin now orange, black dots everywhere. In no pattern she could see. Like the plague. Or some other dreaded disease.

She heard footsteps. Outside. Then a door scraping open. She tensed. Had someone arrived to rescue her?

He stood and turned toward the door. She looked that way.

Two men.

"What are you doing here?" her captor asked.

"We need to talk," the taller of the two said.

Blond hair, more shaggy and unkempt than her captor's, same blue eyes. Were they related?

The two men approached. Each walking around the table. Examining her.

"Remarkable," the shorter one said.

Darker, stocky, more dangerous looking.

"She's beautiful," he said.

Her captor smiled. "I told you she was special."

The tall one ran a hand along her leg, up her thigh. "Amazing."

"Still want out?" her captor asked.

Out? Out of what?

"Did you see the paper this morning?" the tall one asked.

"Sure."

"General Kessler's granddaughter? Are you crazy?"

Her captor looked around. "Let's step outside. It'll be more private."

The shorter one gave a smirk. "Do you think that makes any difference? She'll never tell anyone."

Her heart fluttered. The tension in her body felt as if she had lifted from the table. Floated on some insensible cloud. She had known from day one that she wouldn't survive this. No way he could do this and let her live. But, hearing it said, in so many words, was an affirmation that made it even more real. *God, if you can hear, if you even exist, please, please help me.*

"Okay. There's no way she can be traced to us." He nodded toward Chelsie. "Chelsie either."

"That might be true," the tall man said. "Or not. The problem is that her being so high profile could lead to a more vigorous investigation."

"Relax. I told you. They were both purchased. From someone who doesn't know me. Has no way of finding me. Or you. Truth is, he doesn't know what I look like."

"But, you've met him. Haven't you?"

Her captor shook his head. "Never."

"Then how did you…?"

He raised a hand. "I never met him. The girls were delivered by a couple of his guys. In a dark warehouse. Where no one could see anyone else."

"You sure?"

"I am."

The shorter one now ran his hand over her ribs, cupped one breast. "She's remarkable."

"And she'll be more so once I've finished."

The tall one sighed. "When?"

"Two more days. Three at the most."

The tall man nodded. "Okay."

"I guess this means you're still in?"

The two men exchanged a glance. "We are."

CHAPTER 48

Cain pulled in to the Nashville Airport's general aviation area. After maneuvering past the check point and following the guard's directions, he rounded a hangar and General Kessler's Gulfstream G650 came into view. Nearly 100 feet of high-speed, long-range luxury—the speed being just under Mach One and the range around 7000 miles. The General could get anywhere, in a hurry.

"Wow," Harper said. "I didn't expect this."

"What? Just a regular old Gulfstream?"

"Since you put it that way, yeah."

Cain smiled. "You underestimate the General."

"Wonder what something like this costs?"

"I think it's one of those things that if you have to ask you can't afford it."

Earlier, as Cain left Carlos' place, he had called Kessler. Said Carlos' guys recognized the killer.

"Who is it?" Kessler asked.

"They didn't say who but they know him." Cain explained the photo Harper had taken and how he saw recognition in the eyes of Munoz and Reyes.

"You're telling me the guy who did this is a friend of Martin Stenson's?"

"Looks that way. Hell, it could be Stenson himself."

"I never expected the trail might lead there."

"Every mission has its own surprises," Cain said.

"True. What's your next step?"

"We need to go to Vegas. To see the valet who recommended Carlos to our guy. See if he can pick him out."

Kessler didn't hesitate. Said he'd have the jet spun up and ready within the hour. So, here they were, headed to Sin City.

Cain parked, nose in, near the hangar. They grabbed their overnight bags—because you just never knew—from the trunk, and walked toward the aircraft.

A young lady appeared in the doorway at the top of the stairs. She offered a pleasant smile as they climbed to where she stood. She ushered them inside.

"Mr. Cain. Ms. McCoy. Welcome aboard."

"Thanks," Harper said.

"I'm Brooke."

She turned and nodded toward the cockpit. Inside the pilot and co-pilot busied themselves with their pre-flight checks.

"This is Captain Bart Henderson and his co-pilot Adrian Lindberg."

They turned. "Make yourselves comfortable," Henderson said. "We'll be ready to roll in a few minutes."

Brooke stored their bags in a front compartment and then directed them into the cabin.

Plush didn't cover it. Two rows of white leather captain's chairs, dark wood trim, thick carpeting. Space for twelve in three four-seat groupings, each arranged with two seats facing forward, the other two aft.

Cain and Harper settled mid-way back and sat facing each other.

"Anything to drink before we take off?" Brooke asked.

Cain and Harper declined. Brooke walked toward the front. She closed and sealed the front door and then disappeared into the small galley.

Cain's phone rang. The William Faulkner one. The caller ID told him it was Adam Parker.

"Adam?" he said.

"Where are you?" Adam asked.

"Why?"

262

"We need to talk."

Cain glanced at Harper. "About?"

"I'd rather do it face to face. Not on the phone."

"I'm headed out to Miami right now. But, I'll be back tomorrow. Can it wait?"

Adam hesitated. "I guess." He didn't sound thrilled about waiting.

"Go ahead; tell me."

He heard Adam sigh. "I'm having some second thoughts about all this."

"Oh?" Cain said.

"Maybe I'm overreacting. Or being paranoid or something."

"In this business a touch of paranoia is a good thing. What exactly's bothering you?"

"When I started this, when I hooked up with Carlos, it was all fun and games. I found girls who wanted to make money, he gave them the opportunity. Everyone did well. The girls, most of them anyway, were grateful. Several of them helped pay for their college and living expenses."

"Okay. And now?"

"Cindy Grant changed everything."

The last thing they needed right now, when they might be just a few hours from identifying the killer, was Adam Parker making waves. Making Carlos nervous. Carlos was deeply invested, hungry for money, making him vulnerable. But if Adam created ripples, Carlos might become wary. Might bolt. Cain wanted him fat and happy and clueless.

"How so?" Cain asked, already knowing the answer, but letting Adam vent.

"Carlos sold her. To some guy who did stuff to her. Killed her. I mean, *Jesus*, I don't understand what's going on."

"Did you express these concerns to Carlos?"

"No way. He'd be super pissed if he thought I wasn't sold on this whole idea."

"Probably."

"And, he's scary. Those two guys he hangs with are even scarier."

"Adam, I appreciate your concerns. As you heard earlier, I

share them. I don't like Carlos selling girls locally. Overseas, okay, but not here in his own backyard."

"What happens to those girls? The ones that go overseas?"

"They make money. Some even begin a new life. A plush life."

Cain's lies rolled out easily. He hated it, but it was the only play right now. He had to keep Adam in the fold.

"How do you know?" Adam asked.

"We keep track."

"I see." Adam fell silent.

"Look, I'm going to fix all that. Clean up the mess Carlos made. Get us all on the right track."

"How?"

"Leave that to me. But I want you to lay low for a day or two. Stay away from Carlos. If he calls, tell him you have classes, or appointments with new girls, anything to put him off."

Adam let out a long sigh. "Okay."

"I'll be back tomorrow and I should have a solution worked out by then."

After he hung up, Harper asked, "He getting rattled?"

"Sure is."

"And here I didn't think he had a soul."

Cain smiled. "He's a kid. A punk-ass but a kid."

"You mean not a killer, just a pimp?"

"Something like that."

Brooke appeared. "Buckle up. We're ready to go."

The flight took just under three hours, the sun setting when they landed at the Henderson Executive Airport. A black Lincoln Town Car and driver awaited them.

"Call when you're ready to go," Brooke said as she escorted them to the car.

"Shouldn't take too long," Cain said. "Couple of hours, maybe."

"The guys and I are going over to a little pub we like and grab something to eat. It's nearby, so let me know when you're headed this way and we'll be waiting."

"Sounds good."

CHAPTER 49

Their driver was Raquel Scotto. A tall, fit young lady who wore black slacks and a white collared shirt. She spun the car toward the exit.

"Caesars, right?"

"That's it," Cain said,

Mama B had said Luis Orosco's shift today ran until eight p.m. so he would still be on duty. When Cain asked how she found that out, she replied, "Want to see his pay stubs? His work schedule for the next three months?" Was there anything she couldn't dig up?

Now, Cain and Harper shuffled through the pages of intel Mama B had sent. Originally from Tijuana, Luis had been in the US eight years, and at Caesar's for four. Besides his two pandering arrests, neither going anywhere, he hadn't had so much as a parking ticket.

From his photo he appeared stocky, muscular, with shaggy dark hair and a grin that was actually pleasant. As the Town Car swung into the Caesars's valet area, chaos ruled. Cars unloading way too much luggage, others reloading similar baggage plus multicolored bags of shopping and souvenirs; still others held the routine comings and goings of gamblers and drinkers. The party crowd. The valet guys were hopping, somehow making it all look easy.

Cain spotted Luis near the entry door, phone to his ear. He

pointed.

"He looks almost normal," Harper said.

"He's not."

Another valet approached as Cain stepped out. Harper didn't.

"She's just dropping me off," Cain said.

The guy nodded and headed toward the car that had pulled in behind them.

"We'll circle back in about fifteen," Harper said.

Cain waited until Luis hung up and then approached him.

"Luis?"

He turned, smiled.

"That's me."

"I'm Bill Faulkner. Mind if I ask you a couple of questions?"

His smile evaporated. "About what?"

Cain scanned the surroundings. "Maybe just over here." He indicated an area twenty feet away, near a column, removed from the bustling entrance drive. He walked that way. Luis followed.

"What's this about?" Luis asked.

"Girls."

His gaze cut right and left. "You got the wrong guy."

"I don't think so."

Luis hesitated. "You look like a cop."

"I'm not. I'm a friend of Carlos Campos. You might say we're business partners."

His smile returned. "Oh, I see. What can I do for you?"

"I'm looking for a guy. One you sent Carlos' way."

"Why?" Luis asked.

"Let's just say he can throw a kink into some things Carlos and I have planned."

"Back in Nashville?"

"Yes."

"And I sent this guy to Carlos?"

"Several weeks ago. Maybe a month or two. He was looking for a girl. Not just for the night. Something more long term."

His brow furrowed. "I should call Carlos."

"That's not necessary," Cain said.

"I'd feel better." He slipped his phone from his pocket.

"I'd rather you didn't." Cain smiled.

"What does that mean? Who the hell are you?"

"Bill Faulkner. And I'm trying to solve a problem for Carlos."

Luis glanced at his phone then back up to Cain. "That makes no sense." Again, he began working his phone. "I'd better call him."

"No," Cain said. Luis's head snapped up. "This is a delicate matter and it's best for Carlos if he has no connection, or even knows of this conversation." Again, Cain smiled. "Gives him plausible deniability if things get sideways."

"I don't like this."

"It's simple. Tell me what I need to know and I'll go away. You'll have no other involvement and your name will never be spoken again."

"And if I don't?"

"Then I'll have to follow another path. Perhaps involve the Las Vegas PD. And I'd rather not."

"What the hell did this guy do?"

"Better you don't know that."

Luis glanced back toward his coworkers. One looked his way, raised his shoulders and opened his arms as if to say, "We could use some help here."

"Just tell me about the guy you sent to Carlos," Cain said. "That's it. Then you can get back to work."

Luis considered that for a full half a minute, ultimately saying nothing, just giving a brief head shake.

Cain considered his options. Going hard at Luis wasn't a good choice. Not here. Public place, his friends nearby. But, he didn't have time to woo him. Convince Luis he was a good guy. Not a threat. Finally, Cain pulled out his phone. "Let me show you a photo. Tell me if you recognize anyone." He brought up the image of Stenson's crew and held it toward Luis.

At first he looked away, then gave in, studied the photo. His pupils widened a notch. Recognition. No doubt. He shook his head. "None of those guys look familiar." He looked at Cain. "Who are they?"

"Just some guys. You sure you haven't seen any of them before?"

"I'm sure."

"Okay. That's all I needed." Cain returned his phone to his pocket. "I'd appreciate it if you'd keep this conversation between the two of us."

"Sure." He shrugged. "I got to get back to work."

Cain watched him walk away. Before he reentered the chaos, one of his co-workers rolled down the passenger window of a car he was parking and shouted to Luis. "You going to that party tonight?"

"Yeah, man. Wouldn't miss it." He glanced at his watch. "I get off in about forty-five. Got to run by my place and clean up. I should be there by ten."

The guy gave a thumbs up. "Going to be fun. Lot's of ladies I hear."

Luis waved. "Later."

The Town Car pulled up and Cain jumped in.

"Tell me something good," Harper said.

"He recognized someone. Don't know who. He denied it, but just like Munoz and Reyes, he knows who we're looking for."

"What now?" Harper asked.

"Plan B."

She laughed. "I always love plan B."

Cain gave Raquel Luis's address. She eased into the thick traffic along Las Vegas Boulevard.

Cain's cell buzzed. Mama B.

"He just called Carlos," she said. "Told him some dude—that being you—had harassed him about the guy he had sent to him."

"Harassed? I was polite. Mostly."

Mama B laughed. "Right. Bottom line—Carlos isn't happy."

"I'm not either."

"Let me guess, you're going to have another chat with Mr. Orosco?"

"Chat might be a little polite."

CHAPTER 50

Bobby Blade, Age 9

It started when he was four. Uncle Al's games. Back then, Bobby had no idea they were actually training sessions. He discovered that much later.

Uncle Al began with trees. Not simply scaling them, but ascending without anyone being aware. How to use the trunk, limbs, and foliage for cover. When to move, when to remain frozen. How to avoid the weak branches that might break, or creak, or sway, and seek out those that would not only support him, but wouldn't give away his position. The game was to reach the highest point and not be seen. They practiced in parks, in the woods, even in people's backyards, often while the family was eating just beyond a bank of windows.

He then moved on to ropes, trellises, even sheer walls. Brick and stone were the easiest. They found abandoned houses and Bobby learned to reach the second floor, open windows and doors, move quietly, even across squeaky floors.

Shortly after his ninth birthday, Uncle Al sat him down at their motorhome's dining table.

"It's time," Al had said. "Tonight. I have a place staked out. Should be a quick in and out." He nodded. "You'll be going in with me."

"Really?"

Bobby had never been inside. His role had been the lookout. Hiding nearby, often in a tree, good view of the target house, sounding the selected bird call if the family returned. He'd only had to do that once.

"You're ready," Al said.

His first mission, a two-story house on a quiet cul-de-sac. Easy access from the wooded area that wrapped the backyard. The occupants were away. No alarm system, no window bars, lots of sliding glass. What Uncle Al called a "ripe plum."

Bobby went in first, Al following, checking his every move.

They accessed the second story by way of a crabapple tree that hugged the home, near a small balcony. According to Al, even in houses with alarms the owners often didn't pony up for upstairs window sensors. Save a little money. Fools.

Inside, Al showed him how to avoid any areas that might be occupied—bedrooms, bathrooms, particularly kids' rooms. His take? They kept less predictable hours than did adults. Of course, people on vacation, or at work, or just out for an evening were best, but even if they were home and asleep, Al could get in and out without anyone being the wiser. That was a later lesson.

The night had been a success. Two high-end cameras—Nikons, no less—silverware, some jewelry—not all that expensive, but something—some cash hidden in a sock drawer, where it always was, and a nice crystal bowl. For Dixie.

One of Al's rules was to go for the stuff you could fit in a pocket or could easily carry. TVs and stereos and computers were bulky and selling or pawning them could get sticky. Serial numbers and all that. Cash was king but jewelry could be broken down and that made it untraceable. Cameras fell in-between.

When they returned to the camp, Bobby had been on a high. The anxiety he had felt going in now morphed into a giddiness that made everyone smile. It had been a rite of passage. Into manhood, as far as the family saw it.

Afterward, he went on many outings with Al and Uncle Mo. Learning, getting better. His long arms and legs, and lean build, proved to be assets. He could slide in and out of even the tightest places with ease. He could move quietly through homes where the occupants slept, not knowing he had been there until the next day, often much later.

Six months into his new career, he made his first solo raid. Uncle Al served as lookout. Second floor window. No sweat. He filled his pockets with cash from a wallet and purse, a generous amount of jewelry from a dresser, with the couple sleeping just a few feet away. As he eased the drawer closed, the woman stirred. She raised her head and for a moment seemed to look right at him. He froze.

Another Uncle Al dictum was that, in the dark, stationary objects were invisible. Movement could be tracked. Bobby put that theory to the test. After what seemed like forever, the woman flipped back the covers and swung out of bed. Her back now to him as she seemed to be putting on slippers. Cain eased to his left and folded himself into a ball on the far side of the dresser. His chest tightened, his breathing shallowed. Sweat tickled his neck. He fought to ignore it.

The woman padded past him, merely two feet away, and entered the bathroom. Her flowery perfume trailed behind her. The man stirred, but only to roll over, readjust his pillow. Bobby considered taking a chance. Could he make it across the room and out the door undetected? But Al had often said, once you go to ground, stay put. Get small and wait. An opportunity to escape unnoticed would reveal itself. Through the slightly ajar door, he heard the woman urinating, then the toilet flushed, and again she shuffled back to bed, her slippers scraping across the carpet.

He waited. Time slowed. She flipped and flopped a few times. Her husband did, too. Then finally, thankfully, their breathing slowed, the man snoring slightly.

Cain made his escape.

Over the years, he had other close calls, but that night was imprinted in his mind. He had followed Al's rules and had succeeded in walking away with over ten thousand in jewelry and cash.

Another step toward gypsy-style manhood.

CHAPTER 51

Most people who visited Vegas never left The Strip. Why would they? It had literally everything. Something for every major sin.

But the surrounding area, several blocks deep, was home to a few other major hotel/casinos, smaller boutique hotels, and motels of varying stature. High-end restaurants, to mom and pop ones, to dives and nightclubs. Strip joints. Liquor and convenience stores. Service stations. And apartment and condo projects from large to small, luxurious to run-down.

Luis's condo was only four blocks off The Strip, but it took over twenty minutes for Raquel Scotto to navigate the thick traffic. Cain called Brooke, telling her they had something to take care of so it'd be a bit longer. No problem.

Cain and Harper examined the building schematics Mama B had sent. Luis rented a third floor, corner unit, near one of the pools. No alarm system. At least he didn't have any security contract among his bank and credit card records.

Was there anything Mama B couldn't dig up?

The condo project was okay, neither top drawer, nor ramshackle. Raquel circled its eight buildings. Most parking places were filled, but she found an empty slot on the backside, near a trio of dumpsters. Cain checked the knives he had secreted in hidden sheaths sewn into the seams of his pants, the third strapped to his ankle. The other five he had were likewise well hidden. Harper opened her purse and removed her Glock 17. She checked its clip and chambered a round.

Cain told Raquel to sit tight and he and Harper climbed out. Harper settled the Glock in the back of her jeans, covering it with her windbreaker.

They slipped between two of the identical tan-stucco, six-unit blocks—one being where Luis lived. First floor patios and stacked balconies, giving each unit a slice of outdoor space, were wrapped by a black, wrought iron railing. Similar iron work connected them vertically. An easy climb.

The problem? Thirty feet away a couple snuggled in a Jacuzzi, their backs to Cain and Harper. Blue light lit the water and reflected off two wine glasses on the apron.

"I'll distract them," Harper said. "You get your ass up there as quickly as you can."

Harper walked toward the couple, circling the Jacuzzi, to face them from the far side. They looked up.

"How's it going?" Harper asked.

"Couldn't be better," the guy said.

"I'm looking for a place," Harper said. "Heard good things about this project."

"It's great," the girl said.

Harper continued the small talk; Cain climbed. He easily reached Luis's balcony and dealt with the sliding glass door. Took less than a minute to get inside. Five minutes later, Harper had extracted herself from the couple, circled the building to the entry, and climbed the stairs to the third floor. Cain opened the door and she entered.

"Nice place," she said.

It was okay. Neat and well furnished. Open concept. The living area, the small dining table, and the kitchen separated by a short breakfast bar/counter, were essentially one room. They explored. Short hallway, a washer/dryer alcove along the right side, the single bedroom and bath on the left, nothing of interest.

Back in the main area Harper asked, "What's the play?"

"I'm not in the mood to tap dance with Mr. Orosco."

"And you think I am?"

Not a chance.

"So let's go at him hard," Cain said.

She nodded.

Footsteps approached. The sound of keys.

Cain settled in a chair that flanked a sofa, and faced the front door over a glass coffee table, where he laid two throwing knives. Harper slipped down the hall and into the washer alcove, out of sight.

The door opened. Luis entered, a small gym bag in one hand. He didn't see Cain. Turned toward the kitchen, settling the bag on the breakfast counter. He tugged open the fridge and snagged a beer. He twisted off the cap and took a slug.

Then, he saw Cain.

"What the…?"

"Hello, Luis."

"What are you doing?" His head swiveled. "How'd you get in here?"

"Wasn't difficult."

"Get the fuck out or I'll call the cops."

"No you won't. Sit down. Let's talk."

"Fuck you." He reached out and unzipped the bag.

"Keep your hands where I can see them."

"Or what?"

"I might have to hurt you." Cain scooped up one of the knives and flicked it. It thumped/twanged into the side of a cabinet only a foot or so from Luis's head.

Luis recoiled. Looked that way. Then the gun appeared. In his right hand. He raised it toward Cain as he circled the counter.

"Guess you brought a knife to a gun fight," Luis said.

Cain smiled. "I brought a gun, too."

Luis looked confused. His gaze searched Cain, the remaining knife on the table.

"Really?" he said.

"Really," Harper said.

He jumped, looked her way. Right into the muzzle of her Glock.

"Put the weapon down," Harper said.

"I'll shoot him," Luis said.

"No you won't," Cain said. Luis turned back to him. "She'll

disconnect your spinal cord before you can hiccough." Cain smiled. "She's very good." Luis froze. "Or I'll put this other knife in your left eye. It's your call."

Sweat glistened on Luis's face. His eyes wide. His hand shaking slightly.

"Sit," Cain said. "We only want to talk."

Luis seemed to consider his options. He placed the gun on the dining table, moved to the sofa, and sat. He took a calming breath. "About what?"

Harper yanked Cain's knife from the wooden cabinet, then moved to Luis's right, her weapon down at her side.

"You know what."

Luis swallowed hard.

"I told you not to call Carlos."

"I didn't."

"And here I thought we were going to be friends," Cain said.

"I'm not your fucking friend."

"What you don't want is for me to be your enemy."

"I'm not afraid of you," Luis said.

But, he was. It was all over his face.

"I've killed twenty-seven people," Cain said. "What makes you think I won't make you number twenty-eight?"

Luis had no response.

"She's only up to six," Cain said, nodding toward Harper. "So she might want to do the honor."

"I don't know what you want."

Cain removed his phone, pulled up the photo again, and held it where Luis could see the screen.

"You recognized someone in the picture."

"I didn't. I told you that."

"And you lied. Take another look. Who is the guy you sent to Carlos?"

He studied the image again. "I can't tell for sure. One of these guys." He indicated Stenson, Tyler, and Norris.

"You don't know which one?"

"They look alike. Are they brothers or something?"

"Something like that. Look more closely."

Luis took the phone. He expanded and shrank the picture with his fingers several times. "I can't tell. I've only seen the guy once. And that was several years ago."

"Several years ago?" Cain asked.

"Yeah. He was looking for a girl. One of the bartenders told him to come to me. I hooked him up. That's how I knew him. He would call whenever he was in town and I'd set up dates for him. Not often. After that first time it was all done on the phone."

"So you never saw him face to face again?"

"That's right."

"So why'd you send him to Carlos?"

"He called a month or so ago. Needed a date, so I set it up. The next day he called again. Said he needed a girl for long term. Heard girls could be purchased." Luis shook his head. "Some article he had seen online. Wanted to know if I did anything like that, or knew someone who did."

"And Carlos did?"

"That's what I'd heard. And he's really the only guy I know in Nashville. That's where the dude had said he was from. So I sent him that way."

Cain nodded.

"What happened?" Luis asked. "Why're you busting me on this?"

"Better you don't know." Cain stood. He took his phone back and slid it in his pocket. "We'll leave you alone if you keep your mouth shut. But, if you contact Carlos again and tell him about this little chat, we'll be back." Cain smiled. "Next time won't be as pleasant."

CHAPTER 52

Captain Lee Bradford met Cain and Harper in the fourth floor corridor outside Adam Parker's condo. An older building, but overall fairly well maintained. Except for the wobbly elevator they had taken up. It was nine a.m. They had gotten home from Vegas well past midnight, slept a few hours before Bradford called.

Bradford dismissed the uniformed officer he was chatting with as Cain and Harper walked toward him.

"What's going on?" Cain asked. Bradford had declined to say on the phone, only that they might want to meet with him. Cain knew in his gut what the deal would be. Bradford confirmed it.

"Adam Parker got himself killed."

"When?"

"Last night. ME techs say around midnight would be a good guess."

"How?" Harper asked.

Bradford twisted his neck. "Follow me."

The living room was neat and clean. Looked like Adam wasn't your typical college guy. First off, it was a condo, not some off campus apartment, and it was well furnished and well kept. Guess pimping and selling girls was profitable.

Nothing looked out of place, nothing disturbed. Not so with the bedroom. An ME tech and a uniformed officer stood to one side of the bed. Adam lay on his back. Jockey shorts, no shirt.

Entry wound in his left chest, another smack in the middle of his forehead. An execution.

"Carlos," Cain said.

Bradford nodded. "Probably."

"No probably about it."

Cain told him of their visit to Vegas to see Luis Orosco, Luis calling Carlos.

"Carlos is getting nervous," Bradford said.

"Cleaning house," Harper said.

Cain circled to the far side of the bed. The body position, the double tap nature of the killing, the absence of anything, even the bedsheet, being out place said Adam was likely shot in his sleep.

"Who found him?" Cain asked.

"A friend. Classmate. He came by to pick him up for a racquet ball game. No answer at the door or on his phone. Said the front door was unlocked so he came in."

"Where is he?"

"The back of a patrol car on his way to the station. I want to do an official interview. And record it."

Cain nodded.

"If Carlos is behind this, I wonder who else is on his radar?" Bradford asked.

"Luis the valet," Cain said. "He can connect Carlos to the guy who bought Cindy Grant."

Bradford's brow wrinkled. His jaw set, eyes narrowed.

"What is it?" Cain asked.

"Trying to decide if I need a warrant to go after Carlos, or can justify exigent circumstances. Maybe someone's life is in danger. Like another girl."

"No evidence of that," Cain said.

"But we don't know that. Could give me the excuse I need."

"Or screw everything up," Harper said.

Bradford gave a shake of his head. "True. The search, arrest, whatever could get tossed."

"Might I suggest another way?" Cain said.

Bradford nodded. "Suggest away."

Cain pulled out his phone and brought up the photo Harper had taken. He extended it toward Bradford.

"This is Martin Stenson, his son Tyler, and some of Stenson's bow hunting buddies."

"Where'd you get this?"

"Harper took it. We were at his place. Met the crew."

"Okay."

"Our guy has only been seen, as far as we know, by three people. Luis Orosco and Carlos' two sidekicks, Alejandro Reyes and Hector Munoz. When I showed this photo to Reyes and Munoz, they denied recognizing anyone. But they did. I saw it in the reactions. Luis also denied it until Harper and I explained things to him."

"Explained?" Bradford asked.

Cain smiled. "Let's say we convinced him it was in his best interest to come clean."

"I don't even want to know how that went down."

Cain shrugged. "In the end, Luis said that the guy he saw was either Stenson, his son Tyler, or this guy." Cain indicated Norris. "Guy named Ted Norris. One of Stenson's hunting partners."

Bradford squinted at the image. "They look a lot alike. At least on the small screen."

"They do in person, too," Harper said. "Up close you can tell Tyler is younger, but from a distance, not so easy."

"But this Orosco guy. He didn't know which one?"

Cain shook his head. "Only saw him once and that was a few years ago. Everything else was done over the phone."

"What does everything else mean?"

"Whenever he was in town, whoever he is, he would contact Luis and he would supply him with a girl. Last time, he said he needed to purchase one."

"This Luis guy told you that?"

"He did." Cain glanced at Harper. "We didn't leave him much wiggle room."

"I can get someone on checking travel for each of them. See who goes to Vegas a lot."

"That won't be easy and it'll take time," Cain said. "And a trip to Vegas isn't exactly evidence.

Bradford sighed.

"The main problem is that we don't know who to look at. Right now, we have three possible suspects. And the real one might even be none of them. Could be someone we know nothing about."

"Which makes barging in and taking down these three problematic."

Cain nodded. "Nothing to charge them with. No probable cause for getting a warrant to search their properties. And even trying to do so might put the guy we want on alert."

"And he'd get rid of everything?"

"Exactly. And would get messy. A good defense attorney would have a field day with such a shotgun approach. Wouldn't it be better to know? Have proof?"

Bradford took a slow breath, let it out even slower. "So, what's your plan?"

"Let me talk to Carlos and his guys. Maybe I can convince them to come clean."

"Or get yourself killed?"

"I'm still on the inside. They think I can make them rich. Maybe even clean up this mess for them. If I can persuade Munoz and Reyes to pick out the right guy, we're ahead of the game."

Bradford considered that, then said, "You don't think Luis calling Carlos, telling him you were in Vegas asking questions, might queer the deal?"

"Maybe. But I told Carlos I wasn't happy about him selling girls locally. That I'd make that situation right and in the future all sales would be offshore."

Bradford sighed. "This is some sick shit."

"It is. But if I can show Carlos that visiting Luis was simply part of the plan to clean all this up, maybe I can convince him to let me take care of the buyer. That way Carlos won't have to get his hands dirty. Makes him and his guys free and clear."

"You think he'll buy that?"

"Worth a try."

"Let's say that works. What then?"

"You can have Carlos and his crew. Harper and I will head south. Try to sort out the real killer."

Bradford scratched the back of one hand. "Does Laura Cutler know any of this?"

"She's on our call list," Harper said.

CHAPTER 53

They mustered in the PD's backlot. Bradford, Harper, Cain, a quartet of uniforms, and a six-man SWAT crew, all dressed for combat. Bradford unfolded a map on the hood of his car.

"We'll approach here," Bradford said. He indicated the street that ran along the opposite side of the block from Carlos' cute little craftsman. Three houses from the corner. "We'll park along here." He pointed at the cross street. "All unmarked cars." He glanced at the SWAT guys. "No van. Is that a problem?"

The leader of the SWAT crew, young guy named Vince Givens, shook his head. "None. We got all we need." He held up his automatic assault weapon, a Heckler & Koch MP5.

"Once you get through the door," Bradford nodded to Cain, "we'll deploy. SWAT along the rear and sides, me and the officers out front."

"And me?" Harper asked.

"You'll stay with the cars."

She squared her shoulders. "Not likely."

Bradford looked at her.

"I'll go with the SWAT team. Work my way to the rear door and crack it if need be."

Bradford now glanced at Cain.

"She's been in more fire fights than you can imagine," Cain said. "More dangerous places than this."

"But…"

"But, nothing," Harper said. "If Bobby's going in, I'm going to be close by." She smiled. "We're not negotiating here."

"It'll be fine," Cain said. He looked at Harper. "Even welcomed."

She shrugged. "Just like Kandahar."

"This isn't Afghanistan," Bradford said. "And you're a civilian."

"So is Bobby."

Bradford hesitated. "Okay." Then, to Harper, "Stay with the SWAT guys."

She nodded.

Bradford's cell rang. He answered, walking a few feet away. He mostly listened, then ended the call. "We might have a problem. I had a couple of guys do a drive by. Unmarked car. Two young girls just went inside."

"I'll get rid of them," Cain said.

"How?"

"Leave it to me."

"We can't risk a confrontation if there are a pair of civilians in there."

"They won't be," Cain said. "Just give me a couple of minutes after I get in. Wait until they leave before you deploy."

"Might be best to detain them," one of the SWAT guys said. "Just in case they sense something and make a call."

Cain nodded. "If you can do it without making a scene."

Fifteen minutes later everyone was in place, staged just around the corner. Cain parked at the curb in front of Carlos' place. A VW bug sat in the drive. The girls' ride. He rapped on the door. One of the girls answered, holding it for him as he entered.

She was twenty, max, as was her friend who sat on the living room sofa. Each wore short shorts and tank tops. In the den, Carlos faced his computer and swiveled toward Cain.

"Mister Faulkner. How's it going?" Carlos asked. No smile.

"Fine. But we need to talk."

"Yes, we do."

Cain nodded toward the living room, the girls. "Alone."

Carlos considered that. He yelled toward the door to the living room. "Darla, Simone, get in here."

Cain heard one of them huff out something. Sounded like

"Jesus."

The pair appeared at the doorway. Hands on hips.

"Why don't you guys run over to the liquor store?" Carlos said. "Grab a couple of bottles of tequila."

"We just got here," one of them said.

"And now you're leaving." He dug in his pocket and handed her a wad of crumpled bills.

Another huff. She fisted the money and they left. Not happy.

Munoz and Reyes came from the kitchen area. They stood side by side, Munoz with a gun stuffed in his jeans, arms folded over his chest. Cain didn't see a weapon on Reyes, but no doubt he had one. Probably along his waist in the back.

Carlos swiveled his chair back and forth. "You had a talk with Luis? In Vegas?"

Cain took a chair. "I did." He slid his hand along his right thigh as if wiping away sweat, actually tugging the secret zipper down a couple of inches. Just in case.

"Want to tell me why?" Carlos asked.

"I told you, I need to clean up your mess."

"My mess?"

Munoz shifted his weight, hooked a thumb in his belt near his weapon.

"You sold Cindy Grant to a local," Cain said. "A guy who did some unpleasant things to her. Attracted much unwanted attention."

"So?"

"Not to mention the girl is the granddaughter of General William Kessler."

"Again, so?"

"You don't see the problem there? Kessler's connected. And no fool. And from what I hear, tough as nails. Not someone who would turn the other cheek. And your guy, the purchaser, has put a spotlight on everything." Cain waved a hand. "Created a trail that could come back your way."

"It won't."

Cain raised an eyebrow. "My sources tell me that Kessler has hired someone to track the guy down."

"Who?"

"Don't know. But it means that someone besides the cops is sniffing around the girl's disappearance."

Carlos leaned forward. Elbows on his knees. "We can handle it."

"I told you I would," Cain said. "I've already made some progress."

"What might that be?"

#

Harper and the SWAT guys had gained a position on a small rear patio near the back door. Kneeling and peering over the kitchen window sill afforded her a look through the kitchen and into another room. She saw Munoz and Reyes, their backs to her. Beyond them, Carlos sat in a chair, hunched forward. Elbows on his knees. Talking. To Cain no doubt. He wasn't visible.

Munoz shifted his weight. Shoulders erect. Uneasy. Reyes moved a hand to his back as if scratching. Lifting his untucked shirt. She saw the gun stuffed in the waist of his pants.

"I'm going in," Harper said.

"No," Givens said. "We don't have orders for that."

She turned to him. "Something's getting ready to go down."

"We don't know that."

"I do."

"How?"

"Body language." She reached for the rear door knob and twisted it. Unlocked. She pulled her Glock and eased the door open.

#

"Identifying the buyer is obviously the critical factor here," Cain said. "Luis seemed the best place to start." Cain nodded toward Munoz and Reyes. "Your guys couldn't ID the guy who bought the girls. I figured Luis might."

"Did he?" Munoz asked.

"Almost." Cain looked at him. "He saw the same photo you did. He recognized the same guys you did."

"We told you we didn't know any of those dudes in the photo," Munoz said. A smirk on his face.

Cain sighed. "But you did." Reyes started to say something but Cain waved him away. "Which one was it?"

Munoz's eyes narrowed. Reyes shuffled a couple of steps to his right. Smart move. Creating separation. Angles. His hand was behind his back. Cain had hoped to avoid a confrontation, but the odds of that were declining. He shifted forward on the chair, quietly lowering the zipper a couple of more inches. His hand now lay over the knife's handle.

"We're on the same page here," Cain said to Carlos. "Once this guy is taken off the board, we can get on with our business."

Carlos scratched his chin. "You see, I'm starting to have my doubts about you."

"In what way?" He worked the knife loose, the handle now firmly across his palm.

"You come out of nowhere. Adam brings you here. You have this unbelievable plan. Wave money in front of me, thinking I'll buy it."

Cain shrugged. "If you want out, that's fine. I'm sure we can find someone else in the neighborhood to work with."

Carlos' face went hard. "Probably not."

"I see."

"Do you? I'm thinking we do indeed need to clean house." He nodded toward Munoz. "In fact, we've already started."

"With Adam Parker?" Cain asked. He smiled. "Yes, I know about that."

Carlos gave a quick nod. "Mister Faulkner, I'm afraid you've become a liability I can't afford."

"Too bad."

"Yes, it is."

Things happened fast.

Munoz reached for his gun.

Cain pulled the knife, flung it toward him. It entered just left of his trachea, severing the carotid. Blood erupted. Munoz's weapon discharged, punching a hole in the coffee table near Cain's knee.

Reyes' hand came from behind his back. He raised his weapon.

Cain rolled from his chair and spun behind it. Another

discharge. The bullet tore through the top edge of the chair back and slapped into the wall behind him. He had the other knife in his hand. Coiled, ready to rise and throw.

"Don't fucking move." Harper's voice boomed from behind Reyes.

He turned that way, his weapon following. The bullet struck him in the middle of his forehead and he dropped. Two SWAT guys and Harper entered the room.

Carlos sat frozen, eyes taking up half his face. Munoz, who had been gurgling and writhing on the floor, one hand clutching at the knife, fell silent. Bradford and the two uniforms came through the front door, service weapons in hand.

"Jesus," Bradford said.

Cain stood. "They made bad choices." He waved the knife toward Carlos.

"What the fuck?" Carlos said.

Cain smiled, nodded toward Harper. "We're the ones General Kessler hired."

Carlos visibly deflated. Cain stepped toward him, grabbed a handful of his hair, and slammed him to the floor. His head bounced off the carpet. Cain settled a knee into his chest.

"Cain, what are you doing?" Bradford said.

Cain didn't look his way, keeping his gaze locked on Carlos. Fear now dripped off him. "I have a couple of questions for my business partner."

Carlos heaved, tried to move. Cain leaned into him, driving his knee more firmly into his chest.

"Are you sure you don't know who bought Cindy?"

"No. I told you."

"Why would I believe you?"

"It's true." Carlos was breathing hard now. Sweat frosted his face.

"And you've had no other contact with him?"

A slight flutter of his eyelids, pupils expanding.

"You have," Cain said.

"No."

Cain raised his other knife. He directed it toward Carlos' right eye, resting the point in the soft tissues beneath.

Bradford started to say something, but Harper grabbed his arm.

"Tell me," Cain said. "Or I'll pluck your eyes out right here, right now."

Carlos whimpered. "I told you I..."

The knife point broke the skin, a trickle of blood appearing.

"Try again," Cain said.

"Okay. Okay. He bought another girl."

"When?"

"A couple of days ago. Reyes and Munoz delivered her just like before."

CHAPTER 54

Cain and Harper stood outside Carlos' house. The SWAT guys were packing up; the two girls huddled in the back of a police cruiser. Their expressions were somewhere between fear and bewilderment. Carlos, handcuffed, now sporting a small band aid beneath his right eye, sat in the back of another cruiser. He glared at Cain.

Cain walked toward him, leaned down to speak through the window, lowered only six inches. "You sure you don't know the guy who bought the girls?" Cain asked.

"Fuck you."

"Maybe you should consider your situation. You're already going down as part of a murder conspiracy. If he does something to the girl he has, the one you sold to him, that'll up the ante."

"So?"

"Probably double the time you get. Bump twenty years up to fifty, or life without."

"I don't know the dude. I told you that."

"Never saw him?"

"No."

Cain nodded. "What about the girl? Who is she?"

Carlos turned his gaze toward the front windshield. Thinking, considering. His shoulders relaxed, and he looked back toward Cain. "Chelsie Young. She worked for me for a few months. But started making noises like she wanted out." A one shouldered shrug. "So I figured I might as well squeeze out a final payment."

"You're a real peach, Carlos. I hope they burn you up in court." He smiled. "I know I'll be there to give the jury my part of the story."

Cain walked away.

Bradford approached. "That could've gone better."

"Or worse," Harper said.

Bradford gave a quick nod. "What now?"

"We're headed south. Hook up with Laura Cutler. See if we can find the other young lady before something bad happens." Cain nodded toward Carlos. "He gave up her name. Chelsie Young."

"I take it she worked for him?" Bradford asked.

Cain nodded. "She planned to quit the life. Quit Carlos, anyway."

"I'll get someone on looking into her." Bradford scratched the back of one hand. "You still thinking it's either Martin Stenson, his son, or that Norris dude?"

"That's the working theory. Of course, the trick now is proving which one."

"What's the plan?" Bradford asked.

"We're working on it," Harper said.

Bradford nodded. "I'll need to sit down with each of you and get an official statement soon."

"As soon we get back from Moss Landing."

Cain and Harper swung by home, changed clothes, packed a few more, and stuffed the equipment they might need into two black gear bags. Cain called Cutler, told her they were headed her way, and had some news.

"Good news, or bad?" Cutler asked.

"Depends on your perspective. We have a good idea who we're looking for. At least, the suspect list seems to be down to three."

"Who?"

Cain hesitated.

"Tell me," Cutler said.

"Martin Stenson, Tyler, or Ted Norris."

"What? How did you come up with that?"

"A witness. He couldn't tell which one but it was one of the three."

"Who's this witness?"

"A valet in Vegas. The guy who sent our guy to Carlos."

"Jesus."

"It gets worse," Cain said.

"Of course it does," Cutler said.

"He has another girl."

"Down here?"

"Probably. It's where he lives."

"Are you sure?" Cutler asked.

"Carlos said he sold a girl named Chelsie Young to him a couple of days ago."

She sighed heavily. "I think it's time to go roust the Stensons, and Ted Norris."

"No. Sit tight. We have a couple of ideas on how to prove it one way or the other."

"There's a girl in danger and you want me to twiddle my thumbs?"

"Exposing your hand now might put her in a worse situation," Cain said. Cutler said nothing, obviously considering that. "We're heading out of Nashville right now. I'll call when we get close and we can meet somewhere."

"You sure know how to screw up a day."

"Sorry. See you in an hour or so."

Cain navigated the thick traffic and soon was out of the city, cruising down I-24 toward Murfreesboro. That's when Mama B called.

"You're going to love what I've got," she said.

The phone was blue-toothed through the Mercedes sound system.

"We usually do," Harper said.

"I did some digging into the Stensons and their buddy Ted Norris. The father seems bland and clean. Norris about the same. Not much there. A DUI, couple of parking lot fights. But, Tyler? He's a whole different story."

"Okay," Cain said. "Tell us."

"He definitely manages one of his father's companies. Doesn't seem to take much time on his part. They mostly run themselves.

Lots of free time it seems. He has no record, no run-ins with the law, not even a parking ticket."

"But?" Harper asked.

"I went back a few years. To his days at Princeton. You'd think a kid of his means wouldn't need a job. But Tyler did. Part time."

Mama B liked stretching the spring. Loved to roll out a story slowly. She should write thrillers.

"Do we have to guess?" Cain asked.

"He deposited a bunch of checks from Tootie's Tattoo Parlor."

"What?" Harper said.

"Yep. He did. Essentially once a month for nearly three years."

"He worked as a tattoo artist?" Harper asked.

"I doubt he was sweeping the floors," Mama B said.

"This is a game changer," Cain said.

"Sure gives him the skills," Mama B said.

"And narrows our choices."

"This is amazing," Harper said.

"I've got a little more," Mama B said. "Tyler's spread is maybe twenty acres. Abuts the southern edge of his father's much larger estate."

"I think we saw the entrance to it," Harper said. "Just off the county road."

"That's it. I grabbed some satellite photos. From a friend."

Mama B had friends everywhere. CIA, NSA, everywhere.

"Shows four buildings," she continued. "The residence, a garage, a barn, and another smaller building. Like an equipment shed. I'm sending it all your way."

"Thanks."

"I suspect you'll pay him a visit come nightfall. Be careful."

CHAPTER 55

He was late. He had worked for a couple of hours early in the morning. Just after sun-up as far as she could tell. Then he had said he had some things to take care of but would be back around noon. It felt well past that now. She was hungry. The bacon and egg burrito he had brought her earlier hadn't been very good. She only ate half. Now she wished she had the remainder.

She examined herself for like the five hundredth time. Nearly her entire body had been tattooed a tan/orange color with random black splotches everywhere. Only her abdomen, one shoulder, and her face had escaped his needles. But that was coming.

She stretched out her arms, rotated them. She did look like a cheetah. A fucking cheetah? Her eyes moistened, the splotches now running together as if melting.

She heard footsteps. The side door swung open. She wiped her eyes with the backs of her hands and sniffed. He walked toward her, handed her a white bag.

"Got you a burger and some fries."

It smelled wonderful. She took the bag. "Thanks."

"Eat up. Then we have to get back to work."

Inside she found a thick cheeseburger, a small bag of fries, and a large bottle of water. Maybe the best burger she'd ever eaten. Or perhaps she was simply starving.

Once he had strapped her back on the table, she asked, "What time is it?"

"A little after four."

"No wonder I was so hungry."

"Took me longer than I thought. Means we'll work a little later tonight. Maybe until nine or so."

"I don't know if I can take it that long."

"You'll be fine. Besides, we have a lot left to do before tomorrow night."

She stiffened. "What happens then?"

"Your debut." He smiled. "You'll be completed and ready for the world."

The tattoo gun buzzed to life. She jumped when it touched the tender flesh of her abdomen, just below her ribs.

Again, tears pushed against her eyes.

Don't give him that.

She fought but felt them leak from her right eye, slide across her cheek.

"Are those tears of joy?" he asked.

Was he freaking kidding? Or mocking her? She couldn't tell. The only thing she knew for sure was that he was one demented fuck.

"It just hurts," she said.

"I know," he said. "You've been a real trooper. Not much more. Just this and your shoulder today, then tomorrow morning your face."

A sob escaped. "Then what happens? I don't understand."

"You will. You'll be the star of the show."

She had no idea what that meant. Only that whatever it was, she wouldn't survive it. There was no way he could let her live. No way. Would she get a chance to escape? Would she be taken somewhere, or was this her final resting place? Here in this cold, dingy barn? *Please, dear God, don't let that be true.*

Her parents, her sister, would never know what happened to her. No one would. She would simply evaporate. As if she never existed.

Or would he make a mistake? Lose his concentration? If he did take her somewhere else, would an opportunity arise? Could she somehow surprise him? Overpower him?

Another thought crept in. An even scarier one. Who were those other two guys? They were obviously in on this. Would they be "part of the show," as he put it? Was this some crazy sex game? Would they do all this to rape her? What kind of sick fuck would do that?

She knew the answer to that. The one bending over her, marking her flesh.

"Who were those other two guys?" she asked.

The buzzing stopped, he looked at her. "Friends."

"Will they be part of things tomorrow night?"

"Oh, yes. Definitely."

"But, you won't tell me what it is? What's going to happen?"

"I wouldn't want to spoil the surprise."

The buzzing restarted.

CHAPTER 56

Cain and Harper found themselves back at Flo's Diner. They had called Cutler just after scooting through Lynchburg. Cutler suggested meeting there, saying she was starving. Cain and Harper hadn't eaten since their granola and fruit breakfast that morning, so Flo's worked perfectly.

Flo greeted them, wiping her hands on a red-checkered kitchen towel as she approached. "Welcome back. The Chief said you'd be joining her."

"Smells better than I remembered," Harper said. "And I remembered it being wonderful."

"Love to hear that," Flo said, her face lighting up. She jerked her head toward the back. "She's back that way. I'll bring some menus."

Cutler sat at a table in the far corner. She wasn't alone. Jimmy Rankin sat next to her.

"I invited Jimmy in on this discussion," Cutler said.

"Good," Cain said. "I'm interested in his take on everything."

Flo appeared, menus in hand. She handed one to Harper, then Cain. "These two don't need a menu. They know it by heart." She laughed. "But I'd recommend the meatloaf. Luke Nash brought me some of his famous pork sausage and I ground a bit in there."

That's what everyone ordered.

Cutler waited until she left. "Tell me what's going on."

Cain glanced at Rankin.

"I told Jimmy you suspected one of the Stensons and maybe Ted Norris."

"And I find that hard to believe," Rankin said.

"I think we know which one now," Harper said.

Cutler and Rankin stared at her.

"Let me lay it out," Cain said. "Then you can tell me what you think."

Cutler nodded.

"We know Cindy Grant was tattooed and hunted. Most likely, the teacher, Rose Sanders, was, too. From Cindy's autopsy, the weapon used was an arrow. My guess is a crossbow bolt."

"How'd you figure that?" Rankin asked.

"The nature of the wounds. Small, round, not bullets. Definitely not a hunting arrow. More like a target type, or a crossbow."

"And since bowhunters don't use target points?" Rankin shrugged.

"Exactly. That led us into Stenson's world. Our visit to his place left me with the impression he has a pretty tight group. So we figured the killer was at least known to Stenson."

"Makes sense," Rankin said. He took a sip of coffee.

"We wormed into the business of one Carlos Campos. Up in Nashville. We got there thanks to Adam Parker. He's the one who recruited Cindy into prostitution."

"Your fake website worked?" Cutler said.

"Sure did. We made Carlos an offer he couldn't refuse. Lots of money, lots of girls. From that relationship, we learned Carlos had sold Cindy to someone. Our killer, no doubt."

"Which is who?" Cutler asked.

Flo and one of the waitresses appeared. Plates were eased onto the table. "Get you anything else?" Flo asked.

"I think we're good," Cutler said. "Thanks."

Flo and the waitress left and everyone dug in.

After a few bites, Cain continued. "I'll get to the 'who' in a minute. We learned the buyer was sent Carlos' way by a valet at Caesars in Las Vegas. Guy named Luis Orosco. We paid him a visit. He looked at a photo Harper had taken at Stenson's the other day. He narrowed it down to three people. Martin Stenson, Tyler, or Ted Norris."

"But he didn't know which one?" Cutler asked.

Cain shook his head.

"Ted does look at lot like Tyler," Rankin said. "Martin, too, for that matter."

"Probably why Orosco couldn't say which one for sure," Cain said. "He told us he only met the guy once. Several years ago. After that everything was done over the phone."

"Everything, like what?" Cutler asked.

"Seems that whenever the guy was in Vegas, he'd get girls through Luis. Then a month ago, he asked Luis if he could buy a girl. Apparently he'd read some article about trafficking. Online or somewhere. Luis knew he was from the Nashville area so he sent him Carlos' way."

"And he purchased Cindy from him," Rankin said. Not a question.

"Carlos never actually met the guy," Cain said. "His two sidekicks did. Guys named Munoz and Reyes."

"So they know our killer?" Cutler said.

"They said no. Didn't recognize anyone in the photo. But, they were lying."

"What about this Adam Parker?" Rankin asked. "He know the guy?"

Cain shook his head. "Never met him. All he did was bring Cindy to Carlos." He looked at Cutler. "And get himself killed."

"What?"

"Carlos' two guys. Last night. In his condo."

Cutler gave a slow nod. "You sure it was this Carlos guy and his crew that did it?"

"I am," Cain said. "He told me so. Right before he tried to do the same to me."

"Obviously not successfully," Cutler said. "I assume they're in custody?"

"Sort of," Harper said. "The ME has them."

Cutler sighed. She looked at Cain. "You?"

"Us," Cain said. "Munoz caught a knife, Reyes a bullet." He looked at Harper. "Forgot to say this earlier, but nice shot."

"Lucky," Harper said.

"Right." Cain smiled. "So, we have three bodies and Carlos in

Lee Bradford's hands. But since Carlos never saw the guy, that left us still unsure which of the trio to focus on."

"But now we know," Harper said. "It's Tyler."

"You sure?" Cutler asked.

"After some digging, we discovered that Tyler had a side job while he was at Princeton. At a tattoo parlor."

Cutler couldn't hide her shock. "You're kidding."

"So we have Luis picking out the two Stensons, and Ted Norris, and Tyler with the requisite skills."

"But this Luis guy couldn't say it was Tyler for sure. Right?" Rankin asked.

"No, he couldn't," Cain said.

"You have to admit they look a lot alike," Harper said. "Martin looks much younger than he is, and Norris looks like part of the family, so I can see how he couldn't be sure from a photo."

"I don't get it," Rankin said. "Why on God's green earth would Tyler Stenson do something like this?" He glanced at Cutler. "I mean, he's kind of a pussy."

Harper smiled. "He does seem a little passive. But, I had a nice chat with him. He was against hunting. Gave his father and his friends grief about it. But, he said something odd. He suggested they should hunt each other. Said that would be more fair."

"And that's his motivation?" Cutler asked.

"Maybe." Harper shrugged. "Or maybe he's trying to show daddy up. Hunt real prey. Not simply dumb animals, as Tyler called them."

Cutler pushed her plate away, her meatloaf only half eaten. "Martin can be a little overbearing."

"And Tyler is definitely spoiled," Rankin said. "Never wanted for anything. Privileged upbringing, top notch education, and a very high-dollar career dropped in his lap."

"All courtesy of his father," Cain said.

"Yeah, but always on Martin's terms," Rankin said. "At least that's my read."

"Mine, too," Cutler added.

"It's not an uncommon dynamic," Harper said. "Daddy's demanding. Kid wants to make a statement. Prove he's a man. Maybe one up daddy. That sort of thing."

"Okay, I get that," Cutler said. "But this? Hunting girls?"

Harper leaned forward, propped her elbows on the table. "Think about it. Martin Stenson is a skilled hunter. A big man in that world. He displays his trophies in his home. Like badges of honor. Tyler isn't part of that group. An outsider of sorts. Yet, daddy and his friends are there all the time. Rubbing it in his face. Intentional or not, doesn't matter. To Tyler it's just that. He grows up seeing those trophies, seeing his father bond with his buddies while Tyler's ignored to some extent. So, he decides to do the one thing daddy wouldn't do. Hunt a human."

"And the tattooing?" Rankin asked.

"Two things," Harper said. "One is that it makes them resemble daddy's trophies. Sort of a 'take that' statement. The other, it dehumanizes them somewhat. Makes them truly prey and no longer human. Easier to hunt that way, I suspect."

"Why behead Cindy?" Rankin asked.

Cain sighed. "A trophy. Like daddy's heads on the wall."

"Wait a minute," Cutler said. "You're saying Tyler Stenson has Cindy Harper's head hanging on his den wall?"

"Maybe Rose Sanders, too."

"If not on his wall," Harper said, "somewhere nearby. Where he can enjoy them."

"Enjoy?" Rankin said. "This is unbelievable."

"More than that," Cutler said. "This is a fucking mess." She glanced at Cain. "What now?"

"We need proof," Cain said. "And to find the other girl."

"Maybe raid his place?" Rankin said.

"Not sure we can do that," Cutler said. "We have no real evidence he's done anything. Be hard to get a search warrant with what we have. And going in there empty-handed would put him on alert. Give him time to destroy any evidence he might have."

Rankin nodded. "Including the girl. If he still has her."

"We have another idea," Cain said. "You two are handcuffed. Have to work within the framework of the law." He nodded toward Harper. "We don't."

"You want to translate that for me?" Cutler asked.

"We're going to visit his place as soon as it gets dark."

"And what? Ride in on white horses?"

Cain smiled. "Not exactly."

"Okay. So Tyler sees you out there sniffing around, calls me, and I have to lock you up for trespassing." She smiled. "Maybe even B and E."

"He'll never know we're there," Harper said.

"Really? I don't know his security situation out there but it's his house, his property. Don't you think that gives him a leg up?"

"You don't know us," Cain said. "Our history. And we can't talk about any of it. But, let's say we've carried out too many missions to count. Middle of the night. Very hostile territory. Tip of the spear stuff."

"Black ops?" Rankin asked.

Cain shrugged. "Some tasks need to be accomplished quietly and efficiently. Deep in the bad guy's home court. Off the radar."

Rankin stared at him.

"Bottom line, is that we can get in there and see what's what," Harper said. "Completely off the grid."

Cutler shook her head. "I'm not sure I'm comfortable with that."

Cain caught her gaze. "It's our job. What we were hired to do."

"Weren't you hired to find Cindy Grant? You did. So doesn't that end it?"

"That was part of our mission," Harper said.

"What else?" Realization fell over her face. "No, wait a minute. Does General Kessler want you to take out whoever murdered his granddaughter?"

Cain deadpanned her.

Cutler took a deep breath. "I can't let you go in there if your plan is to kill Tyler Stenson."

"We're going in to gather intel," Cain said. "And hopefully rescue a girl in deep trouble."

"And that's it?"

"That's it. Unless our hand is forced. Hopefully we'll find what you need to make an arrest."

Cutler sighed. "This makes me uneasy."

"That's why you'll be miles away. Completely out of the picture."

Cutler sighed, looked toward the entrance. Cain could sense her wheels turning, wrestling with what to say. Whether to buy into this or not. Finally, she simply said, "It's supposed to rain."

Cain smiled. "Good. It'll provide cover."

CHAPTER 57

The intel and maps Mama B provided proved invaluable. Of the four buildings on the property, the garage and the small shed seemed less likely candidates for locating the girl. Neither appeared to have the space he would need for his work. If the girl was indeed on his property, at a minimum he would require some place to incarcerate her: a locked room, a basement, a cage, something that was secure, and a work area. A table, and ample room for his tattooing equipment. The shed was too small, barely room to stand up much less move around. The garage, a single car version, could work, but it'd be tight.

His home could easily provide the needed elbow room. Four bedrooms and a full basement according to the construction plans Mama B had scooped up. The basement could've been modified to suit his requirements. Tyler wouldn't be the first killer to have done so.

But would he chance that? Have a captive in his home? What if people dropped by? What if the mailman saw or heard something? What if a fire broke out? Many a criminal's career had been harpooned by such odd happenings. Best laid plans and all that. Using his home seemed too risky.

Hell, using anywhere on his property chanced exposure.

Harper suggested he might consider that an acceptable risk. That he wouldn't have his lair too far from home. That he'd want to keep his eyes on it. That completely tattooing someone would take many days and he'd want it to be convenient. A remote location might require him to sneak in and out. The risk of being seen would be real. He did most of his business from home, so nearby, on his property, made the most sense. He wouldn't need to manufacture an excuse for being on his own property.

The barn offered everything. Privacy, security, and it sat only a couple of hundred feet from the house. Close, but not too close.

The maps also provided the best approach angle. The house and the other buildings occupied a flat, oval clearing among a patchwork of pine thickets, limestone outcroppings, and scattered areas of open grass land. A stream ran northeast to southwest a quarter of a mile south of the buildings. The paved road and the house were indeed the ones they had seen a few days earlier while surveying the area. To the north, a dirt road wound through the trees and entered the clearing a hundred yards from the house. A similar road to the south demarcated the southern edge of Tyler's property. That seemed the best approach.

They easily found where the road spurred off the county highway. Calling it a road was stretching the definition. It was simply two dirt tracks, weeds sprouting in the middle. Cain turned on to it. The car gyrated over its deep ruts, the grass scraping the car's undercarriage.

"That's Clovis Wilson's place," Harper said, pointing to their left. "Where Rose Sanders' remains were found."

Cain glanced that way. He could just make out the outline of the stand of trees where the kids had found her leg and Cutler had recovered her rib cage and arm.

Cain jerked the car to a halt.

"What is it?" Harper asked.

"She escaped."

"Rose?"

"Yes."

"How do you figure that?" Harper asked.

"I didn't before, but being here, seeing this, it makes sense." He pointed north. "Tyler's place is about a mile or more from here. That way."

"So she managed to escape, took to the woods, and tried to

outrun him."

Cain nodded. "Made it this far."

"And since hauling away a corpse is no small task, he buried her."

"Exactly. I suspect, she wasn't complete. Not to his satisfaction anyway. That's why he didn't display her. Like he did with Cindy."

"I want to take this son of a bitch out," Harper said.

"Maybe you'll get your chance." Cain looked at her. "But you'll have to be quicker than me."

He moved forward. The road swung north and entered a stand of pines. Cain flicked off the lights, slowed, letting his eyes adjust to the darkness. The half moon filtered through the trees, slid in and out of the broken cloud cover, providing just enough light to stay on course. The road soon gave out and melted into a pile of limestone rubble and brush a good quarter of a mile from Tyler's home.

Cain popped open the Mercedes's trunk. He and Harper were dressed in solid black combat fatigues, each wearing a cap. Cain settled a throwing knife into the sheaths sewn into his pants along each thigh, while Harper checked her Glock, pocketed two extra clips. Each slid small, single-lensed scopes—equipped with night-vision capability—into a zippered pants pocket. Harper stuffed her pouch of lock picks into her back pocket.

A few drops of rain tapped the pine boughs overhead as Harper led the way. They quickly found the stream they had seen on the maps and followed it. The terrain rose slightly, the water tumbling over and around wads of limestone. They soon reached the edge of the clearing where Tyler's home stood.

It was large, two-story, and sat atop the highest elevation in the clearing. A few clusters of landscape lights haloed the house, illuminating scattered trees and flower beds. The entire property seemed quiet, normal. The kind of place a family could put down roots, raise the kids. But was it? Did it hold Tyler Stenson's darkest secrets?

A faint glow fell through two of the first floor windows, the second story dark. Cain scanned the house with his scope. The lights came from overhead kitchen lights and a table lamp in the living room. He saw no movement.

The garage hung off the left side of the house, its door closed. Dark, also quiet. The barn stood a couple of hundred feet way, silhouetted against the night sky, muted by the drizzle. A large, dark-colored SUV sat near one corner. Cain couldn't determine its make, but its size was unmistakable. He knew the small shed was just beyond the structure, not visible from this angle. There was no sign of life anywhere. Was Tyler here? If not, their task would be considerably easier.

"Look," Harper said. She pointed toward the barn.

Cain aimed his scope that way. Narrow ribbons of light slipped between the barn's siding planks. "There's a light in there."

Harper adjusted the focus of her scope. "Someone's in there."

Cain had seen it, too. A shadow modulating the light. "Interesting."

"We just might catch him red-handed," Harper said.

"Unless he's in there woodworking or something."

"He isn't the type. His hands are too soft."

The light in the barn went out.

Cain froze, instinctively dropping behind a pine branch. Harper followed suit.

They switched their scopes to night vision.

"There," Harper said.

Cain watched. Through the night scope lens the world appeared greenish. Tyler Stenson exited the barn and walked toward his house. Unhurried. Head and shoulders forward, confident strides. Once inside he flipped on another light. Cain switched his scope to standard mode. Tyler entered his kitchen. He crossed to a large, stainless steel fridge, grabbed a beer, then moved out of sight.

The rain was now a steady drizzle.

"Let's move," Cain said.

CHAPTER 58

A long day. Fatigue tugged at Tyler. His back muscles knotted from the hours spent bending over the table. He was behind schedule, or rather the timetable had been compressed. Moved forward. Ted and Hank were getting wonky, threatening to walk away. He couldn't allow that. So, he accelerated his next project, the hunt now set for tomorrow night. He needed to drag them back into the fold so time was his enemy.

He had seen the excitement on their faces during the last outing. All he needed was to solidify that feeling. Take them back to the intensity of the hunt. It had been delicious. Intoxicating. Beyond even his imagination. They had also felt it, and now only needed a reminder.

Today's long hours had allowed him to alter the schedule. Now, with only her face left to do tomorrow morning, she would be ready. But her preparation had come at a price.

He twisted his torso back and forth, trying to stretch things out. Didn't help much. Maybe the beer would. He took another gulp as he climbed the stairs. A quick shower then he'd grab something to eat. He entered his bedroom, unbuttoning his shirt with one hand, tilting back the beer for another slug with the other.

Rain peppered the window. He walked that way, peeled back the flimsy shear curtain, and looked out. Last he had heard, the rain wasn't supposed to arrive until after midnight, but the weather folks were never right. The good news was that it was going to blow though quickly and be far to the east by sun-up.

He took another gulp of the beer, let the curtain go. Just as it flapped back into position, something caught his eye. With a finger he parted the fabric once again. Just enough to peer out.

It was dark, the rain misting the exterior lights. He saw nothing. Then, there it was again. Far away. Along the tree line. He blinked. Was it simply the rain and breeze creating shadows? He squinted.

He saw them. Two forms moved along the edge of the trees.

What the hell?

His heart rate clicked up. Who could it be? Why?

The answer to the latter was easy. Someone knew. Or suspected.

What to do? Confront them? Were they armed? Did it matter? They could only be there because he was a suspect. Was it Chief Cutler and Jimmy Rankin? Was it simply a pair of burglars?

Again, did it matter?

Whoever it was would definitely find the girl. Not something he could explain away.

He walked to the bedside table and snatched up the phone. Ted Norris answered after two rings.

"We've got a problem," Tyler said.

"What?"

"Someone's here. Sneaking around."

"What does that mean?"

"It means I just saw two people slip out of the woods near my house. They could find the girl."

"Shit. I told you this might happen."

"Yeah, well, it has. Call Dixon and get over here."

"He's here. We've been working on those new bows."

"Then get moving."

"What if it's Cutler?" Norris asked. "And Jimmy Rankin?"

"What if it is? What if it's a pair of vagrants looking for shelter from the rain? What if it's a couple of kids causing mischief? It makes no difference. Anyone who finds the girl, sees what she looks like, sees her confined to a cage, will know. If it isn't the cops, it soon will be."

"Fuck."

"Exactly."

"Okay. On the way."

"Park up on the dirt road to the north," Tyler said. "I'll meet you there."

"Will do."

"Hurry."

"Ten minutes. Max."

CHAPTER 59

The rain and wind had kicked up by the time Cain and Harper sprinted across the open area and knelt behind the SUV, a massive Yukon XL. Not a downpour by any means, but enough to be annoying. It did, however, provide extra cover.

Up the slope, the house appeared unchanged. Cain scoped it. No sign of Tyler or any movement. Still no second floor lights. Maybe Tyler was in a back room. Cain remembered the house plans indicated three upstairs bedrooms; a fourth downstairs, in the far corner from where they were. Maybe Tyler used it for an office and had taken his beer in there to work.

"Looks quiet," he said.

Harper zipped her combat shirt high on her neck. "You ready?"

Cain nodded.

Harper darted toward the barn. Cain followed. They settled along the wall opposite the house. Each placed an eye to one of the cracks between the boards. As his eyes adjusted, Cain sensed movement. Toward the middle of the barn's open space. He could make out no details.

"See anything?" Harper whispered.

"Something. Can't tell what."

They crept toward the side door. A padlock hung from the latch's loop.

Harper opened her small tool pouch and removed what she

needed. She had the lock open in less than half a minute and eased the door inward. A soft creak. They stepped inside.

And there she was.

In a cage.

Sitting, legs pulled up, arms wrapping her knees, a blanket draped over her shoulders. Her head jerked toward them, a startled look on her face. A small squeal escaped her lips.

Cain moved quickly, grasped the bars. "Chelsie?"

She discarded the blanket and jumped to her feet. She wore what appeared to be thin draw-string pants, a tee shirt, and bedroom-type slippers.

"Don't make a sound," Harper said. "We're going to get you out of here."

"Who are you?"

"Cain."

"Harper."

Chelsie's gaze bounced back and forth between them. Confusion etched her face. "How did you find me?"

"Later," Cain said. "Right now we need to crack this cage."

"I've tried," Chelsie said. "This thing is solid."

It was. A cage designed for large animals. Steel, titanium, or some similar combination. The door latch was sturdy, but no match for Harper's skill. She knew her locks.

While Harper worked the lock, Cain looked round. A metal table. With straps. Three floor lamps surrounding it. His work area. A smaller metal table with a pair of tattoo guns and an assortment of inks. A long, wooden work bench along the wall. More ink bottles, a few tools, a canvas drape, something tenting it in the middle. Cain lifted it. In the dark it took a few seconds to sort out what he saw. He recoiled.

Two jars. Two faces staring at him. Shaved heads. One marked with thick slashes of black, the other similar black and orange stripes. Cindy Grant.

"Oh my god. What is that?"

Cain turned. Harper had obviously cracked the lock; she and Chelsie stood only a few feet away, seeing what he saw.

"Don't look," Cain said.

"But…" Chelsie began.

"But nothing. Let's get out of here."

Harper grabbed Chelsie's arm, spun her, looked her in the face. "You can process all this later. Cry and scream and anything you want. Later. Right now, we have to move."

Chelsie let out a long, almost painful breath. She nodded.

"Can you run a mile?" Cain asked.

"I can run a goddamn marathon if it gets me out of here."

"Let's go," Cain said.

The door creaked. Chelsie yelped, eyes popping wide. Cain and Harper spun. Cain pulled one knife, Harper reached for the Glock she had holstered in the small of her back.

A gunshot sounded, its muzzle flash lighting the barn. A thud against the roof. Three men stood just inside the door. Two held handguns, the third a shotgun, each leveled their way.

Cain stepped in front of Chelsie, shielding her with his body. Harper dropped to one knee, raised her weapon.

"Don't move," the guy in the middle said.

The floor lamp just inside the door flicked on.

Tyler stood facing them. Flanking him were Ted Norris and Hank Dixon.

"Drop it," Dixon said to Harper.

She hesitated. Cain knew she was assessing whether she could take the trio down before they could fire again. Truth was she might be able to. Not likely, though. The wild card was the shotgun Tyler held. Looked like a short barrel, probably only eighteen inches. Meant it had a wide scatter pattern. As Uncle Al always said, "Never argue with a shotgun." To which, Uncle Mo would add, "They're autofocus. Point and shoot." Here, there was little chance of missing a target, even three, only fifteen feet away.

Harper made the same calculation. She laid the gun on the ground, stood, raised her hands.

"Kick it this way."

She did.

"That's better," Tyler said.

"Now the knife," Norris said.

Cain dropped it. He had plenty of others.

Norris moved to his left, circling Cain. He grabbed Chelsie's arm. Cain turned, stiffened. Norris pressed the gun against the side of her head.

"Don't even think about it."

Cain knew he had no good move available. Better to buy time. Wait for a mistake.

"Cell phones," Tyler said.

Harper pulled hers from her pocket, laid it on the floor. Cain followed suit.

Dixon waved his gun. "Down. Face down."

Cain and Harper hesitated.

"Do it," Norris said. "Or she's dead."

They complied.

Dixon gathered their weapons and phones, then carried them to the table and dropped them there.

"What the fuck?" Norris said. He spun toward Tyler. "You kept their heads?"

"They're trophies."

"Are you fucking crazy?"

"You collect deer mounts. These are mine."

Dixon glanced that way. "Tyler, that's some sick shit."

"Really?" Tyler said. "What do you care?"

"You behead them," Dixon said. "Display them. Asking the world to sniff around. That's crazy."

"What I do or don't do with them is my business. The thrill of the hunt is all you need to focus on."

Silence fell. Cain tensed. Would they go at each other? Would they give him and Harper an opening? Maybe he could ramp up the pressure, complete the fracture.

"You aren't going to get away with this," Cain said.

Tyler laughed. "How do you figure that?"

"Chief Cutler knows we're here."

That gave Tyler a momentary pause.

"She knows you're the one," Harper said.

"And yet she isn't here," Tyler said. "That tells me she doesn't know shit."

"She knows enough," Cain said.

"Then we better clean this mess up."

"What've you got in mind?" Norris asked.

"She's not quite ready but she'll have to do. The other two are simply a bonus."

"We going to hunt all three?" Dixon asked.

"You got a better idea?" Tyler said. "Or one that would be more fun?"

"I don't know," Dixon said. "All three? What if one of them escapes?"

"It's a fucking island," Tyler said.

"Still," Dixon added.

"Let's sweeten the pot," Tyler said. "We'll pony up a total of a hundred grand. You could win it all if you bag the three of them."

"What are you talking about?" Chelsie said. Her voice was tight, almost hysterical.

"You don't think I did all this work on you for fun, do you?" Tyler chuckled. "You're simply the prey." He moved to this left, looked down at Cain. "And you guys are the icing." He turned toward the two men. "You ready?"

"Do we really have a choice here?" Norris said. A question that didn't need an answer.

Dixon nodded. "Let's do it."

"Search them," Tyler said.

While Tyler provided cover Dixon knelt beside Harper, ran his hands over her legs, sides, around her waist. He did the same to Cain, finding two more knives—one sheathed along his thigh, the other strapped to his ankle. He tossed them out of the way.

Norris appeared with a roll of duct tape. Options raced through Cain's mind. None were good. Three armed men, he and Harper face down. The main deciding factor was the black hole of the shotgun muzzle that stared at him like a dead eye. Buy time. They were to be hunted. That means released. An opportunity might yet arise.

Norris taped their wrists together behind their backs, before making several wraps around their chests, pinning their arms to their sides. He did the same with Chelsie. The trio then led them outside to the SUV. Tyler lifted the back hatch. The second and third row seats were folded flat. The massive cargo area was empty except for a couple of folded towels and one of those metallic, folding windshield screens.

"Inside."

Cain hesitated.

Tyler stepped toward him, looked up into his eyes. "Either crawl in or I'll have them shoot you and we'll dump your body in."

Cain complied. Harper and Chelsie followed.

"Face down," Tyler said. "All of you. Side by side."

Norris bound their ankles with the tape, then slammed the door. Cain could hear them talking.

"Hank, you go get the boat ready," Tyler said. "Ted and I'll grab the crossbows and meet you at the launch."

Cain heard footsteps crunching the gravel, moving away.

"What are they going to do?" Chelsie asked.

"They're going to take us somewhere and hunt us," Harper said.

"No." Chelsie began to sob.

"Chelsie," Cain said. "Listen to me. Don't panic."

"What? Aren't you?"

"No," Cain said. "For them to hunt us, they have to let us go. That gives us a chance."

"But they have the weapons."

"Not all of them."

"What does that mean?"

"It means that if you keep your head, do exactly as Harper and I say, we just might get out of this."

CHAPTER 60

"I was driving by and I saw your light on," Jimmy Rankin said as he walked into Laura Cutler's office. "What's up?"

"Catching up on paperwork."

Her desk top was empty, only her cell laying there, right in front of her.

"No, you're not," Rankin said.

She shrugged. "Waiting to hear from Cain and Harper."

Rankin glanced at his watch. "Might be a bit early to get all sideways."

"Feels late to me."

"They're out there sneaking around. Sometimes that goes quickly and other times it takes a while."

"Or goes wrong?"

"That, too."

Cutler spun her phone with a finger.

"Want to take a ride?" Rankin said.

She considered that. She was going insane sitting here. Doing nothing. She stood. "I'll drive."

"No, you won't. Your Bronco has those big old gold emblems on the doors and that light bar. Might as well hang a disco ball on the roof and let everybody know we're snooping around."

"Good point."

"My car, on the other hand, is completely invisible."

It was. Rankin drove a plain, vanilla, sliver Taurus. Looked no different than the thousands of others on the road.

Ten minutes later they rolled by Martin Stenson's estate and continued south toward Tyler's place. Rain flooded the windscreen, the wipers fighting to keep up.

"Shitty night for a drive," Cutler said.

"We could've stayed at the station." Rankin grinned. "Your desk was all cozy and warm."

"And boring."

"How you want to do this?" Rankin asked.

"Just a drive by, first."

"Sounds good."

Headlights approached. A large vehicle. It whipped by, its wake rocking the car slightly.

"That was Tyler," Cutler said.

"And Ted Norris."

"You see anyone else in there?"

Rankin shook his head. "Nope." He glanced in the rearview mirror. "Want to follow them?"

Cutler considered that. It wouldn't be possible to do that and stay invisible. Especially at night on quiet rural roads. "No. Let's go ahead."

They passed the road to Tyler's place. His home was barely visible in the distance. The rain blurred the landscape lighting. Another couple of minutes and they reached the road that demarcated the line between Tyler's property and Clovis Wilson's cotton fields.

"Turn here," Cutler said.

"Where?"

"Right there." She pointed. "On that road."

He did. The car gyrated. He came to a stop. "Why're we here?"

"This is the road Bobby Cain pointed out. It's the one he and Harper were going to use."

He nodded and eased forward. "I hope we don't get stuck out here."

"Wimp."

"This ain't no Bronco."

The path rose and fell, the car slipped a couple of times, but they soon saw the rear of Cain's Mercedes. Rankin came to a stop. They climbed out.

Fat rain drops slapped the overhead leaves and pine boughs. Drips fell on Cutler's face. One slid down her back.

"It's all locked up," she said. She walked around to the front of the car and looked into the darkness ahead. "They must still be up there."

"Want to wait?"

She sighed.

"Maybe go take a look around?" Rankin said. "We know Tyler ain't there right now."

"He might come back."

"So? We can just say we dropped by to say hello."

"Like he'd buy that."

"Right about now I don't give a big old goddamn what he buys," Rankin said. "If he's the one that did this to those women, then he's got one up there on his place most likely. To me, that changes things."

"We might interfere with what Cain and Harper are doing."

"Yeah, well, this ain't their job. It's ours."

Cutler nodded. "Let's go."

CHAPTER 61

No, they didn't have all of Cain's weapons. Not close. He still had five blades in his possession. The two throwing knives in the soles of his boots. A simple twist of the heels and they would be released. Two others in his belt buckle. Small, stacked inside the metallic rectangle. What Uncle Al, who had hand-made Cain's first pair, called "T-Pokers," saying, "You never know when you might have to poke someone in the throat, or the eye." T-shaped handles that when grasped in his fists allowed the finely-honed, leaf-shaped blades to protrude between his index and middle fingers. Perfect stabbing, or "poking" weapons. Very lethal. Finally, his favorite throwing knife sheathed high in the back of his shirt, between his shoulder blades.

When someone searched for weapons, particularly someone who was a rank amateur, they checked pockets, shoes, arms, legs, even a grab of the crotch. But high on the back? No one ever thinks of that. Tyler and his crew hadn't. They found three knives, a reasonable number. Enough to satisfy them. Cain never went into a potentially combative situation with less than eight.

As comforting as that was, they were of little use right now. Hands, arms, and legs bound with multiple wraps of duct tape allowed little movement and no chance of slipping free. Hopefully, their bonds would be cut before they were released for the hunt.

Tyler drove, Ted Norris shotgun. Cain, Harper, and Chelsie

managed to shift into positions that were more or less comfortable. Not really, but at least acceptable. Like three rolled carpets. They lay on their sides, knees flexed slightly, Chelsie between them.

The storm had arrived. Rain pounded the roof, its drumbeat echoing inside the cavernous SUV. Cain tried to sense where they were going. Turns, distances, types of roads. But since he didn't really know the area, it was a futile effort. So, better to engage his captors. Try to dig out useful intel.

"Where are we going?" Cain asked.

"Somewhere off the grid," Tyler said.

"And then what?"

"I told you. You run. We hunt."

"Leave Chelsie out of this," Harper said.

Norris twisted in his seat. His weapon rested on the seat back, the muzzle angled down toward them. "She's the star of the show."

"Tell me, Tyler," Harper asked. "What's in this for you? I thought you didn't like hunting."

"I don't like hunting animals for sport. Humans are a different story."

"Oh, that's right. You think that's fairer somehow."

"Isn't it?"

"Yeah, right. Three guys hunting a young, naked, and barefoot girl is so very fair."

"They could escape," Tyler said. "That's part the thrill."

"Escape?" Cain said. "From an island?"

"It's possible."

"You're such a sport," Harper said. "Daddy must be proud."

"Shut up."

Harper wasn't finished. She was going full PsyOps on him. Make him angry. Make him miss something. Overlook some crucial detail. It might work. It might not. They had little to lose.

"Why wouldn't he be?" Harper said. "I mean, his little boy uses daddy's money to buy young girls, mark them up like some childhood coloring book, and play big game hunter."

"I said, shut up."

Norris twisted further, nudged the top of her head with the muzzle of the gun. "You heard him."

Cain picked it up. "Not to mention displaying your work. Sort of like tacking third-grade crayon drawings on the family fridge. Shouting 'look at me. See how clever I am.'"

"And taking their heads as trophies," Harper said. "Like collecting trinkets."

"Yeah," Cain said. "Daddy, look what I made for you in shop class."

Norris rapped the gun muzzle against Cain's scalp. "Shut the fuck up."

Cain did. He and Harper had gotten the reaction they wanted. Best to let Tyler stew on it.

Fifteen minutes later, the SUV turned off pavement onto an uneven gravel road. The behemoth rocked slightly and pebbles pinged the undercarriage. It crunched to a stop.

CHAPTER 62

The house was quiet. Cutler rang the doorbell, knowing Tyler wasn't there, but continuing the narrative that if they were wrong about seeing him and Norris on the road, or if someone else was there, it would look like a more casual visit. As expected, no answer. Peering through the adjacent windows revealed a couple of lights on, but no one inside. She came off the porch to where Rankin stood, surveying the grounds.

They checked the garage, peering through the side door window. Dark, Tyler's BMW inside.

A gravel drive forked off the paved one and led down and around the barn. They walked that way. Also dark, but the side door stood open. Cutler felt an electric current zip up her back. She looked at Rankin. He nodded, unholstered his service weapon.

Cutler pulled her own weapon, pointing it toward the ground, and approached. Rankin moved to her left, keeping a clear line of sight to the doorway.

She peeked inside.

"What the hell?"

"Are you kidding me?" Rankin said.

A large cage dominated the center of the space. Door open. No one there. She saw a blanket, an air mattress, two empty water bottles, and a toilet chair inside.

"Look at this," Rankin said. He stood next to a pair of metal tables. The larger equipped with wide leather straps, the smaller supporting a pair of tattoo guns and an assortment of ink bottles.

"I didn't want to believe it," Cutler said. "Guess I have to now."

"So, where's the girl?"

"You think Cain and Harper have her?"

"Wouldn't they have called?" Rankin asked.

"Maybe they want to get completely clear first."

"So maybe they're working their way back to Cain's car?"

"Possible." Cutler looked around. "But I don't like it."

"You got his number, right? Call him."

She pulled her cell out, found Cain's number in her recent call list, and punched it. It's chirping caused her to wheel around toward a table near the wall. She walked that way.

"What the fuck?" She pointed to the two cell phones, three knives, and the Glock that littered its surface.

"I don't like none of this," Rankin said.

"He has them," Cutler said. "In his goddamn SUV."

"Guess we should've followed him," Rankin said.

"Damn it."

Rankin walked around her. Lifted a canvas sheet. "Oh, Jesus." He tossed the covering aside.

Cutler gasped. "Are you kidding me?"

"Those have to be Rose and Cindy."

"My god, Tyler Stenson has completely split from the program." Cutler shook her head. "Call in a couple of the guys. Get them out here to protect the scene."

"What if Tyler comes back?"

"Wish he would." She led the way back outside. "We aren't visiting or trespassing or whatever anymore. This is a crime scene."

Rankin pulled his phone and made the call. He arranged for a couple of officers to come cover the scene and then asked that a BOLO be put out on Tyler's SUV. They climbed in Rankin's car.

"Tyler's lost his freaking mind," Rankin said.

"I think he did that a long time ago. Right now he's trying to clean up a mess."

"Where to?" Rankin asked.

"Martin Stenson's place. Maybe he can tell us something that'll help find his son."

CHAPTER 63

The boat was nice. And expensive. Sleek white with a dark blue water line, maybe thirty-five feet, covered bridge with a pair of captain's chairs. Perfect for skiing, fishing, or taking the family for a cruise on Tims Ford Lake. All driven by an engine with the horsepower to vibrate the hull.

Vibrations that Cain felt deep in his bones.

He and Harper lay side by side on the galley floor, Hank Dixon charged with keeping an eye on them, sitting at the small table, gun in hand. Chelsie up on the bridge with Tyler and Norris.

The rain and wind had kicked up, churning the water into a washboard that made the ride rough. Cain and Harper bounced against each other. Their wrists and arms were still bound, but the tape around their ankles had been removed. Made it easier for Tyler and crew to herd them on board and for them to descend into the galley under their own power. A strategic error on Tyler's part. Gave Cain and Harper weapons. He was fairly skilled with his feet, Harper more so. If it came to that. If the opportunity arose. Cain knew it just might not.

"You okay?" Cain asked Harper.

"All things considered, I'm peachy."

"Shut up," Dixon said.

Cain looked up at him. "How'd Tyler drag you into this?"

"Who says he did? Maybe it was my idea."

"It wasn't," Harper said. "You're a follower."

Dixon recoiled, his head jerking back. "You don't know shit."

"I know losers. Weak sisters. Seen a million of them."

Dixon turned in his seat. Kicked her hip. "You say another word and I'll splatter your brains all over this boat."

"No, you won't," Harper said. "Not without permission."

He kicked her again. Harder.

"Not to mention that would leave a ton of forensic evidence to deal with."

"Ever tried to clean up a crime scene?" Cain asked. "All that blood and brain tissue; it seeps into nooks and crannies. I can see you mopping the floor, scrubbing the walls, even on your hands and knees with a toothbrush, and still you'll end up on death row."

Dixon tapped the gun muzzle on the table top. "You guys think you're clever, don't you?"

Cain smiled at him. "It's been said. But what I'm unsure about is how clever you are."

Now, Dixon smiled. "Enough so that you're the one on the floor wrapped up like a mummy."

"And you'll be the one in handcuffs," Harper said.

"Not likely. You won't be around to see it anyway."

"So, you're just going to blindly follow Tyler's orders? Let his personal demons lead you to prison?"

Dixon stared at her.

"He's crazy. You know that, don't you?" Harper said. "This is his game, not yours. His pathology. His daddy issues. You can still unwind it. For yourself, anyway."

"I think it's a little late for that. Even if I wanted to. Which I don't."

"So you helped hunt down the two women?" Cain asked.

"Not the first one. She escaped before Tyler finished his work."

Suspicions confirmed.

"But the second one?" Harper asked.

He shrugged.

"Was it your bolt that killed her?" Harper asked.

Dixon shook his head. "Ted won that round."

"So you didn't actually kill anyone?"

"Like that matters."

"Sure it does," Cain said. "If you tell the truth you might buy your way to a lesser charge. With luck and a good lawyer, you might even walk."

Tyler descended the stairs, stopping halfway down, ducking his head, peering into the galley. "Everything okay down here?"

"All good," Dixon said.

"Ten minutes and we'll be there." Tyler climbed back to the deck.

Cain felt the boat veer to starboard, then straighten again.

"Ten minutes," Harper said. "What you decide in the next ten minutes will change your life forever."

"So this is your divide and conquer strategy?" Dixon said. "Convince me to save your asses?"

"And yours," Cain said.

Dixon smiled, nodded. "Exactly how do you see that working?"

"Cut us loose," Cain said. "Give her the gun. We'll take it from there."

"Give *her* the gun? Not you?"

"She's a better shot."

"Never would've figured that. I guess life's full of surprises."

"Eight minutes," Harper said.

"What's it going to be?" Cain asked.

Dixon shook his head. "Not going to happen."

"So, go ahead," Harper said. "It's the plan after all. Tyler's plan. And he's the band leader."

"Actually, the plan is to give you a chance," Dixon said. "Let you run while we hunt you down."

"Your sense of fair play is heartwarming," Harper said. "Bet your parents are thrilled with the way you turned out."

Dixon dug the toe of his boot into her ribs. "You're making this so easy." He stood, looked down at them. "This is going to be fun." He climbed the stairs. Not all the way. Just to the top rung. Still able to turn his head and see them. Raindrops tapped against the bill of his cap.

"Here's the way I see it," Cain said. "They'll release us. Probably all three of us at the same time."

"And if they don't? If they do it one at a time?"

"Then we're in trouble."

"So you don't have a plan B?"

"You and I'll be fine. Either they'll never find us, or we can take them one by one."

"Your confidence isn't very comforting."

"You've been in dicier situations."

Harper gave him a wry smile. "Remind me when that was."

"It's Chelsie that'll need help. She's not cut out for this."

"What's plan A then?"

The whine of the engine dropped, the ride smoothed. A sharp turn to port. The engine idled, then reversed, and soon the stern hull crunched against land.

Dixon came back down the stairs. "It's showtime."

CHAPTER 64

"Martin," Laura Cutler said with a nod.

Martin Stenson stood at his open doorway, his confusion obvious. His gaze moved back and forth between Cutler and Rankin. "Chief, Jimmy, what brings you out on a night like this?"

"We need to talk," Cutler said.

"About what?"

"Maybe inside," Cutler said.

Stenson stepped back. Cutler and Rankin entered the cavernous foyer.

"What's going on?" Stenson asked.

"Maybe we should sit."

Stenson hesitated, his confusion deepening. "Okay."

Cutler and Rankin shed their jackets, hanging them on the coat rack adjacent to the door. Stenson led them into his den. Stuffed heads covered the walls. Deer, boar, Bighorn sheep. A bearskin hung over a wooden rack just left of a massive river-rock fireplace. They sat in deep leather chairs around an oak coffee table.

"Where's Tyler?" Cutler asked, getting right to it.

"Home, I suspect. Unless he's out somewhere."

"He's out," Cutler said. "And he screwed up big time."

"What on earth are you talking about?"

Cutler laid it out. What they had seen in Tyler's barn. That Cain and Harper had been there, Cain's car abandoned, the pair now unaccounted for.

"I don't understand," Stenson said.

"Did you know that Tyler once worked at a tattoo parlor?" Cutler asked. "While he was at Princeton?"

"No. Why would he? He didn't need a job."

"I don't know why. All I know is that he has a bunch of tattooing equipment in his barn. And a cage that's equipped as a prison. Now he's off somewhere with Ted Norris."

"We saw them leaving his place," Rankin said. "In his SUV."

Deep lines creased Stenson's face. "What are you saying?"

"I'm saying it looks like Tyler could be the guy we're looking for." She sighed. "The one that hunted those women."

Stenson shook his head. "No. That's not possible. Not Tyler. He'd never."

"Then he can tell us that," Cutler said. "But right now we need to find him."

"I'll call him," Stenson said.

"We tried," Rankin said. "He's not answering."

"He will if it's me."

Cutler shrugged, waved a hand saying go ahead.

Stenson called, listened for a minute, then said, "Tyler, when you get this contact me immediately." He disconnected the call and laid his phone on the table.

"Any idea where he'd go?" Cutler asked. "He and Norris?"

"If they were trying to whack a couple of folks?" Rankin added.

"Aren't you jumping to conclusions?" Stenson said.

"Are we?" Cutler asked. "I'm open to another explanation of the facts."

Stenson stared at her, saying nothing. His shoulders sagged.

"So, any ideas?" Cutler asked.

He shook his head. "Hank Dixon might know. He and Ted are tight." He reached for his phone. "I can call him."

"Maybe not," Cutler said. "We'll drop by his place and surprise him. Maybe that's where Tyler and Norris were headed."

Stenson leaned forward and massaged his temples, staring at the floor, his pain palpable. He looked up. "You don't really think Tyler did any of this, do you?"

"I don't know." She stood. "That's why I need to talk with him."

Stenson stood, a bit unsteady. He walked them to the door.

Cutler hesitated in the open doorway and turned toward Stenson. She laid a hand on his arm. "Look, we don't know for sure. All we want to do is find him, talk to him, and see if he can make sense out of this."

Stenson nodded.

"I'd appreciate it if you'd call me if you hear from him," Cutler said.

"I will."

CHAPTER 65

They did indeed release the three of them together.

Not before Tyler explained the "rules of the game," as he called them.

Cain and Harper, Chelsie between them, stood on a rocky shoreline; a thick, pine forest waited behind them. They faced the three hunters, each gripping a crossbow. The nearest land Cain could see was a good eight-hundred yards away. Not a viable option since the bad guys had a boat. Not that that would be Cain's choice anyway. Better to get them into the trees. Where he and Harper had an advantage. Of sorts.

The rain now hard, the wind gusting. Felt like a real storm was coming in. Good cover. For both sight and sound.

"You'll get a ten minute start," Tyler said. "Then we'll come. If you get away, you win. If you don't, we do. Simple. Straightforward. Any questions?"

"You can't be serious," Chelsie said. "You're going to hunt us?"

Tyler smiled. "We are."

"And we're just supposed to run?" She set her jaw. "I won't do it."

Tyler took a single step forward. "You will. Or we'll shoot you right here."

A sob escaped Chelsie's throat. "When did you lose your fucking mind?"

Another step forward. "We can either go for a clean kill, or one that's more painful." He smiled. "If I were you, I wouldn't press your point any further."

Cain laid a hand on Chelsie's arm. She flinched.

Cain caught Dixon's eye. Raised an eyebrow.

Dixon smiled. "I'm feeling particularly lucky tonight. I think I'm going to win the entire hundred K."

"Like the Old West," Harper said. "We have a price on our heads."

Tyler gave her a nod. "That's the perfect way of putting it."

Harper stared at him. "So do you."

Tyler raised his arm, pushed up the sleeve of his jacket, and fingered his watch. "Your ten minutes starts…now."

Cain and Harper each grabbed one of Chelsie's arms and dragged her into the trees.

"Where are we going?" Chelsie asked.

"Follow Harper," Cain said. "I'm right behind you."

"We're going to open some distance," Harper said. "So keep up."

They were off. Harper led the way through the trees, over bumps and piles of limestone. Cain flashed on Cindy Grant. Running for her life. Barefoot. At least Tyler had left them clothed and shoed. Another strategic error on his part.

They covered several hundred yards before Harper stopped in a small clearing.

"Why are we stopping?" Chelsie asked.

"Just do exactly as we say," Cain said. "First thing is, we're going to hide you. Then we'll handle these guys."

"They have bows," Chelsie said.

"And they're full-on amateurs," Harper said.

"And you're not?"

"Not even close," Harper said.

"I don't understand."

Cain grabbed her arm and led her into the trees. He found a slight depression in the ground. He nodded toward it. "Lay down."

"What? It's wet and smelly."

Cain gripped her upper arm. "We don't have time to explain everything. If you want to get out of this, lay down. Right there.

We'll cover you with leaves. Don't move, don't make a sound. We'll come back for you."

"You're going to leave me here?"

Harper stepped near her. "Chelsie? Look at me. We can't maneuver and keep an eye on you. You need to be off the radar. Out of sight."

"And if they kill you? What am I supposed to do?"

Harper grasped the sides of her face, got close. "Do what we say. Get down and stay down. We're going to set up an ambush."

"They have weapons. We have nothing."

Cain knelt, twisted the heel of one boot and then the other, removing the two knives secreted inside. He handed one to Chelsie, the other to Harper. "Now we do too."

"I'm scared," Chelsie said.

"Good," Harper said. "Lay down. Now."

Chelsie did. Cain and Harper scooped wet leaves and pine needles over her. To Chelsie's credit, she finally got it, let them do their work. They covered her entire body, leaving only her face exposed. Cain broke off a well-needled pine branch.

"Close your eyes and relax," Cain said. She did and he placed the final piece of her camouflage over her face. "Can you breathe okay?"

"I guess. But it tickles."

"Whatever you do, don't move," Harper said. "No matter what happens."

"I won't."

"We'll be back soon."

"Let's go," Cain said.

The plan was simple. Cain circled left, Harper right. Backtracking and flanking the trio. No doubt the three of them would split up. It was a competition after all, so each was left solo, and vulnerable.

The rain beat against the tree canopy, thunder rumbled overhead. Cain wound his way through the pines, careful to step on the wet needles. He moved laterally until he could make out water between the trees, then backtracked toward the hunters. Flanking their most likely path. A hundred yards father and he veered inland, an encircling move. He stopped, listened. Nothing.

Another fifty yards, another halt. He repeated this until he finally heard footsteps. Heading his way. He settled behind a pair of twisted trees, peered between their trunks. He removed one of the "T-Pokers" from his belt buckle, fisting its handle, the blade protruding between his index and middle finger. He waited.

Hank Dixon came through the trees, angled just to Cain's right. He clutched his bow in one hand, the other pushing aside branches. His head swiveled. On the hunt. Unaware of Cain. He moved forward, gaze aimed down, carefully stepping over the uneven terrain, scattered with limestone and undergrowth. He passed within ten feet of where Cain crouched.

Cain sprang. He slammed his left elbow into the back of Dixon's head. Air whooshed from his lungs and he tumbled forward, face down. The bow slipped from his grasp. Cain was on him.

Cain used his own weight to press Dixon's body against the ground. He felt the firmness of the gun Dixon had stuffed beneath his belt in the small of his back. So much for a fair hunt. He guessed crossbows weren't enough of an advantage for these guys.

Cain grabbed a handful of Dixon's hair, pulled his head back, and pressed the knife's point into the soft recess of his neck. Just over the carotid artery.

"Not a sound," Cain said.

Dixon, initially stunned, now began to resist. Tried to twist free. The blade punctured his skin. He froze.

"Are you feeling lucky now?" Cain asked.

"Please," Dixon said.

"Please what?"

"Let me go. I'll help you find Tyler and Ted."

"I think Harper and I can handle that."

"I'll tell the truth. I promise. Everything. The whole story."

"You mean like how you guys purchased and hunted young women? That story?"

"It was Tyler. He bought them."

"I know. But you and Norris joined the hunt. And placed bets on it."

"I'm sorry. I really am. I'll surrender to the police. Whatever you want."

"Too late for that," Cain said.

"No, please."

"Tell me," Cain said. "Are Norris and Tyler carrying guns, too? Or is it just you that's breaking your so-called rules?"

Dixon hesitated.

"I'll take that as a yes."

"Please. I'll do whatever you want."

In a perfect world, taking Dixon in, letting him spill his guts, would be a viable option. But leaving him here, able to re-enter the fray, yell, whatever, was an unacceptable risk. And, of course, there was that whole karma thing.

"I wish I had time to chat," Cain said, "but I don't."

The blade sliced through Dixon's carotid. Blood gushed and spurted. Dixon bucked, Cain held tight. Twisted the blade, yanked it free.

Took only a couple of minutes for Dixon to fall limp. Done.

Cain wiped blood from his hand on a wad of damp pine needles. He stood. Now to find Norris and Tyler. And Harper. She had no idea that both men were armed with something more lethal than a crossbow.

CHAPTER 66

Ted Norris. Harper heard him well before she could see him. Winding through the pines that were less dense here. He lumbered down the slope toward where she had secreted herself behind a limestone outcropping. He wasn't overly concerned with stealth. She'd seen it before. The arrogance of the hunter when he believed he had all the advantages over his prey. Led to mistakes. Unnecessary exposure to ambush or counter-attack. She couldn't imagine him being a very good deer hunter, let alone humans.

Lightning flickered overhead, strobing off the trees and Norris' face. He recoiled from the flash.

"Jesus fucking Christ," he said.

Thunder rumbled through. Loud and sudden. Almost strong enough to vibrate the cool, damp rocks she pressed her cheek against.

He was now only fifty feet up the slope. He spun, looking in every direction. Not sure which way to go now. Then he casually unzipped his fly and took a leak.

Harper waited. Which way would he go? Hopefully, toward her. She didn't want to track him anymore. She wanted to end this. She pulled the rock she fisted against her chest. *Come on.*

Norris zipped up, propped his crossbow over one shoulder, and shuffled down the slope. Its steepness caused him to step almost sideways as he descended. Loose rocks tumbled ahead of him. Unsure of his footing, his attention focused on each step.

When he reached her, she leapt toward him, slamming the rock against his face. He staggered, but didn't go down. The blood that erupted from his eyebrow looked black in the darkness. He raised his arm in reflex, self-defense, but it didn't help. She punched him in his larynx. He dropped the bow, bent over, and clutched at his throat, gagging and wheezing.

Harper tossed the rock aside and snatched up the crossbow. She stepped a few feet away, removed one of the four bolts that protruded from the holder beneath the right limb, and fitted it into position. She levered back the string and leveled it at the center of his chest.

"Hello," Harper said.

He could finally breathe and straighten up, unsteady on his feet, pain and confusion on his face. "What the fuck?"

"Isn't like hunting deer, is it? They tend not to fight back." She froze his gaze with her own. "Neither do scared and naked young women."

He actually sneered at her. Amazing. "So, what are you going to do? Kill me?"

"I'd like to. I really would. Fact is, you're lucky you ran into me instead of Cain. He wouldn't hesitate."

"So what? You think you can simply march me out of here? Little old you?"

"No. But I can do this."

She shot him in the thigh.

He recoiled, moaned. "What the hell?" He clutched at the bolt, blood seeping between his fingers.

"I can shoot you in the throat if you'd rather." She settled another bolt into position.

"You're one crazy bitch."

"I'm flattered. I truly am."

His hand disappeared behind his back. It reappeared with a Glock, its muzzle swinging up toward her. She shot him. In the throat.

He staggered. The gun thudded against the ground. His chest heaved, each wheezing breath a red spray. He listed left, fell. His gaze found her, eyes wide. His pupils dilated into two unseeing black pools.

She picked up the Glock, stuffed it into her belt, and, holding the crossbow in her left hand, climbed the slope. She didn't get far before she sensed movement. To her right. A form stepped from the trees. Cain.

He walked to where she stood. She pointed down to where the late Ted Norris lay.

"Two down, one to go," Cain said.

"Which one?" Harper asked.

"Dixon."

She nodded. "He have a gun?"

"He did."

She patted the Glock. "Norris, too. So we have to assume Tyler is similarly armed."

"Be surprised if he wasn't."

CHAPTER 67

"You don't really believe any of that, do you?" Rankin asked. "That Tyler might not be the guy?"

They were in Rankin's car headed back toward town, toward Hank Dixon's place.

"No, I don't," Cutler said. "There's just too much that points his way." She shook her head. "He had a fucking cage, for Christ's sake."

"And heads in jars."

"That's too creepy for words."

"I never liked him much," Rankin said.

"I know."

"A fancy pants. And spoiled."

Cutler laughed. "Last time his name came up you called him a pussy."

"That, too," Rankin said. "It's a strange rock we live on."

He turned onto Hank Dixon's street and rolled to a stop in front of his house.

"Looks dark," Cutler said.

"Don't see his truck."

"Or his boat. Doesn't he usually park it over there by the garage?"

"Yep."

"You think he's with Tyler and Norris? Out on the lake?"

Rankin looked at her. "Good place to dump bodies."

"I hate it when you're right."

"Happens a lot." He grinned.

"Occasionally."

"I'll take that."

"Okay," Cutler said. "Let's say that's their plan. Where would they go?"

"The lake's a hundred and seventy miles long. Stretches all the way to Winchester. A ton of hidden coves and out-of-the-way places."

Cutler considered that. "Where do you think they'd put in? We could start there."

"Not down by the marina," Rankin said. "That'd be too risky."

"Nearest other place is Cooper's Landing."

Cooper's Landing was five miles up the road from Moss Landing. Named after Jonathan Cooper who had owned the land before his death decades earlier. It wasn't really a landing. No dock or anything like that. Just a gravel lot off the county road that possessed ample parking and angled down to the lake. Place where fishermen and boaters could easily slide their rigs into the water.

"Want to check it out?" Rankin said.

"Probably should."

Ten minutes later they arrived. It was dark, no one around. Typical for this time of night. Particularly in rain like this.

Made seeing Hank Dixon's truck and boat trailer, and Tyler's SUV, even more ominous.

"I really, really hate it when your hunches are right," Cutler said.

"This time I do, too." Rankin aimed his car out toward the water, cranked up the high beams. "See anything?"

"A lake."

"We need a boat."

"And some idea where to look."

Rankin pulled out his cell phone. "I'll call my cousin Tommy Earl. He's got a nice boat."

"It's late. He might not appreciate it."

"He's up. He watches old movies all night." He bounced an eyebrow. "When he ain't out doing some night fishing."

"Do it."

CHAPTER 68

Shivers racked Chelsie's entire body, chattering her teeth. Even her joints ached. The coldness of the damp soil penetrated deeply inside. Or was it the smothering fear that sent electric ripples through her?

Rain battered the trees, dribbles splatted against her cover, seeping inside, adding to her misery. She tried to ignore all of it, even the insects that crawled over her legs, body, one even trying to invade her nose.

She had thought she'd never be in a worse situation than that cage. But this might be it.

How long had it been? Seemed hours. How much longer could she lay here?

A hard shiver shook her. Her hands and feet felt numb.

What if Harper and Cain had been killed? The three men hunting her would eventually find her, wouldn't they? They had plenty of time. She had seen no signs of life when she stepped off the boat and into this isolated world.

How big was this island? Was there a way off?

Would someone else come to rescue her? Did anyone ever come here?

They had told her to stay put, isolated, buried. Said that she shouldn't move, much less crawl free from this frigid cocoon.

But if they had been killed? What then?

She had heard nothing. No footsteps, no conversations, nothing. No one had come anywhere near where she lay.

An insect bit her calf, causing her to jump.

She couldn't do it. Not just lay here and wait. She'd freeze to death if nothing else.

She sat up and began brushing the leaves and pine needles from her. She stood. Dirt and debris matted her hair, invaded her clothing, prickling her flesh. She shook her hair out.

Lightning pulsed above the trees, followed quickly by a peel of throaty thunder. She looked around. Which way should she go?

She sensed the boat was behind her. But was it? They had run this way and that, right and left, up and down, all seemingly random. And in the dark. If this was indeed an island, any direction would bring her to a shoreline. But, so what? Swim? To were? How far? She wasn't that good of a swimmer. Never really liked water. Never felt comfortable in it. Even a pool. And here? A lake? Middle of the night in a thunder storm?

Tears pushed against her eyes.

No, Chelsie. Don't break. You've come this far. Move. Go anywhere but don't just stand here.

She chose what she believed to be forward, away from where the boat was docked. Maybe the far end of the island offered hope. Maybe it wasn't an island at all.

She had covered only a hundred yards, max, when she sensed movement. Up ahead in the trees. She froze. Even her breathing halted.

Was it Cain or Harper? The police? How would they know what was going on? Should she call out to them?

No. Best to be cautious. She crouched, crab-walked behind a small pine. It offered essentially no cover but it's all she saw.

The footsteps advanced toward her. A form emerged among the trees. A vague outline, no details. Male, female, who? She couldn't tell. Her chest ached. She could feel her heart hammering so hard that it was almost audible.

The shadow pushed between the final two trees and stepped into the clear. Only fifteen feet away.

Her heart flipped and sank. It was him.

"There you are." He smiled.

Her head swiveled, searching for an escape. She coiled, ready to run. When her gaze returned to him, he directed his crossbow at her.

"You take one step, and I'll kill you."

"Please?"

Tyler smiled. "Looks like I win the big prize."

CHAPTER 69

Tommy Earl's boat was indeed a nice fishing rig. And he knew how to handle it. Once Cutler and Rankin were on board, he gunned it out into the lake, bucking the washboard surface as if he'd done it a thousand times. Probably had.

The canvas-topped bridge was tight, just spacious enough for the three of them, but it provided cover from the hammering rain. Lightning streaked the sky but the wind had diminished somewhat.

"Nice night for a boat ride, ain't it?" Tommy Earl said.

"Not exactly my idea of fun," Cutler said.

Tommy Earl laughed. "I figure we'd start by running the far side of the lake. It's fairly narrow here, and there aren't many houses on the north shore along this stretch. Seems to me if they're looking for a place to hide out or whatever, it'd be over on the north side. I mean, if you ain't going to cross the lake, why would you need a boat?"

That made sense to Cutler and she said so.

Tims Ford Lake was one of the most beautiful lakes anyone was likely to see. Long and narrow with a disordered—almost randomly so—shoreline, pocked with finger-like inlets, shallow coves, and a few small islands. It stretched over a hundred and seventy miles from Lynchburg to Winchester. Though there were many pockets of civilization, mainly clusters of cabins, and some impressively larger homes, it was mostly free of habitation. The thick forests that surrounded it draped over the slopes and extended down to the shoreline.

Finding a single boat that was likely secreted in one of the many undulations, seemed an impossible task. Especially at night in this weather. Cutler wasn't optimistic. But the truth was she saw no other options. She no longer had doubts that Tyler, Dixon, and Norris were in this together and they now had Cain and Harper, and the missing girl, with them. She also harbored no illusions about the fact that they would kill all three of them. Probably bury or deep six the bodies. They had to now. Too late to backtrack.

When they approached the far side, a hundred yards offshore, Tommy Lee turned east. Rankin used a pair of binoculars to scan the shoreline. Cutler did the same, sans binoculars.

The minutes dripped by. The rain slackened some and the storm seemed to move to the west, now distant flickers and rumbles.

"I got a searchlight mounted up front if you want to use that," Tommy Earl said.

Cutler considered it. "No. They'd be able to see it for miles. Know where we are."

"And who we are," Rankin added. "Even if they hear or see the boat they'll just think it's someone out fishing or something."

"In this weather? Fishing?" Cutler said.

"I would," Tommy Earl said.

More minutes melted away. Cutler's pessimism grew.

But sometimes the proverbial 'needle in the haystack' rises from the straw.

"Got something," Rankin said. He pointed and handed the binocs to Cutler. "Look along the east end of that spit of land. She did.

"It's a boat," Cutler said.

Tommy Earl cut the throttle, let the boat glide to a stop. "That there's a little island," he said. "Good fishing on the north and west sides of it."

They were three to four hundred yards away. The boat a tiny, ghost-like blur.

"Get closer," Cutler said.

Tommy Earl eased the throttle forward and turned that way. He again slowed, coming to a stop when they were a hundred yards away.

Rankin had the glasses again. "I don't see anyone. Boat's backed up to the shore." He lowered the binocs and looked at Cutler. "What do you want to do?"

"How big is this island?"

"Not very," Tommy Earl said.

She nodded. "Let's take a lap. See what's what."

"We got time for that?" Rankin asked. "I mean, they have hostages."

"They have prey," Cutler said. "They're hunting." She scanned the island's silhouette. "And the perfect hunting grounds. No escape."

"So maybe we should go on in," Rankin said.

"Might just walk into a trap," Cutler said. She nudged Tommy Earl's shoulder. "Give us the scenic tour."

CHAPTER 70

Cain crept through the trees, Harper just off his left shoulder. Back toward where Chelsie waited. Now that there was only Tyler to track down, getting her back in the fold was critical. If they ran across Tyler in the process, so much the better.

They each held a crossbow and each had a Glock stuffed in their waistbands. The advantage was now theirs. Tyler was no hunter. Other than hunting down naked and barefoot women, he possessed none of the needed skills. Cain and Harper did. Each had tracked more dangerous targets in much more hostile environments. Still, Cain knew that in any such mission, surprises were the wild cards. In many ways, amateurs were more dangerous than pros. Less predictable. Would do things that made no sense. But that would sometimes work.

Such was the case when they reached Chelsie's burial spot.

She was gone.

"You think he found her?" Harper whispered.

"Or she got impatient and left. Looking for us, or some path to escape."

"Which means we no longer have a free-fire zone."

True. Meant that before taking Tyler down, they had to be sure it was him and not Chelsie. No shooting at shadows.

"Which way?" Harper asked.

Cain scanned a three-hundred-and-sixty degree circle. "With

someone like her, it's a guess, but I think she'd head away from the boat."

"I agree."

They turned west.

Three minutes later, they heard voices. Ahead. They couldn't make out what was being said. They eased forward until the voices became clear. They stopped, crouched.

"Please." Chelsie.

"Please what?" Tyler.

Cain laid the bow on the ground and pulled the Glock. Harper followed suit. Cain slid a couple of feet to his left. He could see them through the branches of a pine tree. Chelsie on her knees, facing his way; Tyler behind her, gun in hand, pointing to the back of her head. Dicey.

"I won't tell anyone," Chelsie said.

"I know. As soon as Hank and Ted get here, maybe I'll give you another chance to run."

"What if they don't? What if they're dead?"

Tyler chuckled. "I think they can handle themselves. Against a couple of citified P.I.s."

"Dixon isn't coming," Cain said. He rose from his crouch and pushed through the trees.

Tyler recoiled, but recovered. He grabbed Chelsie by her hair, yanked her to her feet, pulling her tightly against him. The gun now pressed against the side of her head.

"Neither is Norris," Harper said as she stepped up beside Cain.

"Don't move," Tyler said.

Cain and Harper raised their weapons.

"I'll kill her."

Cain smiled. "And we'll kill you."

The sound of a boat motor ground through the trees.

"Hear that?" Cain said. "That's the cavalry."

Tyler's head swiveled toward the sound, his panic and confusion rising. "Or maybe just someone out fishing."

"In this weather?" Harper said. "Do you really believe that?"

Tyler hesitated. Cain could almost hear the argument going on inside his head. Shoot, run, what?

"Put the weapon down, Tyler," Harper said. "You can't win

here."

"You don't think I'll kill her?"

"No, I don't," Cain said.

"I have nothing to lose," Tyler said.

Cain knew that was true. Maybe he or Harper could take him. Maybe he wouldn't get a shot off. But he didn't like the odds. Time to decompress the situation. Make Tyler think he'd won. Make him confident. Arrogant. Something Tyler had plenty of.

"Okay," Cain said. "We'll put our weapons down. You let her go. Then we three can find a way out of this."

Tyler stared at them. Considering the situation.

"Why would you do that?" Tyler said.

"It's Chelsie we're worried about," Harper said. "Let her go. You'll still have us."

"There's a trick here somewhere."

"Let me know when you figure it out," Cain said. "All I see is a bad situation. We're simply seeking a solution."

Tyler said nothing.

Cain lowered his weapon, bent, and dropped it at his feet. Harper did the same.

"Hands up," Tyler said. "On top of your head."

He had watched too much TV. Cain and Harper complied. Mostly. Cain actually laced his fingers behind his head.

"Now let her go," Cain said.

"You think I'm stupid? Why wouldn't I simply shoot her, then both of you?"

Cain eased his right index finger and thumb beneath his collar until he felt the handle of the knife sheathed there.

"And then what? Bury five bodies before Chief Cutler and her crew get here?"

"No small task," Harper said. She sidestepped a couple of feet to her right, creating a gap, an angle between her and Cain.

"I've got plenty of time."

Cain tugged the knife up until he had a grip on it.

"The boat," Cain said. "They'll be here in a few minutes."

"I don't think so. I see no way Laura Cutler could know where we are."

Cain glanced at Harper, gave an almost imperceptible nod.

"You willing to take that chance?" Harper asked.

"Like I said before, I don't really have a choice."

"Sure you do." She took another step to her right.

"Don't move," Tyler said.

Another step.

Tyler angled the gun away from Chelsie and toward Harper. "I will shoot you."

Harper coughed. A signal.

Everything happened quickly.

Harper dropped to the ground.

The gun discharged.

Cain flicked the knife.

Chelsie screamed.

The blade entered Tyler's right eye.

He staggered, the gun fell from his hand. He clutched this face and spun to the ground, a few twitches, then he lay there completely still.

Chelsie collapsed to her knees, sobbing. Harper came over and put an arm around her.

"It's okay," she said. "It's over now."

She helped Chelsie to her feet.

Chelsie looked down at the unmoving, un-breathing Tyler Stenson. She turned away, bent over, and dry heaved.

Cain waited until Chelsie regained control, then said, "Let's get out of here."

Ten minutes later they stepped out of the trees and onto the rocky landing site. There were now two boats parked there. And Cutler and Rankin, each on one knee, guns leveled in their direction.

"Don't move," Cutler shouted.

"It's the good guys," Cain said.

"Jesus." Cutler stood. "You nearly got yourself shot."

"You don't know the half of it," Harper said.